Stefanie Lon[...] of contempor[...]
After sneaking several English Lit subjects into her 'very practical' business degree, Stefanie worked in the corporate world. But it wasn't long before she became bored with writing emails for executives and turned her attention to romantic fiction. Stefanie's books have been called 'genuinely entertaining and memorable' by *Booklist* and her writing was praised as 'elegant, descriptive and delectable' by *RT Book Reviews*. Originally from Australia, she now lives in Toronto, with her very own hero, and is currently in the process of doing her best to travel the world. She frequently indulges in her passions for good coffee, lipstick, romance novels and anything zombie-related. For more information on Stefanie and her books, check out her website at stefanie-london.com.

Nicola Marsh is a *USA TODAY* bestselling and multi-award-winning author who loves nothing better than losing herself in a story. A physiotherapist in a previous life, she now divides her time between raising two dashing heroes, whipping up delish meals, cheering on her footy team and writing—her dream job. And she chats on social media. A lot. Come and say hi! Instagram, Twitter, Facebook—she's there! Also find her at nicolamarsh.com.

If you liked
The Fiancé and *Her Playboy Crush*
why not try

Masquerade by Cara Lockwood
Dating the Rebel by Lisa Childs

Also by Stefanie London

Melbourne After Dark

Unmasked
Hard Deal

Close Quarters

Faking It
The Fling
The Rebound

Also by Nicola Marsh

Sweet Thing
Wild Thing
Play Thing
Stripped
Under His Skin
One Wicked Week

Discover more at millsandboon.co.uk

THE FIANCÉ

STEFANIE LONDON

HER PLAYBOY CRUSH

NICOLA MARSH

MILLS & BOON

First Published in Great Britain 2021
by Mills & Boon, an imprint of HarperCollins*Publishers*
1 London Bridge Street, London, SE1 9GF

The Fiancé © 2020 Stefanie Little

Her Playboy Crush © 2020 Nicola Marsh

ISBN: 978-0-263-29787-4

MIX
Paper from
responsible sources
FSC C007454

This book is produced from independently certified FSC™ paper
to ensure responsible forest management.
For more information visit www.harpercollins.co.uk/green.

Printed and bound in Spain
by CPI, Barcelona

THE FIANCÉ

STEFANIE LONDON

MILLS & BOON

CHAPTER ONE

Ava

I DON'T OFTEN use dramatic, sweeping statements—
which is a miracle given my family are gold medalists
in making mountains out of molehills. But I'm going
to use one now:

Today is, without a doubt, the worst day of my life.

I sit across the dining room table from my mother,
matching her determined stare with one of my own.
Seriously, if I could turn the woman into a stone gar-
goyle and stick her on top of a Gothic mansion for the
rest of eternity, I totally would. At least then she could
torture someone else.

"No." I say the word with a conviction that drills
right down into my bones.

"Ava." My mother stretches my name on for several beats, doing her best to infuse it with that guilt-
inducing tone she does so well. "You haven't heard me
out. This could be such a good thing—"

"No," I repeat. "I'm not sure how I can be any clearer."

I glance toward the lounge room where a man is

chatting with my grandmother. I catch a glimpse of him through the frosted-glass sliding door. He's little more than a shadowy figure, but my brain sketches in all the details: receding hairline, puffy lips, sausage fingers and a smile that makes me shiver for all the wrong reasons. His mother and mine are best friends, which means he's been coming around this house for as long as I can remember.

In my head, I call him Anthony McCreeperson.

My mother huffs. "But—"

"I am *not* marrying him." Why do I have to stand my ground on this? "I don't care what you promised him…or his family. I don't care how much livestock they offered you."

My mother frowns, the lines in her forehead deepening. "Livestock, Ava? What are you talking about?"

"Isn't that how brides were bartered back in the day? With goats…or cows or something?" I know I'm not making any sense. I was in a bad mood when I arrived and now, I'm…livid. "And I guess you'll have to let them know I'm not a virgin."

Barely. I was a late bloomer, but she doesn't need to know that.

"You're being ridiculous," my mother snaps, keeping her voice low. "He's a good man with a good job and he comes from a good family. Why is it crazy to think you would make a positive marital match?"

Correction: Anthony McCreeperson is a fedora-wearing sleaze ball with a job at an electronics store owned by his equally creepy uncle. He's thirty-four and still lives with his mother. He once told me he had no plans to leave because his mum still does all his washing, ironing and cooking.

Yeah, he's a *real* catch. Not.

Unfortunately, when it comes to who *would* make an acceptable husband for me, my mother sets the bar so low that even Anthony McCreeperson can stumble over it. Employed? Check. Legally able to marry? Check. Penis? Unconfirmed, but for the sake of this argument...check.

End of checklist.

"Because he's..." I shake my head. "I'm not attracted to him at all."

"Don't be so superficial." She frowns and gives me a pointed look. "None of us are perfect."

I let out an annoyed puff of air. Okay, fine. I'm not exactly a Victoria's Secret model. I'm not skinny or tall and I don't have Barbie proportions. I've got athletic thighs from years of playing netball and my hips like to bump into things. But I'm okay with all that.

No, scratch that. I *like* my body. Some days I even love it.

Being plus size doesn't mean I'm automatically denied a relationship built on mutual attraction. Some guys like a vertically challenged woman with a curvy figure. I don't have to settle for the first warm body who shows interest.

"Wanting chemistry is *not* being superficial. It's a bare minimum." I roll my eyes. "Besides, how do you know I'm not seeing someone already?"

The scoffing sound she makes cuts me deep. Does she really think I'm *that* un-datable? "Well, you haven't brought anyone around. You haven't even mentioned a name."

"Maybe because you and Grandma are like a pack of hyenas with this stuff. It takes a while to figure out whether a person is long-term material, and I'm not going to bring a guy home unless I think it's going somewhere."

"You shouldn't even be considering short term, Ava. Do you think you'll be able to waltz into your thirties and pluck a great guy off a shelf at the husband store? It doesn't work like that. Trust me, I know."

And this is the crux of her argument. She waited too long, rejected a suitable proposal, only to fall for a guy later on who turned out to be a scumbag. He got her pregnant and left her to raise a baby—a.k.a. me—on her own. She ended up a single mother with trust issues who'd "wasted" her youth. By the time she was ready to date again, nobody was interested in a woman with baggage.

Don't get me wrong, I love my mother. I appreciate the sacrifices she made to raise me. I really do.

But I think her still being single in her fifties has more to do with her attitude than the life she's lived. Unfortunately for me, she's become fixated with marrying me off before I turn thirty so I don't follow in her footsteps.

"I'm not you, Mum." I shake my head. "I'm not going to make the same mistakes."

"I never thought I would make those mistakes, either."

Every so often I glimpse the woman she used to

be—the woman I've seen in old photos. Shiny brown hair, a wide smile, hazel eyes with unusual hints of orange-gold…an image eerily similar to what I see in the mirror. She was vivacious and loved to throw parties and go to rock concerts and write achingly beautiful poetry. She was full of life.

Some days I wish I'd met that version of her.

"We're not having this discussion," I say, pushing back on the dining chair so it scrapes against the tiled floor. "I'm not marrying Anthony and I don't need your help finding a man."

"Because you already have one?" The hope in her voice is like nails on a blackboard.

"Whether I do or not is none of your business until *I* decide it's time to make an introduction." Like in the year twenty-never. "I love you, Mum. But you drive me bananas."

"Think about it," she cajoles. "He's a good boy."

"Yes, exactly. He's a *boy*." I pick up my bag and sling it over one shoulder. Time to make an exit. "And if I ever get married, it will be to a *man*."

I pull my mum in for a hug. Despite our differences, I won't ever leave without telling her I love her. Even if I want to shake her. Even if I think she's got her priorities all messed up. Even if she meddles more than the town gossip in a Hallmark movie.

We're close…but we're fundamentally different.

"You aren't going to say goodbye to him?" she asks, incredulous. Her bony, unadorned hand flicks toward the frosted doors sealing off the living room.

"He's your guest, Mum. *You* invited him over." I

plant a peck on her cheek and head for the front door, already digging my phone out of my bag because I need to call my best friend and vent. "I'll see you next week."

Before she can get another protest out of her mouth, I slip outside and glare at Anthony McCreeperson's secondhand BMW with the gaudy personalised plates as I walk down the driveway.

B1GM2N.

I think the *2* is supposed to be an *A*, but obviously someone else got to that number plate first. It takes everything in me not to vomit in my mouth. I would rather die than marry him. I would rather be tied to a post and have one million hungry rats set on me than marry him.

I would rather—

My phone vibrates in my hand, interrupting the slide of gruesome thoughts. Emery. It's like she knew I needed her. I slide my thumb across the screen.

"Hey," I say with a sigh. "You have no idea how much I need to talk to you right now. I've had the day from hell."

"Spill," she replies in that short-and-to-the-point way of hers.

For a minute, I'm totally overwhelmed. You see, my mother the wannabe matchmaker isn't my only issue right now. It's simply the gleaming cherry on top of a giant shit sundae.

"I..." I shut my eyes for a moment. "Shit."

"Take it slow, girl. Tell me everything."

I head toward where I've parked my car on the

street. The footpath is littered with fluffy, yellow wattle blossoms that look like tiny polka dots against the grey concrete.

"I heard back about the teaching job at that school in Epping." I suck on the inside of my cheek. "They found a candidate with more experience."

"After they dragged you through three rounds of interviews? Bastards." She makes a noise of irritation. "I'm sorry. I know you had your hopes up for this one."

"One more rejection letter for the growing collection." I've been surviving on a mix of casual relief teaching shifts, supplementing the inconsistency of that work with catering shifts in the evening. It's been enough for me to make rent, but now... "And I ran into Mr. James today."

Mr. James is my landlord. He's a kindly old man of eighty-three and he owns three apartments in the 21 Love Street complex. He's been giving me the deal of the century on rent because I taught his granddaughter for a term and she loved me to bits.

"How is he?"

"He's selling the apartment."

Silence stretches on the other end of the line and for a second I think the call has cut out. But then I hear something in the background, like a cupboard door closing. "He's selling?"

"Well, he's signing all the apartments he owns over to his children and *they're* selling, apparently. Honestly, my brain stopped working for a minute so I didn't take in all the details."

"How long?"

"Two months." I can't even bear the thought of it. I *love* that apartment. I've filled it with personal things. I've made memories there. Friends, too. "I won't be able to find anything in the city for what he was charging me, either."

Not to mention that without a permanent teaching role, my ability to save has been somewhat hamstrung. Casual work pays well, but there have been weeks where I've had little more than a single shift to live on.

"You can stay with me," Emery offers.

"Oh yeah, and sleep on your couch forever? I appreciate the offer, but that's not a solution."

"What are you going to do?"

I glance back at my mother's house as I unlock my car. The thought of moving in with her, especially after what happened today, is *not* ideal. "I honestly don't know."

"What a shit day! We'll figure something out, whatever you—"

"That's not everything." I slide into the driver's seat and pull the door closed behind me. For a minute I sit there, staring out through the windshield and counting the leaves that have fallen from the big tree hanging overhead. They've gotten caught in the windscreen wipers and they flutter as the wind picks up. "My mother is trying to convince me to marry Anthony."

"Creepy Anthony?"

See, even Emery knows it. "Yep."

"You're kidding me."

"I'm not." I press my head back against the headrest. "If she was any more old-school there would have been a dowry and everything."

"I can't… I don't know what to say to that."

"There's nothing *to* say, Em. I just want today to be over."

"This is messed up." She sighs. "Come over. I'll order pizza and we'll crack open a bottle of wine. Or something stronger."

I glance at my watch. "I can't. I've got a catering shift tonight and it turns out I need the money more than ever."

Emery makes me promise to come by in the morning so she can treat me to brunch. Honestly, the thought of food turns my stomach. I'm barely employable, soon-to-be homeless and my own mother thinks I need to marry a loser so I don't get left on the shelf. It's like the universe is telling me that I should settle for whatever I can get.

But I can't.

I refuse to become like my mother, a broken woman who thinks the bare minimum is something to aim for. A woman who's too afraid to aim for anything at all. I have big goals and dreams. I want to find a teaching job where I can really impact the development and growth of young people. I want to buy my own home and be proud of what I've accomplished. I want to find a love that makes my heart flutter and my soul shine.

I want it all.

And while I have exactly zero ideas on how to make that all happen, I'm not about to lay down my sword. I *will* find a solution…somehow.

CHAPTER TWO

Daniel

I'M THE KIND of guy who's always got a plan, who's prepared for anything. Yet when it comes to my family... I'm stumped. It never ceases to amaze me how quickly they can make my day go from bad to shitstorm. Or, in this case, whatever the hell comes *after* shitstorm.

I white-knuckle a tumbler containing two fingers of Scotch, resisting the urge to hurl it at my brother as he storms away.

But we grew up in the spotlight and I know better. Every moment, including this one, is a chance for the public to feast. I've seen too many people felled by pointless Twitter arguments and unflattering Instagram rants. Too many promising careers dashed because people didn't have the discipline to hold themselves in check.

I won't give the masses any ammunition. Well... any *more* ammunition.

Around me, the party swells with sounds of conversation, laughter and clinking glasses as if reminding me that I'm not alone. Two women in sparkling cocktail dresses brush past, eyes lingering before they sweep into the bar. I *should* be enjoying myself—top-shelf drinks, beautiful women, the glittering skyline of Melbourne stretched out like a gift from heaven.

My company, Moretti Enterprises, has officially opened the tallest tower in the Southern Hemisphere. The Cielo is a 394-metre high, 108-storey luxury apartment building—a massive accomplishment for my family's property development company. And for me as the newly minted CEO.

I *should* be floating on a cloud.

Instead, I'm seething with anger at being accused of the one thing I would *never* do.

"Did you hear that?" I suck a breath in between my teeth, gripping on to my composure though it feels like water sliding through my fingers. "Tell me I've entered a parallel dimension."

Leo sips his champagne. He's my head of operations and is the buffer between my brother's fiery temper and my icy resolve.

"You can hardly blame him for being pissed off with the gossip," Leo points out. "And maybe it wasn't a smart move to fire your own flesh and blood in the middle of launch night."

Marc has made it across the room, drawing curious glances and whispers as he's stopped by his wife, Lily. She attempts to calm him down, but there's no mistaking Marc's furious expression and clenched jaw. Beneath his bespoke suit, my brother is tightly coiled like a tiger.

And just as bad-tempered as one.

This morning I'd awoken to my phone exploding with messages. Photos from a gossip site proclaimed that we, the Moretti brothers, are "at war" over Australia's top model—a.k.a. Marc's wife.

The headline doesn't hold even a grain of truth—not a microscopic speck. But the media can't get enough of a love triangle, even if it's a complete fabrication.

"I didn't fire him," I say through gritted teeth. "I simply asked him why he was letting himself be manipulated."

"You *told* him to let it go," Leo corrects. "You know that's a red flag to a bull, right?"

"It shouldn't be difficult for him to let it go, I'm his fucking brother." I stalk over to a window. We have a phenomenal view. The inky sky is a perfect contrast to the lights, making it look like someone has draped Melbourne in a blanket of diamonds. "I have not and will not *ever* have an affair with a married woman. *Especially* not my brother's wife."

The fact that Marc is entertaining this fictitious piece of bullshit is a blow. Not just any blow, the *ultimate* blow. Our father liked to change mistresses more often than he changed his jocks, and it ruined our family. I'm not like him. And Marc is an idiot for accosting me, "demanding answers" in the middle of our most important company event ever. With the press in the vicinity.

While drunk.

Sometimes he's not the brightest crayon in the box.

But I stood my ground with stoic denial. With unemotional logic. We're opposites like that—ice and fire. I turn to stone when angry and Marc is a volcano. So telling Marc that he was an idiot for believing the media went down like a lead balloon. And unfortunately, he'd taken the argument as a recommendation to resign from the family company.

Hence his storming off.

Now a pink-cheeked Lily heads toward us, the length of her strapless emerald gown gathered in one hand so she doesn't trip as she hurries across the room. She's like the little sister I never had, and we've only ever been friends. But the media doesn't care about any of that. They love the idea of some sordid affair because it sells advertising.

Not because there's a shred of truth to it.

"He's furious," Lily says, shaking her head. She wraps her hand around my arm and her nails dig into my biceps. "He's refusing to talk to me. I've told him nothing is going on... But he says he's seen proof."

I place a hand on her shoulder, doing my best to comfort her but without giving anyone around us more to speculate on. "There can't be proof of something that doesn't exist."

"That's what I told him." She sucks in a shaky breath. "But he won't even hear me out."

"That's his issue, Lily."

"I love him and it's affecting our marriage, so it's *my* issue." Her voice wavers. "And he's your brother, which makes it your issue, too. We have to do something."

"Like what?" My head pounds with the beginnings of a headache. Of all the bloody nights for Marc to lose it, why tonight? "We've both told the truth. That should be enough."

We're in the middle of an acquisition at the moment. An acquisition Marc set up using a personal connection, which will be on shaky grounds without him. I might be stubborn, but I can see how the fallout of this will affect the company.

"Clearly it's not enough. He told me not to come after him tonight. He's...never pushed me away like that before."

"We need a plan," Leo agrees, frowning. "Now."

People are talking. The gossip is taking away from what *should* be a triumphant evening for my whole family and a chance to reward our staff for all the hard work and long hours they've put in.

Everything has been carefully designed for tonight's event. The champagne is flowing. The glamorous "viewing space" holds a replica of one of the lounge rooms of our penthouse suites. People sit and stand as though sketching themselves into their perfect home. It's the culmination of hours and hours of blood, sweat and tears.

But clusters of reporters and photographers have been gathered outside our HQ all day. We've been bombarded with phone calls and emails, requesting comments on a claim made by an "anonymous source" that Lily and I have been sleeping together since before her wedding to Marc. *Sure.* Like one of those morally defunct tabloid columnists didn't make it all up and then claim they had a "source" for their information.

"I'm *not* making a public statement." I scrub a hand over my face. "It'll only add fuel to the fire."

"The longer we let this fester, the more damage it will do," Leo counters. "You need to convince Marc by any means necessary that nothing is going on."

If I had my way, I'd let my hotheaded brother stew in his misery. If he doesn't believe me, that's *his* issue. How he could even think I would do such a thing...

My knuckles tighten around my glass again.

But Leo has a point. And we need Marc. Not only for this deal, but because he has the best head for numbers of anyone I've ever met. The company is better with him in the CFO role. Fact. Not to mention that I can't stand to see Lily hurting, either.

But I have to say, I'm not entirely surprised that their marriage has problems—I'd warned Marc before the wedding that marriage wasn't something to treat lightly. As much as I love Lily and was thrilled to have her officially join our family, my thoughts on marriage are grim. If our parents taught me anything at all, it's that passionate love is a lit match hovering over a pool of petrol.

It will consume everything and leave you with nothing.

I'm *not* going to fall on my sword and beg forgiveness for something I didn't do. But I still need a solution—something to convince Marc that I'm not a philanderer like our dad. Something to convince my brother to come back to work and make sure we get this deal over the line.

"Also, your mum is on her way," Leo says.

Shit. My eyes dart across the room to where my mother is striding toward us. Despite not even reaching five feet, she has the presence of a person three times her height, and the crowd parts like the Red Sea to let her through. Her black dress shimmers as if in warning, and her thunderous expression makes my spine automatically straighten.

"I don't have the energy to deal with her right now," I say, letting out a frustrated groan. "I've got to deliver this speech in five minutes and I need to look like I haven't watched my life crumble to pieces."

"I'll run interference." Leo holds his hand up. "Go."

I ditch my drink and head in the opposite direction, leaving my friend and sister-in-law to deal with the Moretti matriarch. I need a moment to pull myself together. With all the hurt and frustration swirling in my head—things I'll never let the public see—I *can't* stand in front of a room of important investors, industry titans and press unless I've got my head screwed on properly.

This is a critical moment.

The launch of the Cielo is a new direction for Moretti Enterprises. It's a symbol of everything I stand for as a leader. Progress. Evolution. Innovation.

I will *not* have this moment overshadowed by people making up stories about my sex life.

Ducking past a group of waiters coming out of the bar area, I spot a staff hallway across the room. A closet marked Supplies is exactly what I need. It's the last place anyone will look.

Five minutes. That's all I need.

I yank the door back and slip inside, looking over my shoulder to see if anyone has followed me. For a fleeting moment I have some reprieve. But that's shattered the second I find myself staring at a woman covered in streaks of red. Her eyes widen in shock, and she scrambles to close a ruined shirt across her chest. But not before I get a good glimpse of her curvy body, skin generously dusted with freckles and a set of breasts so perfect I have to resist the urge to drop to my knees.

A lace bra in a shade of pale, flesh-toned pink peeks out from between the red-streaked shirt, and the dusky hint of her nipples creates a tantalising shadow.

The ponytail and conservative black pants give her away as one of the waitstaff, but even with history's most boring outfit, there's no denying the sensuality radiating from her. Her eyes are the most unusual mix of warm brown and coppery-gold. And her body...wow. She's curvy, with full thighs and a dip at the waist that's the exact thing that drives me wild.

If I was hoping to find solitude and calm in this cupboard, then that idea has officially been shot to hell.

CHAPTER THREE

Ava

COULD THIS DAY get any more humiliating? I bury my head in my hand—my free one, *not* the one currently trying to preserve my dignity—for a full four seconds, before cracking my fingers open to see if the man has disappeared. Nope, still there.

Ugh, he's one of *them*. Painfully handsome, richer than sin and probably has an entitlement level to match. I deal with his type a lot in this job.

"What happened?" The man steps toward me, heavy brows creased. He has dark hair and darker eyes, like glittering chips of black that are somehow intimidating and sexy at the same time. Which is *not* my usual definition of sexy, mind you.

I like guys who are more like golden retrievers. Fun, good-natured, a bit silly. Loveable. This guy, however, is a Doberman.

Maybe your comparison of men to dogs is why you're still single.

"It's pasta sauce. There was an incident." If I was

any more of a mess right now, I'd be a Jackson Pollock painting.

Of course, the "incident" had occurred because I wasn't paying attention to my surroundings. Anthony McCreeperson was texting me, trying to set up a date so we could talk about my mother's "great idea."

Kill. Me. Now.

If I didn't need this job so badly, I would go straight home to drown myself in cheap wine and pizza with extra cheese, and never leave my house again. But there are certain things about being an adult that suck balls... One of them is how reliant we are on money. Therefore, I need to stay and put on a happy face while I try to ignore the source of my humiliation texting me all night long.

Don't you mean the sauce *of your humiliation?*

Even when I'm falling in a heap, I can find a pun.

"What exactly *was* the incident?" the gorgeous man asks.

"A too-tight Tupperware lid and a sous chef with greasy hands."

His lip twitches. "Right."

"So yes, I'm hiding in a supply cupboard so I can change. Two more seconds and you would have seen more than my bra."

Great, now he's probably imagining me naked. *Why do you have to open your big mouth all the time, Ava?*

For some reason, the thought of my naked body running through his head makes me tingle like a cluster of fizzy champagne bubbles is tracking through my veins. I'm far too aware of the pressure of the clothes on my skin. Of the heat in his gaze.

Now that I look at him a little closer, I think my initial assessment was slightly off. This man isn't painfully handsome. He's not even obnoxiously handsome. It's like he found the damn handsome scale and snapped it over one muscular thigh.

He has the kind of lips made for kissing. Full, wickedly curved like the lines on a fancy sports car. Tanned, olive skin and strong hands that I imagine skimming up the inside of my thighs.

Yeah, obnoxiously handsome doesn't even *start* to cover it.

"So that's me," I say. My voice has taken on that high-pitched quality that happens whenever I get wound up. And right now, staring at possibly the single hottest man on planet Earth, I am most definitely wound up. "What's your story?"

He raises an eyebrow. "My story?"

"The reason you're *also* hiding in a closet."

The man straightens. He's more than a head and a half taller than me and I have to crane my neck to meet his gaze. "I'm not hiding."

"You hang out in supply closets for fun?"

"I was about to practice my speech. This is the only place I could get some bloody peace and quiet and…" His eyes rake over me, burning a path from my lips to the shirtfront bunched in my fist, down over the unflattering black pants my boss forces us to wear. "And look how that turned out."

"Not great, huh?"

His lip twitches again, like it can't quite figure out if it wants to smile or smirk. He ends up somewhere in the middle, which shouldn't make my stomach twist and flip, but it *definitely* does.

This is the kind of chemistry I was talking about earlier today. Looking at this man makes me ache. Everywhere. He makes my mind spin and my hands itch and my pulse pound. Looking at Anthony McCreeperson makes me want to run in the opposite direction.

"No, not great," he replies drily. "Or maybe it's very great, depending on your definition."

Uh, boobs. I'm barely keeping the double-Ds in check right now. Honestly, I know some women have always wanted a bigger bust but I can say firsthand that they are a pain, both literally and figuratively.

I motion for him to turn around, so I can change into a clean uniform. The boss keeps spares on hand in case of "incidents" because god forbid the rich people see someone looking messy. Their perfectly coiffed heads might spontaneously combust.

"So, you're making a speech, huh? Are you introducing the big guy?" I cringe as I peel the soggy shirt from my skin. "Daniel Moretti. He must be having a hell of a night what with trending on Twitter."

I don't know anything about the family who's hosting this event. Of course, I've heard of Moretti Enterprises and the Cielo tower… I haven't been living under a rock. But between relief teaching and catering shifts, applying for every education job in the city of Melbourne *and* trying not to let my relationship with my mother turn into a dumpster fire, I don't have the mental energy for internet gossip. However, the other catering staff *love* to gossip about our clients, and I overheard them chattering about Daniel Moretti's alleged affair earlier.

The man doesn't respond. I slip the new shirt over my shoulders before realising that some of the sauce has soaked through to my bra. I grab a tissue from my pocket and try to get as much off as possible.

"I mean, that's pretty low if he slept with his brother's wife," I say. Getting cheated on is awful. Heinous. Seeing how it turned my mother from a bright and vibrant young woman into someone negatively obsessed with security, I have a lot of sympathy for the brother. "I can't imagine what that conversation would have been like. Brutal."

That's when I realise the man *still* hasn't responded.

A funny thought settles in the pit of my stomach. No, this can't be him. Isn't Daniel Moretti an older dude? This man in the closet with me is no more than midthirties, max.

But the silence stretches on and my stomach knots. Shrugging the paranoia off, I button up the fresh shirt and when I turn, he's still facing the door. But even from behind I sense the change in him. His shoulders are tensed, pushing up toward his ears...like he's about to Hulk out of his expensive-looking suit.

Uh-oh.

"I uh... I'm decent now." I let out a nervous laugh. Dammit, I always give myself away. "You've gone all quiet. I'm starting to worry I've put my foot in my mouth."

"I was curious to see what else you were going to say." He turns and cocks his head. Now his eyes are blisteringly dark. So intense I wonder if it's possible for him to burn me to ash. "What's your take? Do you think it's true?"

He wouldn't have a reaction like this unless it affected him somehow. So either he's the guy accused of having the affair, or the brother who's supposedly been cheated on. Either way, he could cause me a lot of trouble.

Shit.

My heart pounds. I can't lose this job now, not after *everything* that's happened today. If I suffer one more humiliation I might sink into the ground and cease to exist. Besides, I need every penny to make sure I don't end up back at home with my mother.

I'm not sure our relationship would survive it.

"I don't think I should comment," I say, trying to tuck my shirt into my pants. But my hands are clumsy and I can't seem to drag my eyes away from his beautiful, angry, glittering gaze.

"Please." He motions for me to go on. "Indulge my curiosities."

Think, brain, think. How can you get out of this diplomatically?

"Well… I think the media will write whatever sells the most advertising, regardless of truth. And I think the two brothers need to have a serious, honest chat and leave everyone else's opinions to one side."

Very good. Well done, brain.

"So, which brother are you?" The question slips

out before I have time to consider the consequences. Story of my life.

"Daniel Moretti." He sticks his hand out. "Falsely accused."

When his palm slides against mine, sparks skitter pleasantly along my skin. I'm jolted with flashing images of silken sheets and naked bodies and those big, strong hands sliding all over me. The fantasy is sharp and real, and for a brief second it steals my breath.

"Ava Matthews," I reply, trying to keep my voice from wobbling. "Barely employed teacher by day."

He raises an eyebrow. "And by night?"

"Catering waitress who can't keep her mouth shut."

"At least you said it to my face." He rakes a hand through his hair and a crease forms above his nose. "Unlike most people here."

"I'm subtle as a ton of bricks, as my mum used to say." I drag my gaze away from Daniel's exquisite features and continue to tuck my fresh shirt into my pants. Unfortunately, I still look rumpled in spite of my efforts. "But I'll take the compliment."

"You should." His expression is smooth and clear, but his eyes are locked on to mine with an intensity that makes me feel like I'm half-naked. He doesn't seem like the kind of man who simply looks. No. His gaze bores into me. Strips me back. Holds me totally and utterly captive.

I honestly don't remember the last time a man looked at me like that, but it feels phenomenal. Yeah, yeah, I know I shouldn't really want that, especially while stuck in a supply closet with a guy I don't know.

But after the day I've had, to feel seen is…everything.

"I don't know you," I say. "But you seem sincere to me and I believe you didn't do what they're saying. I hope your brother listens."

"Thank you." Daniel nods. "I appreciate that."

"I should get back to work now." I try to ignore the cosmic little tingle of awareness that shoots through my body. Oh boy, I definitely haven't felt like this in a while.

He's hot. It's a natural reaction. But this guy has got more baggage than Southern Cross Station… And so do you, at the moment. Eye on the prize.

"Uh, good luck with your speech," I add with a nod. Daniel's dark gaze stokes the fire in my belly as he watches me. I want to stay and bask in that intensity a little longer, let that pleasant feeling roll through my body like warm water.

"You're a little…" He steps closer, his hands going to the buttons on my shirt. In my haste, I've done them up wrong. "Mismatched."

He pushes one button through its hole, and then another. My breath stutters in my chest—and I'm frozen like an ice sculpture. But inside I'm molten. Wanting. Burning. His hands don't even touch my skin as he corrects the buttons, but it feels so startlingly erotic he might as well be sliding my underwear down my legs.

There's something so intimate. So sensual.

But the moment is shattered when the door to the closet is suddenly pushed open and a bright flash goes off in our faces. "What the…?"

"Daniel!" A male voice cuts through my fog.

But there's another flash, then another. Spots dance in my vision and I blink, trying to see through the lights. The voices come all at once.

"What are you doing with this young woman? Is this another one of your mistresses? Are you still seeing your brother's wife?"

I'm reeling as Daniel slams the supply closet door shut. He leans back against it and lets out a groan of frustration. Outside, voices shout his name again and again.

Something tells me this humiliating day is *far* from over.

CHAPTER FOUR

Daniel

FUCK. THIS IS the *last* thing I need.

I rake a hand through my hair, trying to formulate a plan. My mind whirrs like a broken machine, unable to get a grip on any one thought. It was bad enough having everyone think I'm screwing my brother's wife, and now they think they're catching me *in flagrante* with a catering waitress.

Ava looks at me with wide eyes. I'm guessing she's mid- to late twenties, and in spite of the dull uniform, she's gorgeous—unusual copper-flecked eyes, full lips, a body made for sin. Her fair skin is pink around her cheeks and neck…dammit. Even *I* would think we've been up to no good.

Why can't I be stuck in here with a woman who looks like my grandmother?

"Do they think we're…?" She glances at the door. "Surely not."

I let out a bark of a laugh. In my life, there is always someone looking to take advantage. I can't help but appreciate that she seems shocked by this. Intrusiveness is something I've come to accept as my norm, and it's refreshing to be around people who bring me back to reality.

"If there wasn't a whiff of something sordid, nobody would be standing outside that door," I drawl. "What better way to get clicks than to catch someone like me undressing a woman in a closet?"

I should really keep my mouth shut. Because now I'm wondering what it would be like to push her against the shelves and plunder that sweet little mouth. To hear what her voice sounds like when she croons into my ear. To feel her curves beneath my palms.

You're in enough trouble already.

She blinks. "But we're only talking. I mean, granted I did have my top off, but it wasn't for pleasure and you didn't really see *that* much."

I saw enough.

If this whole situation hadn't come at the worst possible moment, I would be laughing. The universe has turned my life into a circus. Unfortunately, as much as I would prefer to laugh it all off, this whole mess could have serious bottom-line consequences.

Why would anyone trust a CEO to manage a company when he can't even manage his own image?

As it is, there are already old dinosaurs on the board who are waiting for me to trip up so they can prove I'm not up to task. They'll try to devour me whole, given a fleeting chance.

"My boss will freak out if he thinks I've been…well, you know." Ava cringes. "It's against policy to even talk with the clients. I *can't* afford to lose this job."

"And I can't have people thinking I'm screwing every woman in Australia." I let out a growl and move my head from side to side, trying to work out the tension. "Who led them here?"

It's a rhetorical question. My mother had been charging across the observatory like a storm barrelling along the coast. No doubt the press we invited—under duress from my head of communications—were right on her heels. They're supposed to be covering the launch of the Cielo, not adding fuel to the fire about my love life.

What a joke. I've been working so hard I haven't brought a woman into my bed for over a year, and yet I'm fighting off a playboy reputation at every turn.

"Can't we tell them the truth?" Ava asks, keeping her voice low. She wrings her hands, twisting and turning them as if trying to strangle her worry.

"And you think they'll believe it?" I shake my head. "Don't be naive."

"Then what? It's not like they could really think we're together." She laughs, and the sound has a slightly maniacal edge. But then her eyes light up. "Hey, you're rich, right? Can't you pay the press to leave you alone?"

"That's not how it works. They make more from advertisers, and me paying them off would simply make for an even better story." This is getting out whether I want it to or not. That's if it hasn't *already*. "We need to control the narrative another way."

"And how, exactly, do we do that?"

If this story is going to get out, then maybe I can use it to my advantage. After all, I need Marc to believe that I'm not sleeping with Lily. That's going to take some deflection *and* a more compelling explanation than a simple 'I didn't do it.'

But maybe the perfect solution has landed in my lap.

I look Ava up and down—she's gorgeous. Maybe not the kind of woman people would expect, because we don't appear to run in the same circles. But we can get around that. More important, there's a spark to her. *And* a spark between us. I felt it the second I walked in here, like our energy was charging the air with a sexual current. With a ring on her finger and a fabricated backstory... Well, why wouldn't people believe it?

"How much do you make a year, Ava?" I ask, still leaning back against the door. I keep my voice low, ignoring the buzzing and pounding on the other side. Ignoring the flick of the handle and the sound of my name being called.

"None of your business," she replies, tilting her chin up. The pride tells me everything I need to know. Maybe I can make this beneficial for us *both*.

"You're right, and I don't actually care." I fold my arms across my chest. "Name your price."

She blinks. "Why?"

"Because you're going to lose your job the second I open this door."

She swallows, panic swirling in those warm, fiery eyes. "But I haven't done anything wrong."

"It never matters what you've done," I say darkly. "Only what people think you've done."

"What are you going to tell them?"

"That we're getting engaged." This is the only route

that makes sense. It gives this whole situation a more romantic edge. Two people in love unable to keep away from one another, as opposed to a quick-and-dirty screw in a cupboard. The noise outside increases and the door rattles again. "We wanted to keep it a secret because neither of our families knew about the relationship *and* because of all the current media attention."

"What?" Ava squeaks. "Have you lost your mind?"

"I wanted to spare you the circus, but now we've been caught," I continue, the plan starting to unfold in my mind. "You'll pretend to be my fiancée for a few weeks. We'll be seen together, perhaps have a vacation somewhere beautiful. It will be a whirlwind romance and then we'll 'break up' and go our separate ways, reputations intact."

For some reason, the thought of having Ava on my arm, acting like she's mine and I'm hers, strikes something primal inside me. We'll have to pretend to be lovers, to be *in* love. Well, obviously *that's* going to be an act, because I vowed long ago to never let myself feel something as destructive as love.

But being attracted to Ava won't take much effort at all.

"Then what…? We act like it never happened?" Ava looks at me as though I've started talking gibberish.

"Exactly. I'll help you find a job. I know plenty of people looking for good workers and I'll compensate you for your time, of course." I shoot her a confident smile. "Plus, you'll be living it up while we're together. Money is no object."

For a moment she's utterly silent. Her eyes flick

back and forth as if she's weighing the pros and cons. "You're serious? You'd be happy to have a fake relationship to appease the press?"

"If it serves my needs, yes."

"And it's pretend, right?" She nails me with a stare. "Because I don't know what you're used to, but paying me doesn't entitle you to anything physical."

"I don't pay for sex." That's another thing my father did that I despised, and the memory of finding out he'd cheated on my mother with multiple sex workers burns through me hot and furious like a house fire. "I can meet my sexual needs very easily without opening my wallet."

Ava nods, chewing on her bottom lip. In my world, learning to read people is critical. Politicking is part of our DNA, as much as I loathe it. But right now I'm grateful for that skill, because it tells me that for whatever reason, Ava needs this arrangement as much as I do.

"I don't expect anything other than for you to uphold the story while we're in public," I say quietly. Not that I wouldn't enjoy the pleasure of Ava's body. But on the rare occasion I allow a woman into my bed, it's only ever for mutual pleasure.

No business, no money. And certainly no feelings.

"Well, that *would* be quite a good way to shut my mother up." She rolls her bottom lip between her teeth and my curiosity is piqued, but right now the only thing I care about is getting her agreement.

"See, mutually beneficial."

"But we're lying." She frowns.

"Think of it like this—a lie is going to come out

of this situation no matter what we do. *This* lie will at least allow us to move forward with a positive story— I keep my reputation, and you can get yourself a better job and set yourself up financially. Or you can gamble that you won't get fired. It's up to you."

She sighed. "That's not much of a choice, is it?"

"There's always a choice."

My uncle, the man who acted as the mentor I'd always hoped my father would be, had taught me that one special life lesson: *never think you're without choice, because even a boxer in a corner has control over what he does next.* It's the motto I live by. The ruling words behind every move I make, always taking the driver's seat and never letting anyone force me to back down.

"I'll make it worth your while, Ava. Whatever you need in your life right now, I can make it happen."

Outside, chants of *Daniel! Daniel!* gather steam. This is going to be a nightmare regardless of what happens next. But if Ava agrees to my proposal—no pun intended—then at least I can see my way out of it. I'll introduce her to the family, make Marc see I'm not interested in Lily, and then I can get right back to what matters: building my empire.

She nods, her eyes glancing warily at the door. "Okay. I'll be your fake girlfriend."

"Fiancée," I correct. "Congratulations. We're about to get engaged."

CHAPTER FIVE

Ava
Two days later...

I STARE AT the suitcase on my bed. The damn thing is *still* empty and it gapes at me like a wide, open mouth. What *is* one supposed to wear for a weeklong sleepover with their fake fiancé?

Let's be real, there's nothing in my wardrobe that says "yes, I am hot enough to date a billionaire," and no amount of squinting at my closet is going to change that fact. I'm solidly a cute-skirt-and-ballet-flats kinda gal. A "find the best thing on the sale rack at Target" kinda gal. I don't do designer labels and ball gowns and stupid tiny purses that cost more than my monthly rent.

To make this process even *more* unbearable, Emery is sitting on my bed and glaring at me. Her hair—dyed a vibrant blue—is piled into a messy bun on top of her head. "I can't believe you didn't tell me you were dating someone, especially not after all the crap about your mum trying to marry you off. What happened to honesty? Integrity? The lifelong bonds of sisterhood?"

"Talk about a flair for the dramatic," I mutter.

Emery ignores the dig. "I thought we told each other everything."

The worst part of this situation, by far, is having to lie to Emery. I *knew* she'd be pissed at me, but the girl also has a mouth bigger than a barge. No way can I risk her accidentally divulging some incriminating information. Besides, I want this over and done with as quickly as possible.

She'll forgive me...eventually.

Last night I tossed and turned, my brain spinning on the possible outcomes of a week with Daniel. I kept veering to images of his full mouth and the dark, burning intensity of his eyes. To his powerful hands and what his body might look like under his suit. How I felt when he adjusted my buttons, his gaze never leaving mine.

This is a fake engagement, remember? This is about getting your ample butt out of a financial hole and nothing more.

"I'm sorry." I push my hair away from my face and sigh. "It's...complicated."

"A Facebook answer? Wow."

Ugh. Talk about twisting the knife. I *hate* lying. "Em..."

"It's fine. I'm giving you a hard time so you remember this next time you think about lying to me." She grins and I know I've been forgiven...for now. If she finds out that this lie was to cover up an even bigger one, I'm toast.

Guilt churns in my gut. I've always wanted a sister,

and Emery is the closest I've come. We have a great group of friends right here in this building—the two of us, plus a detective named Hannah, a flight attendant named Drew and her twin sister, Presley. The five of us are like a little family and we catch up weekly for games and drinks. Knowing that I need to mislead them all makes me feel sick.

You're doing this for your future.

"I feel bad, okay?" I pluck a simple black dress from my cupboard. It's not fancy in the slightest, but I've always thought it had a bit of an Audrey Hepburn vibe. "Really bad."

Emery watches me closely. "Have you told your mum about all this?"

"Apparently someone saw a picture of me from the launch party and told her." I cringe.

"Oh shit, she found out from someone else?" Emery's face would be comical if I wasn't feeling so anxious about this whole thing. "That's not good."

"No, it's not."

While this whole arrangement has the benefit of getting my mother off my back about Anthony McCreeperson, that doesn't mean the plan is without its downsides. Namely, that I got the earful of a lifetime about not telling her I have a boyfriend. Let alone one who's proposed to me.

Oops.

"She said that she was disappointed that I'd kept it a secret, but at least I had some hope of a stable future."

Emery blinked. "I'm sorry, did we timeslip back to 1952?"

"Story of my life." I roll my eyes. "It's insulting that she thinks I need someone to take care of me. But whatever, that's her issue, not mine."

"Well, I mean he should *take care* of you, if you know what I mean." Emery cackles.

My cheeks burn. I don't need *any* help thinking about Daniel taking care of me in that way, trust me. I woke up in tangled sheets last night with the kind of dirty dream that had me willing my body to go back to sleep. The kind of dream where my legs were spread and his dark head was moving down, hands and tongue and teeth sweeping over me like a storm.

How I'm going to keep my sanity intact while we pretend to be in love is a question I haven't yet answered.

"That red face says you don't have *any* trouble in that area." Emery nudges me with her elbow.

"Can we not talk about my sex life, please?"

Or lack thereof.

I need to keep my wits about me for this whole thing. Yes, I'm lying and I feel guilty as hell. But what options do I have? Allow myself to be evicted from my apartment and move in with my mother because I can't afford rent?

If I do that, she'll be in my ear every day about marrying Anthony and eventually I will either A, give in to shut her up or B, end up stabbing her with a Biro.

Our relationship would *not* withstand us living together. And while I thoroughly *hate* the idea of being paid to pretend to be in a relationship, right now my survival instincts are the ones in the driver's seat.

"I'm going to get out of your hair," Emery says, pushing up from the bed. "Text me when you're back. You owe me a pizza night."

She envelops me in a big hug. For a minute I want to cry—how the hell did my life end up here? I did well in school, planned my life out with goals and dreams and ambitions. I studied hard and I'm kind to people and...

Thinking like this won't do anything. Just bat your eyelashes at a handsome man and then you can come home and get your life in order.

How ironic that no matter how hard I've tried to buck against my mother's ideals, this is where I've ended up.

I won't let Daniel get to me. I won't be fooled into thinking someone like him might want me in the real world. I won't feel *any* affection for a man who can buy his way into or out of anything. My mother fell for a man like that once, and she never recovered from it.

I won't repeat her mistakes.

As I finish packing, the sound of a car door slamming grabs my attention. My apartment overlooks Love Street—that's right, I live at 21 Love Street, and the address has never felt more ill-fitting. A sleek, black limousine is parked out front and the driver steps out, wearing a black suit and a shiny brimmed hat.

Looks like procrastination time is over. I'm being summoned.

Reality settles around me like a boa constrictor. I've agreed to Daniel's deal and it's time to front up.

All you have to do is be seen at a few Michelin-starred restaurants gazing lovingly into his eyes. Easy-peasy.

I can play my part and then go back to my life barely even remembering Daniel's name. So long as I keep my distance the second the prying eyes are out of sight, I'll be totally fine.

I shut my suitcase and check my reflection one last time before heading downstairs to meet my fate.

"Let me help you with your things, Ms. Matthews." Daniel's driver, a guy who introduces himself as Andy, lifts my bag into the boot of the limo like it weighs no more than a bag of chips. "You're a light packer."

My cheeks burn. I'm sure he doesn't mean it as an insult, but it only adds to my growing feelings of insecurity about the whole arrangement, and frankly, I don't need any help with that.

Andy opens the limo's door for me. To my complete and utter dismay, Daniel is stretched out along the back seat, looking like the epitome of male hotness. He's dressed more casually today, in jeans and a touchable white shirt that he's tucked in and secured with a brown belt. It highlights his trim waist and contrasts with the broadness of his shoulders. His black hair is wavy and soft, a little long around the ears.

All in all, he looks like a more attainable version of the man I met the other night—which is a dangerous, dangerous impression. Because *nothing* about this man is attainable.

I scoot into the back seat with all the grace of a newborn deer, trying not to let my skirt ride up my legs. Dammit, why didn't I wear pants instead? My thighs have a life of their own sometimes. His eyes flick over me, hotly assessing every inch, with a subtle quirk of his mouth that makes my pulse pound in my ears.

Everything is fine. I can manage this. I can absolutely ignore the pulse of sexual awareness currently scrambling my brain. Who needs brain cells anyway? They're filler, really. Totally not a requirement to function.

Yeah, you're in deep, deep *trouble.*

CHAPTER SIX

Daniel

EVERYTHING IS GOING according to plan. After the media snapped us coming out of the supply closet on Friday night—dishevelled and holding hands—it was all over the internet by morning.

"Cinderella Story: Catering Waitress Snags Australia's Most Eligible Bachelor."

Funny how I went from being an amoral cheating bastard to "most eligible" in only a night. But it tells me that we're not only making lemons into lemonade, we're slapping a fancy label on it and passing it off as artisanal.

Some tabloids are still touting the affair rumours, but there has definitely been a change of tune across the board, according to my head of PR. She rushed into my office this morning with the good news, and a congratulations, of course. Stumbling across Ava might possibly have been the best thing that could have happened right now.

Although, I can see we have a bit of work to do. Ava

sits so far to the other side of the back seat, her arm pressing against the limo's door, it's almost like she thinks I'm going to bite her. Or worse.

"You didn't have to come to pick me up yourself," she says, eyeing me. Instead of her slicked-back ponytail from the night of the Cielo launch, her hair is loose. It swirls around her shoulders, catching the light. Looking rich like espresso one minute, then warm like burnt toffee the next. "I assumed you'd be too busy."

"And I assumed it might be weird for you to walk into my apartment by yourself," I reply. Truthfully, I *am* too busy to be doing this. But a good CEO doesn't do everything on their agenda; they simply know how to prioritise.

Right now, making Ava feel comfortable enough to play a convincing fiancée is at the top of my list.

"It's weird to be riding in a limo, to be honest. I've never met someone who owned one before," she says. "But I'm guessing this is normal for you."

"It is. Although sometimes I like to drive myself, if I need to get out and think. The Maserati needs to be taken for a spin every so often."

"Oh." She rolls her eyes. "My apologies. I've never met anyone who owns a limousine *and* a Maserati."

I stifle a smile as the car whisks us out of Ava's street and toward the central business district. I live in a penthouse apartment facing the river, in a building I acquired and renovated as my first major project with the family business.

Ava remains glued to the door, even after we've been driving for a full five minutes.

"I don't bite, you know." I watch as her mouth tightens. She doesn't like being called out, apparently. "Unless you're getting up close and personal with that door because you've got some kind of car fetish?"

"No, I don't have a fetish, thank you very much. And I'm sure you don't bite. But I know nothing about you and yet I'm going to stay in your home and…" Her eyes are wide as she twists the hem of her simple floral dress in one hand. But the nervous action drags the fabric up and flashes me part of her thigh. My pulse quickens in response. "It's crazy. I'm like some naive girl in a Liam Neeson film only I don't know anyone with a very special set of skills who's going to save me if you decide to sell me on the black market."

I can't help but laugh at that. "If you're worried that I *am* going to abduct you, then it's probably not wise to tell me you don't have anyone to save you."

"See!" She throws her hands up in the air. "I'm TSTL."

"What's that?"

"Too stupid to live."

"No, you're not. I bet you googled the shit out of me before you left, right?" I shoot her a look and she nods. "See, there's an electronic trail. Plus the whole world knows we're together and they *always* suspect the boyfriend."

"Fiancé," she corrects me with a hint of a smile.

"You're more useful to me alive."

"Gee, thanks." Ava rolls her eyes, but I can still see that smile tugging at the corner of her full lips. She's relaxed against the back seat of the limo now, and I think my charms might have worked on her.

Charms, really?

That's *not* usually a word associated with me. Ambitious, driven, single-minded. Arrogant. They all get bandied around at length, because I refuse to pander to the press who've tortured my family since I was a child. They do *not* see me as charming. Therefore, the world doesn't see me as charming.

Truthfully, the world has no idea who I am behind my suit and my job title. I keep that part of me—the *real* me—locked up tight. Protected. Even from myself.

"Look, we were backed into a corner and a decision had to be made on the spot," I say. "We seized the opportunity to improve both of our situations."

"But what if people ask questions? I didn't even recognise you in the cupboard, so how am I supposed to act like we've been dating for months?"

Good point. Not so much to fool the press, but I have an even bigger, more important audience to worry about: my brother. "What do you want to know? I'll give you the speed-date version now."

Ava shifts on the spot, turning her body so she's looking at me directly. The dress she's wearing is soft and touchable, a light grey cotton with embroidered white and pink flowers and little sleeves that flutter around her arms. There's a subtle V at the neckline that hints at treasures beneath—and unfortunately I saw enough two nights ago to mentally fill in the blanks.

"What's your favourite movie?" she asks.

"The Godfather."

"Favourite food?"

"Pasta *al forno*."

"Favourite place in the world?"

"Tuscany."

Her eyes crinkle with laughter. "Are you just naming Italian things?"

"Are you trying to tell me I'm a cliché?" I slide my hands down my thighs, the thick denim an unusual sight. Most weekdays I wear a suit. But I left the office early, opting to take all my afternoon calls from home so I could pick up Ava. The second she's settled, I need to get back to it. Although she's right, we *do* need to get to know one another. "I also happen to like soccer, gelato and Formula 1."

"You *are* a cliché." The smile lighting her face is enough to power a city. If she's this sweet and charming come dinnertime, then this whole mess might be wrapped up easier than I thought.

Hopefully then my life can go back to normal. No more headache-inducing drama. No more having my brother think I'm nothing but a carbon copy of our father. No more sleepless nights, tossing and turning with fury.

You know Ava is going to cause sleepless nights.

Okay, so having a beautiful woman around 24/7 for the next week will be a distraction...but I'm perfectly capable of keeping myself in check. But even as I think that, I feel anticipation crawling through my bloodstream. It's been too long since I let myself indulge.

"And what do I need to know about you?" I ask.

"Well, I'm a teacher... Although I can only get relief

teaching shifts at the moment. You know, funding cuts and whatnot. I love working with children and helping them learn. It's one thing I'm really passionate about." The tone of her voice is so genuine that for a moment, it sounds almost foreign. "My favourite colour is sea-foam green. I have a sweet tooth. I love B-grade action movies, and my hidden talent is being able to tie a cherry stem with my tongue."

Good lord, I do not *need to imagine that.*

I clear my throat and hope that she doesn't see how my brain tried to short-circuit itself. "See, now we're best friends."

"Except we have to pretend to be *more* than friends."

I might not have any idea how to appear in love—fact is, I've never seen it in the flesh. Not with my parents. Not with any relationship I've ever been involved in. I thought, for a moment, that I *might* have seen it with Marc and Lily.

Pretending to be head over heels in *lust* however... Now that I can do. And isn't that a mark of the newly engaged? They can't keep their hands off one another.

Given Ava's plush lips, unusual eyes and wicked curves, she may as well have been made precisely to trigger my desires. Which is a good thing for our act, and troublesome for my sanity behind closed doors. Perhaps burying myself in this new CEO role to the exclusion of literally everything else for the past twelve months wasn't as smart as I'd thought. Because now it's hard to look at Ava without my mind wandering to what's hiding under that wispy little dress.

"Only while people are watching," I reply, as much for my own benefit as for hers.

"So what's the plan for today?" she asks.

"We've got the afternoon to ourselves, so you can settle in and I'll get some work done. Then it's dinner with my family."

"The *whole* family?" she asks. "I thought we only needed to convince your brother."

It would have been easier if it was just Marc. But no, my mother has gone into full mama-bear mode. Formidable as she is, her sons are her whole world. Our fighting must be killing her inside, because she instilled in us both from a young age how important it was that we take care of one another. But Marc won't let go of the rumours unless *he* believes nothing happened.

No amount of matriarchal interference will change his mind.

"My mother will be there, as will Lily. It'll be better with a bit of a buffer between me and Marc, anyway."

It's sad that our relationship has come to this—we were so close as kids. Now everything is splintered. Fractured.

"No time like the present, I guess," Ava says, clapping her hands together. "Rip it off like a Band-Aid."

"Do you normally spout colloquialisms when you're nervous?"

"I'm not nervous." Her tone is indignant.

"Do you normally lie when you're nervous?" I shoot her a sidelong glance and she frowns, her brows furrowing above an adorably pert nose.

"I feel like you're going to talk circles around me,"

she mutters, turning her face to the window as the world rushes by. "What if your family hates me?"

"It doesn't matter if they hate you. They only need to believe you."

"Don't you care?" She turns and tilts her head, her warm eyes assessing with laser-like focus. She's a woman who could see too much. Get too close.

But my desire to keep people at arm's length has had years to set down roots, to grow strong. Watching my mother fall apart at the seams while my father stomped on their vows by fucking his way around the world solidified my need to protect myself. Watching her cry and beg him to come back after all he'd done... Well, that showed me one important thing.

Love makes you weak.

"If my own brother can accuse me of having an affair with his wife, then why should I care about his opinion? Clearly, he knows nothing about me." I force myself to pause and take a breath. My head might be swirling but I need to keep my focus. I have a job to do and I want it done as quickly as possible. "I need to fix this before it does any more damage to my company."

"To your company." Ava bobs her head. "Interesting choice of words."

Her comment rankles, because I have *always* cared about my family. I spent my whole bloody childhood shielding Marc from the demise of our parents' relationship—distracting him with endless games of soccer in our street while my parents screamed at one another inside. It's the reason *he* still believes in marriage and love...at least, until recently.

The thought of having to face my brother after his accusation makes me feel hollowed out. What happened to the happy-go-lucky guy who was my sidekick from the day he was born?

Maybe Marc is sick of being your sidekick.

I thought we had a good thing going. I took care of the broader company strategy and set the new direction and he applied his brilliant mind to the numbers. We need both sets of skills—my big-picture approach and Marc's intense eye for detail.

And without him, our acquisition of Livingstone Spas is on shaky ground. The small boutique spa company has properties scattered along desirable portions of Australia's east coast, and it's a core part of my strategy to get Moretti Enterprises a foothold in the luxury wellness market.

But Marc is close with Henry Livingstone. If he decides to get in Henry's ear about the "affair," then... I can kiss this acquisition goodbye.

Ava stares at me, clearly waiting for a response while my mind is still spinning.

"I didn't bring you here to judge me," I reply. "And if I don't care about their opinion, what makes you think I care about yours?"

Perhaps it makes me sound like a bastard, but I did *not* become a CEO by worrying about other people's opinions. That way lies a path to poor decisions.

This *has* to go smoothly. I need Marc to come back to the company and ensure this deal goes through. If he does that, then the media should finally quieten down.

As for the mess that is our relationship... Well, that's a whole other story.

One I'm not sure will have a happy ending.

"An evening with the family whose opinions you don't care about," Ava says, looking as though she's trying to muster something. "That should be fun. Not."

CHAPTER SEVEN

Ava

Daniel's penthouse apartment is *not* at all what I expect. I mean, I'm pretty sure his coffee machine cost more than my teaching degree, so *that's* on brand. But I'm expecting a place full of white and silver and glass, sleekly modern and cold. Impersonal. Like a showroom.

What I get is something else entirely.

The old building was once a factory, so the penthouse apartment isn't actually that high up. But due to the fact that we're facing the Yarra River, the view is uninterrupted. One side of the apartment is exposed brick, which contrasts with lighter wood flooring and white walls. The kitchen has stark black countertops. There's a giant metal staircase leading upstairs, and windows so big they run the full length of both floors.

The furniture—a large cognac leather couch, a table and chairs to seat eight, and a coffee table that looks vintage—has personality. On top of the coffee table sits a well-loved classic science-fiction novel next to an empty espresso cup, and a matching saucer sprinkled with crumbs.

"Wow, it actually looks like you live here." I blurt the words out before I have a chance to think about how silly they sound. "I mean…"

"You expected me to take you to a fake apartment?" Daniel looks confused.

"No, what I mean is I expected something different." I turn around to face him and fiddle with the handle of my suitcase. He'd insisted on wheeling it for me, but I already feel that I'm accepting more from him than I would under normal circumstances.

But these are not normal circumstances. These are very, *very* unusual circumstances.

"Like what?" He cocks his head, his eyes tracking my face.

"Something sleeker." I cringe. Now it sounds like I'm insulting his taste. "I mean, this has more personality than I expected."

Oh wow, that's even worse.

"That's a backhanded compliment if I ever heard one." His mouth does that half smile, half smirk thing and my stomach automatically flips.

"Well, it's just that you seem so…modern." Dig up, stupid. "And all your recent projects have been very modern, too, right? The Cielo, that tower down in the Docklands. Oh, and the hotel your company designed near Southern Cross Station."

Daniel raises an eyebrow. "You *have* done your homework."

"Well, maybe I'm not TSTL after all." I nod. "This place is really nice. It's warm."

"Warm and old," he replies affectionately. "I like old things. They have character and a story behind them. I like thinking about their history when I'm shopping for a new piece."

"You decorated yourself? I thought rich people use interior designers."

Daniel motions for me to follow him. "Rich people who don't have control issues use interior designers."

Something about the way he says "control issues" makes my mouth run dry. I try to swallow but find my heart is beating harder in my chest and it's difficult to walk and breathe and swallow at the same time.

You're acting like a complete giddy fool.

"I've set you up in here." Daniel leads me to a room on the bottom floor that's tucked away behind the kitchen.

It's so gorgeous I almost gasp. The window runs from the floor all the way up, flooding the space with natural light. There's a large bed with a wrought iron bedhead and soft cream linen, and a blanket thrown over the foot in a pale dusty blue. There's even a book-shelf filled to the brim, a mix of architecture and art books and spine-cracked novels.

"You've got your own bathroom through there." Daniel points to where an open arch shows a small room with a spa-like shower *and* a claw-foot tub. "It's stocked with shampoos and soaps. My assistant put some other girlie things in there for uh…makeup and stuff."

"Makeup and stuff?" I'm touched by the gesture. Imposing and blunt as Daniel may be, I get the impression he really does want me to feel comfortable here.

"It's been a long time since anyone was here but me, so I'm a little out of touch with what women need in their bathrooms." The cryptic statement has me curious but before I can even think about opening my mouth to pry, Daniel moves on. "Towels are in the drawers. And there's plenty of space for you to hang clothes in here."

An antique armoire is the feature of the room, the rich reddish wood standing out against the white walls and sun-bleached floors. When I pull the doors open, I'm shocked to find a few things already hanging inside. There's a sparkling black dress, one in blue and another in deep purple.

"Tell me this isn't left over from the last woman." I glance at him over my shoulder and the bastard grins at me. He's pushing my buttons.

"Get all the jokes out now, you've got a long night ahead of you," he replies, leaning against the doorframe. How easy could it be to imagine this is really my life—a perfect home, perfect dresses and a perfect man to take them off at the end of the night.

This isn't real. None of this is real.

"How do you even know what my size is?" I raise an eyebrow. "And if you feed me some bullshit about you can tell by looking at a woman's body, I'm going to brain you with my shoe."

"I had my assistant call the catering company to get your uniform size under the guise of wanting to surprise you."

"Oh." That's smart. "You thought of everything, didn't you?"

"At the risk of sounding like a snob, I thought you may not have anything in your wardrobe fit for the opera." He shifts on the spot, like he's acutely aware of how this simple thing highlights how different we are. "In France."

"France?" I squeak. "Excuse me? I must be having hearing problems. It sounded like you said we're going to France."

"That's right."

"As in, France in Europe?"

Daniel watches me from his vantage point, hands jammed into his pockets in a way that encourages me to lower my gaze. "Do you know of another France?"

"Don't be smart."

"I was going to talk to you about it today. I'm supposed to leave on Wednesday for a meeting, and I figured that we should be seen together anyway, so you can come with me and we'll kill two birds with one stone."

I gape at him. "When you said we'd take a holiday, I assumed it would be in a fancy hotel here. Maybe Sydney."

"Why would I stay in a hotel here when my apartment is better than any hotel?" His genuine confusion makes me want to smack him. Or kiss him.

Or push him down to the floor and straddle him and—

"You're looking a little red," Daniel comments, taking a step toward me.

"I'm fine," I snap, holding up a hand to stop him

coming any closer. "You never said there would be international travel involved. What if I didn't have a passport?"

"You don't have one?"

I can't help but bristle at the way he says it like *everybody* would have a passport. Clearly someone as worldly as Daniel Moretti wouldn't consider that international travel might not be in everyone's budget. But I *do* happen to have a passport from my gap year, where I backpacked around Europe with a friend, living on a few dollars a day.

Something tells me this trip to Europe will be different.

"Well, yes, I do have one," I admit. "But I didn't pack it."

"So we'll swing by your house and get it." I can tell he's getting frustrated with the objections I'm throwing up. Clearly Daniel likes to be in charge and he's planning to make all the decisions through the course of our arrangement.

Part of me wants to press on him, to show him that I can hold my own. "And what about tonight, then? I need to be prepared."

All I know about the Morettis is what I gleaned from a few online searches. Loaded…like *seriously* loaded. Divorced parents, father accused of multiple affairs, which certainly explains why Daniel is going to such lengths to prove himself right now. I couldn't find a single picture of Daniel and his father together from the last decade and a half.

He gives me a noncommittal shrug. "They're not going to quiz you."

"Do you want them to believe us or not? Or am I supposed to be a trophy fiancée who doesn't know anything about anything?"

Daniel looks at me curiously, as though he's trying to figure me out. "Is that the kind of woman you think I want?"

"Well, I don't really know because you're about as communicative as a pet rock." I fold my arms across my chest, defensiveness tightening my muscles. "Seriously, for someone who's willing to buy himself a fiancée, you sure seem to resist anything that might help me do my job properly."

"If I'd wanted a 'sit still, smile quietly' woman, then I have failed miserably in choosing you, haven't I?"

"I'm going to take that as a compliment," I reply primly.

"You should." He stares at me for a moment, dark eyes roaming my face and making my body slowly heat as though he's cranking the dial to my internal thermostat.

"I want to know what I'm walking into tonight. They might not quiz me but if you want anyone to *actually* believe we're a couple, then some sense of family dynamics would be helpful," I say. "If it wasn't painfully obvious the night we met, I sometimes put my foot in my mouth."

"Will you stop prodding if I give you something?"

"Yes." *Maybe.*

"My father cheated on my mother for years until

they divorced, which I'm sure you were able to gather when you looked me up. They would fight, but she ultimately turned a blind eye so long as nobody outside the family knew." He snorts, making his stance on his mother's actions very clear. "He brought women into our family home and she didn't put a stop to it. Eventually they divorced. We didn't hear from him for several years, because he wanted to have a 'clean slate' with his new wife and that didn't involve Marc or me. Then he started trying to contact us again out of the blue when I was about eighteen."

"That's horrible."

"I haven't spoken to him in years." His expression is so blank and so careful, I can only assume there's something painful being masked inside him. "And I have no desire to."

"Okay, duly noted. Don't mention your father."

"Needless to say, I have no desire to follow in my parents' footsteps, so this engagement will be a shock to everyone." He pauses, looking off like his mind is lost in the past. "I have no idea why my parents got married in the first place."

"You don't think they loved each other back then?" I ask.

"Possibly, in the early days. But that clearly didn't last, did it?" His voice has a sharp, cynical edge. "That's the thing about love, it's not deserving of the pedestal people place it on."

I bite back my instinct to disagree. Even with my mother's negative experience and all the pressure she's put on me to get married so a man can "save" me, I still believe in love. Real, passionate love. I used to spend hours looking at old photo albums of my grandparents when they were young. The way my grandfather looked at my grandmother—like she was the only thing in the world that mattered—I want that. And I want someone to give it to in return.

"I understand why you would have that opinion," I say. And I do, even if I don't agree.

"I expected you to jump to love's defence," he says, raising an eyebrow.

"Because I'm a woman?"

"Because you're a romantic."

"And what do you base *that* assessment on?"

"Anyone else wouldn't care about winning my family over, given this is a business arrangement. But you want them to like you. And you're worried about lying."

"Doesn't that make me a good person rather than a romantic?"

"It means you have a rose-coloured glasses view of the world, which is inherently romantic."

Daniel seems like the kind of man who once he's made up his mind, nothing short of a gun to his head will change it. And really, why should I care what he thinks of me? As he said, this is a business arrangement.

"How on earth are you going to convince the world that a romantic like me fell in love with a cynic like you?" I ask with a teasing tone.

"I've got a PR manager to help with that." He smooths his hands down the front of his jeans, and I track the movement with my eyes. Everything about him screams self-assurance—from his posture, to the firm grip he has on every conversation, to the way he looks at me with unwavering eye contact, no matter how I prod him. "All you have to do is look like you're enamoured."

I try to resist a smirk. "I might need some practise. You haven't exactly given me much to be enamoured by."

Liar.

"Fine. Let's practise," he says, his tone issuing a challenge. Clearly he's not content to let me do all the prodding.

"Seriously?"

He shrugs. "Why not? It's got to be better than you poking around in my personal life."

"Sorry for wanting to get to know you." I roll my eyes.

Surely it wouldn't hurt to have a little "rehearsal" of how we're supposed to act? Truth be told, I *am* a little nervous. His family belongs to another world. *He* belongs to another world…a world where money can buy anything. Even a fiancée.

And I've never faked anything, not even an orgasm. Because if a guy can't make me feel something real, I'm not going to stroke his ego by pretending.

But if I fail to convince his family, he might not hold up his end of the bargain. Then I'm screwed—no apartment, no catering job to help me get by since my "indiscretion" is plastered all over the internet. I *have* to make this work.

I take a few steps forward and plant one hand against

his arm. The soft fabric of his shirt hugs the curve of his biceps and it's heaven beneath my fingertips. I tilt my face up to Daniel's as though we're about to kiss, and I give him what I hope is a convincing expression of a woman head over heels in love. But Daniel's husky laugh makes me frown.

"Let it come naturally," he says. "Stop trying so hard."

"But—"

My words are cut short when he presses his finger to my lips. His face is close, so close I can see each thick lash framing his dark eyes, and the hint of stubble impressing itself on the skin around his jaw, like darkness is peeking through from inside him.

My breath hitches as he slides his hand around my neck, his fingers driving into my hair. He tilts me back, his thumb brushing my cheekbone and the corner of my lip for a moment that stretches on endlessly. Anticipation winds through my body, tightening like a snake and squeezing. Making me want, need, desire.

Making me ache.

My lips go slack, calling silently to his. Calling for his kiss.

Daniel's head comes forward, his dark gaze holding me captive. In this moment, I am his to command, soft and pliable under his touch. When his lips part, I almost whimper. *Yes*.

But the sound of his ringtone slashes through the moment. Daniel pulls back and digs the device out of his back pocket, cancelling the call. I'm almost burning up. I'm like a flame he's coaxed to life and I hate myself for it. I force myself to push away the pink fog of lust addling my brain.

How does he play me so easily?

"Okay, so…" I square my shoulders like I wasn't about to allow him to kiss me senseless for no good reason. I can't let him see the effect he has on me. "Dinner with the whole family and a trip to France. Anything else I should know about before I unpack?"

"I'm a light sleeper." Daniel's eyes are dark, almost black but not quite. It makes him hard to read, hard to decipher. The man, so far, is full of contradictions—sleek image and a home filled with personality; he acts like he doesn't care about my opinion and yet he stocks my bathroom with everything I could possibly need. I don't know what to make of him. "If you hear me walking around at night, don't worry. We're not getting burgled."

I already know what's going to happen tonight. I'm going to lie awake, listening to the sound of him, wondering what it might be like if he cracked my door open and padded softly into my room to pick up where we left off a moment ago. Wanting to know what it might be like to be burned by him.

Wanting it all.

CHAPTER EIGHT

Daniel

I COME TO find Ava several hours later, right before we're due to leave. One thing I didn't consider when concocting this crazy plan was that I'd need to let a stranger into my very private world. My home, which is my personal sanctuary, and my family, which I keep as far from people as possible.

I jog down the stairs to the bottom floor of my apartment, making a little more noise than normal so Ava will know I'm coming.

It's strange having someone here.

And yet...

The moment we shared in her room was anything but strange. It was totally familiar, intimately familiar. Had my assistant's call not interrupted us, I would have absolutely followed through and kissed her. Her sweet lips have been on my mind all afternoon, ruining my ability to work. Taking my concentration and shredding it to ribbons.

I took myself in hand in the shower, closing my eyes

and thinking about her soft curves and fiery eyes while I stroked myself. I thought about having her there, pinned between me and slick tile, open and willing and wanting. I have to admit, I enjoyed watching Ava battle her attraction—it's not something I come across very often. The women I've dated casually in the past never made an effort to hide what they wanted…which was often what ended up causing the relationship to come to a swift end.

Because wanting my body is fine, and wanting my attention is fine…to a degree. But wanting my money or my commitment is entirely another story.

Those things are off limits.

Hence why I don't date anymore. A year ago I realised that it was impossible to juggle everything, and I've never enjoyed the head games. So that's why this arrangement suits me fine…even if I'm going to give myself blue balls from hell.

I pause outside her door and knock.

"Coming!" There's a thud followed by an *oof* and then the door swings open. Ava's wearing a simple black dress—not the one my assistant procured for her—but it suits her perfectly.

The cut is subtly flared from the waist, so it skims her hips, falling to her knees in a soft, rippling sheet. The bodice crosses over her bust and there's a tie at one hip that strangely gets me hot and bothered. I wonder if I tug on that string whether the whole garment will open up.

"Ready to go? I'll grab my bag and…" Her voice

trails off as her eyes snag on the velvet box I pull from my pocket. "Oh."

"You'll need to wear this until we're done." I'm not sure what the protocol is. I feel like my opening the box for her is a bit too…real. Instead, I hand it to her.

Ava runs her thumb over the velvet before opening it. "Wow."

"Do you like it?"

"I guess it doesn't really matter if I do but…I do." She smiles and it's free and uninhibited and so damned genuine that the breath stills in my lungs. "It's really beautiful."

The ring is unique. When I ducked into the jewellery store this morning, the blue stone immediately caught my attention. It's an oval cut, surrounded by diamonds, and there's something charmingly traditional about it. Which is how Ava strikes me. "It suits you."

She slides the ring onto her finger. "Is it a sapphire?"

"Yes."

"That's my birthstone." Her smile fades a little. "You know, I thought the first time I wore a ring on this finger it would mean something."

I've never considered myself a sentimental person, because such traits are a liability, but hearing that hint of regret in her voice shifts something inside me. Something that I don't want shifted.

"Apparently it's bad luck to wear a ring on this finger before you're married. My mum told me that once," she says with a snort. "Old wives' tales."

"I would think that there'd be a million other things that would cause bad luck in relationships before that."

"Been a while since you had a girlfriend, huh?" she teases. Her fingers toy with the ring, twisting and turning it around her finger so the blue stone winks at me as if it knows all my secrets.

But I won't bite. "I don't talk about my love life."

"Ever?" She cocks her head.

"Ever."

"Why?"

"It's private. And our being together now isn't an excuse to play twenty questions." The words come out a little harder than I intend, but ever since I took the role of CEO of Moretti Enterprises, the press have been relentless. Hounding. Intrusive.

They're all hoping for a front-page-worthy outburst, poking and pushing me so the pain of my past will bubble to the surface. Advertisers might think that sex is the big seller, but I'm convinced pain sells more. And the media preys on it.

"Maybe it would be quicker for you to give me a list of conversation topics that *are* acceptable," Ava says, grabbing her bag from the bed and slinging it over one shoulder. "Because every time I ask a question, you act like I'm interrogating you. Unless, of course, that's your not-so-subtle way of saying you have no interest in talking to me."

"Even if that was the case, something tells me you're the persistent type." I fight back a smile as we walk through the apartment, her heels clicking against the polished boards. Even with the pencil-thin lady stilts, she's still a shorty.

"I can be quite loud when it's required."

I laugh and scrub a hand over my chin. I didn't shave, and the prickles rub against my palm. "So you're a screamer, huh?"

"I don't mean...not like... Get your mind out of the gutter," she says, whacking me with the back of her hand. "I was not talking about *that*."

"That?"

"You know what I mean." Her eyes plead with me not to tease her anymore, but I can't help myself.

"I haven't the faintest clue."

"Well, if your parents never talked about the birds and the bees with you, that's *not* my problem." She picks up speed, walking ahead of me toward the elevator. I hold back, enjoying the way her dress swishes against the back of her thighs in a way that has my pants feeling suddenly tight.

Add that to the growing list of mental images I need to ignore for the next however many days...

I *have* to get my head into the game, if I have any chance at all of salvaging this deal and my reputation. Not to mention my relationship with my brother. I can't let anything distract me from my goals...not even Ava.

CHAPTER NINE

Ava

AND I THOUGHT *my* family was dysfunctional.

This dinner is awful. Unbearable. Seriously, secret service agents should film this as inspiration for torture techniques.

I'm sitting at the dinner table, between Daniel and his sister-in-law, Lily. On the other side sits Daniel's mother, an older family friend named Enzo, and Marc. The silence is so thick I'm worried it might choke me if I open my mouth. The only thing that breaks the oppressive lack of sound is the clack of cutlery against porcelain.

But nobody is actually eating. We're simply pushing vegetables and pieces of tender meat in a red sauce around our plates. Awkwardness is a real appetite killer, it turns out.

Lily is sweet and she attempts to make conversation with me. She's even more beautiful in person, without Photoshop smoothing away the little bits of her that make her unique, like the cluster of freckles on her nose and the mole on the side of her neck. I know her—like most do—from when she was crowned Miss Australia five years ago.

But I can feel her eyes constantly darting across the table to where her husband sits, a stormy expression on his face. We've all been summoned here by Mrs. Moretti, but to what end? I'm itching to get out.

"We need to talk about this," Daniel says eventually, and there's an unnerving stillness around the table.

"There's nothing to say." Marc pushes back roughly on his chair and stalks out of the room.

A second later, Daniel follows him. "This whole thing is ludicrous. I'm your brother for Chrissake."

"And?"

"I have a fiancée," he says, controlling his voice. "Why would I screw around when I have such a beautiful woman already in my bed?"

I feel my face grow hot, and thankfully their voices start to fade as they enter the next room. I'm questioning everything right now—maybe this whole deal was a bad idea. Maybe I should have come out of that supply closet with my head held high, betting that my catering boss wouldn't have fired me.

"I know what I saw." Marc's tone is frosty but only snatches of conversation float into the dining room. "A photo...kissing."

I frown. Daniel was so convincing about not being involved with Lily, but there's a photo? This is news to me, and it hits me like a punch in the gut. I believed him. That first night, when I put my foot in my mouth so hard I almost kicked my own brain out the back of my head, he told me the rumours were false and I believed him.

I turn to Lily, who sits with her shoulders back and her head high, but a tear slides down the side of her cheek.

"We didn't do it," she says, her voice wobbling. "I don't know what Marc thinks he saw."

Across the table, Mrs. Moretti watches Lily. Her expression is impossible to read, but there's something dark in her eyes. Something like hurt. Based on what Daniel told me about their family's past, maybe she's inclined to believe people are capable of anything. The older gentleman with salt-and-pepper hair suggests coffee and coaxes her out of her chair, leaving me alone with Lily.

"I'm sorry you have to see all this," she says, swiping a tear with the back of her hand. A huge diamond glitters on her finger, matching a strand of smaller stones dangling gracefully from her wrist. "It's not how I would want to welcome anyone into this family."

"It's not your fault," I reply automatically.

"I know. But try convincing them." She nods in the direction of where Mrs. Moretti and Enzo have disappeared into the kitchen. "I can't blame her for taking her son's side, but...I've known them forever. Since I was a little kid. Our parents were friends and I used to come here to play. She helped me with skinned knees and told the boys off if they were being too rough. She *knows* me."

My heart squeezes for this poor woman and what

she's going through. Instinctively I want to believe her, as I did Daniel. "Then what photo is he talking about?"

"That's the thing, I have no idea." Lily shakes her head. "He won't show it to me. Hell, he won't even talk to me now. The only reason he came tonight was because his mother lied about who was coming. Part of me wonders if she was pushing Marc's buttons so he'd flip out and divorce me."

"Do you really think that?"

"No, I guess not. Before all this happened, I was close with her. She loves her sons more than anything." She presses her fingertips to her cheeks. "But the whole world thinks I'm a cheating whore, so it's easy to become paranoid."

I don't know this woman at all and I have no real stake in this beyond wanting them to believe Daniel and I are engaged, but something compels me to comfort her. I reach out and grasp her hand, squeezing. "I believe you."

Lily looks up, her eyes watery and her mouth pressed into a line.

"I really do love him," she says, though the words are barely a whisper. "I've loved him since I was ten years old. Marc and Dan... They had a tough childhood, as I'm sure you know. They're not easy to reach."

"I'm seeing that." Every time I try to ask questions about Daniel's life, it's like pulling teeth. He's suspicious, waiting for an ulterior motive to reveal itself.

"The press hounded them when their father split. Imagine that? Asking two teenage boys what they thought of their father having an affair and leaving them."

No wonder Daniel is so guarded. "That's awful."

"It took me proposing to Marc three times before he said yes."

I blink. "*You* proposed to him?"

"Sure, why not?" Lily lifts one shoulder into a shrug and despite the tense situation, a cheeky smile blossoms on her lips. "I'm an independent woman who knows what she wants. I don't need to wait around for him to ask me."

"Amen to that." I reach for my wineglass and hold it up in salute before taking a sip. "Good for you."

"To be honest, I *never* thought Daniel would get married. He's been vocal about it for years and I know he was worried about Marc and me when we tied the knot. So, you must be pretty special." Lily touches my shoulder. "I'm glad he's found someone like you. I can tell you have a big heart."

My stomach churns. I'm categorically *not* special, not when sitting next to a woman with a body fit for modelling lingerie and bikinis. And especially not for a man like Daniel, whose opinions won't be changed by anything. The fact that we're in this outrageous scenario is proof—who would be comfortable faking an engagement, except a person who didn't believe in the sanctity of marriage?

I'm a means to an end. Nothing more.

But does that stop me being utterly intrigued and fascinated by him? Does it stop me wondering what it might be like to be loved by someone like him?

"Thank you." I barely manage to choke the words out. Guilt churns like sea foam in my stomach, whipped up by the storm of my emotions.

I'm lying to these people. I'm lying to my own family. My friends. It's not right.

But before I have a chance to dwell on it too long, Daniel storms back into the room looking like a god about to enter battle. His eyes are blazing chips of onyx and his jaw is granite hard.

"We're leaving," he announces, and doesn't break his stride on the way to the opulent house's front door.

I exchange a glance with Lily and she reaches in to give me a quick hug of solidarity. Something tells me it's going to be a long night.

CHAPTER TEN

Daniel

THE ENTIRE WAY home I don't say a word, and neither does Ava. I've shown her the worst side of my family tonight—the ugliest, darkest parts I've worked my whole life to hide away. The parts I'm ashamed of.

But my brother is a fool. He claims to have seen a photo of Lily and me kissing—a photo that I know cannot exist. Either he's lying...or someone else is lying. All I know is that I never laid a hand—or any other part of me—on his wife.

By the time we make it home, I'm all but shaking with anger. I need a shower and then I need a stiff drink.

"I'm sorry you had to be party to that," I say as we enter my apartment.

Ava grips her bag against her stomach like she needs a shield. I can't say I blame her. "All families have baggage."

The apartment is dark. The huge windows show a view of Melbourne at night—lights reflecting off the rippling river, cars trickling along the streets. The sky is a blanket of navy velvet and for some reason, I think of the ring on Ava's finger.

I shrug out of my jacket and sling it over the back of the couch. "Even yours?"

She lets out a hollow laugh. "Uh, yeah. My mother thinks the only way I can live a decent life is to find a man to support me, and my father is a ghost."

"What does that mean?"

"It means I have no idea where he is." She lets out a sharp, humourless laugh. "I have no idea if he's dead or alive. I couldn't even tell you his name."

Sometimes I wish my father had never been around to inflict the harm he did on my family, but then I hear the hurt in her voice and I know this option isn't any better. "He abandoned you and your mother?"

"Before I was even born. He didn't stick around to meet me, took off the second he found out my mother was pregnant." Her eyes are burning hot, defiant. Angry. "And my mother thinks she partied for too long and that was her punishment. She's worried I'm going to be left on the shelf, and that I'll be miserable like her and die alone."

"Wow." I let out a snort of disbelief. "That's messed up."

"So you're not the only one who's got more than their share of familial baggage, Mr. Moretti." She pokes my chest in a way that's almost playful, daring. Like she's trying to show me she understands without saying the words aloud.

Something deep inside me wants to reach out and touch Ava. To connect with her. To be soothed by her.

I want to lose myself in something good for once, in a pleasure so strong and deep it burns away every bad memory and hateful word, turning it all to ash in my palms.

"I don't have any ulterior motives here," she says softly. "I feel like you keep waiting for me to do something to prove you shouldn't trust me—"

"It's not that." Although maybe it should be. It wouldn't be the first time someone got close to me and tried to use it to their advantage.

"Then what is it?"

She steps closer, her beautiful copper-flecked eyes glimmering like embers. In the dim light, my senses are heightened. I smell the perfume on her skin—sweet and girlish, vanilla and flowers. I feel the heat radiating from her. I sense the flutter of her heartbeat, the quickened pace of her pulse.

"I'm sick of talking, to be honest." I rake a hand through my hair. "Sick of questions."

"What would you prefer?" She steps closer again, her hand brushing my arm. It's all so innocent, so innocuous. And yet... "Silence?"

Need grips me at the base of my cock and I'm harder than I've ever been in my whole life. I want her. I want to be lost in her. I want her cries to erase the worries in my head.

I need...

"We should go to bed." My voice is low, rough as gravel. I'm holding on to the promise I made her—this relationship is for show. Behind closed doors we're nothing to each other. And I expect nothing from her.

"We?" she whispers, trailing her hands along the line of buttons on my shirt, mimicking the way I touched her that first night.

I stand my ground, even though my entire body screams at me to claim her. "You were the one who was concerned about making sure our arrangement didn't include sex."

"I said you weren't *entitled* to it," she clarifies, her big eyes looking up at mine. Moonlight and the flickering city reflect off her skin, creating shadows and hollows. "I wanted you to understand that paying me doesn't mean I owe you my body."

It makes sense. Her mother believes that only a man can give her a proper life and here she is, making a deal with a man for the benefit of her future. It must eat her up inside.

She's going to regret this in the morning.

I know that with certainty.

"Go to bed, Ava," I say, taking her hand and removing it from my shirt. No matter how much I want her—*need* her—right now, what I need more is her playing the part outside my apartment. I can't mess that up. "*Your* bed."

I don't wait to see her reaction. Instead, I turn on my heels and head toward the metal staircase and climb the steps two at a time until I've got enough distance from her. My entire body pulses and aches. She's under my skin already. It's too much, too quick.

It's not her. It's this whole damn situation. You're messed up and it's affecting your thinking.

I head straight to my shower, undressing as I go, trying to think about anything but how I'm never going to be able to fall asleep knowing she's lying downstairs.

But I have to try.

The conversation with Marc tonight was a disaster. He's *so* convinced I betrayed him. And I won't let anyone see it, but... It fucking hurts. It hurts like he's taken a knife and stabbed me right in the chest. He's my little brother and I've loved him since the second he was born. I took care of him for years, taught him all my soccer moves until he did them better than me. I helped him with his homework, taught him to drive a stick, showed him how to tie a Windsor knot.

All the things I had to learn on my own.

I walk naked into my bathroom and wrench the taps until hot water jets out and steam fills the glass cavity. I step under, slapping my palm against the tiles as the hot water hits my back.

How could he accuse me of this? Ever since I was named CEO, things have been different. It's like he resents me getting to be number one. But I'm the first son. My uncle has been grooming me for this since I was a kid.

The water beats down and my muscles start to loosen. I stand there, forehead against the tiles while everything swirls in my head. If I can't convince Marc of my innocence, then I'll have to settle for the next best thing: clearing my name in the media. I need Ava for that. Because as much as I want my brother to believe me, my priority has to be ensuring the family business isn't ruined by this.

I'm in charge for a reason, because I know how to prioritise.

Eventually, the hot water brings me back down to earth. I turn off the taps and step out of the shower. Steam swirls and I swipe my hand across the mirror. My reflection is distorted, dark eyes and dark features warped by anger and condensation.

The apartment is silent.

I almost breathe a sigh of relief. I did the right thing walking away from Ava tonight. As much as it wasn't what I wanted, I need to keep my head in the game. But that doesn't mean I don't have needs to take care of.

I towel my body off and head into the bedroom. The upstairs floor of the apartment is mostly open, like a loft. A low metal railing rings the edge, allowing me to look down into the loungeroom and kitchen below. My king-size bed sits in the middle of the space. I need to be quiet.

What is she doing to me?

I flop down on my bed, the springs squeaking under my weight. The cover is soft against my back and cool air prickles along my damp skin. I lie there for a moment, staring into the fractured darkness, watching the lights shimmer outside. I strain, trying to hear if Ava is awake below me. But there's nothing.

Good.

I run my hand down my stomach and reach for my cock. I'm impossibly hard, even now. The shower did nothing for that—perhaps I should have taken a cold one instead of a hot one. I wrap my hand around myself and squeeze, flexing my hips and tightening my ass. I did this only a few hours ago, but Ava has me hot and bothered again. I can't let this get out of hand… No pun intended.

The drawer next to my bed has a bottle of lube and I squirt some into my hand, rubbing it up and down the length of my cock, coating myself in it. I close my eyes and press my head back against my pillow, letting myself sink. Behind my shuttered eyes, she's there. This time I don't push the fantasy away.

I don't think about what it means, about whether it's real or simply a product of this fucked-up situation. I don't temper myself.

I glide my hand up and down my cock, twisting when I reach the head. My other hand palms my balls. In my mind, she's here. Stripping off that simple black dress and exposing her curves to me, letting her long dark hair tumble over her tits. I love a woman who's got hills and valleys, whose thighs touch.

I was that kid who felt nothing toward the actresses of my day, instead getting hard over vintage films with Sophia Loren and Marilyn Monroe. I've always been attracted to softer women with flared hips, round bums and cleavage for days.

I stifle a grunt as I jerk myself, tugging on my cock in a way that makes the fantasy rich and bright. I pretend it's her hand working me over. Her in my bed instead of empty space.

Sex has no place in this arrangement, I know that. Even with Ava sending me mixed signals, I know better. But my libido—which has been forced to take a back seat this past year while I threw myself into taking over the helm of my family's company—has jumped back into the driver's seat. I'm hungry, wanting.

I want *her*.

Temptation rolls around in my head, like the ball of a pinball machine. She's the one who laid the suggestion down and opened that door.

I'm hard as marble remembering the way she looked up at me, with big, sultry eyes. Lips parted just so. The muscles in my ass and thighs clench as I squeeze myself, sliding my hand up and down slowly. Deliberately.

Flinging my other arm across my eyes, I thrust into my hand. I try to be quiet, stifling each grunt and groan. It will never be as good as the real thing, but this flickering reel of fantasies pulls me in. I can almost feel the softness of her tongue against my cock, and the tight pressure of her mouth.

I pretend she's here with me now.

CHAPTER ELEVEN

Ava

I CAN'T SLEEP. I toss and turn until my skin is damp with sweat and my hair sticks to the back of my neck. Why is it so hot in here? Maybe it's not. Maybe it's just me, burning up with the way Daniel looked at me when I propositioned him.

Unsuccessfully, remember? He turned you down.

And why wouldn't he? His brother is married to freaking Miss Australia. *That's* the calibre of women these brothers will end up with. Not unemployed schoolteachers who come from the burbs. Not Target-wearing, just-scraping-by women who grew up undeniably ordinary.

But I felt something. A connection, a passing of electrical current between us... Didn't I?

I toss again, my legs twisted in the sheets. I should have packed my vibrator.

"Ugh, why do you do this to yourself?" I stare up into the semidarkness. Outside the city lives and breathes, lights shining, cars gliding, people dancing.

I sit up and rake a hand through my hair. I need a drink of water—*something* to cool me down. My bare feet hit the floorboards and already it's a relief to my overheated skin. I walk to the door and pull it open. With all these big windows, it's easy enough to see my way around the apartment. My feet make soft noises against the polished boards as I pad quietly to the kitchen.

Just as my hand reaches for an empty glass sitting on one of the funky open shelves, I hear something that makes my entire body freeze. The sound is undeniably... male.

For a moment I wonder if I've imagined it. I strain to hear, searching for something in the soothing still-ness of the night. There are sounds of life outside, the whisper of tires over road, the faint pulse of music somewhere in the distance. And then...

I hear it. The unmistakable sound of someone re-leasing their breath, followed by the softest gasp that tells me it's not a sleeping sound.

It's a pleasure sound.

Before my addled brain has time to think through the consequences, my feet draw me away from the kitchen and toward the stairs leading up to the second floor. It's like I'm drugged, or maybe controlled by out-side forces. Perhaps some greater being has tied string to my wrists and ankles and is dancing me across the apartment. When I get to the bottom of the stairs, I pause, listening. Now I hear something else—the faint sound of slickness, of skin over skin.

My body beats, pulses. I'm like a ball of aroused

energy. I take one step and my breath catches at the shock of how cool the metal feels against the sole of my foot. I take one step at a time, quiet as a predatory cat stalking through thick, dense green.

You shouldn't be doing this. This is a total invasion of privacy.

If he didn't want me to hear then he could have taken it elsewhere—like in the bathroom. In his shower where a closed door would keep the sound locked away.

Maybe he wanted me to hear.

My palm smooths along the railing as I ascend, unsure what exactly I'm going to find. I'm holding my breath, my heart fluttering like a hummingbird caught in a spider's web, and with each step my mind spins quicker.

When I get to the top, I have to place a hand over my mouth to stop myself from making any noise. He's magnificent.

Daniel is stretched out on his bed, muscular thighs spread. The light from outside plays on his skin, dappling him with shimmering yellow and blue. He has one arm over his eyes and his other hand wrapped around his length. His muscles flex with the up-and-down movement, his hand a tight fist sliding from root to tip.

His chest—smattered with the finest dusting of hair—rises and falls and his abs clench. My gaze slides all over him, taking in every glorious detail. Taking in the hard, curved length of him. Taking in the gleam of something wet, and the way his jaw clenches as he tries not to make a sound.

Holy shit.

It's the most erotic thing I've ever seen. In the past, my ex never let me watch, though I'd asked. Multiple times. I grew up in a house where talking about such things was off-limits. Couple that with a Catholic school education and I felt unprepared for the world of sex and sexuality—so I'd explored on my own, searching for things on my computer and hoping to hell I didn't end up ruining my MacBook with a virus. Then my ex had reinforced the idea that sex was for closed doors and blankets pulled up and lights flicked off.

It had been good. At one time I'd even thought it was enough.

But now...now. There's nothing shameful or perverse about self-pleasure. It's beautiful. Empowering. Exciting. Simply—

"What the fuck?" Daniel is awake—how did I not see his eyes flick open? Too busy looking at what was going on downstairs.

I whirl around, my stomach in my throat. "I got up for a drink of water and I heard..."

"Jesus." The sound of something hitting the floor, possibly his feet, makes me jump. "And what? You thought you'd come up here and investigate?"

What *was* I thinking? Nothing, clearly. I'd been acting on instinct. Impulsive and reckless and intruding on his privacy.

"I'm sorry, I..." I scrub a hand over my face. *Oh god, oh god, oh god.* "That was really uncool."

The silence stretches on as my heartbeat thunders inside me. For a moment, I wonder if he's disappeared.

"So was me trying to take care of business while you were in the apartment," he says roughly. "That won't happen again."

I'm facing the window, watching the subtle shift of the reflection in the large glass panes. I make out Daniel's broad chest and wide shoulders. The shadow on his jaw. My gaze skitters to the floor as heat floods me, and not the good kind. I walked into his bedroom and watched him masturbate.

What the hell was I thinking?

"I can't even blame this on having too much to drink," I say with a shake of my head. "I was so nervous at dinner I didn't even finish one glass of wine."

Daniel lets out a long breath. "Why *did* you come up here? What did you think you'd find?"

"Exactly what I found," I admit. "I'm *so* sorry. That was a complete invasion of your privacy and honestly... I wasn't thinking at all. If I had, then I would have stayed downstairs."

I sense movement behind me, see it flicker in the glass. Daniel bends over, probably covering himself with some underwear. I chew on the inside of my cheek. How am I supposed to face him tomorrow, in the light of day? How am I supposed to keep my shit together when that image of him is going to be permanently seared into my brain?

"It was hard enough saying no to you downstairs," he says, his voice gravelly. "I don't need you coming up here and tempting me further."

Tempting him? My breath catches.

"Why did you say no if you were tempted?" I ask.

"Because this *isn't* a relationship, it's an arrangement. I'm paying you to be here."

Ah.

"And frankly, I don't know if I'm comfortable fucking a woman I'm paying." He moves behind me, pacing. I'm tempted to turn around, but something makes me feel like I shouldn't. "It's…sleazy."

"What you're paying me for is everything *outside* this apartment. When we're in public, with your family… We made it clear what happens behind closed doors is *not* part of the arrangement."

I'd been clear about that before. I don't want to feel like I'm being paid for sex, and I certainly don't want Daniel to feel like he's entitled to anything. But this whole interaction makes it clear that he's a decent guy.

A decent, sexy, hung-like-a-freaking-horse guy.

Stop thinking about his dick.

"I don't like being outmanoeuvred, Ava." He's closer now. I can feel him behind me—not touching, not even attempting to touch. But I catch his eye in the reflection of the glass. "I don't like being put in a position where I'm making decisions with my cock instead of my head."

I swallow and my mouth is completely dry. "You think that's what I'm doing?"

"You came up here, hoping to find me in a compromising position and you do it wearing the flimsiest, poorest fucking excuse for nightwear I have ever seen," he growls.

I glance down at myself. I hadn't even thought about

that. At night, I tend to overheat and so I sleep in as little material as possible. Flowy, thin white cotton. It's a camisole that barely covers my bum and ties at the shoulders in little bows. It's the only thing that doesn't make me feel like a million degrees once the weather starts to warm up.

I've never thought of it as sexy—because in my head sexy equals red and black and lace and satin. Not white cotton.

"You come up here in *that*." He almost spits the words out. "So thin I can see your nipples through it, and so short I'm almost salivating to find out if you're wearing anything at all underneath."

"I'm not."

The sound he releases is so hot and so frustrated that I almost melt. "Are you wet, Ava? Did you get that little pussy all wet watching me jerk off?"

I whimper. "I think so."

"You *think* so?"

The air is so silent and so still for a moment I think I'm going to choke on the tension. My knees feel weak, and my pulse is so wild that I feel like I'm not getting enough air to my brain. Or maybe it's too much air? I don't even know anymore.

"I want you to know, Ava. Not think."

"I…" My brain is scrambled. Words won't form.

"Let me spell it out for you. I want you to put your hand between your legs and stick your fingers there and tell me if it's wet."

He's punishing me. *That's* what this is. I'm being punished for stepping over a line and making him feel like he lost the upper hand for a moment. I shouldn't find this ridiculously hot.

It goes against everything I understand about sex.

But despite all that, I find my hand tracking under the hem of my nightie and up my inner thigh. I gasp when I touch myself, because my excitement is wound so tight that even the softest brush of my fingers has the muscles inside me clenching up tight.

"Yes," I whisper. "I'm wet."

"Louder."

"Yes, I'm wet," I say, louder this time. "I got wet from watching you jerk off."

There's a hum of satisfaction behind me. "If I send you back downstairs now you're not going to be able to sleep, are you?"

"No," I whimper. I'm so aroused I can feel my clit pulsing, desperate to be touched. The need to come is like a snake lashing out inside me, snapping and writhing and slithering.

"You need to get some release." His voice is smoother now, almost hypnotic. He's back in control and he likes it. "You need to relieve some of that tension or else you're going to ruin those expensive sheets I put on your bed."

"Yes." The word is like a hiss of steam releasing from a pressure cooker.

"Go on, then."

What? He wants me to do it…now? Here?

Punishment, remember? You watched him so he gets to watch you.

"But…"

"Take your fingers and touch yourself until you come."

Fuck. I'm almost panting with need now—it won't take long to get me over the edge. But I can't do this, can I? I can't get myself off in front of him. For some reason this feels more intimate than sex. More vulnerable.

"Ava." He stretches my name out. "If you want to play this game, you have to be willing to take your turn."

I nod. I *do* want to play. Because I know even if I don't, the pressure from this will make me explode at some point. I want to see what effect I have on him.

Swallowing my nerves and excitement, I widen my stance and tease the tip of my forefinger through my sex. I'm so wet. So slick with need. I drag the moisture up to my clit, swirling it around the swollen bud in a way that makes me gasp. This won't take long at all. I'm almost there already, just from watching him. From his words.

"Oh my god…" I pant. I move my hand, flicking the spot that makes everything tighten inside me. My sex clenches, unfulfilled. Wanting to be full with him. I imagine the thick length of him sliding into me.

"Yes, that's it." His voice is a little choked up now. There's movement behind me, but I can't focus on the reflections. My eyes flutter shut as I pleasure myself for him. For me.

The squeak of bedsprings makes me think he's sitting or lying down. I hear that slick sound again and I know he's touching himself. I let that image—coloured by my memory from moments ago—flare to life in my head. His big hand, stroking up and down. I take it further, allowing myself to imagine him finishing. His muscles would bunch up, his biceps bulging as he squeezes himself tight, hips jerking up into his grip one last time.

The head of his cock would be rich with colour, all the blood pulsing underneath his skin. With a shuddering gasp he would let go, emptying himself in long, jetting streams across his stomach.

"Oh my god," I gasp as the image flickers and fades, my release blanking everything in my brain so that I can focus only on the orgasm rippling through me. My thighs clench around my hand. "I'm coming. Daniel, I'm coming."

There's a grunt behind me, crude words and pleasure sounds mixing into a guttural mélange. And I hear my name. *Ava, Ava, Ava.*

My orgasm is strong and I press one hand against the window to brace myself. My sex is so wet, dampness clings to my inner thighs, coating my fingers, as well. As my breath finally starts to slow, I come back down to earth.

"Go to bed," he commands. "We'll deal with this in the morning."

CHAPTER TWELVE

Daniel

I SPENT THE night dreaming about her, about what might have come next if I hadn't managed to hang on to one shred of control. Never mind the fact that I tugged on my cock while watching her put her hand between those sweet, trembling thighs. Never mind the fact that I came so hard I almost saw stars. Never mind the fact that the one glance she gave me over her shoulder as she left was enough to have me haunted for life.

I'd been cavalier that first night—thinking that if she offered her body to me, I'd enjoy it. Thinking that if sex was on the table, then I'd take it without a second thought. Without worrying that it would affect me.

But I've been ambushed.

Because Ava has surprised me. I was unprepared last night, caught in the headlights. And instead of simply doing what any guy would if he was hot for someone—give in to the feelings and have some dirty, impulsive sex—I got all Sergeant Commander on her.

Christ.

That is not good news. One look at Ava will tell you she's a forever gal. A wants-a-*real*-ring-on-her-finger, walk-down-the-aisle kinda gal. And yeah, while she's obviously attracted to me, I've probably ruined this whole thing by letting my true self out on night one. If I find her room cleaned out and the apartment empty this morning, I won't be surprised.

I shower quickly, then pull on a pair of jeans and a black T-shirt. Staring at my reflection in the bathroom mirror, I second-guess myself. Black might be too harsh, so I change into a white one instead. Pathetic, right? But I shove aside the self-deprecating thoughts. I'm better than that. Better than some animal who lets his base instincts control him.

I can fix this.

I jog down the stairs and, to my surprise, I find Ava sitting on my couch. She's wearing jeans with a hole in one knee, and an oversize cardigan. Her dark hair tumbles over her shoulders and she sits, engrossed, reading a book from my shelf, *Broken Angels* by Richard Morgan. There's a bowl of cereal half-eaten on the coffee table.

"That's the second book in the series," I say, and she jumps. "You should read *Altered Carbon* first."

"Are you a stickler for reading order?" Ava slides a bookmark between the pages. It's not mine—the little strip of leather has a fringe at one end and the initials *AM* embossed.

"I would assume you are, too, if you're the type of person who carries a bookmark wherever you go."

"Touché." She stands and pushes the sleeves of her

cardigan up, but they almost immediately slide back down over her hands, and there's something strangely endearing about it. "I've already read *Altered Carbon*. I'd been meaning to continue the series, and I got excited when I saw the second book on your shelf."

"I'm surprised you're still here, to be honest."

A delightful flush tints her cheeks but she squares her shoulders as if fighting the visceral reaction. "Why?"

I head over to my kitchen and press the button for a short black on my espresso machine. This conversation needs coffee, a strong one. The machine whirrs to life and I grab a small porcelain cup from the cupboard above it. It's white trimmed with a fine line of gold—a gift from my mother when I first moved into this place.

"Last night was…unexpected," I say as I watch the dark liquid slowly fill the cup. I sense movement behind me and hear the soft fall of Ava's footsteps approaching the kitchen bench.

"Yes, it was."

When the machine finishes pouring the shot, the apartment is eerily quiet. And yet, I can sense the cogs turning in both our minds so strongly it may as well be death metal blasting from my sound system. I don't normally have these conversations.

Especially not here, in my home.

Whenever I'm with a woman, it's a nighttime affair only. Fancy dinner or maybe a show, drinks, a luxury hotel room. Easy to get away if I need to—and easier for her, too. I'm not the kind of guy who assumes all women are looking to shackle me with a gold band.

Plenty of the women I know aren't looking for marriage or even long term, and are quite happy to approach sex the way I do: as something fun and temporary.

But something tells me Ava is different. The questions she asked about my family, the story about her mother... It all points to one thing: she is not the kind of woman who wants to settle for less than she deserves.

"I should have handled it different," I say eventually. I grab my coffee and turn around, breathing in the aroma and hoping it'll help my brain work better.

"You wouldn't have needed to handle it at all if I hadn't come up the stairs."

"I don't want this to change our arrangement," I reply, pausing to take a sip of my drink. "I know the dinner last night was a bust, but even if I can't get Marc to come around, I still have my public image to consider. I can't have speculation about my personal affairs affecting public confidence in Moretti Enterprises. Not with everything I have planned."

"Big goals, huh?" She smiles.

"Always."

Ava traces a vein in the marble countertop with her fingertip, her gaze intently focused on the winding, natural line. It gives me a moment to observe her—I really thought she'd be running scared this morning. And the fact that she's not intrigues me.

"I had big goals once," she says with a sad sigh. "Get a teaching job at my old school, buy a beautiful house in a leafy suburb, make a life."

"What stopped you?"

"Do you ever feel like you have a picture in your

head and then…everything goes wrong?" She looks at me, then laughs. "No, you probably have no idea at all what that's like."

"I would say that describes my current situation quite well, actually," I quip.

"That feels like my whole life. I took some time off to travel after high school, and I spent a year backpacking around Europe. When I came back, I got a teaching degree and then… There were no jobs. No one willing to take on a fresh teacher, anyway. I got a maternity leave contract for one year, but that finished and then there was no position for me." She shakes her head. "I've been getting by on relief-teaching shifts and working as a catering waitress. *Then* my landlord decided to sell my apartment and…"

I realise she's right. My current situation *might* be crappy and unfair, but I've never had to worry about these things. I've never worried about getting a job, because my whole life I was groomed to be CEO. I've never worried about where I would live, because my family owns this building. I've never worried about what my future might hold, because I could stop working right now and have plenty to live on until I was a hundred.

I want to help her, more than just upholding our side of the arrangement.

"If I live with my mother, I have a very real fear that I will never need to worry about where I live ever again," she adds. "Because I will be in jail for murder."

A laugh shoots out of me that's so real and natural I almost startle myself. "I know that feeling right down to my bones, trust me."

Ava bites down on her lip, but it does nothing to stifle the smile that reaches all the way up to her warm, sparkling eyes. "Ah, family. Can't live with 'em, can't live without 'em."

"Truth."

She looks so relaxed sitting at my countertop, face fresh and clean, hair loose. It strikes me as so normal and familiar that I almost wonder how this isn't my everyday reality. "So, last night…"

Yeah, *that*.

"I'm not going anywhere," she says. "I plan on holding up my end of the bargain. It's not like I have other options at this point."

"I'll take care of you," I say, but then I automatically want to crush the words under my tongue. "I mean, with helping you figure things out. My assistant's husband is actually a principal at one of the private schools in Camberwell, and we've got some apartments on hold for private use at the Cielo. You don't have to worry."

"I can't afford a building like that," she scoffs.

"We'll work something out, I promise."

"Can you fix any problem?" she asks, shaking her head in wonder.

"That remains to be seen." I drain the rest of my coffee and put the cup into the sink. "Now, I have to head into the office this morning and deal with some things. I assume you can amuse yourself for a few hours?"

"I've got a book and a coffee machine, what more could a girl want?" Ava grins and I feel the sunshine of it punch me right in the chest. What *is* she doing to me?

"Good. Take a few minutes to pack your bags before I get back. We're flying out tonight," I say. "There are plenty of things to do in Nice and you and I need to be seen together."

"How did you get a ticket for me at the last minute?" She blinks. "That must have cost a fortune."

I don't say anything, but I'm betting the look on her face when we pull up to our private jet will be pretty damn priceless.

CHAPTER THIRTEEN

Ava

THAT EVENING, I understand why my question had amused Daniel and encouraged another one of his annoyingly sexy half-smirk expressions. His private jet had been prepared for our flight. Of *course* he has his own damn plane.

If there's any more proof required for me to fully understand that Daniel and I do *not* come from the same world, this is it. That fleeting thought I had of him looking attainable when he picked me up from my apartment? Poof! Gone. The moment we shared in his kitchen this morning where I thought I felt something real pass between us? A delusion.

And don't even get me started on what happened in his bedroom. I don't know *what* to call that.

Oh, and did I mention that he's taking me to France? Actual France. Baguettes and champagne and Chanel France.

"Macaron pastry, Macron president." I've been going over that for the last twelve hours so I don't embarrass myself. I push the door of the limo open and step right out onto the airport tarmac. No long security lines, no pat downs, no shitty airport food. "Macaron pastry, Macron president."

"What on earth are you muttering to yourself?" Daniel asks as Andy hands our luggage off to the crew. We walk toward the stairs leading up to a small but fancy-looking jet.

"Nothing," I grumble.

I climb the stairs slowly, my flat sandals clacking against the metal steps. For a second, I feel like a heroine in one of those old romantic movies—hair billowing in the breeze, dress flapping around my legs. All I need to complete the look is a silk scarf tied around my neck and some big sunglasses.

That's right. Concentrate on the fantasy, not on the fact that you're about to be stuck in a tin can shooting halfway across the world with a man who's watched you masturbate.

To make matters worse, I feel him behind me. His presence is a warm burn at my back. Even when he's not touching me, my body is a radio tuned to his frequency, sensing him at all times. When I falter, my sandal catching on the edge of a step, his big hands go to my waist, steadying me. The feel of his touch— confident and sure—shoots my body temperature up a few billion degrees.

"Welcome, Ms. Matthews." The flight attendant smiles and takes my denim jacket, which normally makes me feel cool, but now makes me feel like a little girl amid all this luxury. "Can I grab you a drink before we take off? Champagne, wine?"

"A water would be great, thank you." I need to keep my wits about me. I'm feeling turned around and upside down and inside out. Daniel has me dizzy and spinning, and I'm not sure I'll ever feel steady again.

"Absolutely." The flight attendant turns to Daniel and gives him the same professional treatment.

God, even his plane is more impressive than my apartment. Not that I've ever seen a private jet before, obviously, but it's even better than I imagined. There's a cluster of seats to one side, two pairs facing a table, with a further two rows behind it. On the other side of the plane is a sectional lounge that looks to be made of buttery-soft leather.

"That turns into a bed," Daniel says, coming up behind me. "So if you're feeling sleepy later, I'll have the staff do a turndown for you."

A turndown. My brain goes straight to my pyjamas. *So thin I can see your nipples through it, and so short I'm almost salivating to find out if you're wearing anything at all underneath.*

His words swirl in my head. For some reason, thinking about Daniel watching me climb into bed, seeing those secret parts of me that I touched for him, sends a shiver down my spine. A dull ache gathers between my thighs, but I squeeze them together.

For a second, I have the sense I'm floating, looking down on myself in some kind of out-of-body experience. Am I really on a private jet about to fly across the globe? Am I really thinking about a guy who isn't simply out of my league, but is basically another species?

"There's only one bed," I mutter, completely meaning to speak those words only in my head. But when a darkly amused chuckle comes out of Daniel's mouth, I suck in a breath. Is he thinking about last night, too? "Just an observation."

Smooth, Ava. Like forty-grit sandpaper.

"Yes, there's only one bed," he replies. His dark eyes glitter, as if his mind has gone *exactly* where mine has—straight into the gutter. "Don't worry, I'll be a gentleman."

I wish you wouldn't.

I clear my throat and whip around as though I have something *very important* to dig out of my handbag. "Good, well that's…excellent."

"I've got to get some work done," Daniel says, settling in to one of the plush leather chairs and plugging his laptop in. "There's a TV screen back there with movies and TV shows preloaded. I saw you'd raided my bookshelf, as well."

Busted. I've stashed the rest of the Takeshi Kovacs series into my carry-on, along with two Philip K. Dick novels. "What can I say, you have a large collection."

Large. Couldn't you have used literally any other descriptor?

"I'm glad you appreciate my large collection." His eyes sweep over me, and though I'm wearing a simple dress that keeps me perfectly covered, I feel like he can see every inch of me. "I'm rather proud of it."

I try to swallow, but my mouth is bone-dry. "You should be."

Daniel's lip twitches, but he turns his attention to the screen in front of him, mercifully giving me a chance to die of embarrassment without his onyx eyes picking me apart. How have I been reduced to thinking about sex no matter how innocent the conversation?

I scurry to the sectional sofa and settle in, slipping a pair of headphones on and trying to find something to watch that won't have my mind leaping to anything *large* belonging to Daniel. They must have kids on the plane sometimes, because there's a collection of Disney movies. I pop *Moana* on and smile at the flight attendant as she delivers my water, along with a little plate of fruit and cheese.

I can do this. Spending a couple of days in France in complete luxury won't be a hardship, and I know I should try to relax and enjoy the experience. This tension between Daniel and me is nothing more than animal instincts. He's hot, single and we're in close proximity. It's not surprising there's sexual chemistry.

But even as I think those safe, logical thoughts there's a dark corner of my brain that whispers to me, telling me I'm wrong. That this is more. That Daniel lights up something inside me that nobody else ever has. When he got his sexy revenge for me watching him, the way it turned my body liquid, the almost forbidden nature of it... That was new.

Which means I am well and truly screwed. Or rather, I want to be.

CHAPTER FOURTEEN

Daniel

I ALMOST DOZE off between combing through documents for the acquisition negotiations that are supposed to take place next week. But Henry Livingstone is avoiding my emails and I can feel the deal slipping through my fingers. Even if Marc hasn't gotten in his ear, one look at the media makes our company seem like we're one bad headline away from having our own trashy reality TV show.

And the worst thing of all… I feel numb.

My heart is hollow and my brain spins like a tire slipping against an icy road. Everything I have worked for, everything my grandfather and uncle built our company for…is family. Even while my parents' marriage fell apart, my mother would hold Marc and me and tell us over and over: family is everything. Blood is thicker than water. You must love each other.

But maybe familial relationships are just as risky as love relationships. When your guards are down, you're inviting someone to take aim with their strongest weapon.

Shaking off the pointless ruminations, I reach my hands above my head and stretch. My body is tight from hours of sitting. Ava has spent the first part of the trip watching movies, her giggles cutting through the silence every so often in a way that makes me smile. But when I look at her now, she's curled into the couch and her eyes are shut. The flicker of the screen makes light play over her face.

She can't be comfortable squished up like that. What's the point of owning a luxury jet if you can't have a decent sleep on an overnight flight?

I push up from my chair and go to her. She's snoring lightly, her long hair tangled beneath her head. At some point she's kicked off her sandals and they lie haphazardly on the floor. She looks so peaceful. Content.

I push a button on the wall to call one of the staff and a second later the cabin chief, Marisa, appears. "Can you make the bed up?" I ask.

Marisa's eyes drift down to where Ava is currently sitting on the couch that is to be transformed into her bed. "Sure, let me grab the pillows and blankets."

I contemplate waking her, but a gentle shake of her arm results in nothing. Not even a murmur of discontent about being interrupted. Literally nothing.

"Ava?" I try again, but she remains completely surrendered to slumber.

Sighing, I slide an arm under her legs and one behind her back and lift her up. Her curvy body presses against mine, suffusing me with warmth. The rub of her breasts against my chest stirs something primal inside me and the enticing peaks of her nipples through the fine cotton of her dress—stirred by the cool air-conditioning—has all the blood in my body rushing south. I hope she doesn't wake up now and feel my cock growing stiff against her like some fucking pervert. Her eyelids flicker, like she's dreaming, and for a minute I think she might wake. But she doesn't.

Chalk that up to things I'm learning about her: she sleeps like the dead. Thank god.

Marisa makes the bed and I lay Ava down onto the fresh sheets, pulling the blanket up over her. She's got a pair of earrings in with those long backs that look like they might poke into her skin. So I slip them out and place them on the little table beside the bed. Immediately, she snuggles into the covers, wrapping herself up like a human burrito.

It's better for me this way, with her fully clothed and covered in blankets. Easier for me to think of last night as something I dreamed up while getting off. Easier for me to keep *that* version of Ava totally separate from the sweet and spirited woman I see during the day.

I turn to head back to my chair but I halt when I hear a rustling behind me.

"Daniel?" Her just-woken-up voice is sexy and husky and my poor cock leaps to response. "What happened?"

When I turn to face her, she's sitting up. Her hair is a fluffy cloud around her shoulders and she scrubs a hand over her face.

"I put you to bed."

Is it my imagination or do her eyes seem to get darker?

"You were asleep on the couch," I continue, refusing to let my brain catch on anything that might tempt me to get closer. "I thought you might be more comfortable in a proper bed."

"I was just resting my eyes." She yawns and stretches, causing her bust to strain against the confines of her cotton dress.

"You should rest more than your eyes."

"What about you?" She's slipping her cardigan off her shoulders and the bare skin of her arms is way sexier than it should be.

"I have work to do."

Ava frowns. "You said the work never ends. Does that mean you never sleep?"

"Are you asking me if I'm immortal?" I try to make light of the situation. I know what she's doing.

"Are you avoiding sleeping because of me?" Her eyes nail me with a direct look. She has no hesitation in calling me on my bullshit.

"You made a comment about there only being one bed, so…" I gesture in her direction. "I always want my guests to feel comfortable."

"Don't be ridiculous. It's like, what—" She gropes for her phone "—five in the morning? You have to sleep."

"I need less sleep than the average person."

She makes a noise of frustration and gets out of the bed. "I'm going to put my pyjamas on and when I get back, I expect you to be changed and in bed."

I blink. "Excuse me?"

"We're engaged, remember," she says softly. "Don't

you think the airline crew will find it odd that you re-fused to get into bed with your fiancée?"

Well, fuck.

"It's not unusual for a man in my position to work through the night," I reply crisply. "It's part of the job."

"And part of your job as a future-husband is to get into bed with your soon-to-be wife." She plucks her carry-on bag from the overhead compartment and with-out another word heads in the direction of the bathroom at the end of the cabin.

For a moment I stand there, my feet stuck to the spot like roots are holding me in place. Lying next to Ava all night long, knowing what it sounds like when she comes, is going to be pure torture. I feel like we're playing chess, each maneuver analysed and countered. And just when I thought I have my strategy under con-trol, she queens me.

I almost choke at the double entendre. Christ. I re-ally need to get a grip.

Yeah, you do.

Cursing under my breath, I stalk up to the crew's section and inform Marisa that Ava and I are both turn-ing in, so not to disturb us until it's time for breakfast service. Then I pop the buttons on my shirt and toe off my shoes. I toss my clothes messily onto one of the chairs, which is *highly* uncharacteristic. But I want to be in bed before Ava gets back so I can avoid seeing her wriggling those perfect, ample hips as she walks out of the bathroom.

Part of me wants to call her bluff. I'm not one for losing at games, and I certainly don't enjoy letting others get the upper hand. If Ava wants to play with fire, then I'll show her that I don't burn.

Not for anyone.

I slip into bed and a second later the cabin becomes dim as Marisa turns the lights to sleep mode. Only the safety lights along the walkway are lit, which is a good thing. It means I don't see Ava in great detail when she climbs into bed beside me. I only feel the shift of the bed and the rustle of the sheets. I smell the sweet vanilla on her skin and feel the gentle brush of her hair as she gets comfortable.

But my head is filled with flickering images of her standing at the top of my staircase, watching me. It's filled with the way her body shuddered and trembled as she touched herself. It's filled with the reflection of her in my bedroom window, the perfect O her lips made as she sought release by her own hand.

My cock is so hard I'm sure I'm tenting the blankets.

I force myself to stare into the darkness, lying still. Keeping my distance. This whole situation is outside the realms of how I view sex—which is for recreation. No emotions. No future. But I can't draw that neat little line in the sand with Ava, because we're going to be together for a while.

Forced proximity. Right now it feels like a challenge of willpower.

"Are you not attracted to me?" Ava asks in the darkness.

I growl. She's determined to push me, this woman. "What kind of a question is that?"

"A genuine one."

"Do you think what happened last night…" I shake my head. "Yes, I'm attracted to you."

While I don't believe that anyone has to stick to a "type," there are certainly common attributes in the women I'm attracted to—I like a woman with a curvier figure. I like a woman who has something to say and speaks her mind. I like a woman who's herself. Some of the women I've been with in the past seemed to change from one day to the next, like chameleons always trying to be what they think others want. I prefer to know someone honestly, whether it's for a romantic dalliance or something platonic. I prefer to know the real them, so I know *exactly* whom I'm dealing with.

Unfortunately, that becomes less common the older I get.

"I'm attracted to you, too," she says, though I don't need the confirmation. I could see it in her eyes the night we met.

Under the sheets, I feel something brush the back of my hand. It's her knuckles, her fingers, searching mine out.

"I keep thinking about last night," she says and I press my head back against the pillow, wanting to groan in pent-up sexual frustration. "About…"

"What?" I snap.

She sucks in a breath. "About how I wish you hadn't ordered me away afterward."

"And what would you have preferred, Ava?" I've been trying to be a gentleman, but she's making it very fucking hard to keep my wits about me.

"I would have preferred for you to come up behind

me," she says. "I would have preferred for you to put your hands between my legs and feel for yourself how wet I was."

I reach down and squeeze myself under the covers. "You were the one who didn't want this arrangement to include sex."

"Maybe I've changed my mind. You're…" The bed shifts as she turns. My eyes are adjusting to the dark and I can tell she's facing me. "I want to explore this attraction between us."

What if it feels far too risky to sleep with Ava and then continue being around her? What if it feels way too risky because she speaks to me on some level that goes beyond sexual? Beyond the lines I draw carefully around myself so I have complete control over my life?

"If I touch you now and you're not hard as a rock, then I'll leave it be," she says softly.

Check fucking mate.

I feel her warm breath puff over my skin and the subtle movement of her hand beneath the sheets. She's getting closer to me. I feel the brush of her fingertips at my thigh, then up and over. Inching closer.

Closer.

When her palm skates over the hard ridge of my cock, every muscle in my body grows tight. But it's the sharp hitch of her breath that undoes me. It's the crackle of tension that builds and builds until it's so explosive and bright I have no hope of stopping it now.

"Fine. You want to play games, Ava?" I growl. "Then let's play."

CHAPTER FIFTEEN

Ava

FOR A MOMENT I wonder if I've bumped my head. Maybe there was unexpected turbulence while I was changing in the bathroom and I've slipped and fallen. Maybe I'll wake up to the harsh, fluorescent lighting and this will be nothing more than a trauma response.

But I feel Daniel shifting position and then one possessive palm is at my hip, and I decide I don't much care whether this is real or not. I want this man and I will take him any way I can get him.

"You've tested my willpower, thoroughly," Daniel says, his voice low and ragged. He pulls me closer, so I'm on my side and he's on his.

Our bodies are lined up against one another and I feel the prickle of his leg hairs against my smoother skin. I feel the pressure of his fingertips at my hip, the slow creep of his touch around to my backside. And yes, I feel the hard length of his erection digging into my lower belly. I want to touch him there again, to feel that hard, powerful length twitch beneath my fingertips.

I'm desperate for him. Desperate in a way that I've never been desperate for another person before. Everything about him is a drug to me—the faded scent of his cologne, the roughness in his voice. The angry glitter in his eyes.

"Kiss me, Daniel," I whisper. "And tell your willpower to bugger off."

His throaty chuckle sends a ripple of awareness through me, but thankfully he doesn't make me wait any longer. His hand sweeps up my body, finding my jaw and then my head, fingers tangling in my hair as he crushes his mouth down to mine. *Yes.* My tongue darts out to meet his, tentative at first but I grow bolder with each second. He kisses like he's making love to me already, and his hips canter toward mine, rubbing his hard length against me.

I groan into his mouth, my senses so overloaded my poor brain doesn't know which sensation to focus on first. Taste, scent, touch. *Touch.* Daniel smooths his hands back down my body, tracing the line of my neck, the curve of my shoulder, then down my arm, to my hips and then behind me, cupping my backside and pressing me flush against him.

Oh.

He's impossibly hard. Pulsing. I feel him strain against me, with little more than two thin layers of fabric between us. His fingers knead my backside, allowing him to grind against me as we kiss. I'm dizzy from it all.

"Daniel." My breath comes in short bursts, my breasts rising and falling against his bare chest. I plant my hands there, seeking out the light dusting of hair and the flat circle of his nipples, exploring him in the dark.

I tilt my head back, encouraging him to kiss me there. He trails a blazing path up to the sweet spot behind my ear, a spot I know makes my body shiver. His rough stubble-coated jaw is heaven against my skin, the nip of his teeth making me tremble before we've even gotten to the good stuff.

"You wanted to feel how excited I am." He takes my hand and presses it to his length. My fingers flutter for a second before curling around him. "So feel it, Ava. Take responsibility. My cock has been aching for hours because of you."

"You were the one who made me come in front of you," I shoot back. Yes, I lit the match. But *he* was the one who tossed it into the air, setting everything ablaze.

He curls his hand over mine, working my fist up and down the length of him. But I don't want any barriers between us—I want him skin to skin. I want to feel everything. I reach for the slit in his underwear and free him, gasping at the hot slide of him against my palm.

"Don't act like you didn't want it," he says roughly. His hand runs down to the hem of my nightie and draws it up, his fingers creeping between my thighs. "You were so wet I could practically see it dripping down your thighs."

The breath leaves my lungs. For some reason, the hint of resentment in his voice, the unexpectedly sharp touch of anger, good lord... It makes my sex clench. He's annoyed that I tested him. That I pushed him.

And that makes me want him even more.

"Says you. The only reason I even came upstairs was because I heard you jerking off." I meet his gaze in the dim light. As my eyes adjust, more of him is revealed. The beautiful angles and hard-edged planes of him.

I squeeze his cock and he thrusts into my grip.

"You were thinking about me," I challenge.

"Yes, I was."

A gasp escapes my lips as his hand reaches for me, cupping my bare sex. The heel of his palm grinds against my clit and I almost explode on the spot. "Tell me what you imagined," I gasp, squeezing my eyes shut.

"No." The word is a harsh slash across this intimate moment. We may have sex, but he won't let me in.

"Afraid I'll use it against you?"

"Yes." He tugs on my bottom lip with his teeth. "Now open those lovely thighs up for me."

I shift, allowing him to touch me more easily. His fingers graze over the most sensitive part of my sex, and I swallow back a groan. He drags one finger between my lips, gathering moisture on his fingertip and then lowering his hand to rub circles over my clit. Stars flare behind my shuttered lids and I arch into his touch. "Please."

But Daniel isn't a man to be rushed.

"You're like a fucking fountain," he says, his lips brushing my ear. "These poor staff are going to have to clean up these sheets tomorrow, you know. Sheets that will be soaked in you."

Oh god. Why is that so hot? It shouldn't be. A flutter of embarrassment flares through me and I already know I'm going to strip the bed on my own in the morning before they get a chance to. But I can't help it, Daniel has the remote control to my body and when it comes to him…I'm powerless to resist.

His finger continues to pluck at my clit, driving me higher and higher. It's like he's taunting me for pushing the issue. Getting payback. I flop onto my back and spread my legs for him, not even caring how it comes across. I need him to make me come. Now.

"That's it, surrender." He looms over me and pushes my nightgown up to my stomach, totally exposing my thighs and my sex. "You're so wound up I bet you won't even last a minute."

I want to argue. I want to shove him in his chest and tell him that he's not so powerful… But there's no point. He's right. Ever since I walked in on him, my body has been like a rubber band pulled to extremes.

The dim light reveals his broad shoulders and chest, finely sculpted muscle. He's perfection. Now he's between my legs, his knees nudging my thighs wider while he uses his hand on me. There's a wicked glint in his eye, something that tells me he likes playing this role—dark seducer. The one in control.

That he likes having the upper hand…no pun intended.

He bows his head and blows cool air across my hot, swollen sex. I almost jolt with the contrast, and goose bumps ripple across my skin. His thumbs rub over the area, teasing the tight bundle of nerves and parting me in a way that feels incredibly intimate.

"Fuck that's a pretty pussy," he says. "I'm going to enjoy eating you, Ava. Try not to make too much noise, okay? I don't want the staff listening in."

He runs his tongue between my folds, drawing a line that makes me bow against him. My hands immediately fly to his head, fingers driving through his hair. "Oh my god. That feels…"

He raises his head, dark eyes laser focused on mine. "Say it."

"So good," I gasp. "So very good."

How the hell am I going to keep quiet? I had an ex once tell me I was a screamer, and he didn't use the label as a compliment. I can't help it—when something feels good the noises just come out of me.

His tongue drives me to the edge, each precise swirl designed to push me to the limit of my pleasure. The flicking motion makes all the blood in my body rush to that one spot and I pant, trying to keep quiet. Really, I *am* trying.

"Put a fist in your mouth, Ava," he says. "Or use a pillow. Because I'm going to make you come now."

Before I have even a second to react, he pushes two fingers into me and sucks my clit between his lips. Hard. I jam my hand into my mouth and clamp down, trying to stifle the shocked sound of my orgasm exploding. My muscles clench and when I come, it feels like my body is about to split in two. I actually see flashes of white behind my eyelids as the waves roll and roll and his mouth is relentless, pushing me to the point of it being too much, so that I squirm beneath him.

When he finally releases me, I'm liquid. No longer fully in control of my body. There's that smug half-smirk expression again as he drags a hand over his mouth and jaw, wiping me from him.

Bastard. He enjoys having me at his mercy.

"How was that?" he asks softly, but the cocky tone is no less clear even with the reduced volume.

"It wasn't obvious?" I meet his stare, unwavering despite the fact that I just had the strongest orgasm of my entire life. "I really had to work to get there. I thought you'd be better."

He laughs. The bastard actually laughs. "You've got spark, Ava. I like that about you."

"And you clearly like role-playing as an asshole."

"It's not role-play," he murmurs. "Unfortunately."

But it is. I've seen him—the man who loves to read and who cares for his family and who's hurt by his brother's accusations. Daniel might like to hide behind his hard exterior—and I'll let him, because honestly... it turns me on—but I know a facade when I see it.

"I hope you brought a condom for this grand seduction," he says.

I did. I always have one in my wallet just in case, and I reach for where I've stashed my bag in the little unit next to the bed. When I hand Daniel the foil packet, he sheaths himself while never letting his eyes leave mine.

He handles himself like a man who's intimately familiar with his own body. Like a man who gets intimately familiar on a regular basis. He's hung. *Well* hung. And I know a lot of women don't find the male anatomy to be physically attractive but… Daniel's drawn a winning card in the dick lottery.

He comes down on top of me, settling himself between my legs and bracing his body on his forearms so our faces are mere centimetres apart. This feels like a pivotal moment—maybe where I'll really know for sure if this sexy asshole gig is a lie or not.

"You done punishing me yet?" I ask, tilting my face up to his.

He rubs against me, dragging his cock through my wetness and bumping against my still-sensitive clit in a way that makes me shiver. "No."

"Are you usually like this?"

His dark eyes search mine. In the dim cabin lighting they look almost black, like the sheer drop of a cliff edge at night. "No, not usually."

His words warm me. Why is he different with me? I guess it's hard to say. This whole situation is anything but normal. It feels divorced from reality, somehow. A simulation of another life.

And yet I feel more alive than ever before.

He kisses me long and deep, his tongue delving into my mouth, and I taste myself on his lips. "Think you can be quiet this time?"

"I managed before."

He kisses my neck, dragging his teeth from jaw to collarbone, and I arch against him, trying to encourage his cock inside me. But he holds back—making me wait. Maybe he wants me to beg.

"You were louder than a B-grade porno before," he says with a wolfish grin. "I bet they were all listening."

"I was *not*!" I try to shove him, but he chuckles and pins me down, holding both my wrists above my head.

"You let everybody know how well I ate that sweet little pussy."

"Oh my god…"

"What's wrong? Maybe you were right. It *would* seem weird if I wasn't eager to service my wife-to-be." He's turning my words against me, using them to taunt me. "But now I want to finish what we started, Ava."

Yes. The word slithers through my body and I press up against him, widening my thighs and rolling my hips under his. I need to be filled. I need to be fucked.

"But first you have to tell me how much you want it," he says.

Is this a power play? A head game he likes to play in bed? I'm not sure I even care anymore. All I need is him inside me, his hands all over me, mouth all over me.

"I want it, Daniel." I try to move my arms, but he has me pinned and the resistance, the little struggle, gets me so hot my sex is practically crying out for another orgasm. "You have no idea."

"Then tell me. If you want me to put my cock in you, then you'll tell me how much you want it." His words are so soft, little more than puffs of breath against my ear. But they work. My body is a spring wound tight. Waiting, waiting, waiting.

"I want it so bad I've been thinking about nothing more than this all day," I say, staring up at him defiantly. "I want it so bad that if you don't take me right now, I'm going to torture you by making you listen to me getting myself off again. Only this time, you won't be able to order me away afterward."

With a groan, he pushes into me in one smooth stroke, seating himself so deep that for a moment I can't breathe. For a moment, we're both still as my body accommodates him. Then when he moves, I light up, sparkling like the stars and the entire solar system. He hooks a hand under my knee and lifts my leg over his hip so he can ease in deeper. Eyes shut, I press my head back against the mattress and roll my hips up to his.

There's a flash of pain—it's been a while...too long—but soon the pleasure edges it out. With each slow, smooth thrust I burn on the inside, like a fire drawing oxygen and growing. That feeling grows until my whole body is warm and pliable and soft. Daniel moves over me, his lips marking my skin—my neck, my breasts, my hair. He plucks at my nipples and touches every part of me, like he's learning my body.

Pressure builds inside me, my muscles clamping down on his cock as he thrusts into me. I don't normally come like this, but there's no mistaking the tightness gathering between my legs. No mistaking the needy ache that pulses inside me.

"Greedy girl," he murmurs against my neck. "Can you stay quiet?"

"I don't know," I gasp. It's coming on so strong and so quick—it's foreign and beautiful. Different from a man using his fingers or mouth.

Daniel clamps a hand over my mouth and it's possessive and commanding and hot and I shatter instantly. I let my cries be blunted by his hand and keep my eyes on his, watching him lose himself to our lovemaking. My body shakes as I splinter, squeezing and bucking against him.

"Fuck, Ava." Daniel grunts as he thrusts into me, hard and smooth. But his movements become jerkier, edgier. "You're too perfect. Too…"

The word dissolves on his lips as he buries his face against my neck, driving deep one last time and following me over the edge.

CHAPTER SIXTEEN

Daniel

AFTER WE ARRIVE in Nice, France, things between Ava and I are...different. We're somehow more *and* less comfortable with one another. We're sleeping in separate rooms, but every time we pass one another in the airy, light-flooded villa there's a tension that crackles. A little spark that threatens to catch if I don't remain vigilant.

The day after we arrived, I took Ava out for a tour of the Promenade des Anglais and talked about the varying architectural styles which spread from Paris to Nice and other parts of France during the Belle Époque period. She soaked it all in, eagerly asking questions until I found myself lost in my personal passion for historical architecture.

It's not often I get to geek out with a willing ear, let me tell you.

Then we had dinner at a small, intimate restaurant and she told me all about the gap year she spent backpacking around Europe. We've been to many of the same places and we swapped stories about our favourite piazzas in Italy and the Christmas markets in Germany and Austria. By the following morning, there were several pictures of us floating around online and I have to admit that if I didn't know any better…I would assume we were in love.

But ever since I showed Ava the images, she's been distant. Standoffish. I know it must make her uncomfortable—media attention isn't something I've gotten fully used to myself. My uncle sat me down a few years back, and explained that attention is like a tool. It's sharp-edged and dangerous if you're not careful, but when wielded by someone with skill it can accomplish great things. Ever since then, I've tried to view it for what it can give me: exposure for my company, recognition for the hard work of my staff, raising the profile of my family name.

"If only that's where the focus stayed," I mutter to myself as I stare at my laptop screen. A second later, the familiar ringtone of Skype slices through the quiet air. It's Marc.

Bracing myself, I accept the call. My brother's face fills the screen. He's sitting on a balcony. I recognise the glittering view behind him—the line of lights along Chapel Street, the growing cluster of towers from the CBD in the distance. These days he lives in the city with Lily, but this view is from his old apartment. An apartment I thought he was planning to sell.

"You can stop what you're doing, Dan." He rakes a hand through his hair in a way that's like looking into a mirror. "I see through your bullshit, okay? Even if the media doesn't."

I clench my jaw. I knew Marc would be a tough sell, but I'd hoped there was some part of him that still wanted to see the best in me.

A part you were hoping to exploit?

I shove the inconvenient thought to one side. "Excuse me?"

"I know your relationship is a sham," he says bluntly. "And I know you think diverting my attention will make me forget about you and Lily."

I throw my hands up in the air. "This whole thing is ludicrous. I'm your brother."

"And?"

"I don't need to steal anyone's wife," I say, controlling my voice. "Why would I screw around when I have such a beautiful woman already in my bed?"

Do not think about Ava being in your bed. Do not think about Ava being in your bed.

But the image forces its way through all the dark emotions simmering inside me, as if she's a ray of light parting storm-heavy clouds. At dinner she'd reached for my hand, her eyes alight as I talked about my travels.

It's all for show, I know that.

"You have a beautiful woman that you're *using* to prove a point," Marc accuses, jabbing his finger at his computer screen. The image flickers for a second while his internet connection stalls. "I hope, for her sake, that she knows what this is all about."

A guilty lump forms at the back of my throat. But

I can't worry about Ava—she *does* know what this is about. Neither one of us went into this blind.

"I really hope you're not selling her a lie, Daniel." Marc shakes his head. "You've always had a fucked-up relationship with commitment."

"Says you," I spit.

"I got married," he counters. "I was ready to give Lily everything."

"What about me? We're supposed to be brothers and you treat me like the enemy." I shake my head. "You've only ever wanted what I had and when you don't get it, you throw a tantrum and make shit up to drive a wedge between us."

"I know what I saw." Marc's tone is frostier than usual.

"That's right, the mystical photo." I roll my eyes.

Marc lets out a growl of frustration—the sound is inhumane. Born of real, true pain. The kind of pain you can incur only when you make yourself vulnerable to another person—the way Marc has with Lily. The way my mother did with my father.

The way I will never allow myself to be.

"Show it to me." I stare at the screen. "If you think you have proof, then I want to see it."

A second later an email notification pops up on my screen. There's nothing in the subject line, no text in the body. Just an attachment. Inside is a picture—a *convincing* picture—of what looks like Lily and me in a close embrace, almost kissing. She's wearing a flowing red dress, her hair pulled back into an elegant twist. There's a timestamp on the bottom of the photo, indicating it was taken three months ago.

For a moment, I can't breathe. If it was anyone else in the picture, I would believe the story it told. "I swear this never happened. The photo is doctored."

Marc doesn't bother to argue with me. Of course, he called knowing I would deny it. "You've done something that can't be undone."

The finality in his words hits like a punch straight to my gut. "If you really believe that then you don't know me at all."

Marc's eyes are like fire. "You're so far up in your ivory tower *nobody* knows you."

The acid-edged accusation eats away at me, dissolving my usually cool veneer. Why *would* I let anyone know me, when it's clear the closer people get to you, the more havoc they wreak on your life? My own brother, the flesh and blood I've fiercely protected since we were children, thinks I'm capable of the ultimate betrayal.

As far as I'm concerned, *I'm* the smart one. I've known from an early age how to protect myself, and I've never wavered. Not once. Not for anybody.

And that sure as hell isn't going to change now.

"If you really think I'm capable of this, then…" I scrub a hand over my face. "I don't know what to tell you, Marc. Maybe this is your way of getting out of a marriage you knew was a bad idea in the first place."

For a moment I think he's going to hang up on me. I shouldn't have let my mouth run off, but dammit, I'm angry. I'm furious. I'm so filled with rage and resentment that I want to take the bloody laptop and hurl it through a glass pane.

"You think I *want* to believe my own brother would

take my wife away from me?" He lets out a bitter laugh. "Why wouldn't I believe it? You've taken everything else. Zio gave you the CEO job without even *considering* that there might be a better option. Without even considering that you would run the company the way you do everything else in your life, without an ounce of emotion."

"So *that's* what this is about, the fact that I got the job you wanted." I had known Marc would be hurt when I was promoted above him, but this is my place. My role.

"It's about *you*, Daniel, and how you think the world should be grateful for your existence. Your ego is stifling." He shakes his head. "And the fact that you plucked some poor woman out of thin air to pose as your fiancée, in an effort to dodge responsibility... It's disgusting. Dad would be so proud."

I'm about to spit fire and brimstone at my brother when the call disconnects. Typical Marc, he never stands his ground in a fight. He's happy to set everything on fire and then run away. And he thinks *I* won't take responsibility.

Bullshit.

I stare at the photo for what feels like an hour. It's fake. But how can I prove it? Marc will believe what he wants to believe.

A second later, there's another email from him in my inbox. The subject line reads: *Don't drag Ava through this bullshit. Let her go and I'll make sure Livingstone upholds his end of the bargain.*

Marc has always been a bleeding heart. But he needn't worry about Ava. She knows what this is.

I put my head down and vow to forget about Marc for the rest of the day. After spending another hour taming my inbox and making sure everything is running smoothly back home in my absence, I close my laptop.

Shaking my head, I stalk out onto the terrace that overlooks the gardens. Lush greenery fills every corner of the space, and a big orange tree sits heavy with fruit, scenting the air with tart sweetness. Below, the pool glimmers in the light as a body slices through the water with almost surgical efficiency. Ava's back is mostly exposed, save for the straps of a skimpy swimsuit she bought on our day out yesterday.

For a moment I can only stare—she's like a mythical creature, so beautiful and graceful it captivates me. Memories flash of our night together, the way her body undulated beneath mine. The way she had no shyness in letting me know what she wanted. Thinking about that is enough to make something primal and white-hot filter through my system.

It blanks out the feelings about Marc and the disaster that is our family right now. And for that, I'm grateful.

I head downstairs. Two large double doors sweep open to the gardens and, at that moment, Ava is getting out of the pool. She twists her long brown ponytail. Water runs in rivulets down her curvy body, making her skin sparkle. There's a whole lot of straps doing crisscross things, but the swimsuit hides nothing—not the fullness of her breasts and the peaks of her nipples, nor her strong shoulders and shapely hips.

I try to swallow but my mouth is devoid of moisture.

I want her. Again.

My cock pulses behind my dress pants. I want to bend her over one of the banana lounges and yank her swimsuit to one side.

I clear my throat and shove the images away. "Good afternoon."

"Is it afternoon already? Wow." Ava wraps a towel around herself and smiles, oblivious to the rampant attraction running through my veins. "I couldn't resist taking a dip. It's such a beautiful day."

"You swim very well."

You swim very well?

What kind of a comment is that? Jesus. Whoever thought I was a smooth lady-killer should see me now. Ava has me so tied up in knots, I sound stiff as a board. Hell, I *am* stiff as a board. This is ridiculous. I'm acting like I've never seen a woman in a swimsuit before.

"Thanks." Mercifully, she doesn't seem to notice my inner turmoil. "I can't even remember the last time I was in a pool."

I watch the water drops slide over her skin, tracking across her freckles as though playing connect-the-dots. With her hair darkened by the water, her eyes look even more vibrantly warm, the coppery flecks glinting in the sun.

"We're going out tonight," I say, stuffing my hands in my pockets.

"To the opera?" An honest and open smile filters across her face as I nod. "I've always wanted to see one. Good thing I decided to pack those fancy dresses."

I don't want her in a dress. I want her naked and writhing beneath me. Inappropriate thoughts zip across my brain. I'm angry at my brother, that's all. This is nothing but a survival mechanism—focusing on what feels good. What tempts me.

And Ava tempts me more than any woman I have ever known.

"You okay, Daniel? You look a little…flushed." Her lips curve into a wicked smile. Gone is the remote woman who's been avoiding me since the pictures came out. At any sign that she might get the upper hand, the seductress comes out to play.

"It's warm out," I say.

"You're right, it *is* warm."

I've stepped into her web, played into her trap. Ava releases the towel and it slithers down her body, showing me all that wet, white fabric clinging to her. Showing me the shadow of her nipples and the sweet little vee of her sex.

I'm going to have her again.

I know it even before my brain has the chance to refute it. Tonight, I'm going to taste her again even if it's the riskiest thing I could possibly do. Because dammit, I deserve something decent in the clusterfuck that is my life right now. I deserve something that makes me feel whole and good.

And Ava is my something good.

"Wear something that shows off your legs," I tell her. "The black dress with the slit."

Her nostrils flare and her eyes are like twin flames, but she says nothing. *That's right, Ava. Don't forget who's boss here.*

CHAPTER SEVENTEEN

Ava

I STAND IN the middle of the opulent bedroom suite, staring at the dress. It's a black, glittering sheath with intricately beaded fabric, a high neckline and a slit that goes all the way up to midthigh. With each step I flash the full length of my leg, but the modest neckline and dark colour keep it chic. I've never been thin and there have been times when I've dreaded dressing up because clothes never seem to look on me the way they look on a model or a mannequin.

But this dress is made for curves. It hugs me, enhances me. It makes the most of my best features—my broad shoulders and my strong, muscular legs developed from years of playing netball—and it skims over the bits that I don't feel so confident about.

Am I playing dress-up? Am I hoping the fine fabric and daring shape of this dress will help me appear glamorous and worldly when I'm anything but? Maybe.

I bend down and slip my foot into my trusty black stilettos. These shoes have seen me through weddings and other dressy events. They fake an extra few inches, and somehow...I look like someone who goes to the opera all the time.

I glance at the clock. Five minutes and we're supposed to leave. I lost track chatting to Emery, filling her in on everything that's been going on here...well, everything but the truth of Daniel and me. She told me I seem happy. Happier than she's ever seen me. It's hard to write that off as good acting, because I've never been good at faking it.

Grabbing my clutch, I check my reflection one last time. After a day in the pool, my skin has taken on a warm, golden glow.

Emery's right, I *am* happy.

"Sex and sunshine will do that," I mutter to myself as I head downstairs to meet Daniel.

Holding the length of my dress in one hand and clutch in the other, I take my time navigating the villa's big, sweeping staircase. My heels click and the rustle of beaded fabric fills the quiet, cavernous room.

Daniel is waiting at the bottom, his head tilted up toward me. He looks magnetic—a black tux fits his muscular body perfectly and not even the bow tie softens his darkly masculine edge. He's clean shaven, and his jaw is razor sharp. Dark, smouldering eyes draw me down step by step, as if I'm being pulled toward him by his will alone.

"Wow." He shakes his head and holds his hand out to guide me down the last few steps.

I allow him to help me, more because I love the feel

of his hand in mine than because I need it. "You're looking pretty wow yourself."

"I said it first."

I laugh. "Is this the part where we call shotgun and race for the car?"

He chuckles, and the warm, rumbling sound skitters along my spine. How is it possible for a man to be so damn handsome?

"I'm glad you wore the dress," he says. "I've been dying to see how it would look on you."

"And?"

"Reality makes my fantasy look pale in comparison."

I don't know how to explain it, but even as the sexual tension between us hums and snaps and fizzes, I feel something else. Something more. Something... tender. I'm not sure I've ever experienced that before.

"It's a beautiful dress." I draw in a shaky breath. "I feel guilty accepting such an extravagant gift. All the dresses and the other bits... I can't keep them, of course. They're a loan."

"Well, I certainly won't have use for them after we..."

And like that, the fairy tale is shattered.

Don't fool yourself. It was never going somewhere.

But that doesn't stop the clench in my gut.

"I want you to keep them," Daniel says, but his eyes are colder now. Like the off button for his emotions has been tapped.

Should I be surprised? Daniel has made it clear that he's emotionally unavailable, and despite the fact that I keep pushing and pushing... He doesn't want me knowing about his private life, because that stuff is real. The dresses and the private jet and the luxurious holidays are superficial. Meaningless. Safe.

Another way that Daniel throws money at his problems.

And what about the fact that you've come alive in his arms?

That was neither real nor superficial. It's something wholly and uncomfortably in between.

"We should get going," I say, closing myself off, too. "I don't want to miss the start of the show."

Daniel presses his hand to my lower back, and my traitorous body fills with fluttering warmth. I think we need a team meeting—brain, heart and lady bits all in a room so we can, once and for all, get on the same damn page.

Remember why you're doing this.

For the life I want to build—a career that fulfills me, a home I can make my own, and the desire not to settle for security when it comes to love. This is a lifeline and nothing more. It's a safety net that will stop me from ending up back at home with my mother and ruining that relationship. And it's proof that while some people may be okay with a hollow relationship, I *do* need more than sex and money.

I need a lot more.

Outside there's a car waiting. Daniel holds the door and I climb in, sliding along the back seat and watching as he follows. The weight of his gaze is like a warm bath. I want to sink lower, deeper. I want to drown in him.

This is temporary. Don't forget that.

* * *

The Opéra Nice Côte d'Azur is stunning, with columns and ornate detailing artfully lit to make it stand out against the inky night sky. Inside, the sheer beauty of luxury from another era steals my breath. I've always had a fascination for old buildings. It was one of the things that drew me to Europe after high school. Backpacking around countries with rich heritage and crumbling structures and craftsmanship that doesn't exist anymore was like falling into a fairy tale. But being here, having balcony seats to one of the most prestigious operas in the world, is a whole other experience.

A grand staircase complete with red carpet takes us up to the floor where the balconies are located. Rows and rows of red seats fill the area below us, and there are velvet curtains and gold decorations as far as the eye can see.

"What a magical place." The balcony has three seats in front and two behind, and I hope we've got the ones right at the front. I don't want to miss a thing. "Do you know the other people joining us?"

"No one will be joining us." Daniel shakes his head. "I made sure we had a section ourselves, because I don't want anyone interrupting our time."

My mind immediately wanders into the gutter. "You bought five seats for two of us? Seriously?"

He shrugs. "Why not? The theatre gets their money and I don't have to deal with people I have no interest in talking to."

I laugh. His world is…something else. "Do you do that often?"

"Solve problems?"

"Throw money at things unnecessarily." It shouldn't annoy me. After all, he's entitled to do with his money exactly as he pleases.

Daniel raises a dark brow. "It's not unnecessary if it's something I want."

Ah, that old chestnut. I didn't exactly grow up in poverty, but the life of a single parent isn't easy. My grandmother took care of both my mother and me, ensuring we never went hungry, but I've never had the privilege of being able to focus wholly on my wants.

"I'm not judging you," I reply.

"Yes, you are." He leans back in his chair and his hands rest lightly on his knees, a heavy silver watch poking out of the cuff of his shirt. He's never without a watch, I've noticed, and never late. "But it doesn't matter. It won't change my behaviour. When I want something, I find a way to get it."

"That must be nice."

"You're very disapproving for someone who's also benefitting from this situation."

"Okay, maybe I am. It's hard not to be a little jealous."

"Don't be too jealous, it's not like money solves all problems. It won't fix the problems with Marc and me." He rubs a hand along his jaw. "Nothing will fix that. If we can get it to a point where he's civil to me in public, I'll take it."

"That seems like a low bar." I frown.

"I'm ambitious, not stupid." He shoots me a look. "Marc and I have been at odds for a while. You know, sibling rivalry and all that. Apparently it was a much bigger issue than I realised when I got promoted instead of him."

"He wanted the CEO job." Suddenly the reason for Marc's animosity makes a little more sense—if he thought Daniel had taken a job from him, the rumour of Daniel stealing his wife must have been like salt on an open wound.

"I've been groomed for this role since I was old enough to hold a spoon. The job was never Marc's to have." Daniel looks at me, as if wanting to say more. But then the shutters go up, like always.

"Why don't you tell me what this opera is about?" I lean toward him, my bare arm brushing against him.

The scent of his cologne is like a magnet drawing me closer. In the shadowed booth, there's an intimacy as if we're completely alone, rather than sitting in a full theatre. Right now, I'm not upset that he paid to keep the seats around us empty.

"Don Giovanni is a young nobleman who seduced thousands of women in Seville in the mid-eighteenth century," he says, warm breath skating over my skin. Below us, the opera is about to start. "Anything he wants, he takes."

"Just like you," I quip.

Daniel levels me with a stare but continues, "Don Giovanni was written by Mozart and it's based on the Don Juan myth. Basically, he's a womaniser and thug. The story is about what happens after he kills the father of a woman he wants to seduce, and his bad behaviour finally catches up with him."

"Ah, so there's a moral."

He chuckles. "There's *always* a moral."

The lights suddenly go dim, and a hush falls over the theatre. Our conversation is cut short by the opening scene of the opera. I decide to let all my worries take the night off. This is a once-in-a-lifetime opportunity. I need to stop feeling annoyed at Daniel for not being open with me, when he owes me nothing beyond what our arrangement entails.

And I need to stop feeling guilty about accepting his offer.

If other people are so comfortable doing whatever it takes to get what they want, then why shouldn't I do the same?

I'm enthralled by the opening of the opera when I feel a pressure at my thigh. Daniel's hand is there, touching the skin exposed by the slit in my dress, his thumb tracking a soothing arc back and forth.

I glance at him, and his eyes are on me. They're dark, bottomless. Burning. It's like there's nothing happening on the stage—no music, no singing, no acting. If I hadn't understood why he wanted us to be alone in these seats before, now it's very clear.

He leans over. "Sit on my lap."

"No." I glare at him, but it's no more effective than throwing marshmallows at an avalanche. And it's bullshit. I want him to touch me, but I also feel the urge to resist him long enough that he knows I'll do only what *I* want, not simply what he tells me.

"Ava, I would like you to sit on my lap because I very much want to make you come with my fingers."

Good *lord*. This man… This arrogant, sexy, entitled man.

"Or you can stay sitting and I'll get on my knees and do it with my mouth."

"Stop," I hiss. He's speaking so low that I can barely hear him, so the chances of anyone else hearing is nonexistent. But the thrill of being in public still winds through me, slow and forbidden. "People might see us."

"They're watching the show. Nobody cares what we're doing." He takes my hand and I slip over to his seat, settling my backside into his lap as if I'm asking Santa for some naughty wish. The hard ridge of his erection digs into me. How is he already hard?

He's been thinking about this. Planning this.

The thought makes me shiver. We may want different things out of our lives, but when it comes to sex we're *highly* compatible.

"This is why you told me to wear this dress," I say, my lips brushing his ear. His hand tracks up my inner thigh, fingers walking along my warm flesh. "Easy access."

In the near darkness, his smile is so deliciously wolfish, I feel myself growing wet. His fingertips brush against my sex and the silky underwear that cost me a pretty penny when I went shopping yesterday.

"You're already damp." He slides his finger along the length of my seam, feeling me through my underwear. "I bet you'd let me slide right in if I wanted to fuck you right now."

My breath stutters. I can act as in-charge and girl-power as I want, but the fact is this man has me pant-

ing for him. Desperate for him. Wanton and willing
and ready for him.

"I would." I let the words whisper out, my lips trailing over his neck, and I feel him grow even harder beneath me. "I'd let you bend me over and fuck right into
me without any resistance at all."

Daniel makes a rumbling sound that sends goose
bumps skittering over my arms and legs. "Temptress."

"Brute." I press my mouth to his just as he breaches
my underwear, pressing his finger between my lips and
seeking out my entrance. "Arrogant, entitled, bossy
brute."

He chuckles darkly. "You love that about me."

I know he doesn't mean love as in the capital *L* kind.
I can't love him, I barely know him. But I *do* love how
he makes me feel. I do love how he touches me.

He slides a finger inside me and I gasp. "Watch the
show, Ava."

How can I possibly concentrate? I tremble as he
slides his finger in and out, curling it to hit the spot
that makes me want to shatter. His lips are at my neck,
his other hand palming my breast, taking his fill of me. I
wish we were back at the villa, with privacy. And space.
I want to take him inside me—and not just his fingers.

"I can feel those thighs shaking. You're squeezing
me so tight."

I shift in his lap, trying to give him better access,
but instead he turns me ninety degrees to face the
front of the balcony. I see the show and the audience, and my dress is hiked up around my hips. His
hand snakes over my leg, slipping down the front of

my underwear this time, and when he circles my clit I almost explode.

"You like that better." He's telling, not asking. "You're so wet, Ava. I can tell how much you want it."

I do. I want it so bad I could scream.

He teases me, circling the sensitive bundle of nerves, over and over in sweeping, lazy strokes. It's enough to have me writhing but he pulls back the second I get too close. Bastard. He loves being in control, loves pleasuring me until I bend to him. Loves making me wait.

"Tonight," he whispers into my ear, warm breath drifting over the back of my bare neck. "This is just a taste of what's to come. I'm going to make you mine."

The way he assumes I'll say yes gets under my skin. Or at least, it should. It should bother me that he feels so comfortable making assumptions about what I want. What I need.

But he knows me better and more intimately than any other man before. It's like we've had years instead of days exploring one another.

"Get ready, Ava."

At that very second, as though he timed it perfectly, the opera swells, and perfect clear voices ring like bells through the theatre. So loud they consume my cries and the sound of my pleasure is lost in the fray. I quake against Daniel's hand, release rippling through me like waves, and when I melt back against him, sated and yet desperate for more, I feel the curve of his smile against the back of my neck.

CHAPTER EIGHTEEN

Daniel

FOR THE REST of the opera, Ava is riveted. When Don Giovanni kills the commendatore, she gasps and reaches for my thigh. I managed to resist the temptation to draw her hand up higher, because that is for later. I want tonight to be about her enjoyment, of both the carnal and cultural variety. So I hold her hand until intermission, and when we head to the bar area for a glass of champagne, I listen to her talk at length about what a horrible character Don Giovanni is.

When we make our way back to the balcony, her copper-flecked eyes are dark and tempting. The second we're inside and the lights dim, she leans over and kisses me with such force that I seriously consider pushing her to the floor and taking her right then and there.

Soon.

After the second act is over, we blend into the well-dressed crowd and make a slow exit from the opera house. I hold her hand as we take the steps, the length of her dress gripped in her other hand.

"I don't think I've ever been so happy to witness a character die since season four of *Game of Thrones*." She shakes her head. "I mean, what a tool!"

The comment earns her a snooty look from an older woman draped in diamonds who walks slightly ahead of us. But Ava is undeterred.

"A moral to the story, indeed! I mean, he treated those women like a game. They were nothing but objects to him." She tilts her face up to me and I can't help but smirk at the angry glitter in her eyes. "Don't you think? Getting dragged to hell by a statue of your murder victim hardly seems enough. I want a sequel."

"A sequel?" I chuckle.

"Yes, *Don Giovanni Suffers in Hell for All Eternity*. It's got quite a ring to it, I think."

Another woman turns around and nods. "Hear, hear."

I slip an arm around her waist and run my fingers over the beading of her dress. It feels disarmingly easy, being with her. And it's one thing I never expected at all: fun. Ava has a sense of humour that calls to me, she's unafraid to speak her mind and she holds her own against me...something I don't encounter very often.

The crowd moves slowly, and eventually we make it down the last few steps to where ushers hold open the doors. We're among the last to leave. A warm, balmy breeze skates over us. It's easy for a fraction of a second to think this is a night out between lovers.

But a set of flashes goes off right in our faces, and I hit the hard ground of reality with a spine-jolting thud. I knew the PR team was going to have something planned, some kind of media presence. After all, the point of being with Ava is to be seen, even if I prefer everything we do when no one's watching.

"Who's this lovely lady?" A man with a British accent holds his phone out, and another man beside him has a camera pointed in our faces. There are a few others, with cameras and smartphones pointed in our direction. The other theatre guests are looking at us to see what the commotion is. This isn't real news, just a bunch of tabloids and gossip websites looking for clickbait opportunities.

"Is she your fiancée?"

A stone settles in the pit of my gut and I wonder if this whole thing is a giant mistake. I feel Ava seize up beside me, drawing closer—which might make it look like we're a team, but I feel how uncomfortable she is.

You dragged her into this.

"Yes, Ava and I are engaged." I sound stiff. Like a robot doing a poor imitation of a human.

After everything I went through with my parents, I'm an intensely private man. That's why I've resisted Ava's questions and why I've always resented having to court the media. It makes me feel like a piece of meat. Like nothing is truly mine.

And worse, now I'm spreading that awful experience to a sweet, joyful woman who did nothing worse than being in the wrong place at the wrong time.

"Does this mean you've broken things off with your brother's wife?" A burly man with a French accent steps forward, his phone in one hand.

"I've never been in a relationship with Lily Moretti."

The words come out through clenched teeth. "Now, if you'll excuse us—"

"How do you feel about getting married to a man who's sleeping with his brother's wife?" The British guy steps toward Ava, blocking her path.

Ava's eyes flick to me and for a moment I'm worried that she might be intimidated by all this. But instead her gaze is hard and glittering. She's furious and it radiates off her in glorious waves.

"No comment," she says, meeting the man's intense stare.

"Do you need his permission to speak, love?" The guy chortles, egging her on. "Are you his puppet?"

Now even more people are watching. Passersby pause on the street to watch the sordid affair. Heat blooms in Ava's cheeks.

"How dare you." She balls her hands by her sides. "All we wanted was a romantic evening out, and you're trying to ruin that by perpetuating false rumours so you can sell advertising. It's despicable."

No, *I'm* the despicable one. My team set this up. I knew what we'd face, and I allowed her to walk straight into shark-infested waters. None of the men before us look even remotely admonished. Why would they? They're soulless creatures. Relentless vultures.

I need to get her away from this.

I've made a terrible mistake. Marc will never believe me, and the press won't let go of the affair because it's more salacious than anything else I can offer them. Maybe I've reached the point of no return... I'll never live this down. And all I've done is make Ava suffer.

My hand tightens around hers, and I attempt to lead her down the steps. But she digs her heels in. Literally.

One of the cameramen smirks. "False, eh? That's not what people say."

"Even in the face of all these lies, Daniel is still trying to walk on with his head held high. He's still trying to repair the relationship with his family that *you* have all damaged." She's almost vibrating with anger. I try to move her again, but she yanks her hand out of my grip. "And if you have any idea what we did in our balcony seats tonight, you wouldn't be questioning where his loyalties lie."

Fuck. That is *not* something I need hitting the internet.

Australian Business Mogul Has Raunchy Sexcapade during Opera Show.

"Ava," I growl, grabbing her hand again. "That's enough."

I drag her through the crowd, shirtfronting the British man on my way through. He gives a satisfying *oof* when my shoulder connects with his chest, bumping him out of my way. Yeah, it's a caveman move but I need to get us both out of here, before my darling "fiancée" tells the world any more about our sex life. The tabloid mongrels follow us, shouting for more information, wolf-whistling Ava and asking if I'm good in bed.

Thankfully, our car is waiting right on the side of the road and I yank the door open before the driver has even made it out of his seat. Bundling Ava inside, I slam the door shut behind us, cutting the sound off with a harsh bang.

"You shouldn't have taken their bait," I say as the car pulls away from the curb. "It's only feeding the beast."

Ava leans back against the leather, her dark hair looking a little wild from the mad dash. Strands fall around her face in soft, springy curls. As if she wants to torture me, she reaches behind her head and pulls out a pin that sends the rest of her hair tumbling around her bare shoulders. The black silk and beading on her dress shimmers, enhancing her perfect shape and parting over one thigh, where the split reveals a shapely leg. I'm immediately reminded of how the fabric parted for my hands not too long ago.

"Why should they have the last say?" she asks indignantly.

"They print the words. They *always* have the last say." I narrow my gaze at her. "Especially when you allude to the fact that I used our private balcony for something *other* than watching the opera."

"But it's true, isn't it?"

"Sometimes the truth is more dangerous than the lie."

I'm starting to realise that. Because the lie here is that I feel nothing for Ava, that this is a means to an end. That she's a glorious distraction from the shitstorm that is my life. But the truth of it—the truth of this passionate woman who knows what she wants and isn't afraid to wear it on her sleeve—is far more complicated.

And if there's one thing I don't want for my life, it's more complications.

"But the lie is what put us in this position. One lie

brings another, they breed like rabbits." Her gaze drifts
to the window, where lights flicker as we drive by.
They play against her skin, mingling with the moonlight to make her look even more goddess-like and
ethereal. "Isn't the truth simpler?"

"Maybe for someone like you."

She raises an eyebrow. "For someone like me?"

"Someone who doesn't have to worry about being
in the spotlight."

"Ah," she says with a bitter laugh. "A social peas-
ant."

"That's not what I said."

"But it's what you meant. I'm beneath you in all this,
someone you've dragged up from obscurity to plunge
into your glittering world for the sake of selling the lie."

"Is that what you really think, that you're *beneath*
me?"

She snorts. "Let's face it, Daniel, this dress cost
more than my tertiary education and the last time I was
in France, I lived on bread and black coffee because
it was all I could afford. You may not think of me as
being beneath you, but I am."

"The only way you'd be beneath me is if you wanted
me to fuck you in that position. That's it." I drag a hand
over my face. How she could even believe the bullshit
coming out of her mouth? "Otherwise, we walk on the
same ground. I do *not* view you as less than me simply
because you don't come from money. That's the kind
of classist shit my father believed in."

"How *would* I know what you believe—it's not like
you tell me anything real. The second I ask questions

you clam up harder than a toddler who doesn't want to let go of his toy." She shakes her head. "And I don't care what you say, there is *no* way you would have noticed me if we didn't end up in that closet together. I wouldn't have even registered on your radar."

"No," I admit. "You probably wouldn't have."

Hurt splashes across her face like red paint. But my answer isn't what she thinks.

"The fact is, I haven't looked at *any* woman in more than a year. And that's not by chance." I watch curiosity flicker in her eyes, like embers warming in a fireplace. "After my dad left, my mother…"

I swallow, but it feels like I've got a peach pit lodged in my windpipe. There are so many things I've never told another person, so many things I've bottled up for years and years so that they ate at me from the inside, corroding who I am. What I want.

"I found my mother passed out on her bedroom floor, unconscious in a pool of her own vomit. She'd taken a bottle of sleeping pills and chugged god knows how much vodka…" I still remember the smell of it— the sticky, acrid scent of the puke mixing with Chanel No.5. The sight of all the pills half-dissolved. "The alcohol saved her, because she threw everything up before it had a chance to work."

"Oh my god." Ava's eyes are wide, almost cartoonish. "That's…horrible."

"I called an ambulance, but we had to keep it quiet, because the media would have had a field day. We told people she'd fainted and hit her head in the shower."

"Sometimes the truth is more dangerous than the lie." She echoes my words.

"I didn't even tell Marc." I protected him, like always. I shielded him, bore the brunt of my family's fucked-up nature and let my own shoulders sag under the weight of it. "The thing I never understood was that she didn't once try something like that while she was married to my father and he was screwing anything with tits. Him *leaving* her was what pushed her over the edge. She wanted him to stay, even if it meant he broke every vow they'd made to each other."

Ava scoots over to me and I have to fight my instinct to push her away, to put up the walls. She's here because of all this—because of my views on relationships, because of my family's inability to trust one another. I owe her an explanation, at the very least.

Even if sharing these dark parts of my history makes me want to find the nearest bottle of whiskey and numb myself until I can barely stand.

"You didn't have to tell me all that," she says, putting a hand on my arm. "I know you prefer to keep things private."

"You said I never told you anything real, so there you go." My eyes meet hers and she's so close. Too close. I can count the freckles on her nose and feel the heat of her body infusing mine. She's thawing me, this woman. Breaking down my barriers and cracking open the shell around my heart.

She's under my skin.

Sometimes the truth is more dangerous than the lie.

"You're *not* beneath me, Ava. Can you promise not

to say bullshit like that ever again?" I cup the side of her face. I want her again, my body calls to hers in pulsing waves and my cock grows hard. Blood rushes in my ears as I anticipate her touch.

"I don't know if I can promise that," she whispers. "Maybe you should keep my mouth busy so that I can't say anything at all."

Christ. This woman...

"You're insatiable." I lean forward to kiss her, but she presses a finger to my lips, halting me. If I was any harder, I'd be at serious risk of damaging these tuxedo pants beyond repair.

"That's not what I meant."

Ava fists the length of her dress in one hand and slides off the back seat, dropping to her knees at my feet. I'm in sensory overload. She looks up at me with sultry eyes, long lashes casting shadows on her cheeks. Thank god the partition is up between us and the driver, because in this moment she's mine and I'm not sharing.

She reaches for my zipper and slowly draws it down, then I raise myself up so she can pull my pants and jocks down, exposing me. I never thought I'd be in this position—stuffy tuxedo jacket on top, junk out. If those gossip website vultures could see me now...

But the only thing I care about now is getting Ava's lips around my cock.

Ava runs her fingertips up and down the length of me, teasing me. Is this payback? Whatever it is, I let myself be lost in it. She presses her lips to me and draws me in, sliding the swollen head of my cock so far back I'm sure I bump the back of her throat.

"Bloody hell, Ava." I burrow both hands into her hair, controlling the bobbing motion of her head. It's pure, unadulterated bliss.

She closes her lips around me, sucking, flicking her tongue, and her hand grips me with thumb and forefinger around the base of my cock. Hot wetness consumes me. It's everything. My ass clenches and I thrust into her mouth, letting out a soft groan. I'm sure the driver can hear us. But it's impossible to stay quiet. Ava's nails dig into my thighs and a sharp spike of pain bleeds into the pleasure, blurring everything.

With each flick of her tongue, each tight stroke, I get closer. Too close. Pressure builds at the base of my cock and I feel the familiar pull of an orgasm sneaking up. But when I try to pull back, she holds me tight, the snug ring of her mouth sending dizzying shock waves through me.

"Ava," I pant. "If you don't let go…"

She pulls me out of her mouth and licks the underside of my dick. "I know. I want you to."

I groan. "Seriously?"

"Yes. I want you to come in my mouth."

Her lips are on me again, her hand working me in wet, smooth strokes. I widen my legs and let my head roll back, my hand tightening in her hair. This woman. This up-for-anything, daring, sexy woman…

The second I get her back to that villa, I'm going to bend her over the nearest surface and hike her dress up.

I'm going to tear that silky underwear with my teeth and then I'm going to fuck her senseless.

"Oh god." I'm so close. She sucks on me, tongue flicking, and when she bobs her head back down, driving me all the way to the back of her throat, I'm done.

I send my release into her mouth, jetting in hard spurts until a sense of relief and calm and utter contentment washes over me. I drag her up, needing to have her in my arms in a way I haven't experienced in a long time.

Maybe ever.

I don't just want her, I need her.

This is the dangerous truth.

CHAPTER NINETEEN

Ava
One week later...

I'VE TAKEN DODGING my mother's calls to a whole new level, including setting her ringtone as the *Imperial March* so I know not to answer. But the time has come. I can't avoid her anymore.

"I really don't feel comfortable doing this," Daniel says as we walk up my mother's driveway.

"You think I wanted to bring you here? Uh, no," I scoff. "You're raising my mother's expectations so high that after we break up, no other man will ever have a hope of meeting them."

Even thinking about the breakup sets my stomach churning. I can't explain it, since the deadline has been approaching from the very beginning. But ever since we returned from France, things with Daniel and I have been...

Wow. I think I've had more orgasms in one week than in my whole life prior. We can't keep our hands off one another. It's sex like I've never experienced before. We fit. We're so compatible we keep ruining his bedsheets and we can barely make it through a meal without touching.

And yet, there's something else simmering away. It's not *just* the sex. It's the fact that we talk until late into the night, lying naked, hands entwined. It's the looks he gives me when he thinks I don't see him—the looks that aren't simply heat, but curiosity and confusion and wonder.

They're the looks I secretly give him.

"I'm *that* good, huh?" He winks in such an exaggerated manner that I can't help but laugh. "Ultimate husband material."

I ring the doorbell and roll my eyes. "You go in first. The doorway isn't big enough for you, me *and* your ego."

"Ah, my favourite threesome." He grins and I grin back, feeling my stomach flutter and my hands get a little sweaty like I really *am* about to introduce the man I intend to marry to my mother.

But it's a lie. All of it.

Daniel has the meeting with Henry Livingstone tomorrow to talk about acquiring his company. Marc has promised to stay out of it, apparently. Not for Daniel's sake but for their mother's. For everyone at the company who deserves for this deal to go well.

The media is on our side. Turns out my little outburst at the opera went down a treat—I'm a fierce woman in love and the internet clickers are eating it up.

Daniel almost has everything he wants... And then he'll no longer have a use for me.

"Ava!" My mother opens the front door wearing the biggest, most charming smile I've ever seen. It's entirely for him. "And you must be Daniel."

"It's a pleasure to meet you, Ms. Matthews." He sticks his hand out while keeping his other palm at my back. "I'm sorry it's taken us so long to visit."

"Oh, well...of course." My mother is flustered in the face of such smooth charm. "Come inside so we can get to know you better."

My mother always keeps her house spotless, but it's even shinier than usual. The scent of something delicious wafts from the kitchen and the table is laid out with the "good" china. I'd tried to convince her to meet us out, but she'd refused—insisting that if Daniel were to be part of our family then he would need to come to the family home.

"I was surprised to hear that my daughter was engaged, I'll be honest," she says as she motions for us to sit.

I immediately reach for the bottle of red wine in the middle of the table and pour myself a huge glass. I can't get through this without booze.

"That's on my shoulders, I'm afraid," Daniel says, rubbing my back in slow circles. I have no idea if it's because he can feel my tension or if he's playing the part—whatever the reason, his touch soothes me. "My life is a circus at the best of times and I was reluctant to expose Ava to that side of things. It's an ugly thing to be in the spotlight all the time."

My heart cracks a little at Daniel's honesty. Over the past week and a bit I've come to see the toll such pressure takes on him, how he walls himself away from the world. How each night when he returns from work, he transforms into someone lighter, happier.

"I can imagine," my mum says with a nod. She brings a big pot of homemade bolognaise pasta to the table, along with a fresh hunk of parmesan cheese and bread. "It's been that way for you since you were a kid, right?"

"Unfortunately, yes."

At that moment, my grandmother hobbles out of the lounge room, roused from her nap by the scent of dinner. She's walking slower these days, her cane permanently stuck to one hand, but her eyes are still wickedly sharp. Before I have the chance to even think about getting up to help her, Daniel is out of his seat and offering his arm.

My grandmother titters. "It's been a while since I had someone quite as good-looking as you on my arm," she says.

"Nan!" I scrub a hand over my face.

"What? Just because I'm old doesn't mean I'm dead, dear." She looks him up and down. "If you're as pretty under those clothes, then I can see why my grand-daughter wants to marry you."

Daniel bursts out laughing and I will the ground to split open beneath me so I can disappear forever. "Kill me now."

"Don't be such a prude," my grandmother says as Daniel helps her into a chair. "This is a wonderful thing. And to think, not a few weeks ago your mother was trying to marry you off to that stupid lump, Anthony."

The entire room goes so quiet. I hear the rushing of blood in my ears, and flames crawl up my neck and pool in my cheeks.

"Mum." My own mother steps in, looking as embarrassed as I am.

"He really wasn't good for Ava, though," Nan continues on, undeterred. "He was a little soft, if you know what I mean. Not too bright, couldn't really think for himself. Oh, and he dressed terribly, wore those stupid hats all the time."

I glare at my mother. This is *all* her fault—the fact that I felt compelled to take Daniel's offer in the first place, that I'm here now being humiliated. Sometimes I wonder if she wants me to be miserable.

"Now *you*, on the other hand." Nan nods appreciatively. "I bet you can think for yourself. Plus, you have good bone structure, very strong and muscular."

"He's not a horse, Nan. Jeez." I gulp down half a glass of red wine in one go. I have never been more mortified in all my life.

"I hope you take care of her...in *all* the ways." My grandmother winks at Daniel. Actually. Freaking. Winks.

"This is..." I plonk the wineglass down on the table so suddenly I'm surprised it doesn't shatter the stem. "This is so inappropriate."

But Daniel grabs my wrist and shoots me a look, telling me not to walk away. How is it that after such a short time we can communicate like this—through a touch or a look? It's as though there's a level of intimacy that shouldn't be. It's too soon. Too much.

Especially considering none of this is real.

"What?" Nan shrugs and holds her plate out to my mother, who simply sighs and starts dishing up the meal. I lean back in my seat, even though I'm tempted to walk out of there and never return. "A woman should know when she's got a good thing, that's all. Consider yourself lucky, Ava."

"Actually, *I'm* the one who's lucky," Daniel says. "Ava found me at a moment where I was truly alone in the world…or at least I wanted to be."

I can't help but smile at the secret in his words, the little message of truth that only I will understand.

"It's like she appeared right when I needed her most and every day since has been…surprising." He looks at me and for a moment, my heart skips a beat. How can this not be real? Is he really so good at faking it? Need and want and joy shimmer inside me but I try to shut those feelings down.

This is no different from that day when I walked through my mother's doors and she informed me of her plan to arrange a marriage for me. It's a lie. A solution to a problem that doesn't necessarily need solving.

You know that's not true. You want love and marriage and babies and all of that.

I do. But I also want it to mean something, and I can't settle for a man who sees me only as a means to an end. Yet I can't help feeling this is something more. Something…so close to what I want I'm not sure if I'm staring at fantasy or reality.

"I'm a different person with Ava," he says, still not taking his eyes off me. "A better person."

I reach for his hand, and it's entirely out of instinct and nothing to do with the two sets of eyes watching us. It's nothing to do with keeping up appearances or selling the story or any of that stuff. It's because I want to connect with him. Touch him.

"That's all well and good," Nan says, sticking her fork into her spaghetti and twirling the long strands. "But it certainly doesn't hurt to have an ass firm enough to bounce a tennis ball on."

Laughing and shaking my head, I raise my glass into the air before downing the rest of it in one fell swoop. Lord knows I'm going to need more wine to get through this evening.

We walk out of my childhood home a few hours later. The mortification continued through the meal, dessert *and* coffee after that. Daniel had good-naturedly sat through stories of my failed childhood crushes and looked at pictures of me as a baby and taken flirty-borderline-inappropriate comments from my grandmother on the chin.

We'd driven over in Daniel's Maserati and I notice some of my mother's neighbours watching us through their front windows, blinds cracked enough that I see familiar faces left and right.

"I don't know whether I should thank you for putting up with that or throttle you for putting me in this position in the first place," I say. We pause outside his car and for a moment I'm struck by how almost-perfect this is…emphasis on the *almost*.

The suburb I grew up in isn't fancy. The houses are

very '90s and the Maserati sticks out like a shining Christmas bauble among forgettable Fords and Holdens. But the late spring air is mild and honeysuckle-scented, and the evening sky has that lovely purple tinge to it, with only the first few stars popping out to sparkle the night away.

This is how I imagined my life would be one day—a gorgeous man, family dinners, long, languid pauses as a prelude to kissing.

"Your grandmother is hilarious." He grins and the smile is so genuine it makes my heart ache. I always thought there was something sexy about a brooding guy. But Daniel has shown me the true beauty of that same man offering you a glimpse behind his walls. "I would have dinner with her *any* night of the week."

"You can have her," I joke. "One grandma going cheap."

"Your family is great, Ava. You should be thankful."

"That's *very* easy for you to say when you've only seen the good bits."

He slings an arm around my shoulder and pulls me close, leaning against the side of the car and holding me tight. "You *have* good bits…which is more than I can say."

"I love my mother and grandmother, I really do. It just feels like sometimes they don't really know me. Or what I want. They're trying to foist their ideas of marriage on me when they needn't bother. I *want* to have a relationship and get married… But I want it to be for the right reasons and with the right person."

"So not soft Anthony with the bad hats, then," Daniel teases.

"God no." I shudder. "The fact that my mother thought that was the best I could do... It's insulting."

"Ah yes, well now you have a man with good bone structure and nice muscle definition." He chuckles and pushes the hair back from my face.

"Don't forget an ass firm enough to bounce a tennis ball on," I quip, trying my hardest not to let the swirling worries get to me.

What's going to happen when Daniel and I call things off? How can I come back here and explain to my mother that...it's over? That it was all a lie. I can't tell her that, can I?

The thing is, selfishly, that's not the main thing I'm worried about in breaking up with Daniel. I'm worried about *me*. I've grown closer to him than any other man before and, in some sick twist of fate... I feel like I'm falling for him.

Seeing him tonight, charming my family and doting on my grandmother and being the wonderful man the rest of the world can't seem to recognise... I want that life. I want him. Not as a means to an end. Not for now.

But for real.

"Maybe we should hurry home so you can test that theory," he says, lowering his head to mine and capturing my lips in a searing kiss. He tastes sweet, like the fruity red wine and chocolate brownie we had for dessert, and his hands are hot and greedy.

I feel my body anticipating him, my hips flexing toward his where he's already growing hard against me. My hands thrust into his hair as I kiss him back, pouring all my worry and lust and my wishes and fantasies into this kiss.

"Fuck, Ava," he growls against my neck as I rock against him. "We need to get you home now before I give your neighbours anything more to gossip about."

"Yes, take me home." I gasp as his hand finds my breast and squeezes, his lips trailing fire over my jaw. "I'm all yours."

He looks at me with blackened eyes and need tightening all his muscles and I know, in that instant, that I am totally and utterly ruined. Walking away isn't going to be easy. When he leaves, he'll take a piece of me with him.

And I might not ever get it back.

CHAPTER TWENTY

Daniel

With all the confusing shit swirling around in my head, the frustrating, negative things that I face all day in the office…Ava is my bright spot. When I left work earlier today I was wrung out and hollow. The deal with Livingstone is moving at a snail's pace, and it's taking all my concentration to inch it forward.

Ordinarily, I'd be like a lion snapping my jaws and roaring until I had what I wanted. But with every day that passes, work feels like a waiting room until I can get to the "real" part of my day.

The part with her.

With Ava in my arms I'm alive and refuelled and I feel like I can take on the world. I know those are red flags. I know it and yet…

I'm powerless to resist.

We walk through the front door to my apartment and she immediately wraps her arms around my waist, pressing her cheek to my chest. I smooth my hand over her hair—fighting the comfort it gives me. I don't want to feel anything for her. I don't want to be soothed by her presence. I don't want this to mean anything.

But it does.

Tonight—meeting her family and laughing over their jokes and stories—was a punch to the gut. I could sketch my own memories onto that scene—dinner with my mum and Marc, Lily popping in to visit with her hair in braids. The giggling, sneaking items off one another's plates when Mum wasn't looking. Hiding our peas under napkins.

I've lost that version of my family. Maybe that's why being with Ava feels so good—it's like reclaiming the part of my life I've been grieving for the past year. Several years, in fact.

You have to end it. You can't drag her further into your shit, because you'll only end up hurting her.

But when Ava lifts her head, her warm copper-flecked eyes wide and inviting, I'm obliterated. I lean forward, lips finding hers hot and open and willing. Maybe the physical might help me forget the emotional, might clear the slate for tomorrow so I can think about the path forward.

I've made no promises and neither has she.

"Come to bed with me," she whispers against my lips, her hands fisting my shirt.

I can't speak. There are no words left. So I take her hand and lead her upstairs, her curvy body like fire to my ice-weary heart. When we reach the loft, I kiss her senseless, letting my hands roam her body. The insistent press of her curves has me hard. Ready. Desire burns, slower than before. Slower than I've ever been used to. But it's more insistent. Harder to ignore because it's burrowing deep.

"I want you," she whispers. "I want this."

It feels like there are words missing, like she wants to say more. But neither of us can go there. That is a door we can't open.

I draw her to the bed, placing her down gently. Buttons line the length of her dress and I take my time opening them, kissing her skin as I undress her. She sighs and hums. Her nipples press against her bra, little peaks demanding my attention, and when I suck one into my mouth, she arches against me.

"Yes," she breathes.

My hands work faster, sloppily pushing the buttons open until I have her mostly bare. Cotton underwear covers her and when I press the heel of my palm between her legs, rubbing her in slow circles, I can feel how soaked they are. I need to have her. Now.

"You've been waiting for me." I trace my finger along the edge of her underwear. Her eyes are blackened and wide, drinking me in. Urging me on. "Dirty girl."

"Yes." Her breath comes quicker, her eyes bright and wide and hungry. "I've been thinking about this all day."

It's like a punch to the gut. Knowing she was thinking about me—about this—waiting and waiting while her pussy got wet for me... Fuck.

You could have this forever.

No, I can't. Because forever is a lie.

It's the devil's hand leading you down the wrong

path. A path decorated with fantasies and wishes and desires all designed to trick you. What I feel for Ava might be real—terrifyingly real—but this life I'm being promised isn't.

But I can't take my eyes off her. The breath vanishes from my lungs as I part her thighs, spreading them wider and wider. I press my cheek to the inside of her leg and she makes a delightful *hmm* sound. The gentle pressure of my fingers climbing higher up her thighs, the wet slide of my tongue following, draws a soft groan from her.

I press a kiss to her through the thin cotton underwear. I can make out the outline of her sex through the soaked material clinging to her.

"Please, Daniel." She arches into me, hips rolling.

I'm not patient today and I have no strength for games. I tear the underwear from her, splitting the material and snapping the elastic with my hands, then I bury my face into her. Her orgasm rushes up, swift and brutal. She comes with a cry that's so loud it feels as though it shakes the very foundations of the building.

On any other day I'd be itching to get inside her. I'd be spreading her sex and dragging my cock through her juices, ready to plunge into her. But in this moment, I want her to melt in my arms. I want to cherish her.

I crawl up beside her, wrapping Ava up and holding her close. Her lips find mine and we kiss, my tongue delving into her mouth and my fingers driving through her hair. We stay like this, connected and connecting. Together.

Tomorrow I have to end it.

Because this woman has the power to destroy me. She's peeled back my layers, put thoughts into my head that have no business being there. She's gotten under my skin, inside my heart.

I think I love her.

My body rejects the idea so brutally that my hands automatically clench, yanking on Ava's hair so hard it makes her gasp. But the minx that she is, she doesn't even miss a beat. She pushes me back against the bed and undoes my pants. I lift my hips so she can yank them and my underwear down, and then she's on top of me. Her hair trails over her breasts and I sweep it back so I can see all of her. Every glorious inch.

"Ava." I press my head back against the bed and she rocks against me, working my cock into a frenzy.

"I want to feel you bare," she says.

We've used a condom every other time. "Are you... protected?"

She nods. "I'm on the pill and I keep up my tests. Single gal's gotta protect herself."

Single gal. My gut clenches and I pull her down, smashing my mouth against hers. "I'm clean, too. I get a physical every year. And it's been..."

So long. Now it feels light-years away. I can't imagine having anyone else here. I don't *want* anyone else here.

And the thought of her being with another man...

The visceral sound in my head is almost inhumane. Without hesitation, I flip us over and pin her beneath me. Parting her, I drag my fingers through her moisture, preparing her. When I push one inside her, then two, she clenches around me.

"Oh god," she gasps. The pulses come quicker now as I stroke her. "No. Not like this, Daniel. Please I want… I want…"

I press into her, sliding easily against her slick flesh. The feeling of her being so full and so tight is almost too much. Too perfect. I press my face into her neck so she can't see the conflict swirling in my head—the mix of white-hot pleasure and shadowy pain. I touch her everywhere. My hands are at her back, her butt, her breasts and hips.

"You feel so good." My words are soft and rough against her neck, as though it's a secret for us to share. "So perfect."

I thrust into her harder, picking up speed and chasing the pinprick of pleasure dancing behind my eyes. I let myself be lost in her. Be undone by her.

Be irrevocably marked by her.

I seat myself deep inside, all the way to the hilt, for the last time. For the very last time.

This can't happen again.

After a moment of pure stillness, I wrap my arms around her and roll us so she's on top, her head resting against my chest. My hands are in her hair, stroking and cradling her head. When she sighs in total and utter contentment, it's the purest, most alive I've ever felt.

CHAPTER TWENTY-ONE

Ava

THE NEXT MORNING, I stretch my arms above my head, enjoying the delicious pull in my muscles. Last night was…incredible. After we got home, we made love, showered, drank more wine on the balcony overlooking the city. We didn't speak and yet it was the most comfortable I have ever been. Daniel keeps much of himself under lock and key but every day I see a little more. Learn a little more.

I could spend *hours* in his arms. By his side. Being quiet with him.

Everything feels so right. What started as lust has blossomed into something more. Lust is like love's two-dimensional cousin; similar on the surface, but not the same. *Far* from the same. And last night, watching him be vulnerable with my family, watching him be open and honest… It slayed me.

With him, I feel beautiful. Cherished. Appreciated.

I know I have to return to real life. In fact, I have an interview set up with one of my dream schools today thanks to him. A school that would never have looked at me before is suddenly interested in my skills and experience. If I can secure that job, then my whole life could finally click into place: the career I want with kids I can nurture and develop, a salary to afford me some more secure housing, a perfect man.

He's perfect...until the expiration date.

Sitting in the expansive bed, I hug the crisp cotton sheet to my body. Why can't I have it all? I let my eyes slide over to the empty space where Daniel slept last night, the sheets rumpled in a rough outline of his incredible physique. Why can't this be real?

I deserve love. I *want* love. And I feel things for Daniel I've never felt before. I'm in deeper, *much* deeper. To me...this could be love.

It could be everything.

But it won't be anything unless I understand whether I'm in these feelings alone. I need to know. The clink of metal and porcelain downstairs draws me out of bed. I pull on my dress from the floor, smoothing my hands over the creases, and head quietly downstairs.

For a moment I stand at the bottom of the steps, quiet as a mouse so I can watch. Could our life be like this? Early mornings scented with coffee, sitting at a kitchen island together talking and making plans for our future?

But the smile on my lips falters as I look closer, because he doesn't appear to be a man floating on a cloud. His shoulders are bunched, the muscles pressing up around his neck as he scrubs a hand along his jaw.

"You look very tense for a man who spent all night

doing what we did," I say as I walk over and slide a mug under the spout of the coffee machine, jabbing the button for a double shot. It whirs and the noise makes me jump, even though I'm expecting it. My nerves are frayed.

I don't want this to end. Not yet, I'm not ready.

"We need to talk," he replies.

"We're already talking." I pick up the cup but can't find the strength to bring it to my lips. Instead I let the warmth seep from the china into my palms.

"I'm moving on from this thing with Marc... He's obviously not coming back to the company. The deal with Livingstone is moving forward, albeit slowly. But I think I've done as much damage control as I can there." He sighs and rakes a hand through his hair. "As for the reputation damage, there are still detractors, but I think I've put you through enough."

Sunlight streams in as if it's the most perfect day in existence. Just more proof that the world continues to turn, no matter what.

"I can handle it," I say, even though inside I feel like I'm doing anything *but* handling it. "You don't have to worry about me."

"It's not your responsibility to pay for my mistakes," Daniel says darkly. "You don't owe me anything."

It feels like some cruel message from the universe, some dark foreshadowing. Like a higher being is trying to tell me the very thing I already know: *you want something he can't give you.*

"What does that mean for our plans?" I sip my coffee, but it tastes like nothing.

"It means that we can transition out of this arrangement."

Arrangement. The word hits like a cricket bat to the stomach. "It seems a little callous to call it that now, don't you think?"

"Does it?" He spears me with a look.

This is it. He wants to know where I stand, and I don't think it's for the same reason I want to know where *he* stands. He's in damage-control mode. Protection mode. My access to the soft space behind his walls is gone. A door has been slammed in my face.

"Well, I know it *was* an arrangement at first but…"

"We got together because we both had a problem to solve. Our being together was a solution."

How could he reduce what we've shared to such binary terms? My blood boils, because I *know* exactly what he's doing: pushing me away. "Was last night a solution? Or the week before? Or in France?"

The cool facade cracks and for a brief flash there's something real and raw. He's determined to shut me out. To keep me in my place.

"The sex isn't business, you know that." The sigh he lets out is long and weary. "I'm incredibly attracted to you and it curbed my judgement. I had a moment—several moments—of weakness where I gave in and I shouldn't have. I'm sorry."

Sorry. Like he accidently bumped into me in the hallway. Sorry, like he spilled some coffee on my book. Sorry, like we're acquaintances instead of lovers.

"Well, I'm *not* sorry. I'm not sorry we slept together and I'm not sorry I told you everything I did. This might have started as a 'business arrangement' but that's not how it's going to end. At least not for me."

There, I've opened up the floodgates. No turning back now.

"Ava—"

"I know there's something between us and you feel it, too. The way you look at me…" To my utter horror, I feel tears prick the backs of my eyes, but I will be *damned* before I cry in front of him. I put my coffee down and square my shoulders, mustering every ounce of courage I have. "It's not fake. It's *not* for show."

For a moment he says nothing. That's Daniel, always processing…like a computer.

Let me in.

I know he won't. But I can't be like my mother, always doing the thing that feels safest. Always putting security before passion. Always being frightened of getting hurt.

If I never chase what I want, then I'll be hurting anyway.

"It's lust. You turn me on more than any other woman I've ever known… But I can't give you more than that. I won't make the same mistakes as every other idiot in my family." His face is like carved ice, like marble and stone and concrete. Glittering and hard. "If I don't learn that lesson, then what was the point of any of this?"

"What lesson, Daniel? That people are disposable? That they can be bought?"

"What else was this if not a transaction?" He gets off his stool and paces across the room, muscles coiled and tight. "And why is that such a bad thing? We both needed something from each other, and we set limits. We're two adults who walked into this with our eyes open."

"Then tell me this means nothing to you *now*. All I'm asking for is the truth." I lick my lips, my heart pounding so hard it feels like there's a bongo competition in my chest. But I won't back down now. I need to know.

"Do you even think it's possible to love someone in less than two weeks?" He tosses his hands in the air. "That's ridiculous. It's Hollywood bullshit."

Maybe so. It's quick and I can't explain it. Can I call it love? I'm not sure. But I know true feeling when I see it. I know potential when I see it. I know a future when I see it.

And I see all of that with Daniel.

"I never said the *L* word," I say quietly. "*You* said that."

He looks at me and I see it then—fear. He's shown me his hand, because I didn't even bring love into the equation and yet that word was already in his head. It fills my heart with hope. I wasn't wrong, there *is* something between us.

"It's mutual attraction and nothing more," he says stubbornly. "I like you, we had fun together and we solved a few problems. Today you'll get that job and move on with your life and that will be it. That's all it ever was."

Even though I knew it was coming, the words still sting. It hurts even more knowing that he's lying to me, and to himself. That he's using these words to hurt me because he doesn't want to deal with what's really here.

"I never asked you to make this ring on my finger mean something real. But don't reduce what we shared to a lie," I say, turning the sapphire around and around. "You're better than that."

The muscles in his jaw twitch. "You don't know me as well as you think you do."

"I know a good man when I see one."

"Then maybe you should get your eyes checked."

"You can try to downplay what we shared as much as you want, but that won't change how I feel about it. You can't take it away from me."

"There's no point letting this drag on. I don't want to hurt you, Ava." He raked a hand through his hair, but his face was closed off. His dark eyes emotionless. "I should never have pulled you into this in the first place. I've been trying so fucking hard to put up this perfect image and to battle all the lies and the accusations and I'm sick of it."

Despite my frustration that he's pulling away, my heart bleeds for him. "You're not that person. You're not your father."

"And you're not your mother, Ava. Don't settle. Find a man who can give you what you want, who can give you all of him, because it's what you deserve. But I'm not that person."

That's when I feel it—a slicing sensation, like someone is dragging a blade across my heart. *Swish.* Then an awful gut-clenching. The hollow, yawning ache. It's so much more physical than I thought it would be—

so much more real. Not a metaphorical pain, but real, visceral pain.

He's right. I can't be like her.

"Can't you admit it, Daniel? Admit what you feel even if you don't want to act on it." I know I need to let this go. It's over. Even if we have to go on playing for the cameras a little while longer, sharing his bed—his life—*that's* over.

He stares at me for a long moment, like time has frozen him into a perfect replica of a man. "I have to get to work."

I nod, my heart slowly breaking in two.

"It might be best if you head back to your place for the next few days. I'm sure you need to pack anyway. I'll have my assistant get in touch about setting you up in one of the Cielo apartments, and we can figure out a lease agreement later."

Lease agreement. His assistant will call me. Packing my things.

"For what it's worth," I say, staring him dead in the eye as I tug the ring off my finger, "I could have loved you, and I'm not afraid to admit that."

Before he has a chance to respond, I place the ring onto the kitchen counter. Then I turn and head into the room I haven't slept in since those first few nights. I need to get out of here and collect myself before this interview. Today, I start building my new life. A life where I don't settle and I keep fighting for what I want, even if the man I want most in the world can't admit out loud what we share.

CHAPTER TWENTY-TWO

Daniel
Three weeks later...

EVER SINCE AVA walked out of my apartment, I've been in a fog. And by fog, I mean a state where I have lost interest in all things that previously gave me pleasure—eating, drinking, negotiating deals, seeing my team achieve great things. I'm reaching into my bag of fucks and coming up empty.

Life after Ava is like stale bread.

I've been keeping tabs on her, torturing myself with it. She got the job she wanted at her dream school. It had nothing to do with me—I only made the introduction. From all accounts, the kids love her already. I'm not at all surprised.

But she refused my offer of an apartment in the Cielo, instead wanting to find something on her own. She refused my money as well, and every cheque has come back return to sender. Our arrangement, in the end, left us both with half-measures. My brother doesn't believe me, and she's still looking for somewhere to live.

The deal with Henry Livingstone is hanging on by a thread—true to his word, Marc has stayed out of my way. But there's been delay after delay. I know cold feet when I see it, but I can't find the energy to properly reel him in. And truthfully, without Marc, the financial side of our business is sluggish. But I can't pull the trigger on a replacement, either. Our head of accounts is acting in the CFO role, but the guy is no Marc.

Not even close.

The fact is, I want my family beside me. Even after everything that's happened. But relationships are the downfall of good men...even familial relationships, because they can be tinged with as much animosity and jealousy as romantic relationships.

A sharp knock at the door startles me. I've been thinking aimlessly for over an hour—neglecting emails and board papers and the speech I'm supposed to run through for some charity event. None of it seems to matter now.

"Daniel?" My assistant pokes her head through the door. "Your brother is here to speak to you."

If she registers the shock on my face, she doesn't say anything, and a second later Marc walks into my office. He looks stylish as ever—his signature light grey suit a stark contrast against his overlong brown hair and full but neat beard. The facial hair is new, and when I look closer, I spot the hollows under his eyes. He looks rough. Ragged, even.

"What are you doing here?"

"We need to talk."

Lord knows what kind of speculation is flying

around the office now—I announced Marc's depar-
ture in a short, undetailed statement last week that
led to much office chatter. No one has dared breathe
a word of it to me directly. Still, it hasn't stopped the
whispers or conversation that halts abruptly when I
walk into a meeting room.

Marc takes a seat, popping the button on his suit
jacket and folding his long-limbed body into a leather
chair on the other side of my desk. How many times
have we sat here, tension thickening the air as our relationship slowly disintegrated before my eyes?

"I thought you'd said everything there was to say," I
respond coolly. I have no idea where this conversation
might go, but I'm done trying to placate my brother.
Done trying to be the glue in this family.

"I know what happened," Marc says. "I finally got
to the truth."

Great. Now what fresh, new bullshit does my
brother believe? "I won't keep defending myself—"

"I know you didn't sleep with her."

For a moment, I can only sit in stunned silence.
"That's what I've been telling you this whole time."

I've never seen Marc look so broken before—he's
like a man who's watched the world burn to the ground.
Like a man who's lost the only thing he'd ever cared
about. He pulls out the photo—the one supposedly de-
picting Lily and me in a close embrace.

"You said the photo was doctored, and you were
right." Marc points to a small detail—the cuff link
on "my" shirt, which pokes out from the sleeve of my
suit jacket. It's tough to make out the design, but they

appear to be round with a dark stone in the middle. I squint, but they don't look familiar to me. "Nonno gave me those cuff links before he passed away—he hardly ever wore them because he hated how he fumbled putting them on. But they were a gift from his big brother and he thought they should remain with the youngest Moretti."

"Okay."

"I could have put it down to you borrowing them, even if that does seem unlikely. But I know it can't be true," Marc continues. "Something about the date didn't seem right. I've had them in for repair for months. The gemstone fell out and they've been waiting for a replacement to come in because I was adamant about having them colour matched. They would have been in the shop at the time this picture was supposedly taken."

Such a small detail, but so significant.

"It only clicked when I got the call to pick them up a few days ago," Marc continues. "It triggered something in my memory, and I went back to look at the photo. If the date was fake, then how could I believe any of it?"

He tells me the story—admitting the source of the photo is someone close to us. A confidant. A friend of our uncle's and a board member of Moretti Enterprises. He'd stood next to me at my grandfather's funeral, hand on my shoulder.

A board member who's been quietly objecting to me stepping into the CEO role.

"Turns out the photo is old," Marc adds. "I found the original online. It was from a charity event about four years ago that I don't even remember. I've attended so many of the damn things they all blur into one in my head."

White-hot burning rage filters through my system as I listen to the betrayal, to this morally corrupt board member's plans to oust me. Apparently the "affair" was step one of his wider plans to degrade trust in my ability to lead the company. Marc had been a puppet, blinded by his own jealousy.

"He used me," Marc says simply. For once, his emotionally charged communication style is dampened. Muted. I've never seen him like this before. "He knew that we were at odds over your promotion, and he used it to his advantage. Because he knew you wouldn't let him run the show here, like our uncle did. He knew you couldn't be bought or manipulated."

The underlying message is there: this man thought Marc *could* be manipulated. And he was right.

This must be painful for him. Marc is headstrong, with an aptitude for numbers and an ego the size of a continent. To find out he was tricked…

"He fed off problems that were already there," I point out. "We've been at odds for longer than that."

"Ever since I married Lily."

"I was *never* jealous of you two—I wanted you to be happy."

"You told me I was crazy to get married." Marc throws his hands up in the air. "The night before my wedding you told me I had to protect myself and that I could always get out if things started to go bad."

It was true, I *had* said that.

I remember the conversation now. I was genuinely worried for Marc and Lily—genuinely worried, because I care for them *both*. And the thought of them going down the same dark path that my parents did… I was panicked. Furious that they were so blinded by love as to risk themselves like that.

"I shouldn't have said that," I admit, shaking my head. "I didn't want you two to end up hating one another. I didn't want to lose either one of you over it."

"I thought you were in love with her." Marc's face is pure fire—not anger directed at me, but shame. Regret. Disbelief. "And then when I heard these whispers that you were sleeping together, my brain joined the dots. I thought that whole conversation was because you were already with her behind my back."

"Never." The word comes from down deep; from a dark place packed to the walls with bad memories. "I don't know how much you remember about Mum and Dad's divorce…"

Marc's lip curls. "I remember enough."

"Do you remember that I used to herd you out into the street at all hours to play soccer? Didn't matter if it was midnight and we should have been in bed hours ago."

"We used to throw rocks at Lily's windows to get her to come and play with us." A ghost of a smile slips over my brother's lips.

"It was never about the soccer." I tilt my head up to the ceiling, trying not to drown in remembering. "I did that so you wouldn't have to listen to Mum and Dad screaming at each other. So you wouldn't have to listen to Mum crying that Dad was screwing another one of his assistants. So you wouldn't accidentally walk in on him with another woman in our mother's bed like I did."

Marc's eyes widened. "You're kidding me."

"I'm not. I couldn't shield you from the fact that they were going to split up—nobody could. But I damn well didn't want you to *see* what was going on between them. I didn't want you to be totally messed up by it."

Silence settles over us and I take in a slow breath to calm the rapid drumbeat of my heart. I've never told Marc *half* the things I witnessed. We were young at the time and much of the conversation and subtext had flown over my head. But I heard it all. Absorbed it all.

"I never wanted you to see that Mum *knew* about all the affairs and yet she did nothing. It was almost like a game for him, to see how far he could push her." I hate my father, for the cruelty he exacted on my mother, and indirectly on us. "I think he wanted to see what it took to break her."

"And he did, didn't he?" Marc's gaze drifts to the window behind me, where hazy Melbourne sunshine floods into the office. "I remember that she didn't leave her bed for weeks at a time. She wouldn't let us answer the front door and the phone was always off the hook."

"I never wanted you and Lily to go through that." I sigh. "But I managed to put a hand into your relationship when I should have given you a chance to survive without my baggage. I was worried I'd have to choose between you."

"And who would you have chosen?" Marc asks.

Pain spears my heart so sharply it feels like an actual blade.

"Of course I would have chosen you, Marc. Christ." I put my words together carefully. "I love Lily dearly. Platonically. She's like a sister. But you *are* my brother. You're my blood. Of course I would choose you."

Tension clogs the room like a thick soup. My hand twitches and I have to fight the urge to snatch up the letter opener on my desk and slash through the air just to break it up.

"I know you think I don't care about this family," Marc says. "But I do. I *also* wanted to feel like I had a role here, that I wasn't simply playing your understudy."

"I can't change being born first."

"I know. That's my issue, not yours." Marc looks at the desk. "I should have believed you."

It strikes me then that even though I've wanted to hear those words, I had no idea just how much I *needed* it. "Does this mean you're coming back to the company?"

Marc shakes his head. "I need to do my own thing. Build something for myself, for my own family."

"And Lily?"

"I've been terrible to her…" He shakes his head. "If I was her, I wouldn't take me back, but…"

"But?"

"She's pregnant."

I blink. For a moment it's like I can't breathe, can't even think. "You're having a baby."

"Yeah, she told me the night of the Cielo opening."

Everything falls into place. This wasn't just the fact that he believed I was having an affair with Lily… He thought I might be the father of her child. A child he had *desperately* wanted since they started trying as soon as they were married.

And he'd seen it as one more thing I'd taken from him.

"Congratulations," I say, finding my throat tight.

"I'm going to be a dad." In spite of everything, Marc smiles. "And you're going to be an uncle."

"Zio Daniel has quite a ring to it." I shake my head. Marc made a huge error by believing the wrong person, but I know his coming here now to admit his mistakes must have taken a lot of courage.

"I…" He rakes a hand through his hair and swears under his breath. "I know I've messed up, okay? But I want you to be part of my kid's life. I'm going to fix things with Lily and I'm going to be a better dad than what we had growing up."

All I'd ever wanted was for us to be a real family. But I'd never considered how my taking over the company might affect Marc, and I'd meddled in his relationship by pushing my baggage onto him. Those were my mistakes to own.

"I'd like that," I say. "And I know you'll be a far better dad than him."

For a second, I catch a fleeting glimpse of the cheeky boy I knew from my childhood. "It's a low bar and you know I always liked a gimme."

I shake my head, laughing and feeling like my old self again.

"I don't know where we go from here," Marc says, rubbing his hands up and down his thighs.

"Forward."

Marc and I finish our conversation and as he leaves my office, realisation settles over me, like dust finding the earth after a storm. In every other part of my life—with the company and my dreams—I look forward. Move forward. But when it comes to my personal life, I'm firmly rooted in the past. In the hurt my parents inflicted on us, in the baggage I've shouldered trying to care for Marc.

I've let the past dictate my choices in the here and now. And I planted a seed that might very well have killed my brother's marriage and our sibling relationship. I pushed Ava away at a time when I needed someone like her in my life. Someone who communicates openly, who wears their heart on their sleeve.

I need to stop letting the past control me. And, most of all, I need to trust myself.

I am *not* my parents. The same as Marc and Lily are not my parents.

Even when it hurts, family *is* the most important thing in my life. Only I've been stubbornly looking back at the mistakes my parents left behind, thinking my role was to make up for their deficits. But this conversation with Marc has proved one thing: it's possible to forgive and move forward.

But would Ava forgive me for being pigheaded and blind? For being so stuck in the past I wouldn't allow myself to see a future with her in it? She was the catalyst for me to break out of my old ways. A woman who loves so hard and so fearlessly she makes me reconsider everything. She's changed me, irrevocably.

I can't fix my father's mistakes, but I *can* learn from them.

I can be the man who builds others up, instead of tearing them down. Who loves with everything he has. Who could be worthy of love. *Her* love.

But first I have to tell her the truth.

CHAPTER TWENTY-THREE

Ava

"Thanks for letting me stay." I lug the last box into the garage and stack it against the wall where everything else I own—sans clothing and toiletries, which are in the house—will sit in boxes until I move again.

My mother leans against the brick wall, watching me. She wears an apron over jeans and a T-shirt, with a pair of dirty old runners on her feet. Gardening attire.

I look at the boxes, each neatly labelled with what they contain. My heart feels heavier than a cruise liner, but I'm trying not to seem affected.

Trying…and failing.

"I don't know why you didn't tell me about the issue with your apartment earlier, Ava." My mother frowns. "You *always* have a place here. This is your home as much as it is mine."

Guilt twists like a furious dragon in my belly. I know my mother and I have a relationship complicated by our different ideals, but we're family. We love one another underneath it all and sometimes I don't give her enough credit.

"To be completely honest, I was worried that us living together might…" I sigh.

"Cause irreparable damage?" she offers and I laugh, surprised her mind went there, too.

"Yeah."

She looks so different from the day that Daniel came to visit—gone is the styled hair, which now sits like a poufy brown cloud around her ears. Gone is the lipstick and the gold earrings and the neatly pressed blouse. She's got a smear of dirt on one cheek and a little hole in the neckline of her T-shirt and a pair of shears poking out of the pocket of her apron.

I love seeing her like this, because the garden is my mother's happy place. She could spend hours out there, tending to her flowers and her hanging plants and the herbs she grows along the fence. It's like when her hands are in the dirt, every bad memory in her brain gets paused.

"I know we don't always see eye to eye." She comes closer and pulls me into a hug. It smells like my childhood—fresh earth and petunias and lemon and black coffee. "Matthews women are stubborn and strong, and that's why we survive. But it doesn't always make for an easy living situation."

I swallow and there's a big lump in the back of my throat. "Are we too stubborn?"

"No, darling. Because stubborn means we want something, and where would we be if we didn't want for a better life?" She brushes the hair back from my face the way she used to when I was a little kid.

"I thought you would be mad at me for walking away." I haven't told my mother the relationship was for show. I haven't told Emery or my other girlfriends, either.

Because as much as Daniel and I made an arrangement in the beginning, it doesn't feel that way to me now. And I don't think it matters how it started; only what I felt in the end. I don't know how to label it, exactly... But Daniel means something to me, and this breakup is real and painful.

"You know I want to see you married and secure, but I also want to see you happy." She pulls away and motions for me to follow her into the house. The entryway is cluttered with my suitcase, overnight bag and two extra boxes of clothes and books and makeup. "I know you think I was wrong to suggest that Anthony might make a good match, but I really *did* believe you could be happy together. You used to be friends when you were kids."

"Do you really think I'd be happy with a man who's so attached to his mother?" I say, shaking my head. That whole situation is still a prickle under my skin.

"What's so wrong about a mother having a child who adores her? Some mothers crave that."

And then I understand it. My fierce need for independence, which was fostered by being raised by two strong, self-reliant women, is the very thing that has driven me to make my own life *away* from her expectations. It's what drove me away from her when we had fundamental disagreements about relationships and life.

It's why I sent Daniel's cheques back and refused to take an apartment in the Cielo, despite that being the entire point of our arrangement. The only thing I did take up was the connection for a job interview, because he could open the door but only *I* could get them to hire me.

Calling my mum to ask if I could move in while I got settled in my new job had almost broken me. Asking for help always made me feel like a failure.

Maybe that's why Daniel's refusal to admit his feelings cut so deep—because it was like being pitied. *I* allowed myself to be vulnerable and he didn't value me enough to do the same. One-way emotion always made me uncomfortable like that, so leaving was necessary.

Even if I miss him more with each passing day.

"You were always a girl with your own mind, Ava. It's something I admire about you as much as it drives me crazy. I always felt like you did the opposite of what I told you, even if you actually wanted the thing I was offering." My mother laughs and shakes her head. "I know you want to get married and have a family and sometimes I worry that you shy away from it because it's what I've pushed you toward."

"You're right, I *do* want those things… But on *my* terms. I don't want a marriage for security, I want it for love. I don't want to be with someone as a means to an end, I want to be with someone because they truly believe they can't live without me. And I want to feel that same way about them."

"And Daniel wasn't that person?" She looks sad and I feel like the worst daughter in the world for selling her a lie.

"He was," I say, blinking back the tears prickling my eyes. "He just couldn't see it."

"Sometimes these things take time."

"Well, now he has all the time in the world." I pull my shoulders back. I *refuse* to dwell, even if my heart aches with every beat. I have to keep moving forward. I have to prove to myself that my dreams are worth being stubborn for. That folding and settling is only going to make me unhappy in the long run. "I can't swim in place simply because he can't see past his own baggage to what we could be."

"What would you tell one of your students if their friend was being difficult but they cared about the relationship?"

My mother's question strikes me, not only because it's insightful but also because she knows my passion for teaching goes far beyond ABCs and 123s. I care deeply about the emotional development of my students, about helping them become well-rounded little humans who can march off into the world with confidence and positivity and…empathy.

"I would tell them to give people a chance," I admit. "That everyone has their own way of dealing with things."

"We're all striving to be better, Ava. It just takes some people more time to figure out what that looks like." She bobs her head as if agreeing with herself.

"Hell, it's taken me almost my whole adult life to realise that I was alone because I made myself that way."

My eyes grow wide but I don't dare say a word. My mother has never admitted anything so vulnerable before.

"When you got engaged and I didn't even know about the man you were seeing, it…hurt. But I did some thinking and I understand why you might feel like I'm too opinionated about your life. I don't want to push you away, Ava. You're my only daughter and I love you. I want you to be happy."

I rush forward and squeeze my mum so tight it makes my arms hurt. I know that despite battling against one another for my entire life, our love is stronger than our opinions. Our love is worth a few arguments here and there.

"I'm sorry," I whisper against her hair.

"I'm sorry, too, baby." She hugs me back and we stay there like that for a long moment.

Eventually I hear the shuffle of small feet and see my grandmother coming out of the lounge room, her cane making even little *thunks* against the tiled floor. "I don't know why we're all hugging, but I feel left out."

Laughing through my misty eyes, I reach my arm out and pull her into the fray. Three generations of imperfect, opinionated and stubborn women all entangled in one giant hug. I haven't been the best daughter I could be, but I'm going to make that change now— not by carrying my mother's baggage, but by trying to understand her point of view. Trying to be more empathetic and accepting and kind.

And all the while I'll keep striving for a better life. For all of us.

Later that day, I press my back to the wall of my temporary bedroom and slide down to the floor. Even knowing that I have the job I've always wanted, that I have a roof over my head and that I'm about to be in a better financial position than I've been in in *years*, I can't feel totally happy. Because the one thing I've *always* known, deep down to my very core, is that stability and happiness are not the same thing.

Don't get me wrong, I'm glad I'm repairing things with my mother. And sure, stability is a privilege. Knowing I'm not going to get booted out of my living situation again is a weight off. But it doesn't change the big, gaping Daniel-shaped hole in my heart.

Across the room, I catch my reflection in the mirrored wardrobe doors. It's a sorry sight. Hollows under my eyes, limp hair pulled into a scruffy bun. I've done nothing but go to work and pack my things for the last few weeks, and every day I collapse into fitful, subpar sleep.

I miss him.

The thought is a repetitive echo, day in day out. It never seems to fade.

It seemed too crazy to think I might be in love with a man who's only been in my life a short time—but when I think about him, my heart aches. And it feels so utterly broken I have no idea how to put it back together.

"You gave him a chance to confess how he felt," I mutter to myself. "And you got your answer."

But without Daniel my bed feels cold and empty, my palms reaching for him every morning. And it isn't just sex—although I *definitely* miss that, too. It's the way we learned things about one another, no matter how big or small. Like how he geeked out over historical architecture and could talk for hours about the influences of a particular architect.

The closer I looked, the more beauty I saw. The more goodness. Daniel has the biggest heart of anyone I've ever known, and yet he keeps himself chained up. Inaccessible.

The sound of a car door slamming outside startles me out of my reverie and I need to finish unpacking before dinner. But when I push up from the floor, I catch a glimpse of bright red outside. Bright red like the custom paint job on a very fancy sports car.

"Shit." My breath catches in my throat as I see Daniel get out of his Maserati.

Like a manifestation of my wildest dreams, he stalks up to the house. But he looks different—he's unshaven and his mouth is set in a grim line. He looks worn down, emotionally ruined.

Exactly how I feel.

I have to get to the front door before my mother or grandmother can make it. I scoot out of the bedroom, my sock-covered feet skidding on the tiles as I catch my mother dragging my grandmother into the living room and sliding the frosted glass door shut. She winks at me before disappearing. A second later, the TV is turned on and the sound of a game show gives me a veil of privacy.

Thanks, Mum.

Daniel knocks and I give myself a moment, steeling my heart against seeing him again, before I open the door. Up close, I see even more details of how he's changed—the darkness under his eyes, the crease between his brows. He's wearing a long-sleeved T-shirt in inky black that hangs perfectly so I can admire the muscles in his shoulders and arms and across his chest.

That's a power move if I ever saw one.

"Can we talk?" he asks.

"You could have called for that." But I step back and hold the door, fortifying myself against the crackle of electricity shooting through me. But there's no use— I'm like a woman starved and at the first sight of him, my body demands more. "How did you even know I was here?"

"Gut instinct."

"How could you possibly think that? The whole point of…what we did was for me to avoid this."

"You love your mother, Ava. I could see it plain as day when I came for dinner. You have a good family."

The words pierce and twist. "So… Why do you want to talk? I thought we said everything there was to say."

We're standing in the entryway, and I don't dare take him one step farther into the house.

"I wanted to see how you were doing," he says.

"You don't have to act like you care anymore." There's no sting in my voice—just a sense of resignation. Trying to act unaffected 24/7 is exhausting and I have nothing left.

My mother has hovered around me all day, which tells me I'm *not* doing a fantastic job of hiding my emotions. But the well of my heart is so empty, nothing can cover it up.

"I was worried when you refused to look at the Cielo apartment."

Sending the keys back had been one of the hardest things I'd ever done—because, for the first time, I had to rely on my mother instead of finding my own way. But accepting Daniel's help was out of the question. Neither the email with the details for the apartment inspection nor the cheques had come with a personal note. He was doing what he always did—throwing money at a problem.

Using money to avoid his feelings.

"It's not your duty to keep watch over me."

He looks like he wants to argue further, but he shakes his head instead. "I'm trying to uphold my end of the deal."

The deal, because that's all he'll ever let us be. A business arrangement. It stings, even now, that he can't admit what he feels.

"What do you want?" I fold my arms across my chest. As far as I'm concerned, I've done enough talking. If Daniel wants anything out of me, then he needs to ask for it.

Or maybe beg. I wouldn't mind seeing that.

We face off like two animals sizing one another up—Matthews women *are* stubborn, my mother was right about that. This is one area where I can't compromise. Having Daniel on the fringes wouldn't be enough. Having a half relationship of living together without love wouldn't be enough, even if the sex is hot enough to melt the ground beneath my feet.

"I have something to say." His dark gaze meets mine without hesitation. Without reservation.

I motion with my hand, trying my hardest not to let him see how hurt I am. "Don't wait for an invitation."

"I've always had trouble opening up about my feelings," he begins and I shoot him a look that says *uh, duh!* "Growing up, my house was chaos. My parents' marriage was tumultuous, and their divorce was even worse. Marc needed someone to keep the stability, so I became a pseudo parent and tried to be the rock in his life."

I don't want to feel compassion for him, but it bubbles up immediately. I can easily imagine him as a young boy—proud, protective of his little brother. An adult too soon.

There's that big heart of his.

"I managed to trace every problem in my life back to a relationship—my father's affairs, my mother's love for a man who would never give her what she wanted." He stares at me with those intense black-brown eyes and this time there are no walls. Daniel is laying himself bare in front of me. "I thought I needed to be the one to put my family first, like nobody else had. I appointed myself as 'protector' of our family. I felt responsible to fix things."

I understand that need right down to my bones.

There'd been times when, as a child, I'd tried to set my mother up with my teachers, thinking it might make her happy. Thinking it might stop her from crying at night.

"Only I realised recently, that while I was looking back trying to fix the mistakes of others, I was making a whole lot of mistakes myself. I wanted my family back, and I was pushing away the beautiful woman standing in front of me." For a moment his expression falters, and his true vulnerability shines through. "I found out yesterday why Marc didn't believe me. One of my board members was feeding him lies to stage a hostile takeover."

I blink. Now *that* I was not expecting. "What the hell?"

"Marc was his pawn, because someone wanted me out of the CEO position. I'm too difficult to manipulate, apparently," he says with a distinct note of bitterness.

"I would have thought that was a point of pride."

"I guess it should be, only I feel as though I've let my logic and morals deteriorate some other important aspects of my life. Like my ability to trust people. My ability to love." He comes toward me, reaching for my hand, and I allow him to touch me. "You were right to call me on my bullshit. I was using the arrangement to protect myself from what I was feeling. To protect myself from the thing I've been most afraid of. But the truth is…"

His pause seems to stretch on forever—so important that it slows down every cell in my body.

"What we've shared is like nothing I've ever experienced before, and I don't mean the sex…amazing as that was. It was everything that came before and after—the things I told you that I've never told anyone else." When he looks down at me, it's as if I'm turning my face to the sun. No longer is Daniel shielded by icy remoteness, he's real. Raw. Open and bare right in front of me. "I couldn't believe how quickly we connected, because I never let anyone in. Not even my own family."

The realisation is in his voice—he finally sees why his efforts to "fix things" are always unsuccessful: because he acts without emotion and expects everyone else to do the same.

"But I want to let you in. I want to be the kind of partner who's emotionally available and loving and not afraid to reveal himself. I want to give you back what you've given me." He draws me closer and brushes the messy strands of hair from my face. His fingertips trace my hairline and my ear and the ticklish spot on my neck. "I know neither of us had great examples of what love could be like—"

"Understatement of the century," I say with a shaky laugh.

"But that's a good thing for us."

"It is?"

"We've seen the mistakes. We've learned our lessons the hard way about what *not* to do, so we know what to avoid. We know how to do better."

Is this really happening? I want to shake myself to see if I've fallen asleep in my bedroom and this is nothing but my brain's way of trying to resolve my hurt.

"I haven't been able to stop thinking about you," I

admit. "Every day I've hoped and dreaded that you'd come to your senses."

"Why did you dread it?"

"Because I don't know if I'm strong enough to withstand you changing your mind." The hollow feeling is so vast and so black and so all-consuming that it terrifies me. "What if it turns out your feelings are false? A mistake?"

"There's nothing false in how I feel about you," he says, resting his forehead down on mine. The touch is tender and perfect. "You've changed me, Ava. You've helped me to see all the ways I was holding myself back, all the ways that I set myself up to fail. I'm a better man because of you."

"How?" I need to know the details, to know exactly how he's changed. To know that this change means there *is* space for me in his life.

"I wouldn't have given my brother a chance to explain before," he says. "What he accused me of… It's the biggest, most painful insult anyone could have hurled at me. In my eyes, it was unforgivable. I only wanted him to know I was not having an affair with Lily because it was important to the company…because I didn't want people to gossip."

He draws a long breath, as though it pains him to be so raw. So open.

"But when you called me on my inability to be vulnerable, I realised I was doing the same thing my mother had done all those years ago. By worrying more about what outsiders might think, I was letting bad feelings fester. I wanted Marc to come back to the company, but I never had any intentions of forgiving him for what he said."

"But you *did* forgive him?"

"Yes. I understand why he believed the lies and…" His Adam's apple bobs. "I understand the role I played, unintentional as it was, in why he didn't trust me. Before you, I would never have had the conversation with him because I have always loathed talking about my feelings. I never saw the point in it, because the discomfort was too great. But it's worth it. Letting you go because I was too scared to say how I felt would be a crime. The fact is, I don't know what the future holds, but I do know that *we* are in charge of it."

"We are," I echo.

He lowers his head down to mine, capturing my mouth and kissing me deeply. He backs me up against the wall and I let him in. His lips are firm and his tongue demanding, and he slides his arms around my waist.

"Can you forgive me, Ava? Our business arrangement was done the second you came up those stairs." He closes his eyes for a moment. "Saying I felt nothing was the biggest lie I've ever told."

"I forgive you."

"I want us to build something wonderful together." The raw intensity of his voice makes my body hum with excitement. With anticipation for a bright and beautiful future. "I want us to have a home that is ours and make a family there."

I smile up at him, letting all the heat coursing through my body bubble to the surface. "We should probably start practicing, then. For making a family, I mean."

He laughs and kisses me deeply. Out of the corner of my eye I catch the living room sliding door creep open, where my grandmother pokes her head out and gives me the thumbs-up. Laughing and cringing and feeling all things perfect and awkward and wonderful, I grab Daniel's face between my hands. "But let's not do that here, okay?"

"We can go anywhere you want, Ava. We're starting over, right now."

"Right this very second?" I loop my arms around his neck. "Why, Mr. Moretti, I have to say I've heard some terrible, wicked things about you."

He quirks a brow. "Don't tell me you read internet gossip."

"I don't. But I did hear you've got a thing for curvy women with big mouths who like to sneak up when they're least expected."

He entwines his hands with mine and looks at me so long and so deep it's a miracle I don't melt right at his feet. "You have no idea."

"I have *some* idea." I grin. "So, want to stay for a bite to eat before we escape back to your place so I can have my wicked way with you?"

"Yes. But don't forget, it's *our* place now. You can come up the stairs anytime you want."

"I plan to, Daniel. Every single night from now until forever."

* * * * *

HER PLAYBOY
CRUSH

NICOLA MARSH

MILLS & BOON

HER PLAYBOY
CRUSH

For my mum,
who instilled her love for fashion in me, and never
goes anywhere without a fab lippy!

CHAPTER ONE

'RYDER'S BACK IN TOWN.'

Four words designed to strike fear into Polly Scanlon's guarded heart as she glared at her brother Archie, smirking knowingly at her from his perch atop the stepladder.

'So?'

She shrugged, well aware that Archie of all people wouldn't buy her forced nonchalance for a second as she handed him a hammer.

'Just thought you'd like to know.' He grinned, well aware of her never-ending mortification at the hands of his charming friend.

Ryder Beale had been born to make her life a misery. A fact he'd never let her forget during her painful teenage years and beyond. He'd teased her about everything, from training bras to geeky grades, his sole aim being to make her blush.

God help her if Archie knew the rest.

'You should've defended me all those years,' she said, propping herself against a sheet-covered armoire.

'Encouraging a guy like Ryder is like giving a kid red cordial and letting him loose in a lolly shop.'

Archie chuckled. 'You're the only little sis I have. Par for the course I'd get a laugh out of seeing you squirm.'

'Bastard.'

'Love you too.' He winked and blew her a kiss. 'Now pass me the pack of hooks, please.'

She wondered why Ryder was back in town. It had been over five years since he'd last come home. She'd initially been glad when he'd left Sydney after high school; at least that's what she kept telling herself. She'd been a pining sixteen-year-old at the time, her crush on her older, sexier next-door neighbour a secret she'd shielded behind clever quips and constant sparring.

Ryder had never failed to get a rise out of her, but it had been their thing and she'd missed it after he'd left. He'd returned to Sydney intermittently since then and their banter had only intensified: lots of smartass word play, too much sexual tension on her part. He'd never treated her as anything other than an annoying friend.

Now Ryder was back in town and her ovaries couldn't help but leap for joy.

She handed Archie the hooks. 'So what's the PITA doing in Sydney anyway?'

Not that she was interested. Much.

'The pain in the ass is here to plan my thirtieth, apparently.' Archie hammered a few nails through the first hook's eye and she winced at the noise. 'Something a sibling should do, you know.'

Polly flipped her middle finger at him. 'You hate parties.'

'Not the kind Ryder organises.' He tossed the hammer and caught it, a move he'd got down pat since he'd started renovating his place six months ago. 'When one of his private school buddies turned twenty-one he had the top ten placed girls in a local beauty pageant attend.'

Polly snorted and ignored the stab of jealousy at the thought of Ryder anywhere near beauty pageant contestants. Then again, she'd seen enough of the kind of women he'd hung out with over the years. Ever since he'd become a life coach much in demand on the talk show circuit, he'd been featured in magazines and articles online, some of which depicted him attending parties, usually with a beautiful woman on his arm. His playboy reputation had escalated along with his fame and while she'd never begrudge him his burgeoning career, she could do without seeing the gorgeous, glamorous women he favoured these days.

Not that she should care. They'd never been more than friends—he'd never given her the slightest hint he knew about her crush or reciprocated it—but seeing Ryder with those women made her yearn for a dartboard. It was crazy, considering she was older and wiser now, and someone like him would never go for someone like her, even if she was foolish enough to indulge her old crush a tad.

'You know you'll more than likely get a stripper-gram and a case of tequila.'

Archie slipped the hammer into his tool belt and rubbed his hands together. 'Counting on it.'

She rolled her eyes. 'Don't say I didn't warn you.'

'It'll be a blast.' He came down the ladder. 'Maybe you can both be party planners together?'

'Not bloody likely,' she blurted, earning another wide-eared grin from Archie.

If she didn't know any better she'd think he knew about her long-term crush on his best friend. But that couldn't be right because if Archie knew he would've warned her off Ryder and teased her endlessly about it.

He dusted off his hands and wiped them on a towel tucked into his tool belt. 'Why don't you ponder helping Ryder throw me the best thirtieth party ever while you make a start on sanding the skirting boards in the guest bedroom and I make a quick trip to the hardware store?'

'Fine,' she muttered, agreeing to the physical labour. Pondering anything remotely to do with Ryder? No way in hell.

'Back in ten,' he said, unbuckling his tool belt, grabbing his keys and heading out the door.

Leaving Polly doing exactly as he'd instructed: pondering working alongside Ryder to plan Archie's party. As if.

She may not have spent much time with Ryder in five years, but he'd been the bane of her existence for fourteen years before that. She'd been eight, Archie ten, when the Beales had moved in next door and Ryder and Archie had been besties ever since.

While she'd struggled socially, he'd been the most

popular boy in school. While she'd sucked at sports, he'd excelled at football, cricket, soccer and hockey. While she had still been trying to break into her coveted field of statistics, he'd managed to build a stellar career in life coaching, completing his psychology degree and becoming a revered speaker.

Ryder had appeared in countless online magazines, had been interviewed by the talk show elite and had cut a swathe through gorgeous women from Rome to New York. He'd led a charmed life. Hers was finally kicking off at the ripe old age of twenty-seven.

She'd landed her dream opportunity at Sizzle, Sydney's hippest fashion house. Now all she had to do was kick ass with the upcoming fundraiser she'd been placed in charge of and she could climb the corporate ladder to where she wanted to be: number crunching in the glam fashion world to which she'd been drawn her entire life.

A long, low wolf whistle interrupted her musings. 'Looking good, Pollyanna.'

Polly stiffened, the muscles in her neck tightening so fast they hurt. That voice. Deep. Taunting, with a hint of huskiness that never failed to send a shiver of longing through her. She turned slowly, reluctantly, to find Ryder leaning in the doorway from the kitchen to the lounge, grinning at her like he'd just spied his favourite dessert.

'That's not my name,' she said, sounding cool and collected, feeling anything but.

There was something about the way Ryder looked at her, had always looked at her, that made her want to apply lashings of mascara, slick crimson gloss on her lips and slip into something a lot less comfortable.

'It should be, considering your altruistic view of the world.' He straightened and strode towards her, making her hormones do a weird little jive. 'Still seeing everything in black and white?'

'Nothing wrong with cold, hard facts,' she said, her fingers digging into the wood of the armoire to anchor her in a world suddenly off kilter.

Her pulse raced and her palms grew clammy, physical signs of a purely visceral response whenever this guy got too close. She should be over this, over him. Not that there was anything to get over beyond a lot of fanciful notions in her own head. But she'd spent too many teen years secretly lusting after him to pretend he didn't affect her, because this grown-up version of Ryder was even sexier than his younger counterpart.

'No room for grey, huh?' He stopped two feet in front of her. Close enough to smell his designer aftershave with a hint of spice. Close enough to see the green flecks in his hazel eyes. Close enough to want to touch that broad chest and lean waist and...lower.

She'd seen him bare-chested before, when he'd kick the soccer ball around with Archie in their backyard, and over the years when she'd give in to the temptation of searching his name online and find pictures of him standing on top of a cliff face he'd just scaled or diving with sharks. In both those instances his glorious bronze chest had been on full display and she'd ended up having a restless sleep because of it.

It was stupid to still be fantasising over him all these

years later, but those naughty notions in the middle of the night were nothing on having him this close.

Would his chest be as hard as it looked?

Would her hands fit in the dip of his waist?

Would the clearly delineated lines of his abs be traceable with her fingertips as she dipped beneath his waistband?

How big would he be…?

Polly swallowed and a fine sheen of perspiration broke out on her forehead.

'You're blushing.' The tip of his thumb grazed her cheek, sending a jolt of longing so strong through her body that she almost swayed towards him. 'What's got you all hot and bothered?'

If he only knew. But Polly could never let on how he made her feel. She'd had enough mortification in her life when it came to guys to let the uber-confident Ryder Beale figure out her pathetic crush and how many times she'd imagined riding him until he made her scream.

'I'm not blushing; I've just been working too hard being Archie's slave.'

She fanned her face regardless because her cheeks were flaming. Like that would help. She needed a dunk in an ice bath to cool off.

'Don't let him push you around.' His mouth quirked into a sexy smile as he reached out and tugged the ends of her shoulder-length hair. 'This is new.'

Damn, she wished he'd stop touching her—or at least make it count.

'I lost the pigtails about ten years ago, and you've

seen me since then,' she said, hating how her breathlessness at his proximity made her voice squeaky.

'You didn't have this layered look last time I saw you,' he said. 'I like it.' He wound a few strands around his fingers until they reached her hairline. 'I like it a lot.'

What the hell was he doing? He never touched her, ever, and she'd wondered whether to be grateful or insulted. She'd seen the way he'd been with other girls all those years ago, playful and flirtatious, charming the pants off them—probably literally. She'd been jealous and yearning, hiding her envy behind cutting quips. But he'd never flirted with her; instead he'd tease her the same way Archie did. She'd hated being treated like his younger sister too.

So what had changed now? Had he grown tired of his playthings around the world and wanted a new challenge?

Because that's the only reason he'd be toying with her like this. He knew she was off limits and disinterested—she'd faked it well in the past—so was this some kind of warped game to him, to see how far he could push the geeky younger sister of his best friend?

His fingers wound her hair tighter slowly, gentle tugs that had her biting back a groan at the sensuality of it. When his fingertips grazed her scalp, Polly's knees buckled a little so she reacted how she always did when Ryder disarmed her.

'Back off, bozo, or I'll make you.'

He laughed and leaned closer, his breath fanning her cheek and setting off all kinds of reactions, most of them between her legs. She throbbed with wanting him.

'It could be fun for you to try,' he murmured in her ear, his lips grazing her skin and sending a delicious shudder through her body.

When his teeth nipped her lobe, she froze. He was actually doing this, seducing her, and she had no idea how to react. It had to be a game to him. He'd never shown the slightest sign of wanting to get physical with her before.

'So what's it to be, Pol? Want to take me down?'

He blew on her ear and this time she couldn't prevent a low moan escaping her lips. She didn't want to take him down. She wanted to go down on him, and have him return the favour.

But this was crazy. Until she figured out what game he was playing, she had to put a stop to this teasing.

'You're full of it,' she said, stepping back. She couldn't think, let alone formulate coherent sentences, when he was that close and he knew it.

How many times had she pushed him away over the years? Too many to count. Toying with her amused him; he liked to see how much he could rattle her. By her predictable reaction, the answer was a lot.

But this heightened awareness was new. He exuded a sexual magnetism that drew many women to him, according to the online tabloids, and it irked that it worked on her too. She shouldn't be this attracted to him. Her crush should've waned. If anything, the way her skin tingled and heat flushed her from the inside out, her lust for him had only intensified.

Not good. She needed a distraction, fast.

'Archie says you're here to plan his thirtieth.' She strolled to the corner where her brother had stacked his DIY paraphernalia, putting some much-needed distance between them.

'Want to help me? It's been a long time since I've hung out with Arch and you'd know what he's into these days better than me.'

That was all she needed—to spend one-on-one time with him. Especially after the weird flirty thing he'd been doing a few moments ago that still had her body buzzing.

She should ask him about it. Her ear lobe still tingled from his teeth nipping it in the briefest of bites. But did she really want to have a discussion that could end in her revealing how much she'd like him to nip her all over?

'Can't, I'm too busy with my new job.' She snagged a few sheets of sandpaper, needing to keep busy if Ryder insisted on waiting for Archie's return. 'But I'm sure you'll be the hostess with the mostest.'

His chuckles at her sarcasm warmed her blood, making her slightly giddy. 'Let me guess. Your new job involves calculating the probability of Australia winning the next World Cup. Or you're wowing the Prime Minister with enough statistics to promote you to his deputy? Or—?'

'I'm working for Sizzle,' she blurted out, hating how he never failed to make her feel like the nerd she was.

Growing up, he'd teased her about always having her nose in a book or getting straight As. While he'd been kicking a football in the backyard with Archie after school, she'd have her homework spread out on the kitchen table, trying to concentrate while sneaking glances at the way his jersey moulded to his chest. When he came into the kitchen for a drink she'd feign indifference, trying to ignore how good he made her feel when he asked insightful questions about her homework.

She'd known he was smart back then and had wondered why he'd hidden it, pretending to act the fool and goof around with Archie who'd never had aspirations beyond getting through his final year at school and scoring a building apprenticeship.

She'd attended the local high school with Archie while Ryder had gone to an elite private school several suburbs away, but he'd never lorded it over them and he'd underplayed his intelligence.

'Sizzle?' His eyebrows rose to a satisfying height. 'The fashion house?'

'The one and only.' Smug that she'd managed to surprise him for once, she folded her arms, only to lower them to her sides when his gaze zeroed in on her chest. That was new too, his awareness of her as a woman. She'd secretly wished he would notice her over the years but he'd never hinted at anything untoward. Even his teasing had been annoyingly platonic. Then again, considering his choice of girlfriends over the last few years, she'd never measure up in the glam stakes. 'Maybe you should drop by some time and update your wardrobe?'

She'd meant it as a funny jibe—he'd always looked

good in whatever he wore, even as a kid—her dry humour a defence mechanism. She'd always needled him when she'd felt disconcerted, but she realised it had backfired when a spark of interest lit his eyes.

'Is that an invitation?'

'No, it was me trying to be snide.' She glanced at the dark denim moulding long, lean legs and the navy polo shirt hugging his muscular chest, then wished she hadn't when the heat in her cheeks intensified. 'We both know your outfit cost more than my monthly wage so you definitely don't need a wardrobe update.'

He tilted his head, studying her, the gleam in his eyes speculative. 'In my profession, it pays to keep abreast of the latest fashion.'

'What profession's that? Winning women and influencing friends?'

He tsk-tsked. 'Mixing metaphors and being snide? Not your style, Pollyanna.'

Polly huffed out a breath, annoyed she'd let him get to her yet again, and desperate for him to leave her alone. Physically, she'd always found him attractive but when he sparred with her, she wanted him even more. 'Archie should be back soon if you want to wait in the kitchen.'

'When I'm having so much fun here?' He shook his head and grinned. 'I'd rather see you climb that ladder so I can ogle your legs.'

Discombobulated by his sudden interest in her attributes—first having a quick perv at her boobs and now mentioning her legs—Polly muttered, 'Yeah, a regular supermodel, that's me,' as she tried to brush past him on her way to the guest room.

But his hand shot out and gripped her upper arm, making it impossible to move. 'Why do you do that?'

Her skin prickled where he touched her, every nerve ending on hyper alert, yearning for his touch all over.

'Do what?'

'Undersell yourself.'

His pupils dilated, almost obliterating all that beautiful hazel, and she glanced away.

He didn't stop staring at her but she didn't dare meet his gaze for fear of seeing what she'd glimpsed a moment ago.

Desire.

She must have imagined it. A result of years of pent-up sexual frustration, him touching her arm, and wishful thinking.

Because if she couldn't handle Ryder teasing her, no way could she handle him wanting her.

Guys like him didn't want girls like her.

Beauty and the Geek. And she sure as hell wasn't the beauty.

'You're something else, Polly.'

His audible sincerity undermined her almost as much as the use of her name without the usual teasing addendum, and she couldn't help but look at him.

What she saw blew her away.

Heat.

Pure, unadulterated heat that made her want to lean into him, stand on her tiptoes, and devour him.

'You always have been,' he added, so softly she barely heard, as his hungry gaze focussed on her lips.

Polly swore her heart stopped. Her chest felt tight. Her throat closed. Her eyes watered. Since when had their teasing turned sexual?

Something indefinable pulsed between them as he lowered his head. Every muscle in her body locked. She should flee but she was damned if she wanted to. She'd imagined how his lips would feel for so long that she wondered if the reality would surpass the fantasy.

Firm, commanding, a master who'd had more practice than she had. And in that moment, with a palpable electricity arcing between them and her body straining towards his, she knew kissing Ryder would be a dumbass idea.

He could have any woman he wanted. So what the hell was he doing toying with her?

Time to flee before she blubbered as well as pashed him.

'Still a charmer.' She patted his cheek for a moment, savouring the illicit thrill of stubble scraping her palm, before easing away. 'Nice to know some things never change.'

She slipped out of his grasp, grateful when he let her go.

She only just caught his murmured, 'I've changed,' before she fled.

CHAPTER TWO

RYDER LET POLLY GO. He had to. Because he had a feeling his best mate wouldn't appreciate it if he came home to find him fucking his sister on the lounge room floor.

That's exactly what Ryder wanted to do right now. Fuck Polly. Repeatedly.

She was still the same geeky, awkward woman he'd secretly idolised years ago and had wanted with a ferocity that hadn't dimmed—if the current situation behind his fly was any indication.

She'd lost the waist-length pigtails she'd persisted with until she was eighteen and the mid-back straight style she'd favoured the last time he'd seen her, which was over five years ago; now she'd opted for a modern layered shag that made him want to shag her. The softer style framed her face, made her caramel-brown eyes look impossibly huge, and drew attention to her mouth.

That mouth…how many nights had he lain awake as a teenager, fantasising about what Polly Scanlon could do to him with that mouth. Wondering what her soft freckled skin would feel like. Wishing he could see that adorable blush he never failed to elicit flush across her naked body.

It had felt wrong at the time, secretly lusting after his best friend's sister. Guys knew the unspoken code—never screw the crew—and that included workmates and sisters. It's a line he'd never crossed. Archie's friendship meant too much to him. Yet Ryder couldn't help but wonder how Archie would feel if he broke the code now. They were older, wiser, and his mate regularly mentioned how Polly rarely dated and how he wished she'd find a guy to make her happy.

But deep down he knew Archie would bust his balls if he so much as glanced at his little sis.

Archie had mentioned their bizarre sparring over the years but Ryder had laughed it off, implying he saw her as his little sister too.

Nothing could be further from the truth.

Ryder couldn't help his almost visceral reaction to Polly and seeing her after five years was like a roundhouse kick to the gut. He remembered the hollow ache well, from a martial arts class as part of his high school's team-building initiative in his final year, when his sparring partner had aimed for a kick and ended up connecting with his stomach.

Back then he'd lain on the floor for a full minute, winded and gasping. And that's exactly how he felt now, moments after he'd almost kissed Polly.

He'd wanted to. Damn, had he wanted to. She'd been so close, staring at him with those big doe eyes, lips plump and tempting, the same apple fragrance from the shampoo she'd used as a teen wafting over him.

In an interesting turn of events, she'd wanted it too. He'd expected her to shove him away when he'd focussed on her mouth, craving one illicit taste. Instead, she'd leaned into him, waiting, her eyes sparking fire, and he'd been powerless to resist.

He should be glad she'd had second thoughts because if she hadn't shrugged out of his grasp when she had they would've kissed.

A kiss that would've changed everything.

He usually eschewed complications of any kind and kissing Polly would be one giant fuck-up. With his cock still pulsing from wanting to be buried inside her, he needed to remember it.

He hadn't been short of a date for a long time, not since he'd swapped scaling cliffs for chasing skirt. Not that it had been a conscious decision but being robbed of his favourite extreme sports meant he'd sought the adrenaline rush in other ways and losing himself in a willing woman gave him a similar high.

But Polly was different from the women he dated and he damn well knew it. She was off limits, the kind of girl who wanted for ever, not for now. Wrong for him in so many ways. She was a challenge he had to walk away from no matter how badly he wanted to see how far he could push the boundaries between them.

He ached with wanting her even now and for the first time he'd seen her respond like she wanted him just as badly. It was a heady thought—enough to make a guy run to the fridge in search of a lager—because if he didn't slake his thirst with an icy beer he'd be following her into that guest room and taking her up against the newly painted walls, Archie's renovations and his own reservations be damned.

'Hey, pisshead, get your own beer.'

Ryder grabbed another lager, straightened and handed a beer to Archie. 'Who you calling pisshead?'

'You, butt-face.' Archie popped the top off his beer and clinked bottles with him. 'When did you fly in?'

'This morning. Or, considering I'm still on London time, should that be yesterday evening?' Ryder took a slug of beer, glad Archie had arrived home when he had. Another second with his disastrous thoughts and there was no telling what he may have done with the delectable Polly.

'Did you see Polly?'

Ryder nodded and hoped to God his expression wouldn't betray him. Then again, he'd managed to hide his lust for Polly from Archie all these years. Why should now be any different? 'Yeah. She's being your reno slave in the guest bedroom.'

Archie chuckled. 'Thought she might be hiding out in there, trying to avoid you giving her a hard time.'

'She loves it.'

'You both do,' Archie said, locking gazes with him. 'If I didn't know you guys any better I'd say it's fore-play.'

Ryder's laughter sounded incredibly forced. 'You know me. I'm like that with all the girls.'

Archie's speculative stare didn't waver. 'Yeah, but you two have been at it a long time now. Ever thought about it?'

Ryder didn't like where this conversation was heading. Not one frigging bit. 'About what?'

Archie snorted. 'You and Polly getting together, dickhead.' His eyes narrowed with suspicion. 'Or are you playing dumb because you know I'll beat you to a pulp if you go there?'

'Like to see you try, pee-wee.' Ryder downed the rest of his beer. Guess that answered the question of how Archie would feel about him dating Polly. Not that there'd be dating involved. He wanted a woman, he charmed her, he slept with her. Short-term fun guaranteed to obliterate the memories of what he couldn't have any more. With Polly, he envisaged having a hell of a lot of fun.

Eager to change the subject, he said, 'You still keen for me to throw you the biggest thirtieth Sydney has ever seen?'

'As long as you've got scantily clad women lined up, I'm there.' Archie finished his beer and lobbed it into the recycling bin. 'Want to grab a paintbrush and help?'

Ryder winced and flexed his knee. 'You know how bad this is.'

Archie snorted. 'Mate, just because you broke that leg *five years ago* and managed to fool everyone into feeling sorry for you it doesn't mean you can't do some manual labour for once in your charmed bloody life.'

'Harsh, but true.' Ryder grinned. If Archie only knew how breaking his leg, and what had happened afterwards, had changed his life. 'Sorry, got to see a man about a party.'

'Flaky as well as lazy,' Archie muttered, making

an L shape with his thumb and forefinger against his forehead. 'Pub dinner tonight?'

Ryder wanted to say yes. But if he had his way he'd be otherwise occupied. He had every intention of taking Polly up on her offer of visiting her workplace this afternoon. After that? The night was young.

Logically, he knew starting anything with Polly was idiotic. But he'd never backed away from a challenge and after the spark of interest he'd seen in her eyes earlier, he knew she felt the attraction between them as much as he did. He'd pushed the boundaries by nipping at her ear, a startling reaction to her proximity after years of pent-up sexual frustration. At best he'd expected her to ask him what the hell he was doing, at worst to slap him.

Instead, she'd looked seriously turned on and at that moment he'd known he had to go for it. Life was too short and if she wanted this as much as he did… They were both adults who knew the score. Little Pollyanna was all grown up and more tempting than ever. It would be fun seeing how far they could take this thing between them.

'Rain check? Jet lag's a bitch.'

'Yeah, must be real tough sleeping in those first-class flatbed compartments.' Archie snorted and shooed him away. 'Get out of here and let me get back to work.'

'I'm gone.' Ryder rarely faked anything in his life but he summoned his best acting skills now. Because he had to make a date with Polly and there was no way in hell he'd leave here until it was done. 'Once I say bye to Polly.'

'Knock yourself out.' Archie waved, already turning his attention to the bag of hardware paraphernalia he'd bought. 'Text me if you want to catch up tomorrow, doofus.'

'Done,' Ryder said, grateful that no matter how many countries he visited, no matter how many auditoriums he packed for his motivational presentations, no matter how many five-star hotels and functions he attended, he could rely on his oldest mate to make him feel grounded.

Archie had been there for him throughout everything: moving in next door while he'd still been reeling from the death of his grandfather, being ignored by his grandmother who didn't know how to grieve and acknowledge he was still around, coping with a new school where the pricks only valued mansions and portfolios.

Archie had kept him grounded through it all and later, even after he'd left Sydney behind without looking back and had suffered the leg break that had shattered his confidence and the near fatality that had made him re-evaluate everything, he'd been there remotely. After the accident, Archie had been the one to encourage him to finish the part-time psychology degree he'd started in his late teens overseas. He'd been floundering, lost in a sea of guilt and recrimination, and finishing his degree had been the best thing for him.

After he'd got his head on straight with the help of a shrink, his new career had been born and he'd been motivating people ever since. He'd been a life coach and consultant to major companies around the world, utilising the fame he'd acquired as an extreme sports enthusiast who'd survived a major accident and combining it with the psych research he loved. His bottom line? Employee morale often made or broke a company and once his methods had got results, he'd been invited to speak at countless conferences and beyond.

He liked his life. Liked the freedom and the privileges he could afford. Liked being on the move and not being stuck in one place for too long, outrunning his demons. Liked his varied dating life courtesy of his fame.

But he also liked a petite brunette with freckles dusting her nose, and after all this time she'd finally responded to him as something more than a friend and that gave him the impetus to pursue her. Besides, he was used to getting what he wanted.

Traversing Archie's light-filled Southbank apartment, Ryder imagined Polly's reaction to what he was about to say and grinned. She'd totally unsettled him with that flash of interest earlier. Time to return the favour.

By the time he reached the guest room, he had a plan: ascertain if she'd be at work this afternoon; organise a visit; ensure she'd have dinner with him.

However, his plan hit a snag when he paused in the doorway, his gaze riveted to her butt as she knelt on all fours, sanding a skirting board.

There was nothing remotely sexy about the denim overalls she wore over a frayed grey T-shirt but seeing her in that position, with her cute ass in the air, had him hard in an instant.

'Nice view,' he drawled, and she jumped so fast she toppled over.

'Haven't you left yet?' She glowered at him as she stood and dusted off her hands, another delightful blush staining her cheeks.

'Why so eager to get rid of me?'

'Because I don't like you,' she said, her dart-away glance making a mockery of that declaration.

'Liar,' he said, stalking across the room towards her, not surprised when she backed away. 'You like me just fine and the feeling's mutual.'

'Piss off.' She held up her hands. Yeah, like that would stop him. 'I need to finish up here, head home to clean up, then go to work.'

Ryder snapped his fingers. 'Perfect.'

Her eyes narrowed with suspicion. 'What?'

'I'd planned on taking you up on your invitation to update my wardrobe and this afternoon seems as good a time as any.'

Her blush faded, leaving her pale. 'You're not serious?'

'Dead serious.' Knowing she was likely to slug him—it had happened before in a not-so-friendly game of touch rugby—he tweaked her nose. 'And once we finish up at Sizzle, you're having dinner with me.'

'I'd rather eat dirt,' she blurted, her chest heaving with indignation, providing him with a very nice image of what that would look like sans the tatty overalls and

T-shirt. Generous C cups for his hands and mouth to explore in erotic detail...

'Then I'll make sure to bring you a doggy bag from the garden,' he said with a jaunty wave, aiming for a light-hearted tone to defuse the mind-numbing lust slamming through him, making him want to flip the lock on the door, tear those overalls off and do more than kiss. 'See you around three.'

'I don't work in the showroom,' she shouted at his retreating back.

'I'll find you.'

He chuckled as he strolled out of the bedroom, the sounds of her kicking something echoing in his ears.

CHAPTER THREE

POLLY WAS IN HEAVEN.

Surrounded by cast-offs of last year's spring collection in Sizzle's sample room, touching the softest silks and shiny satins, the plush velvets and finest lace, the sheer chiffons and crisp linens, made her feel glamorous in a way she could never achieve any other way.

She often ducked in here at the end of a long day when her feet ached and her head throbbed from running errands for her boss, Andrina. It was her new go-to place and far removed from the comfort she usually derived from numbers.

Numbers were her life, statistical analysis her forte. She loved the cold, hard logic when numbers coalesced into factual brilliance. But a number-crunching role at her old university the last few years hadn't been satisfying so she'd taken the drastic step of quitting.

Archie had been shocked by her impulsiveness; she'd shocked herself. But then, while setting up a job-seeker profile on a site, she'd seen the ad for a job in Sydney's leading fashion house and had been hooked. Logically, it didn't make sense applying for a job far beneath her pay grade and level of expertise. But she'd been bored in her old workplace and this one glittered like a shiny new bauble in front of her, just out of reach…so she'd done the second crazy thing in a month and applied.

She'd been hired after saying all the right things, but ultimately she had a bigger goal—to combine her two great loves, figures and fashion. Working as a PA to Sizzle's CEO was a step towards her dream job: ensuring Sizzle became the foremost fashion house in Sydney and beyond. She knew she could do it. But first she had to wow the boss from hell during her three-month trial.

No one could believe she'd landed a job at hip Sizzle. Her, the geekiest of the geeks. It had been fortuitous spotting the ad, but her favourite uni lecturer had also called to tell her about the job opening. He knew Andrina, knew Polly was bored assisting statistics lecturers amid crunching probabilities and outcomes, and knew of her not-so-secret passion for fashion magazines.

When he'd mentioned a possible job as Andrina's PA, Polly had thanked him and hadn't hesitated. Combining her two loves would be a dream come true. There was only one problem. Well, several, but the major one was that she was a dork with no sense of style. She'd never had it, which was why she'd spent the bulk of her teenage years poring over fashion mags, escaping into the glossy world she craved but could never have.

She was denim and cotton whereas every Sizzle employee was leather and lace. She'd pretended it didn't matter at the start, but the ongoing sniggers behind her back, and Andrina's condescension, had her questioning the wisdom of following this path.

But then she would come in here, breathe in the intoxicating fabrics and steel her backbone to face another day. Another day filled with the stress of ensuring the fundraiser gala that Sizzle was sponsoring went off without a hitch.

The fundraiser for which she was responsible.

Polly knew the stakes. If the fundraiser was a success, Andrina would listen to her pitch for statistical glory. Fail, and she'd probably be out on her ass.

To make matters worse, Ryder was back in town and determined to make her life hell. If he dared show up here, she'd throttle him.

But that would mean getting close enough to wrap her hands around his neck and considering how badly she'd wanted to jump him at Archie's that morning... Hell, why couldn't she have a crush on gorgeous movie stars instead? Ryder was almost in the same league and just as unobtainable.

It had been bad enough he'd tease her incessantly when they'd been teens. Now he'd added flirting to the mix, she didn't stand a hope.

Because when a guy like Ryder looked at her like he was genuinely interested, when he nipped her ear, when he almost kissed her, it made a sensible girl like her think decidedly insensible thoughts.

No red-blooded woman in her right mind wouldn't find Ryder attractive with his dark brown, just-out-of-bed hair, his stunning hazel eyes with the perpetual twinkle, his killer smile and hot bod. Ryder was a walking, talking fantasy.

And she'd had more than a few of those.

That was the only downside to her glossy mag fetish: seeing photos of Ryder. Ryder in a tux, Ryder at the polo, Ryder on stage delivering his famed motivational speeches, and the worst, Ryder squiring stunning women to various events.

He'd been in her face, silently taunting her, from the pages of magazines or on the internet. Now he was back, bigger, bolder and more brazen than ever.

She was in big trouble.

Not because she thought Ryder would seriously make a move—she knew he valued his friendship with Archie too much to do that—but because faking indifference all these years had taken its toll.

She couldn't fake it any longer.

'Polly, where the hell are you?' Andrina's screech, clearly audible through the thick steel door, made Polly want to climb into the accessories trunk and shut the lid.

Taking a deep breath to steel her inevitably shaky nerves around her boss, she opened the door. 'I'm right here, Andrina.'

The CEO's disapproving glare zeroed in on her from twenty paces away, where she stood at the semi-circular reception desk, hands on hips. 'Get your lazy ass over here and give me a rundown of the guest speakers for the fundraiser.'

Uh-oh.

Polly had tried schmoozing celebs on the phone, she'd taken a soap star to lunch and had sat through high tea at Sydney's plushest hotel with the most self-absorbed talk show host on the planet. But none of them had agreed to speak at the fundraiser, which meant she was about to get yet another ass-kicking from Andrina for her pathetic negotiating skills.

Hating how Andrina berated her in public, Polly trudged towards her, wishing she'd worn heels rather than ballet flats today. Andrina towered over her at five-ten; add the four-inch stilettos she wore daily and Polly was at her most vulnerable.

The closer she got to her boss, the more Polly's gut tightened. Andrina—no last name, trade secret apparently—looked formidable in her sprayed-on red leather pants, black bustier and signature bold make-up. Combined with the back-combed, teased bouffant, she looked like a giant.

'Well? Who have you got lined up?' Andrina snapped, her heavily emerald-kohled eyes narrowing.

'Uh...'

As if her day couldn't get any shittier, Ryder chose that moment to stride into Sizzle's showroom.

Andrina caught sight of him a moment later and Polly braced for a verbal flaying once her boss learned he was there to see her. Instead, a miracle happened. Andrina lost the perma-frown and her lips uncurled from their residual sneer.

'Ryder Beale, it's a pleasure to meet you.' Andrina stuck out her hand as Polly wished the floor would open up and swallow her. 'Andrina, at your service.'

Polly's nose wrinkled at the thought of Andrina, service and Ryder in the same sentence.

Thankfully, Ryder didn't make a smartass remark directed at her. He shook Andrina's hand and flashed his most practised charming smile.

'Nice to meet you.' He shot Polly a subtle WTF glance when Andrina took for ever to release his hand.

'See, Polly? Ryder is just the type of guest speaker you should be organising for our fundraiser, if you weren't so incompetent.' Andrina's predatory gaze swept Ryder from head to foot. 'He's perfect.'

Ryder rarely showed any emotion other than his usual laid-back charm. She'd never seen him angry or riled. But that changed as Polly saw colour suffuse his cheeks at Andrina's putdown and a small part of her wanted to hug him for being outraged on her behalf.

'Actually, Polly is extremely competent.' Ryder edged away from Andrina and closer to Polly. 'In fact, she's the only reason I agreed to be a guest speaker for your fundraiser.'

The blood drained from Polly's head and made her sway slightly. Had Ryder just done what she thought he'd done?

'That's why I'm here, to finalise details with Polly,' Ryder continued, blithely unaware of how he'd dumped her further in the crap.

Because when she had to come clean to Andrina eventually, that Ryder wasn't on board, she'd be out of here so fast her head wouldn't stop spinning for a week.

'That's wonderful,' Andrina said, still staring at Ryder like she wanted to gobble him whole. 'Who knew Polly had it in her to woo a speaker of your calibre?'

Ryder bristled, his shoulders drawing back like he

was about to enter a boxing ring. 'Maybe if you knew the capabilities of your staff better, you'd know Polly is brilliant at whatever she puts her mind to.'

Polly progressed from wanting to hug Ryder to wanting to kiss him.

'Well, yes, she's new but—'

'Polly and I have things to discuss,' he said, cutting Andrina off and Polly almost laughed out loud as her boss's stunned expression gave way to outrage. 'I wouldn't be here if it wasn't for her so you should remember that the next time you put down your staff in front of strangers.'

Kiss Ryder? Hell, Polly was ready to leap into his arms, wrap her legs around his waist and do him on the foyer floor.

Eager to escape before Andrina fired her regardless, Polly gestured to her shoebox office. 'Please come with me, Mr Beale.'

'Lead the way, Miss Scanlon.' Ryder winked as he turned his back on Andrina and Polly had to suppress a giggle.

But her amusement soon faded as they reached her office and Ryder closed the door, immediately shrinking the small space, and faced her.

'You can thank me later,' he said, that familiar teasing glint in his eyes. 'Over dinner.'

Polly shook her head and pointed at the foyer, where Andrina still eyed them curiously through the small glass window of her office door.

'What the hell were you thinking?'

CHAPTER FOUR

'WHAT'S THAT?' POLLY glared at the bottle of champagne Ryder had ordered like it was poison as a waiter placed it on their table with two flutes.

'France's finest.' Ryder had counted on bubbles still being Polly's drink of choice. Because the way she'd berated him during the three-minute walk to this gourmet pub, he needed all the help he could get. 'Thought you might be thirsty after that verbal flaying you just gave me.'

'You deserved it.' Her eyes narrowed as he handed her a filled flute. 'And don't think for one minute this will soften me up.'

'What will?' He clinked glasses with her and tried not to focus on the way her lips pressed against her flute. 'Because I'll do it. Whatever you want. Get down on my knees and beg forgiveness. Crawl across cut glass. Rub your feet every night and morning for the next decade.'

To his delight, she blushed. 'You have no idea the pile of shit you've dumped me in.'

'Considering the way that bitch of a boss treated

you, I think I do.' He shook his head, hating that he'd
been privy to a dressing-down. Nobody deserved to
be spoken to that way, and especially not in front of
other people. 'Why do you let her talk to you like that?'

'Because not all of us can be charming playboys
swanning their way around the world with the luck
of the devil.' Her eyes narrowed, almost like she despised him. But then he glimpsed the sadness behind
her stare and knew she was channelling false bravado
so he wouldn't pity her. 'Some of us have to work.'

'I work,' he said, well aware of how the public
viewed his fortunate life.

Travelling the world, delivering motivational
speeches to large crowds, hired by celebrities for life
coaching. He mixed in interesting circles and to many
it would appear he led an exciting, glamorous life.

If they only knew.

'Yeah, spouting your cookie-cutter psychobabble
for the gullible. Like that's work.' She snorted. 'Give
me a break.'

A sliver of hurt lodged deep. He'd worked his ass
off when he'd busted his leg—a bad break that had
ended the adrenaline-fuelled pastimes he loved, closely
followed by a close call with death that haunted him
most nights when he woke drenched in sweat and con-
sumed by guilt.

He could've taken the easy route and resumed his
old lifestyle. That was the one thing he could thank
his emotionless grandparents for—a sizable trust fund
enabling him to do whatever he pleased. Instead, he'd
completed his psychology degree, a subject that had

always fascinated him courtesy of his dysfunctional upbringing.

Sure, he'd traded on his infamy after escaping death in the accident, getting gigs other graduates wouldn't. He'd found his niche fast, motivating others to give one hundred percent and ultimately improve their lives.

That was three years ago and in that time he'd become a renowned motivational speaker in demand worldwide. He had more validation than he could've wished for. So why did the opinion of one woman matter so damn much?

He'd known he would see her this trip; planning Archie's thirtieth ensured it. But he'd expected their occasional social meetings to go the same way they had the last few years: a bit of witty repartee, some good-natured teasing and not a hint of sexual tension.

But Polly had shot that plan to shit when she'd looked at him with desire rather than derision after he'd pushed his luck and pulled that stunt of nibbling on her ear. She'd changed the boundaries of their long-standing friendship earlier today—so had he, by nibbling her ear in the first place—and he'd known then nothing would be the same again.

He downed the rest of his champagne, hating the acid burn. He'd always been a lager man. 'I am giving you a break.' He rested his forearms on the table and leaned forward. 'By saving your pretty little ass, remember?'

Her intriguing blush was back, evoking naughty thoughts of how far it extended when she got excited.

'You really want to be a guest speaker at a fundraiser for a fashion house?'

'Why not?' He shrugged. 'I'm in town for a while.'

'How long?'

'As long as it takes.'

'For what?' Her gaze locked on his, tentative yet interested, and he decided to push the boundaries again.

'To get you to agree to a date with me.'

He threw it out there, daring her to verbalise what had happened between them at Archie's that morning, trying to gauge her reaction to it and whether she'd be amenable to more, a lot more. Starting with the two of them naked and ending with her screaming his name.

'Yeah, right.' She rolled her eyes, the beguiling colour suffusing her cheeks intensifying. 'What's the real reason?'

Her complete disdain made him doubt his earlier assessment of the shift between them. At Archie's, he could've sworn she felt the spark and wanted to fan it into a flaming inferno. Now? It looked like she'd rather go on a girls' weekend with Andrina than hang out with him.

Perhaps she didn't think he wanted to take her out. Then again, he'd never given her any reason to. It wasn't her fault he'd lusted after her for years and had had a momentary lapse of his tenuous self-control this morning, causing a major shift in their friendship. She probably thought he was teasing as usual.

He should set the record straight.

But what could he say? *I've been having naughty fantasies about you for years and the moment I saw you today with your ass in the air all I could think about was fucking you?*

The way she continued to stare at him with suspicion, it was clear that now wasn't the time to reveal that particular gem, so he settled for a safer answer. 'I'm sticking around for a while because I'm writing a book.'

Her eyebrows shot up. 'Seriously?'

He nodded. 'A motivational self-help guide.'

Something he hoped would help survivors of trauma, like him. He'd been guilt-ridden at the time, knowing he should've died in that car accident had it not been for a twist of fate. He'd been listless, aimless, disinterested, until Archie had given him a pep talk via a video conference call and he'd woken the hell up. 'I've got a publisher lined up.'

'Good for you,' she said, and actually sounded like she meant it. 'But about the fundraiser—'

'I was trying to save your ass back there, but if you don't want me…' He managed to look suitably humble, while inside he yearned to hear her say she wanted him.

They cared about each other as friends, always had. She'd welcomed him into her home as much as Archie and their mother Babs, when he'd gravitated towards the Scanlons as a coping mechanism for the icy, frigid ambience at home. His grandmother had gone into emotional lockdown after Pop had died, and at the time when he'd needed her most she hadn't been there for him.

Archie and Polly had been his best friends, their lack of artifice and normality a big drawcard consid-

ering the pretentious twats at school. They'd been buddies, but things had changed in their teens. He became
aware of her as a woman, a woman he wanted but
couldn't have.

He hadn't seen her much during his brief visits to
Sydney before the accident. Archie would organise a
dinner or drinks at the pub to get them together and
while Ryder would look forward to seeing her, he'd
also regret it when she continued to be immune to him
while he still lusted after her.

He'd wondered if his yearning for her would've
waned over the five years he'd been away. But it hadn't,
and now he wanted her more than ever.

He shouldn't pursue her because nothing had
changed. She was still Archie's sister and technically
off limits. But since cheating death, he found he wanted
to make the most of every moment and not live with
regrets. He dated extensively because of it, enjoying
life to the max. And right now, with Polly returning
his interest for the first time, he knew he'd regret it if
he didn't make a move.

Oblivious to his tumultuous thoughts, she said, 'It's
a charity gig so we can't pay you.' Her fingers traced
gouges in the wood of the table. 'And we'd have to
work together a fair bit, coordinating your speech so
it fits with the image Andrina wants to portray for the
evening.'

Work with Polly one on one? He had to bite down
hard to prevent himself from grinning. When he'd im-
pulsively jumped in to save her from that unjust lam-
basting her bitch of a boss had given her, he hadn't

envisaged all the consequences, namely spending time with this intriguing woman who'd become his number one challenge.

He managed a diffident shrug. 'Sounds doable.'

'I feel like I'm taking advantage of our friendship.' She frowned, and the corners of her mouth turned down, making him want to kiss her into smiling. 'I suck at my job. My clothes are wrong. My hair's a mess. My make-up is a joke. And the only reason Andrina didn't fire me on the spot back there was because you pulled a knight-in-shining-armour routine that I'm still not sure whether to be grateful for or not.'

To his horror, Ryder thought he glimpsed the sheen of tears in her expressive eyes. He'd only seen her cry once before, when she'd thought she was alone. She'd been about fourteen, sitting in the corner of the garden, flicking through magazines while casting longing looks at the house. He'd had no idea what was behind her tears and he'd wanted to barge over there and comfort her but she'd looked so forlorn he hadn't wanted to intrude.

Now he was willing to slay dragons to make her happy. Go figure.

'I only take her crap because I have to kick ass for three months so she'll take me seriously when I pitch for a statistical analyst job.' She sighed and blinked rapidly, hopefully staving off those tears he'd be hopeless with. 'I've always loved fashion—not that you can tell by looking at me.' She gestured at her shapeless navy shift. 'I'm clueless when it comes to style but it makes me feel bloody brilliant to be surrounded by all that glamour.'

When she raised her stricken gaze to his, Ryder could've sworn the barrier around his guarded heart cracked. He'd never been in love and a big part of him wondered if the much-touted emotion existed. He'd certainly never experienced it, from family or otherwise. But when Polly looked at him with those big brown eyes filled with uncertainty and more than a hint of pain, he started to view her as more than a challenge... and it wasn't good. If she was up for it, he'd enjoy shaking things up with her, getting dirty, indulging in his longstanding crush. But anything beyond a fling? No way in hell.

'I'm still the same geek I was as a teenager. How's that for pathetic?'

Ryder's hand instinctively shot out and covered hers where it rested on the table. It was an inadequate substitute for how he'd really like to comfort her, obliterating her moroseness by licking her all over until she forgot her own name. 'You're working hard to get where you want to be. Nothing pathetic about that.'

She sniffed and he resisted the urge to slide along the booth next to her and distract her with the kind of hot, open-mouthed kiss that would take her mind off her work stresses. 'Do you give style lessons along with your motivational spiel? Because I'd be your prime candidate.'

And just like that, an idea shimmered and coalesced. An outrageous idea Polly would never go for, but an idea all the same.

It would be shitty to take advantage of her when she was feeling this low, but technically he'd be helping her. She'd virtually asked for his help with that throwaway comment. Besides, getting to spend more time with her wouldn't be a bad thing. They could reconnect. Strengthen their friendship. And if it turned into something more... Yeah, he was going straight to hell but this was Polly and he wanted her more than he'd wanted anything before.

'I don't like your boss,' he said, leading into it gently.

'That makes two of us,' she said, staring at his hand covering hers as if she'd only just noticed it.

'So what would you say to a makeover that would knock her stilettos off and ensure she took you more seriously when you made your pitch for your dream job?'

Polly's gaze snapped to his. 'What are you talking about?'

'Me, giving you the full consultation I reserve for the companies that hire me.' He squeezed her hand, trying to reassure her before she fled. 'It's what I do. See what needs to be done and subcontract out to experts. Part of that is often giving employees style makeovers to boost confidence. And I'm damn good at ascertaining how best to help people, if I do say so myself.'

The crease between her brows deepened. 'Why would you do that?'

He wanted to say, *Because I want you; I always have.* But Ryder wasn't a complete fool. If he told her the truth Polly would think he was taking the piss. He needed to couch this in more acceptable terms.

'Because I need your help, so it'd be a quid pro quo agreement.'

She snatched her hand out from under his like she didn't buy his bullshit for a second. 'You need my help?'

'Yep.' Here went nothing. 'I need someone to collate the facts and stats for my book. I've got notes and files up to here—' he made a chopping gesture at his neck '—not to mention the documents saved in disarray on my PC.'

He steepled his fingers, hoping it made him appear more professional. 'I was going to hire someone to do it but this way we both get what we want.'

When she continued to stare at him like he'd lost his mind, he continued. 'It's a simple business arrangement, Pol. Making good use of each other's skills to further our careers. What do you say?'

'You're out of your mind,' she said, but he saw her shoulders loosen and the tension ease around her mouth. 'We'll be in each other's faces practically twenty-four seven.'

He was counting on it.

Linking his hands behind his head, he leaned back and grinned. 'Consider it a perk.'

'Perk, schmerk,' she muttered, the corners of her mouth curving upwards into the smile he loved. 'This is insanity.'

'This is going to work and you know it.' He lowered his hands and topped up their flutes with more champagne. 'Do we have a deal?'

After what seemed like an eternity, Polly picked up

her flute and nodded. 'You're nuts. You've always been nuts. But I guess we can help each other out.'

She clinked glasses with him and downed her champagne in three gulps. 'How bad can it be?'

If half the raunchy thoughts pinging around his brain came to fruition during his one-on-one sessions with Polly, Ryder had every intention of being very bad indeed.

CHAPTER FIVE

ALLOWING RYDER TO take her home was a bad idea. Not because Polly didn't appreciate chivalry, but if being confined in his car wasn't bad enough during the fifteen-minute ride to her tiny studio apartment in Cronulla, having him walk her to the door and not inviting him in would really test her wavering resolve.

He'd bamboozled her over dinner, getting her to agree to collate his book research in exchange for makeover advice, ensuring they'd be spending more time together than necessary for however long he was in Sydney.

What had she been thinking?

She hadn't been and that was the problem. Sitting across from him at an intimate table for two, pretending to be immune to his sense of humour and sexy smile while he'd teased reluctant responses out of her, had confused her to the point of making rash decisions.

Including this one, where he opened the passenger door and waited until she stepped out before placing his hand in the small of her back. An innocuous, gentlemanly gesture he'd probably done for other women a thousand times before, but any time Ryder got this close to her, let alone touched her, she wanted to jump him.

As if sensing her wayward thoughts, he said, 'Everything okay?'

'Fine,' she muttered, sounding anything but as she strode towards her front door. 'I'll take it from here.'

'You're not getting rid of me that easily.' He matched her eager steps, waiting until they reached the door to lower his hand. 'And in case you were under any illusions, I'm coming in.'

A lick of heat shot through her and she had to stab her key into the lock twice before it worked. 'Don't you know it's rude to invite yourself in?'

'Don't you know it's rude to lie to an old friend?'

Puzzled by his comment, she finally unlocked the door and opened it. 'Lie?'

He waited until they entered her studio before reaching for her and kicking the door shut with the back of his heel.

'We can keep dancing around each other for however long I'm in town for, Pol, or we can treat each other with the respect we deserve.'

He gripped her upper arms, leaving her little choice but to raise her gaze to his. His eyes blazed with lust and her breath caught as she saw every raunchy, decadent thought she'd ever had regarding this guy reflected back at her tenfold.

Ryder wanted her.

In the same way she'd wanted him for years.

So what was she going to do about it?

Play it safe, like every self-preservation instinct insisted she do? He was Archie's best friend; he wasn't a keeper; he was used to supermodels.

Not to mention the salient fact he'd agreed to be the keynote speaker at the fundraiser on which her job promotion rested.

Sleeping with him would be a giant complication she didn't need. But the key word in that sentence was 'need'. When was the last time she'd given in to impulse to indulge herself out of pure need rather than necessity?

She rented this practical studio rather than splurging on the harbour view she craved. She wore comfortable clothes and practical heels rather than experimenting with the avant-garde fashion she lusted over in magazines. She still played the dependable, sensible sister to her impulsive brother, even though he was older than her and was happy in his life.

Could she say the same?

Staid decisions may lead to an even-keeled life but with Ryder staring at her with desire, maybe it was time to step outside her comfort zone and live a little larger?

'What do you mean treat each other with respect?' Her tongue darted out to moisten her bottom lip and his gaze riveted to it.

He muttered, 'Fuck,' as he reluctantly dragged his gaze from her lips.

Her heart pounded, the intensity behind that curse hinting at Ryder being barely able to control himself for wanting her, and it empowered her like nothing else could.

'Does treating each other with respect mean we acknowledge there's something beyond friendship between us and get this attraction out of our systems with one night of sex?'

She tilted her chin up, daring him to disagree, because she glimpsed wavering in his eyes: duty to Archie fighting lust for her; wanting to do the right thing battling with an urge to throw caution to the wind.

When he remained silent, she knew she'd have to make her feelings on the situation perfectly clear. She didn't have as much to lose as he did. Archie would give her crap for mucking around with his best friend, but he loved her and he'd do it because he was over-protective. But Ryder could lose his friendship with Archie because of the bro code that guys had and she understood if he didn't want to go through with this.

His tortured expression indicated exactly how torn he was over this so she'd have to give it to him straight, otherwise she'd regret not saying something.

'Because I'm up for it if you are.' She held up her index finger. 'One night. No complications. No second-guessing.' She made a zipping motion over her lips. 'And nobody needs to know but us.'

'You are…' He shook his head, before hauling her closer and resting his forehead against hers. 'I won't sugar-coat this, Pol. If I see something I want, I go after it, and I get it. This morning, when you didn't punch me in the nose for coming on to you, I knew something had shifted between us. I thought about putting the moves on you tonight because I've fantasised about you for years, but I still expect you to be the sensible one and tell me to go fuck myself.'

Buoyed by his admission, she eased back to eye-ball him, leaving him in little doubt of her intentions. 'Why, when it'll be much more fun if you fuck me?'

She'd never said anything so raunchy in her life and it galvanised him. 'Hot as fuck,' he murmured, haul-ing her closer, his lips commanding hers, his hands everywhere.

Polly had imagined this moment for so long that she half expected to be disappointed.

She should've known better.

Ryder kissed in the same way he did everything else in his charmed life: with exquisite precision and an expertise that defied belief.

His tongue swept along her bottom lip, a long, strong stroke that made her knees go weak, taunting her, teas-ing her, and when she opened her mouth it swept in to command, slow and sinuous and sexy as hell.

Hedonistic, hot kissing that went on for ever, ad-dling her brain and making her crave more with every cell in her body.

He backed her up against the wall, plundering her mouth over and over as his hands slid under her skirt and kneaded her butt.

She let out an embarrassingly loud moan as he toyed with the elastic of her panties and for a second she wished she went in for those racy lacy numbers in all the magazines rather than sensible cotton.

Not that Ryder seemed to care. He tugged them down regardless, leaving her wet and ready. He found her clit with unerring precision, exerting the right pressure with his thumb as he slipped a finger inside.

She wrenched her mouth from his, gasping for air. 'Ryder, please...'

'Only because you asked so nicely,' he said, holding her chin with one hand so he could watch her come as his other hand picked up speed, pushing her higher and faster until she tumbled into an orgasm that made her knees buckle.

'Sexiest damn thing I've ever seen,' he said, brushing a surprisingly soft kiss across her lips. 'Bedroom?'

'Here,' she said, breathless and wobbly but not wanting to wait. 'Now.'

His eyebrows rose but he didn't move. Instead, he slipped his wallet from his pocket, extracted a foil packet, and slid the wallet back before reaching for his fly.

'Let me.'

This was her fantasy come to life and she intended on making the most of it.

She cupped him through the denim, empowered by his guttural groan. Her fingers traced him, the size of his bulge making excitement pool deep within.

'Pol, you're killing me.'

Emboldened by his audible desperation, she popped the button on his jeans and toyed with the zip, before easing it down slowly. The sound of metal teeth unfastening mingled in the air with their shallow breathing, and when she finally had him unzipped she slipped her hand inside his jocks.

He groaned again, louder this time as her fingers wrapped around his hard length and slipped him free. Thick, long, hard, velvet. Perfection.

She slid her hand towards his balls, then up again, her thumb brushing over the tip.

'Fuck me,' he muttered, stilling her hand and sheathing himself in record time, before backing her up against the wall again. 'You are… This… You and me…'

'Never heard you lost for words before,' she said, hooking her leg around his waist, holding her breath as he nudged at her entrance. 'First time for everything.'

'You got that right,' he murmured, a moment before he slid into her to the hilt, filling her in a way she'd never anticipated but gloried in.

Then he slid out and did it again, over and over again, slow, smooth, seductive, until her muscles pulsed with the pleasure of it.

'You are divine,' he said, a moment before his mouth claimed hers again, and he pounded into her with a ferocity that left her clinging to him, craving more.

He gave it to her, pushing her towards another orgasm so fast her head spun. This time he joined her, his fingers digging into her butt as he lifted her clean off her feet. The back of her head thumped against the wall as he cried out her name, but if her head hurt she didn't register it.

Because she'd just had mind-blowing sex with Ryder

Beale, the guy she'd wanted for as long as she could remember, and all was right with the world.

For now.

She'd leave the inevitable self-analysis and recriminations for later.

CHAPTER SIX

RYDER HAD DONE some dumbass things in his lifetime.

Bungee jumping off a rickety platform in South America, race-car driving on rain-slicked, windy roads in Monaco, abseiling down cliffs in Thailand with ropes that had seen better days.

But none of those rivalled fucking his best friend's sister.

No, that took a special kind of stupidity and he had to own up to it. He'd never shied away from the hard stuff, but coming clean to Archie made his gut churn. They'd been best buds for a long time and while they never discussed the nitty-gritty emotional stuff—most guys didn't—he'd been there for Ryder in a way nobody ever had.

He remembered the day he moved in next door to the Scanlons. He'd been reeling from his grandfather's death and the way his gran had operated on autopilot most of the time since. A financial company had taken care of selling their old house—a mansion akin to a mausoleum that he'd hated—and assisted in purchasing the one next door to the Scanlons. He'd liked the new house on sight, its cream rendered walls, duck-egg-blue trims and bright, cheery feel compared with the dark grey of their old place.

His gran had barely looked at the exterior before stomping inside, leaving him to watch the removal team carefully extract the few pieces of furniture his gran had kept. Most of them were ugly pieces his pop had owned, like a mahogany grandfather clock, a roll-top desk and a sideboard where he'd kept his whiskey. Ryder had hated that sideboard the most, because his grandfather would drink half a decanter of whiskey every night and that was when he'd get really mean.

While Ryder had been watching their furniture being taken into the new house, Archie had stuck his head over the fence between their houses and brandished a cricket bat. 'Want to play?' his new neighbour had yelled, and that had been that. They'd bonded quickly, being the same age, become inseparable, and Ryder had grown to like the new place even if his gran moved around the house like a ghost.

He'd met Polly that day too, a shy, nerdy eight-year-old who'd sat on the front step with her nose in a book, only glancing up if the ball came near her and Archie insisted she throw it back. Her quietness had struck him the most that day. She had emanated a kind of peace he craved in his topsy-turvy world and he'd found himself sitting next to her after the cricket game ended, asking questions about the pony book she was reading because he wanted to listen to her soft, soothing voice.

When he'd eventually wandered home his gran

hadn't even noticed he'd been gone for hours. But at least she'd stocked the fridge so he'd made himself a ham and cheese sandwich, washed it down with a glass of chocolate milk and explored the house.

He'd liked its simplicity and its compactness. It hadn't been hard figuring out which room was his. The door had been left open and his stuff had been dumped in there. At least his bed had been made and as he flopped on top of the covers he'd replayed every moment with his new friends next door and whispered a soft prayer of gratitude that Pop had died, enabling his new life.

He'd immediately felt guilty, before remembering all the rotten ways his grandfather had made him feel inadequate, and was glad all over again.

That had been almost nineteen years ago and now he had to tell his best mate he'd screwed his sister.

Not that he'd couch it in those terms exactly, but he wanted to tell Archie some semblance of the truth. He liked Polly. He wanted to date her. If Archie decked him, so be it.

That was why he'd taken the coward's way out and asked to meet at the trendy pub on Circular Quay. He hadn't been home in five years but the pristine white sails of the Opera House never failed to soothe him. This part of bustling Sydney had always been his go-to place. However, as his glance flicked between his favourite icon and the door, he couldn't help but wonder if he was doing the right thing.

After the wild up-against-the-wall sex back at her place last night, Polly had virtually bundled him out the door. She hadn't met his eyes and a blazing blush had stained her cheeks so he hadn't forced the issue. He'd wanted to. He'd wanted to tell her how incredible she was and how she'd surpassed his fantasies. But she'd been awkward and embarrassed and he hadn't wanted to push his luck.

So while he wanted more of that scorching sex, he had no idea if she felt the same. Polly was all about facts and he knew she'd be analysing every detail, weighing up the pros and cons—and probably find him lacking.

Fact: he moved frequently so whatever happened between them could only be a short-term fling.

Fact: they were opposites in every way.

Fact: Archie would probably kill both of them.

Fact: he didn't give a shit about any of it because he wanted Polly, always had, and after the way she'd reciprocated last night he had every intention of exploring their connection while he was in town.

But first he had to tell Archie.

His best mate strolled through the door and Ryder raised a hand in greeting. Archie nodded and wended his way through the tables to reach him.

'Hey, bozo.' Archie slapped him on the back before taking a seat opposite. 'You know this window table is wasted on me because this isn't a date?'

'Who'd want to date your ugly mug?' Ryder pointed at his barely touched lager. 'Beer?'

'Make it a light. I'm driving.' He screwed up his nose. 'That DIY project I've got going on at home is a major pain in the ass and I'm about to drop another exorbitant four-figure sum at the hardware store after we've finished here.'

'In that case, lunch is on me.'

'You'll get no complaints from this side of the table.' Archie didn't look at the menu. 'Chicken Parma for me.'

Ryder grinned. His mate had been ordering the same pub grub for as long as he could remember.

'Coming right up.' Ryder made his way to the bar, placed their order and grabbed a light beer for Archie before heading back to the table.

The smart thing to do was wait until they'd eaten before broaching the tough stuff, but he knew Archie. He'd go ballistic if he found out Ryder had made small talk while they'd eaten without revealing the real reason he'd invited him to lunch today.

Archie rested his forearms on the table and eyeballed him. 'So Polly tells me you're helping her out with a fundraiser she's organising.'

Ryder's sip of beer caught in his throat and he cleared it, searching Archie's face for any clue he knew. But his friend wore the same goofy expression he always did and Ryder hated that what he had to say would wipe it.

'Yeah. Her boss is a real bitch and it seemed the right thing to do when I popped in to see her yesterday and the cow was giving her grief over it.'

'You're a good guy.' Archie raised his beer in a toast. 'Some of the time.'

'What's that supposed to mean?'

Archie laughed and shook his head. 'Man, you've

been away too long. I remember the way we used to tear up the nightclub and pub scene while you were living in Sydney.' He wiggled his eyebrows. 'You had the girls lining up, and the way you loved 'em and left 'em made you the bad guy in their eyes, while I always thought you were a legend.'

Shit, this wasn't good. Having Archie remember how he used to chase skirt wasn't conducive to revealing his attention was now solely focussed on his sister.

'That was a long time ago, mate.' He chugged his beer, taking three big gulps before being somewhat ready to tell Archie the rest. 'These days I'm only interested in one woman.'

Archie rolled his eyes. 'Who's the lucky lady?'

Here went nothing.

'Polly.'

Archie guffawed and thumped the table. 'Good one. You two have been doing that dance for so long it's inevitable you'd eventually go nuts and imagine something actually happening between you two.'

Archie made circles at his temple with his finger. 'You're crazy if you think Polly would go for someone like you.'

An unexpected hurt lodged in his gut, swift and deep. But before he could ask what he meant, Archie continued. 'You know what she's like, all facts and figures, carefully weighing every decision. She'd never date someone impulsive and transient.'

'But what if I want to date her?'

Archie's grin faded as the importance of what Ryder was saying slammed into him like a slug to the gut.

'What the fuck, man?'

'It's none of your goddamn business who I date but I'm telling you because we've been mates a long time and I don't want to screw it up.'

Archie glared at him through narrowed eyes, his lips thinning into an unimpressed line. 'You're a selfish prick for doing this.' He thumped his chest. 'She's my sister, man. This is fucked up.'

Knowing this would be hard but determined to be upfront, he said, 'You know I'd never hurt her, but for however long I'm in Sydney I want to hang out with Pol.'

Archie made a disparaging sound, half snort, half growl. 'I should punch your lights out, you dickhead.'

'You could, but you're the closest thing to a brother that I've got and I wanted to be upfront with you and not sneak around like a dog behind your back.'

Archie glared at him across the table, a frown marring his brow. An awkward silence stretched between them, until he finally relaxed a tad and sat back.

'I respect that.' A glint of admiration lit Archie's steady gaze. 'But that doesn't mean I have to like it.'

'I'm not asking you to.' Ryder held up his hands like he had nothing to hide. 'But know this. I respect Polly. I care about her—'

'Yeah, yeah, okay, I get it.' Archie tipped half his beer down his throat in one gulp. 'I have to admit, I've always wondered if the animosity between you two meant you'd already hooked up.' Archie's eyes narrowed, his glare speculative. 'And as much as we're bros, if you hurt her, man, I'll have to kill you.'

'Understood,' Ryder said, glad the conversation had gone better than expected, and determinedly ignoring the niggle of worry that all the words in the world would mean nothing if his relationship with Polly ended badly.

CHAPTER SEVEN

POLLY LOVED FASHION but she hated shopping.

Retail therapy was more like torture for her, but as she entered the air-conditioned mall she knew she couldn't leave without ticking a few items off her checklist.

Entering the first boutique she saw, she slipped the piece of paper out of her bag and unfolded it.

She wanted an outfit like the one she'd torn from a magazine, desperate to prove to Ryder she didn't need his help.

Because he'd done more of a makeover on her last night than any stylist could. And she still had tiny finger-mark bruises where he'd grabbed her butt tight to prove it.

Last night… She may have made an ass of herself by bundling him out the door after he'd made her come, twice, but she didn't regret what had preceded his hasty exit one bit.

The sex had been phenomenal.

Better than her countless fantasies.

But what she didn't understand was why he'd done

it. He dated gorgeous women worldwide. Why would he want a nerdy statistician who gave him nothing but grief whenever they saw each other?

Maybe that was it. He saw her as a challenge. He'd flirted his way around the world, according to the tabloids. What had changed last night?

'Can I help you?'

Polly blinked and focussed on the stick-thin, immaculately dressed blonde staring at her with an imperiously raised eyebrow. With her flawless make-up and sleek hair, the sales assistant was everything Polly wasn't. Yet surprisingly she didn't feel intimidated as she usually would entering a boutique like this…because she'd screwed Ryder Beale last night and it had been stupendous.

Struggling to hide a smug grin, Polly held out the magazine page. 'Do you have something like this?'

The assistant glanced at the page, then ran a critical eye over Polly. Surprisingly, she didn't screw up her nose like Polly half expected.

'Not exactly, but we have a similar outfit that would look great on you.' She pointed to the back of the store. 'Go on through to the dressing rooms and I'll bring it in.'

'Great, thanks.'

As the assistant moved away to riffle through racks, Polly wended her way through the store, admiring crisp linens in warm autumnal colours, the lightest silks in classic navy, white and black, and a dazzling array of sparkly and shimmery evening wear in vibrant emeralds and turquoises that made her want to touch them all.

Lush fabrics in bold colours reminded her of her mum and the only thing that had ever bound them. Nobody had understood why the geeky girl loved fashion magazines so much, but Sunday afternoons spent poring over those glossy pages with her mum was the closest thing to happiness she'd felt as a kid.

She'd never liked playing second best to golden boy Archie but for those few hours, flipping pages with her mum, she'd felt special.

She'd barely made it to the dressing room when the assistant entered. 'Let me know how you get on with sizing.'

After hanging the clothes on hooks, the assistant left and Polly tugged the heavy satin curtain across to give herself some privacy. After quickly stripping down to her underwear she reached for the first item, an ebony pencil skirt that took a bit of wriggling to get into. The dove-grey silk shirt slid over her skin like a sensual caress and she slipped a fire-engine-red fitted jacket, nipped in at the waist, over it.

When she'd tucked the shirt in, zipped up the skirt and adjusted the jacket, she turned to face the mirror.

Her reflection shocked her. Even in her ballet flats, no make-up and her hair snagged in a low ponytail, she looked different. Smarter. Almost pretty.

She loved it.

Half turning away from the mirror, she admired the cut of the clothes that gave the illusion of an hourglass figure even from the back.

These clothes had to be magical.

This outfit would be the perfect thing to wear when

she convinced Ryder she didn't need his help. Not that she'd renege on her offer to collate his book research, but having him arrange some weird makeover with his experts seemed too…intimate. Which was crazy, because he'd been inside her last night and that connection had been the most intimate of them all.

But he'd never understand that having sex with him had ripped away the flimsy barriers she'd erected over the years and left her feeling exposed and vulnerable in a way she hadn't anticipated.

Swapping banter with Ryder was one thing, swapping bodily fluids another entirely.

She'd opened herself to him and while she wasn't stupid enough to expect a repeat, she knew their interactions moving forward would be tainted with the memory of how damn combustible they'd been for an all-too-brief moment in time.

'How are you going in there?'

'Everything's fine, thanks,' Polly said. 'I'll be out in a sec.'

'Okay.'

As the click of the assistant's heels faded, Polly stared at her reflection again, knowing no amount of designer clothing could hide the truth blazing from her eyes.

After sizzling sex with Ryder, her crush wasn't going away any time soon.

CHAPTER EIGHT

RYDER DIDN'T KNOW the first thing about lingerie, other than how fast to take it off.

But he would fake knowledge if it got him some one-on-one time with Polly. Besides, she didn't need some stylist telling her what made her look good beneath her clothes.

That was his only regret about last night, that he hadn't got to see her naked. They'd been so hot and heavy for each other they hadn't even stripped.

He planned on rectifying that the next time they got together in the privacy of his place, or hers, because the damnedest thing had happened.

He'd expected sex with Polly to take the edge off his curiosity. Fantasising about her and finally having her should've had him moving on to the next challenge. It had happened before. A one-night stand that exceeded expectations but wouldn't be repeated. How fast she'd shoved him out the door afterwards proved it.

But that one scorching encounter with Polly hadn't assuaged his curiosity. He wanted more; he wanted to know the sounds she made when he went down on her, wanted to know if she preferred to be on top or underneath him, wanted to know if prim, proper Polly liked dirty talk.

There were so many enticing scenarios he could explore with her for however long he was in town...if she was up for it.

Though she was still avoiding him. He'd texted twice and she hadn't responded. That wouldn't deter him. He knew Pol; she'd be embarrassed or floundering or both. They needed to confront what had happened last night, deal with it and move on. To more sex, if he had his way.

In his many motivational talks over the last few years, he'd lectured about being assertive to get what you want.

Right now, he wanted more of Polly.

He didn't believe in fate or coincidence, but when the stylist texted him saying Polly couldn't keep her appointment they'd scheduled at a particular store and had to cancel, he'd taken it as the perfect opportunity to confront the woman who was avoiding him. A surprise confrontation. Perfect.

He strode into the lingerie shop and spotted her instantly, riffling through a rack of granny bras. Beige and white, neutral colours she'd never wear if he had his way.

A rich burgundy or peacock blue would look stunning against her skin and he spotted just the thing a few feet away. The sheer burgundy bodysuit would accentuate every curve while providing a feast for the senses, while the satin blue knickers and bra set had naughty peepholes scattered throughout the fabric. Perfect.

Guessing her size, he snaffled the two sets and made his way towards her. She hadn't caught sight of him yet but as she half turned and he glimpsed her profile, teeth worrying her bottom lip, something kicked in his chest, hard.

She was pretty rather than classically beautiful with her straight nose, thick chocolate-coloured hair hanging past her shoulders, slightly olive skin and rich brown eyes that reflected every emotion she ever had. He knew she underplayed her features, rarely wearing make-up, but it didn't matter because to him she'd always been beautiful.

'These will suit you much better,' he said, biting back a grin as she jumped and whirled on him, one hand pressed to her heart.

'What the hell are you doing here?'

'You cancelled the stylist.' He shrugged, mustering up his best bashful expression. 'So being the stand-up guy I am, I stepped into the breach to help a friend out.'

Her eyes narrowed but he glimpsed the corners of her mouth twitch. 'Was that list of stylists you gave me yesterday even real? Because it seems to me it's mighty convenient she agrees to meet me here, at a lingerie shop of all places, then you show up instead.'

It was his turn to clutch his chest in mock indignation. 'You wound me with your mistrust.'

'Considering you've got a hide like a rhino, I seriously doubt that.'

Her gaze dropped to the lingerie in his other hand

and the faintest blush stole into her cheeks. 'And if you think I'm taking underwear advice from you, you are wrong on so many levels.'

'I happen to be an expert on underwear.'

'I bet.' She rolled her eyes. 'Seriously, I can do this myself.'

'Yet you agreed to be contacted by the stylist? Interesting.' He tapped his bottom lip, pretending to think. 'Is there some lucky guy you're hoping to impress?'

The blush intensified and he yearned to lean down and press his lips to her blazing cheeks. 'I've read that wearing this frivolous stuff underneath clothes can make a woman feel sexy and powerful, so that's why I'm here.'

He stepped closer to murmur in her ear. 'Trust me, babe, you don't need any help in the sexy department. You've got it covered.'

He could feel heat radiating off her and smell her subtle floral perfume, tempting him to swipe his tongue along the underside of her jaw towards her ear, in order to elicit a sharp gasp.

'We're in public,' she said, but she leaned into him so that their chests brushed, sending a jolt to his cock.

'Not for long.'

He snagged her hand and tugged her towards the dressing rooms, discreetly tucked into the back of the shop.

'You can't come in here...' Her protest died when he did just that, flipping the lock behind them.

'Relax,' he said, gritting down on the urge to strip her naked and see if that tantalising blush extended all over her body. 'The people who work here must be used to seeing men checking out their women in the dressing rooms.'

'Pervert,' she muttered, but a coy smile curved her lips. 'Though it's kind of kinky and I've never done this before.'

'Strip down to your underwear for a guy?'

The blush intensified. 'Buy risqué lingerie.' She squared her shoulders and held out her hand. 'Give me those.'

Her boldness surprised him and he handed the sets over, his pulse pounding in anticipation.

'Turn around.' She made a spinning action with her finger, before jabbing him in the chest with it. 'I'll let you see the finished product but only if you don't peek.'

'Spoilsport,' he muttered, folding his arms in a mock sulk, so she jabbed him again.

'Or I can boot you out of here. Your choice,' she said, with a nonchalant shrug.

There was zero chance he'd be leaving this dressing room without seeing her in that lingerie, absolutely none, so he spun around, lust thrumming through him.

If he'd thought watching her undress would be a massive turn-on, it had nothing on listening to the sounds of her disrobing. The unzipping of her skirt, the buttons slithering through the buttonholes of her blouse, the rustling of stepping out of panties…

He gritted his teeth and bit back a groan. This so wasn't him. He'd liked plenty of women over the years and while he wasn't a man whore he didn't do relationships beyond a few dates. But Polly was in a different category altogether because of their longstanding friendship, and their sizzling encounter had only served to make him want more.

He wanted to know all her secrets—where she liked to be licked, where her most ticklish spots were, what she tasted like...

His cock strained against his fly and a fine sweat broke out on his brow. He knew once he turned around and caught sight of her in that sexy get-up it would take every ounce of self-control not to fuck her on the spot.

'Okay, I'm done,' she murmured, soft and uncertain.

He took a deep breath and blew it out before swivelling around.

Hot damn.

The image of Polly standing in front of him, the sheer burgundy lace revealing more than it hid, the way it clung to her curves, would be burned on his retinas for ever.

Her timorous expression made him want to hug her tight but her eyes didn't lie; she was just as turned on by this sexy little parade as he was.

When he finally unglued his tongue from the roof of his mouth, he murmured, 'Wow.'

It was a totally underwhelming response because Polly in that sexy lingerie was beyond wow. Considering his thundering heart, pounding pulse and straining cock, it was closer to catastrophic.

'I've never done this before.' She rubbed one foot on top of the other, endearingly bashful. 'You're definitely a bad influence on me.'

'Sweetheart, you have no idea the influence you're

having on me in that get-up,' he said, covering the short distance between them to snag her hand and press it against his fly. 'Or maybe you do?'

A sexy smile played about her mouth. 'Yeah, I had a fair idea.'

'Vixen,' he muttered, brushing a kiss across her lips. 'Turn around and face the mirror.'

'Why?'

'You'll see.'

He loved it that she trusted him. There was a lot to be said for almost twenty years of friendship, even if they'd been at each other's throats for most of that.

This woman had alternated between teasing him and infuriating him for so long they'd fallen into some kind of weird prolonged foreplay. Last night had been a release, a culmination of all that pent-up sexual tension. He may not be in town for long but he could think of nothing better than having sex with Polly, repeatedly, as a way to distract him from the tension of being back in a city he'd rather avoid.

'Beautiful,' he murmured, pressing his front to her back, sliding one arm around her to splay his hand against her stomach, the other pressed lower. Grazing her with the lightest brush of his fingertips. Tugging on the lace so that the buttons on the crotch popped.

Her eyes widened in delighted surprise. 'I didn't know it did that.'

'Most bodysuits do.'

'A man who knows his lingerie. I'm pretty sure I should be appalled but I kind of like the fact you're so knowledgeable.'

'Why?'

Their gazes locked in the mirror. 'Because I'm a very willing student and I'm sure you'd be up for teaching me.'

'So does that mean you're up for dating?'

'Who said anything about dating?' She lowered her hand and slowly peeled the bottom of the bodysuit upwards and he let out a groan as his hungry gaze zeroed in on her pussy.

Trimmed, neat, but a full bush, such a rarity in these days of Brazilians. He loved it.

'Is it the lingerie making you this bold or have you been hiding your inner sex kitten from me all these years?'

'A little of both,' she murmured, taking hold of his hand and sliding it lower.

It was such a fucking turn-on having her take charge and having her watch as he slid his middle finger between her folds, zeroing in on her clit.

She gasped as he applied pressure, circling the hard nub over and over until she made small panting sounds, while his other hand palmed her breast.

She arched back against him and he lowered his mouth to nibble on her neck, short, sharp bites followed by slow, soothing sweeps of his tongue that had her writhing.

'I'm close, Ryder,' she whispered, their gazes locking in the mirror. Her willingness to let him finger her to orgasm in a dressing room proved exactly how much he'd underestimated this amazing woman all these years.

His finger circled her clit faster as he plucked at a nipple through the lace between his thumb and forefinger, over and over, until she made a small whimpering sound and tensed.

'Shh… I've got you,' he murmured, a second before she came apart, biting down on her bottom lip so hard he saw a speck of blood.

When she sagged against him, he gently turned her around and kissed her, slow and sensual. But he had to stop because they'd been hiding in here long enough and he had no intention of being busted by the lingerie police. The next time he and Polly had sex, he wanted to make it last.

'We need to get out of here.'

Dazed, she lifted her head. 'What about you?'

'We have all night.'

He intended on making it count.

CHAPTER NINE

POLLY LOVED SYDNEY'S hip vibe but she rarely spent time in the city centre, let alone trendy Circular Quay, so it was surreal to be sitting on the balcony of Ryder's plush suite-only hotel overlooking the Harbour Bridge with the lights of Luna Park twinkling in the distance.

She knew he'd made a success of himself but this one-bedroom suite with the million-dollar view was next level.

'Here you go.' He handed her a glass filled to the brim with milk and pulled up a seat close enough that their knees touched.

'I can't believe you remembered my favourite drink.' She raised it in his direction. 'Thanks.'

'And I can't believe anyone would drink milk with cocoa, doctored with brandy.'

'Don't knock it till you try it,' she said, taking a healthy slurp and smacking her lips. 'So good.'

'You're a lunatic.' He smiled and shook his head. 'With very bad taste.'

'Especially in men, present company included,' she

said, with a smirk, raising her glass in his direction. 'I'll drink to that.'

He laughed, reminding her how much she'd missed this. She'd always loved their sparring and, thankfully, getting physical hadn't tampered with it.

It had been her greatest fear all these years and one of the reasons why she'd never made a move. She'd been terrified that sex with Ryder would change their friendship and she'd end up regretting it. And while she may have been avoiding him today because her head was spinning from last night, the fact she'd urged him to give her an orgasm in a public dressing room an hour ago made her feel wanton and alive in a way she never could've anticipated.

'You're thinking about the lingerie,' he said, raising his beer to his lips and taking a deep pull before lowering it.

'How do you know?'

'You get this look in your eyes...' His gaze fixed on her mouth, before lifting to meet hers, hot and intense. 'It's a big fucking turn-on.'

'So I noticed.' She deliberately stared at his dick and he waggled a finger.

'Stop doing that. I want to take this slow tonight.'

'Why, when last night's quickie was so much fun?'

The glint of amusement in his eyes faded, replaced by something she could almost label as tenderness. It was crazy, because they didn't have that kind of relationship. What they had was two friends having sex. A fun, light-hearted connection for however long it lasted. Not that she'd anticipated anything beyond one night but her brazen behaviour in that dressing room, combined with the fact she'd agreed to come back to his place, pretty much guaranteed they'd end up in bed.

It would've fazed her once but it didn't because the sky hadn't fallen in and the earth hadn't split open after they'd had sex. If anything, it made their banter more fun and that was what she needed in her life right now. A little healthy distraction from the fact she was failing at work and wouldn't get a shot at her dream job.

For an intelligent, independent woman, there was something about her ogre boss that made her feel inadequate and she hated it. She'd felt the same around her mum and that soul-destroying feeling of not being good enough was hard to shake, even after all these years.

'Are we going to discuss the fact we had sex and what's going to happen because of it?'

Uh-oh. The conversation they had to have but the one she'd been dreading. Talking about it could lead to him learning about her long-term crush and that was the last thing she wanted. He'd instantly pull away because he'd fear he would hurt her in the end and last night had been too good, too much fun, to quit now.

'I know what I'd like to happen.' She batted her eyelashes. 'The sex was pretty damn exceptional and I want more.'

His eyes glittered with excitement and something she could almost label as caution. 'You know that sex is all it ever can be, right? I'm not a keeper.'

She rolled her eyes, trying to ignore the sliver of hurt at hearing him articulate the truth even if she already knew it. 'You like playing the field, I get it.'

He arched a brow. 'It doesn't bother you that sex could complicate our friendship?'

'Considering we haven't kept in contact in years, beyond seeing you when you occasionally visit Sydney and Archie organises something, I'd say our friendship isn't that much of a big deal.'

Her dry response garnered a short burst of laughter devoid of amusement. 'Still the same pragmatic Polly.'

She hated how he viewed her that way, good old rational, sensible, logical Polly. She'd sex that view out of him if it killed her.

'And in the spirit of pragmatism, I understand last night was just about sex. For some unfathomable reason, you set your sights on flirting with me on this trip rather than our usual caustic sparring, I responded and we ended up screwing.' She felt heat flush her cheeks and wished she wasn't so damn easy to read. 'Nothing more, nothing less. The sex was great, I want more, so let's shelve this discussion because there's no chance of emotional entanglement, okay?'

He pinned her with an astute stare that had her resisting the urge to squirm. She took a long slug of brandy-infused milk, desperate to calm her thundering heart.

Because she'd lied. Sleeping with Ryder would inevitably involve emotions—mainly hers getting trampled on—considering how long she'd wanted this, wanted him.

'You talk the talk, Pol, but I really hope you mean it.' He emptied half his beer. 'We like each other. We'll date for as long as I'm in Sydney, but that's it. I can't give you anything else.'

She schooled her face into a neutral expression despite her disappointment. Of course he couldn't give her anything else. The renowned playboy would leave sooner rather than later in search of his next challenge. She knew the score and she was willing to play the game.

'Dating is a euphemism for fucking, yeah?'

His eyes widened in surprise before he chuckled. 'Of course. I told Archie I wanted to *date* you. I had to make it sound legit.'

Shock rendered her speechless, before she gave a quick shake of her head. 'You did *what*?'

'I told him at lunch today.' He shrugged, like it meant little, him facing up to her overprotective brother. 'After what happened last night I knew I wanted you again and keeping it from him would be deceptive, so I told him the truth.'

'You told him we had sex?' Her voice had risen to a screech and he chuckled.

'Not exactly.' He clinked his beer bottle against her glass. 'He didn't seem all that surprised.'

Archie may act like a layabout builder who told rude jokes on building sites and hung out with the boys at sleazy 'Schnitz and Tits' nights at the pub, but he'd always been intuitive when it came to her. She knew he'd probably suspected her crush on Ryder, though he'd never mentioned it.

'He's seen the way we spar. The doofus probably misread it as sexual tension.' Which it had been on her part for a long time. 'Can I ask you something?'

'Sure.'

'Why now? Why flirt with me this time when you've never done that before?'

He hesitated, his gaze shifting away before refocussing on her with a cheeky glint. 'It's my thing these days, Pol. Flirting comes as naturally as breathing to me and when you responded I couldn't believe my luck.'

It was exactly as she'd suspected. His flirting had meant nothing; she'd let her own latent feelings flare, and he'd run with it. She didn't blame him; what guy wouldn't want to take things further when given the go-ahead? But it irked just the same that she was nothing more than yet another one of his women in a long line that had succumbed to his charms.

'So we're good?' His goofy smile made her want to clamber onto his lap and hug him tight. 'We hook up while I'm in Sydney and walk away at the end, no hard feelings?'

He made it sound so easy. It would be, if she didn't let her stupid heart get in the way of a good sexcapade.

'As long as something else is hard.' She deadpanned, and he laughed.

'You always had a great sense of humour,' he said.

'One of my many good qualities.' She drained the milk, savouring the burn of the brandy warming her from the inside out. Or that could be Ryder's smouldering gaze. 'Seeing as we're being so honest with each other, tell me why you're staying in this fabulous suite and not at your gran's place?'

Just like that, Ryder shut down.

Shadows clouded his eyes, his lips compressed into a thin line and he half turned away to stare at the incredible view of Sydney at night.

He sat ramrod straight, his back rigid, his shoulders bunched with tension. His jaw jutted slightly, as if he was clenching his teeth too hard. She knew he'd never been close to his gran. He wouldn't have spent all that time at their place otherwise and he'd never talked about her. But Polly had definitely hit a nerve with her innocuous question and she wished they could regain the easy-going camaraderie of a few moments ago.

When he didn't answer, she tapped his knee. 'Hey, what's up?'

'Nothing.'

His short, sharp response held a hint of pain and she mentally cursed herself for changing the mood. He'd switched from playful to shut off in an instant.

'Problems with your gran?'

His jaw clenched, a tiny vein pulsing near his ear, before he eventually answered. 'Do you remember much about her when we were neighbours?'

Considering Edie Beale rarely left the house, Polly didn't. She would catch the occasional glimpse of the well-dressed woman with coiffed hair, but Edie had never acknowledged her. At one stage Polly had made it a game, to give an exaggerated wave every time she saw the woman, but Edie would always stare straight ahead and stride down her path with purpose before getting into a car that had a driver.

She'd teased Ryder about it. The first time he'd squished a spider on her head in retaliation, the second he'd dumped a bunch of wriggling worms in her lap, so she hadn't pushed for a third. But she figured the Beales had a lot more money than her family, though Ryder didn't act like it. It made her like him all the more.

'I remember your gran being aloof, that's about it.'

'She was like that with me too,' he said, so softly she had to lean forward to hear it. 'When Pop died she shut down.'

'I'm sorry—'

'She blamed me.' His bark of laughter held no amusement. 'Apparently my behaviour made his heart give out. Which was a total crock of shit considering the old man hated my guts and never held back.'

He shook his head, disgust twisting his mouth. 'Not a single day went by when good old Fred didn't berate me for being a burden on them, for taking attention away from him, for being a financial drain even though the old coot had millions.'

'No offence, but your grandfather sounds like an asshole.'

'He was. He actually told me why he didn't like me once.' He drained the rest of his beer and slammed the bottle down on the table. 'He said I was nothing like my father and it was my fault my parents died in a car crash because they were on their way to check out a boarding school for me in rural New South Wales when it happened.'

'Shit...'

Polly couldn't comprehend lumping that much vitriol on a child, let alone a child left in your care. Ryder's grandparents had a lot to answer for. She mightn't have been as close to her mum as she would've liked, but Barbara had never made her feel unloved or a burden.

'I was four when the car accident happened and I barely remember them, but Pop never let me forget what a useless waste of space I was.'

Wishing she'd never probed at this obvious sore spot, she said, 'What was your gran like when he was alive?'

He shrugged, his eyes glazed as if lost in memories. 'She seemed to like me. Then again, he reserved his hatred for me in private, when she wasn't around.'

Hating the injustice of a grandparent taking his grief out on an undeserving child, her eyebrows rose. 'And she didn't pick up on his animosity other times?'

'If she did she never let on. Fred was her world. They were old school. He controlled the money, she ensured his home was perfect. A match made in heaven.' He snorted, an ugly sound ripped from deep within him. 'Pity living with them was my version of hell.'

It all made sense now—how Ryder would spend every spare minute at their place, how he'd linger until dinner time and quickly accept if her mum asked him to stay, how he'd accompanied them on most of their outings. It made her wonder if Barbara had known about the situation next door and that was why her mum had treated Ryder like another son.

At times Polly had resented the bond between her mum and Ryder, as her mum had lavished him with the attention she'd rarely paid her daughter. Back then, she'd liked Ryder but she'd been a tad jealous of him too. Now her heart broke for what he'd had to endure and she was glad her flighty mum had welcomed him into their family.

'I had no idea,' she said, resting a comforting hand on his forearm.

He stared at it for a moment before shrugging it off. 'Nobody did. I preferred it that way.'

'Will you visit her while you're in Sydney?'

He jolted like she'd prodded him with an electrical current. 'Considering we haven't kept in touch since the accident, it's doubtful.'

Shocked, Polly struggled not to gape. She may not be close to her mum but they kept in regular contact. And whenever Barbara visited Sydney they caught up, usually over high tea and a shopping jaunt. Babs may still be critical of the clothes Polly wore and her lack of style, but her mum made time to see her and that counted for something.

'So you haven't been in contact for over five years?'

'Something like that.' He grimaced and swiped a hand over his face. It did little to eradicate the tension. 'The only reason I know the battleaxe is still alive is because she withdraws the money I regularly deposit in her bank account.'

Despite his shuttered expression, Polly saw hope

warring with anger. Ryder may be livid at his gran but he still wanted to offer support any way he could and for him that involved money.

Not that it was any of her business, but a small part of her wished she could facilitate some kind of reunion between them.

'That's a good thing you're doing—'

'I do it for me.' He thumped his chest with a closed fist. 'Because I don't ever want to feel indebted to her.' He sniggered. 'I guess it's my way of flipping the old man the finger, proving that I owe him nothing.'

Polly's heart ached for his overt pain because he wouldn't be this bitter if he didn't care. She racked her brains for the right thing to say and came up blank.

He stood abruptly, the back of his chair slamming against the concrete wall behind him. 'Do you mind if we call it a night? Jet lag is catching up with me and I've got a shitload of work to catch up on.'

She wanted to call him out on shutting down and in turn shutting her out. If he reacted this way from merely talking about his grandparents then he'd bottled up his resentment for too long. But he was the one with the psychology degree, not her, and she didn't have the faintest idea how deep his bitterness ran. Besides, he'd made it perfectly clear they were nothing beyond sex and she had no right to delve.

'Not a problem,' she said, rising to her feet, wishing she could turn back the clock fifteen minutes so their playful banter would've led to something else instead.

She'd done this with her big mouth and inquisitive questioning. Idiot. He wanted to be alone. She saw it in every tense line of his body, in the bunching of his neck muscles. If they were a real couple she'd stay and comfort him.

But they weren't. They were friends who'd agreed to have sex and right now her friend needed her to leave. She wouldn't push it.

'Call me if you need me,' she said, planting a soft kiss on his cheek, before trudging to the door.

So much for a fun night. She'd screwed it up royally, rather than screwing him.

CHAPTER TEN

RYDER HAD FUCKED that up.

He'd planned a sensual, romantic evening with Polly in his suite but now the strawberries, champagne and hand-crafted chocolates that had been delivered lay on the table, taunting him.

He could be in bed right now, exploring her body, driving her crazy, sating his relentless lust for her, obliterating the memories he'd dredged up by losing himself in her.

Instead, he'd shut down.

When she'd asked about Gran he should've given her a trite answer and moved on, changing the subject quickly. Instead, he'd taken one look into her dark eyes, glimpsed the genuine interest and had opened up like a geyser, spewing forth all sorts of family secrets better left untold.

Then he'd asked her to leave.

Smooth.

Not.

He'd been tempted to go after her but he was no good to her in this mood and from past experience it would take time before he shook it off—time, and a bottle of bourbon.

But the thought of drinking alone left him cold and he turned his back on the chocolates and strawberries and stomped back out to the balcony.

The view was something else, and no matter how many cities he visited around the world trying to inspire people to be better versions of themselves, this vibrant city held pride of place in his heart.

It irked that he hadn't been back in five years, but once his career had started taking off he'd been on a constant whirlwind of motivational speaking tours and empowering employees of companies in need of a makeover.

Breaking his leg and nearly being killed had given him a wake-up call that had changed the direction of his life, but rather than coming home and confronting the past he'd used his new lease on life as a lesson in avoidance.

As long as he made regular deposits in his grandmother's bank account, and as long as she kept withdrawing the money, he believed he was paying his dues. She may not have bestowed love on him as he'd been growing up but she'd put a roof over his head and he owed her. That was what the money was ultimately about. He knew she didn't need it—his grandparents had been rich in their own right from savvy investments—but every time he checked the account and saw she'd taken the money he felt vindicated in doing the right thing.

So why was he still so hung up on the past?

Before he could second-guess his impulsive decision, he strode back into the suite, picked up his keys and headed out the door.

As Ryder drove the winding streets through Cronulla he remembered the first time he'd made this trip. He'd never understood why his gran had always used a driver if Pop wasn't around, until Pop died and he realised Gran couldn't drive. He'd hated sitting in the back seat of their fancy car, staring at the back of the driver's head. The guy had worn a cap, just like in the movies, and it had made Ryder uneasy that he got chauffeured around when most kids had taken the bus or ridden a bike.

On that dreary Saturday a few weeks after Pop died, he'd been filled with excitement. He'd hated their old house in Double Bay. It resembled a museum with its vast halls, sweeping staircase and dusty paintings of old folk. He'd never been allowed to bounce a basketball or kick a footy. In fact, he hadn't been allowed to do much of anything when Pop was around. Besides, it had been easier not to draw attention to himself and avoid the old coot, because if he'd spotted Ryder he'd inevitably heap unwarranted criticism on him.

'Why can't you be tall like your dad? Why can't you get better grades? Why can't you win the top prize for academic and sporting excellence?'

The questions would be biting and endless, and Ryder had soon grown attuned to his grandfather's footsteps and would do anything to avoid him.

If Gran had noticed she'd never said, though at least

she'd been more affectionate before Pop had died. She'd praise him and smile and save him the best cut of roast lamb on a Sunday. But Pop dying had changed her in ways he couldn't fathom. She'd shut down and shut him out.

It had gutted him.

But for him, Pop's death had been a reprieve, almost a godsend, and he'd anticipated being a tight-knit team with Gran moving forward. Instead, she'd looked right through him most days, not caring if he'd spent most of his time with the Scanlons next door.

Archie and Polly's mum, Babs, had lavished attention on him. No surprise why he'd gravitated towards their house every chance he'd got. He'd loved hanging out there after school, doing homework with Archie while teasing Polly. Babs would give them milk and cookies, and she wouldn't hover. And the evenings she'd asked him to stay for dinner they invariably had chicken nuggets and chips or frozen pizza. It wouldn't have mattered if she'd served him crap on a plate, he would've stayed because the raucous family atmosphere around the Scanlons' dining table had made him feel alive.

He often wondered if not having parents made him crave the kind of family Archie and Polly had. And even though their father had done a runner when they were young, they seemed unaffected by it. Archie revelled in his role as man of the house while Polly was Polly regardless: quiet, studious, geeky, with a sharp wit she directed mostly at him.

As he turned left into his old street, one block away

from the beach, his heart gave a betraying leap. This was foolish, a ridiculous whim, but as he pulled up outside his gran's house and killed the engine a wave of nostalgia swamped him, leaving him gasping for air.

He knew where she'd be: in the front room, in a recliner by the window, reading. His gaze drifted across the front of the house, noting the general air of neglect in peeling paint and faded trim, before finding the window.

There she was, silhouetted by the ornate lamp near the window, her head bent, her shoulders rounded. He couldn't see much of her beyond that but the familiarity of it all brought a lump to his throat.

The only time his gran had remotely acknowledged he existed back then had been the evenings spent in the front room, reading. She'd be in that same chair, poring over a boring biography, and he'd lie on the couch, his head on a pillow, his legs hanging over the end, reading comics or adventure novels.

He'd catch her watching him at times, a small smile on her face, and that brief glimpse of almost-happiness had ensured he joined her in that room, with a book, whenever he wasn't next door.

He would've rather been gaming or watching videos online, but the emotional distance between them had been so great that if those evenings reading together were all he got, he took it.

He didn't know how long he sat in the car, watching her, but it somehow soothed him knowing she was okay and stuck in her routine.

He would confront her, but not tonight. He had to

gather his thoughts and get rid of the funk plaguing him before he could see her.

They had a lot to resolve and this time he wouldn't leave without saying his piece.

CHAPTER ELEVEN

ARCHIE RARELY DROPPED BY, especially not at nine p.m. They led very different lives. He went clubbing and pub-crawling and did exciting things like visit escape rooms with his mates. Polly stayed in and ate way too much chocolate while watching English crime dramas.

So the fact he'd texted her, saying he'd be around in fifteen minutes, could only mean one thing.

He wanted to lecture her about Ryder.

For as long as she could remember Archie had been protecting her. She guessed it had something to do with the fact their mum had labelled him the man of the house even before he'd hit his teens and he'd grown into the role—warning her off boys, sneaking looks at her texts, pulling a major intimidation act when she'd coerced a guy to be her date for the year eleven formal.

She'd been annoyed by his overprotectiveness growing up but had known it came from the right place. But at almost twenty-eight she didn't need his opinion on who she should and shouldn't date, and she'd be telling him exactly that.

Ironically, she'd just arrived home and had been

glaring at the lingerie bag when her brother's text had arrived. She'd wanted to make an excuse, in no mood to see him after the way her evening with Ryder had been cut short thanks to her delving into his private life.

But she knew her brother and if she fobbed him off tonight he'd think something was wrong and would hound her even harder tomorrow.

So she'd stowed the bag with her lingerie purchases in the back of her wardrobe and slammed the door shut, as much on her memory of what had happened when she'd lost her mind in that dressing room and turned into a wanton goddess as to hide the evidence from Archie.

She didn't wear risqué lingerie like that burgundy bodysuit but seeing Ryder's reaction when she'd put it on had ensured she'd purchased it along with the blue satin knickers and bra he'd chosen too.

She'd model that other combo for him next time— and keep her big mouth shut. Probing into his past had ended their evening prematurely and she'd been kicking herself ever since. It annoyed the crap out of her that she couldn't turn off her analytical side most of the time and it had resulted in Ryder shutting her out.

No guy liked to be pitied and she was pretty sure he must've read every distressing feeling on her face when he'd told her about his grandparents and what he'd gone through growing up. She'd wanted to hug him but his body language had been as closed off as his expression.

She'd made a monumental blunder in pushing him for answers and no way in hell would she make that mistake again, despite wanting to know every little thing that made him tick.

A loud rap at the door had her squaring her shoulders, ready for battle. If Archie thought he could lecture her, he had another think coming.

Mustering her best blasé expression, she opened the door. 'Hey, Arch. What are you doing here when you could be out indulging in your usual nocturnal debauchery?'

He didn't laugh as he usually would and a deep frown grooved his brow. 'You know why.'

He stalked past her and headed straight for the lounge room, where he dropped unceremoniously into an armchair. 'What's all this crap I hear about Ryder wanting to date you?'

She sighed, closed the door and joined him in the lounge room, sitting across from him.

'Do I ever voice an opinion on the myriad bimbos you date with a never-ending revolving door policy?'

He flipped her the finger.

'The point is, I don't. So what gives you the right to question anybody I choose to hang out with?'

'Come on, Pol, this isn't some random guy you're hooking up with. It's Ryder.' He gave an exaggerated shudder. 'It's gross.'

'Why? Because we've been friends for ever and we respect and like each other?'

'Stop being so damn logical.' He folded his arms and slouched further into the chair. 'It could get messy.'

'We know what we're doing.'

'Do you?' He hesitated, his forehead crinkling in

concern. 'Because Ryder's a player, sis. It's who he is. He's dated extensively over the last few years. It's what he does, always chasing the next best thing. He doesn't do long-term relationships and he'll leave Sydney sooner rather than later.' He grimaced and swiped a hand over his face. 'I don't want you to get hurt.'

She didn't blame him for worrying about her because everything he said about Ryder was true. But she was a big girl sick of playing it safe and being with Ryder lent her life some much-needed excitement. She'd be a fool not to go for it. 'I know what Ryder's like and that's the beauty of this. I have absolutely no expectations.'

A blush crept into her cheeks. 'He's not taking advantage of the situation, because we're both going into this with our eyes open.'

Archie eyed her with respect, but he hadn't lost the frown. 'You're talking the talk, sis, and it's admirable, but aren't you kidding yourself?'

'What's that supposed to mean?'

'I'm not blind. I reckon you've had a crush on Ryder since we were kids. So don't tell me you're not emotionally involved and will happily watch him board a plane and not return for another five years? Or move on to the next woman a week after he dumps you?'

Since when was Arch the logical one? It wasn't like she hadn't contemplated this very scenario. She knew the risks involved and that was exactly why she was doing this. She'd never been a risk-taker, ever. She dealt in cold, hard facts as a statistician and weighed decisions in her life as carefully.

But working at Sizzle had been a giant step out of her comfort zone and dating Ryder was another. She needed to do this, for her, otherwise she'd regret it for the rest of her life and always wonder 'what if'.

Ryder wanted her. That was enough.

She had no illusions of happily ever after or other such nonsense. She knew the score. They'd hook up while he was in Sydney, then he'd leave. The end.

'I'm not an idiot, Arch. I know what I'm getting into.'

The worried dent creasing his brow deepened. 'Do you? Really?'

'Yeah, and as much as I appreciate the concern, I need to do this and nothing you say will change my mind.'

'Fine,' he huffed, throwing up his hands in resignation. 'But you're both being incredibly selfish, putting me in an untenable situation.'

'How do you figure?'

'Well, if he hurts you, I'm honour bound to defend you, and I'll have to kick his ass.'

She bit back a smile. Ryder had several feet on Archie and a lot more muscle. She'd like to see him try.

'I'll be fine,' she said, ready for a change of topic. 'Hey, did Ryder ever talk to you about his gran when we were growing up?'

'Fuck no, guys don't talk about shit like that.'

'What do you mean?'

'Well, I knew something was wrong with his home life considering he spent all his time at our place. And we never saw his gran so I asked him one day if he'd made her up and if he lived in that place by himself.'

'And what did he say?'

'That his gran was a crazy old bat who hated his guts and he avoided her at all costs.'

'Ouch,' she said, struck again by how awful Ryder's upbringing had been.

Hers hadn't been a walk in the park but at least she'd bonded with her mum over their mutual love of fashion. Their relationship hadn't been overly effusive or affectionate but she never got the feeling her mum hated her. She felt sorry for him. Not that she'd make the mistake of telling him.

'What are you thinking?'

She sighed. 'Sounds like Ryder had it tough growing up and we didn't know.'

'I had an inkling.' He shrugged. 'He hid it most of the time.'

She'd been clueless, and it struck her at that moment that maybe all his teasing and joking around had been his way of deflecting attention away from himself. Maybe he'd hidden his pain behind laughter and it made her feel even guiltier she hadn't noticed something.

'He hasn't been in contact with his gran in five years.'

Archie's eyebrows shot up. 'He told you that?'

She bit back her first retort, 'Yeah, Einstein, we're not just screwing,' but settled for a more sedate, 'We're still friends.'

A glint of admiration lit his eyes. 'Have to say, it doesn't surprise me, you two hooking up.'

'You've made reference to it before.'

He managed to look sheepish. 'Yeah, that's because I had my suspicions and I was fishing for intel, knowing you'd be more likely to crack than that doofus.'

She chuckled. 'Who knew giving each other grief was one giant exercise in foreplay?'

'Ew, too much information.' He screwed up his nose and leapt to his feet. 'That's my cue to leave.'

Polly grinned and followed him to the door where he paused, staring at her intently, as if searching for answers she hadn't given him.

'You're happy, Pol, yeah?'

'I am,' she said, and embraced him in a quick hug. 'Now go, before I mention the *F* word again.'

He shuddered. 'I'm outta here.'

She laid a hand on his arm. 'Thanks, big brother, for looking out for me.'

'Anytime, sis.'

As Polly watched him stride down her path and disappear from view, she couldn't help but wonder if there was more behind Archie's visit.

Was he just being overprotective or did he have genuine concerns considering he knew Ryder better than her?

Would the man she'd lusted after her whole life ultimately break her heart?

CHAPTER TWELVE

RYDER HAD HONED avoidance to a fine art over the years, and the day after he'd mucked things up with Polly was no exception.

He knew he owed her a phone call at least but every time he reached for his mobile he'd stop. In the past, his MO would be to laugh off the way he'd acted like a jerk in shutting her out, or to ignore it and pretend it had never happened. He'd become an expert at it and the fact that she and Archie rarely questioned him about his home life was testament to how damn good he'd been at hiding behind his jovial persona.

But he'd opened up to Polly last night in a way he'd never done with anybody and it had changed the dynamics completely. She wouldn't be fooled by dismissive laughter this time. So he did what he always did when in need of a distraction.

He threw himself into work.

Not that his book was work, technically, more a labour of love. Anecdotes and snapshots and tales gathered over the years when he'd been an adrenaline junkie, chasing the next thrill. Breaking his leg in a skydiving accident wouldn't have been a big deal in itself but narrowly avoiding death a few days later had shaken him to his core.

The fact he'd known the people who'd died right in front of his eyes in the accident had changed him. He hadn't known the three young abseilers well, but he'd climbed with them on several trips through Europe and they'd been good people—two guys and a girl in their early twenties with stars in their eyes and adventure thrumming through their veins.

He should've been in the car that had got totalled by a driver who'd taken a bend too fast and smashed into them head-on. But the girl in his crew had taken a shine to one of the guys and she'd asked him to swap out. He'd teased her about it at the time, warning against guys with wanderlust who'd break her heart. Ten minutes later, that erratic driver had broken her body along with everybody else's who'd been in the car. Three young lives wiped out, just like that.

The accident had happened almost six years ago and not a day went by that he didn't hear the screech of brakes, the impact of metal on metal, and see the fireball explode before his eyes.

He'd had a lucky escape that day on a mountainside in Spain and it had changed his outlook. He'd finished his psychology degree, combined his love of travel with life coaching and never looked back. Chasing the next high on a mountain had turned into finding it in the arms of a beautiful woman, losing himself in sex, blotting out memories he'd rather forget.

That was the last time he'd spoken to his gran, not

long after the accident, when he'd called her to...what? Mend fences? Tell her he wished things were different? To touch base with the only family he had? He'd mentioned the broken leg and she'd lectured him about the foolishness of indulging in ridiculous pastimes, before hustling him off the phone like she had more important things to do. He hadn't had a chance to tell her about narrowly missing death. Then again, would she have cared?

The fact she hadn't reached out to him since spoke volumes so he'd given up contacting her out of obligation. She didn't care about him, probably never had. But to put the past to rest once and for all he would visit her while he was in Sydney. His emotional reaction to seeing her through the window at the house last night reinforced it.

His phone buzzed with an incoming message and he glanced at the screen, his heart giving a weird little kick when he saw Polly's name pop up.

U busy? This morning @ work has kicked my butt. Would luv 2 escape office and have lunch.

He shouldn't. It was too soon after last night. But he found himself snatching up the phone and tapping a response with his thumb.

C U @ one?

Her response came quickly.

GR8. Meet U out front @ Sizzle

She didn't want him coming in? Interesting. Then again, if he could avoid a run-in with her cow of a boss it would be a good thing. Polly was the sweetest, smartest woman he knew and she didn't deserve to be treated the way her boss treated her. He hadn't intended on doing any speaking gigs while he was in Sydney but he'd make damn sure he kicked ass at Sizzle's fundraiser so Polly could ram it down her boss's throat.

After riffling through more information for the book, he realised the task he'd assigned Polly was bigger than he'd anticipated. There was a lot of sorting to do before he would be ready to sit down and start structuring the book, and considering all he had to do was give a speech at a fundraiser Polly had definitely got the worse deal.

It took him thirty minutes to reach Sizzle's offices and as he pulled into a parking space he spied Polly standing out front. She clutched a giant black bag to her chest like a shield and he hoped it wasn't as protection against him.

Then again, he had treated her pretty shabbily last night. She'd done nothing but ask simple questions. It wasn't her fault the complex answers made his chest ache with regret.

Determined to keep conversation over lunch lighthearted, he locked the car and strode towards her. Her first reaction when she saw him would tell him a lot about how she felt about last night.

She glanced to the right at that moment, caught sight of him, and waved, a welcoming smile on her face and he exhaled in relief, unaware he'd been holding his breath.

Of course she'd be okay. In all his travels he'd never met anyone quite like Polly Scanlon: warm-hearted, genuine, with a dry wit beneath her deliberately plain exterior. She was pretty yet played down her assets and he'd always wondered why.

'Hey, Pol.'

He touched her arm and leaned down to kiss her cheek. It was a remarkably staid gesture considering what they'd done up against the wall in her apartment and in that lingerie store's dressing room. 'Ready for lunch?'

'You have no idea how ready,' she said, glancing over her shoulder at the entrance. 'Get me out of here, pronto.'

'Bad morning?'

It seemed the most natural thing in the world to take hold of her hand, the gesture surprising her by the slight widening of her eyes.

'You could say that.' She grimaced. 'There's a trendy café around the corner from here. One of their giant chicken schnitzel focaccias will go some way to soothing my soul, then I'll tell you all about it.'

'Deal.' He squeezed her hand as they fell into step. 'I'm glad you asked me to lunch.'

A cheeky glint lit her eyes. 'That's what friends who *date* do, right?'

'Right,' he said, joining in her chuckles, grateful she was making this so easy for him.

She wouldn't rehash last night, she was too clever

for that, and it made him even more thankful for their friendship and the ease with which they'd slipped into something more.

They'd barely rounded the end of the block when he spied a café with wrought-iron chairs and tables filling every inch of the sidewalk. 'This it?'

'Yeah, though I'd rather sit inside.'

'Why?'

'Because if I see Andrina walk past I may be tempted to hit her over the head with one of those chairs.'

'Okay then, inside it is,' he said, biting back a grin at her bristling indignation. She looked incredibly cute with her face flushed and her mouth pursed in disapproval.

Thankfully, there were three empty tables for two tucked into the back of the café and they made a bee-line for the one furthest away. 'This okay?'

'Perfect.' She semi-collapsed onto a seat and dumped her bag on the floor.

'Want a coffee to go with that focaccia?'

'Make it a chocolate milkshake and I'm yours,' she said, her shoulders slumping as if an invisible weight rested there.

'Pity a place like this doesn't stock brandy.'

'I need to start carrying around a hip flask if I keep working at Sizzle.'

Her mouth turned down and the urge to march back to Sizzle and give that uppity Andrina a piece of his mind was strong.

'Offloading to me will be better than alcohol, trust

me.' He winked and headed to the counter to place their order. As the waitress rang up it up, he glanced over his shoulder to find Polly resting her chin in her hands and staring at the far wall. She looked forlorn and nothing like her usual upbeat self. Damn that Andrina woman.

After paying and taking a number, he made his way back to the table, hoping he could cheer her up. He didn't do deep and meaningful conversations as a rule. Moving around a lot, living on the road, didn't breed close friendships and the adrenaline junkie crowd he used to hang with would spend their downtime boasting about exploits or watching extreme sports online rather than talk. And he never let the women he briefly dated get close enough to want to open up to him.

But seeing Polly so morose stabbed at something deep inside and he found he wanted to make it better for her.

When he resumed his seat, she straightened and lowered her elbows from the table, but her posture remained defeated.

'Tell me what the she-devil did.'

'Rehashing it will only make me feel bad all over again,' she muttered, with a shrug. 'Though it might help to get it off my chest.'

'I'm all for getting things off your chest, especially if it's your bra,' he deadpanned, relieved when she laughed.

'That is so lame.'

'Yet it had the desired effect.' He reached across the table and traced the curve of her lips. 'Your smile is gorgeous.'

'Thanks.' Her smile widened as she swatted his hand away. 'You wouldn't know this, but you always had the ability to cheer me up when I was a kid too.'

'Really?'

This was news to him, considering she had seemed perfectly happy back then. Serious, and a bookworm, but happy. He'd rarely picked up on any sadness.

'Yeah. Your infernal teasing would snap me out of whatever funk I was in, and it looks like that hasn't changed.'

He snapped his fingers. 'So that's what this lunch invitation was about. You don't want me for my body, you want me for my sense of humour.'

A blush stole into her cheeks, alleviating the paleness he hadn't liked earlier. 'I think you know exactly how much I want your body.'

'Still nice to hear you reiterate it.' He winked again and snagged her hand across the table. 'We need to go out on a date.'

He'd given her the perfect opportunity to broach the subject of last night and how he'd screwed up, but once again she'd put him first and didn't take it.

'By date you mean taking me up against the wall again, right?'

His cock hardened at the memory and his hand snaked under the table to rest on her thigh. 'That will definitely be happening, but I thought it might be nice to do the real thing too.'

He didn't like how her eyes narrowed in suspicion. 'You don't have to do that. I'm not expecting all that romantic rubbish.' A faint blush stained her cheeks and he wanted to nibble it away. 'I'm fine with our original version of "dating".'

Usually, this would be Ryder's idea of the perfect woman. No expectations. Great fucking. No complications. But he'd known Polly for a long time so taking her out for a meal seemed natural.

'Pol, if we're going to *date* all night, we need to keep up our strength, and there's nothing wrong with two old friends sharing a casual meal.'

She worried her bottom lip, an innocuous gesture that had his cock straining. 'I can do casual. What did you have in mind?'

'Hmm…' He tapped his bottom lip, pretending to think, when in fact he knew the perfect place, something she'd loved as a kid and he hoped she still did. 'Are you free tonight?'

Some of the light in her eyes died. 'I will be, if the boss from hell doesn't dump another shitload of work on me.'

'Tell me if she does and I'll drop a hint or two that if she doesn't lighten up on you I won't be speaking at her precious bloody fundraiser.'

'You can't do that; she'll think I'm some kind of tattletale.'

'Too damn bad, she's a slavedriver and a nasty piece of work.'

'Work being the operative word.' Polly groaned and slumped back in her seat. 'I'm not sure if she's trying to test me or to get me to leave so she doesn't have to stick to her promise of hearing me pitch for a permanent position at the end of the three months, but whatever she's doing she's driving me nuts.'

'So how was this morning any different?'

'One of the designers had a meltdown and quit, then a shipment from Milan went AWOL, and somehow both were my fault and I have to resolve it or else.' She toyed with the sugar sachets, rearranging them within their circular holder. 'I know she'll cool down later—she always does—but she has unrealistic expectations and I'm starting to believe the rumours.'

'What rumours?'

'That she goes through a new PA every few months, and that's despite the cachet of working at Sydney's leading fashion house.' She sighed. 'I'm going to stick it out because I know I can make a difference to their bottom line once I move away from PA and into the role I covet, but one more morning like today and...'

She made a slitting action across her throat. 'Andrina may find herself extracting a wire coat hanger from an orifice where it doesn't belong.'

He laughed and after a few moments she joined in.

'You are the strongest person I know, Pol.' He leaned over to brush his knuckles down her cheek. 'You can do this. I believe in you.'

'Now you're going all life coach on me,' she said, but her eyes had lost the haunted look.

The waitress arrived with their order, a Greek salad for him, focaccia for her, with two chocolate milkshakes.

She waited until the waitress left before pointing at his salad and smirking. 'Girly food?'

He pretended to be offended. 'I treat my body as a temple.'

A sly expression crossed her face. 'As long as I get to worship at it, eat all the rabbit food you like.'

He laughed, loving her sense of humour. 'At the risk of souring the mood, I need to know details about the fundraiser so I can tailor my speech accordingly. What's it for and how long do you want me to speak?'

'As long as we're not discussing Andrina I'm fine.' She took a slurp of milkshake and visibly brightened. 'There is absolutely nothing that a good chocolate hit can't fix.'

She took another sip before continuing. 'The charity supplies clothes and essentials to women and children who are victims of domestic abuse. Often they've been forced to flee their homes with nothing but what they're wearing, so the charity provides them with a new wardrobe, toiletries, that kind of thing.'

'A worthy cause,' he said. 'Can I give a cash donation too?'

'Absolutely.'

The admiration in her gaze made him feel like an all-conquering giant-slayer.

'As for your speech, you're the keynote speaker, but it doesn't have to be long. Maybe fifteen minutes?'

'Done,' he said. 'Any particular topic?'

'You're the expert, choose whatever you like, as long as it's inspirational.'

Ryder had given motivational speeches all around the world to various groups over the last few years but he'd never felt the pressure to perform as much as he did now. Polly made him want to be a better man, but he couldn't tell her that. Fucking between friends didn't foster heartfelt declarations. It would only lead to complications when he walked away at the end.

'Can I ask you something?'

Shit. She'd lulled him into a false sense of security. If she started rehashing last night, this wouldn't go well.

'Yeah.' He sounded hesitant and they both knew it.

'Why life coaching?' She picked at a piece of lettuce poking out from the end of her focaccia. 'You were jumping out of planes and scaling cliffs one minute, the next you busted your leg and completed your psychology degree.'

'So Archie told you about the leg?'

A faint pink stained her cheeks. 'I used to ask about you. We're all friends, you know.'

He wanted to tell her about the accident and how it had changed him. He wanted to tell her about the on-going nightmares and the implications of witnessing something so horrific and the never-ending guilt that he should've been in that car. He wanted to tell her about the anger, the unexpected bouts of rage at the injustice of being robbed of his passion and having to find new ways to get his adrenaline fix—most of them involving frequent sex with different women.

But he couldn't. On the heels of last night's revelations about his upbringing, it would only lead to more questions and he couldn't face that, not from her. Polly was uncomplicated and that was what he craved right now, a brief interlude that would clear his mind and remind him of the good of home to sustain him wherever his travels took him next.

'Rehab for the leg took longer than expected, I got bored, so I decided to finish my degree.'

'And leave the life of an adrenaline junkie behind?'

'The leg has never been the same so I didn't want to risk it. Not from any fear for myself but if you're on a mountain or out on the sea, not being fully fit can put other people in danger and I didn't want to do that.'

It was a valid, trite response she approved of if the understanding in her eyes was any indication, but a broken leg had been the least of his problems back then. Bones healed, scarred psyches not so much.

'Life coaching presents challenges of a different kind,' he said, stabbing at a cherry tomato and spearing an olive. 'I never expected to enjoy it as much as I do.'

'You're lucky.' She sighed. 'I'd give anything to do a job I love and I'm hoping that by suffering through three months of Andrina's torture I'll get the opportunity.'

He hated to be a downer, but it had to be said. 'Won't that mean you'll still be working with her? Is that what you really want?'

'Moving into the financial side of things, using my statistical knowledge to improve the company's bottom line, will garner a hell of a lot more respect from her than being her lackey.' She snapped her fingers. 'And I won't have to do what she says. I'll have a different boss. A sane one.'

He chuckled and held up his hands. 'Fine, as long as you've thought this through. Because that woman scares the hell out of me and working in the same building as her would be too close in my opinion.'

'I have to give it a go,' she said, hoisting her milkshake glass. 'To following dreams.'

'To following dreams,' he echoed, tapping his glass against hers, leaning across the table to murmur, 'Especially raunchy dreams involving you and me naked.'

A crimson blush stained her cheeks. 'You cut last night short and it left me…'

'Horny?' he supplied helpfully, and she nodded, her eyes gleaming with excitement. 'After dinner tonight, I think I can help you out with that.'

She lifted her chin and eyeballed him. 'Why wait until then?'

His cock had subsided to half-mast during their chatter and it surged to life in a big way at her innuendo. 'What did you have in mind?'

'This is mostly an industrial area but there's a motel not far, probably for overseas workers who come to consult.' Her blush intensified. 'Or maybe for horny people like us who can't wait until tonight?'

Man, she blew him away. He never would've expected prim Polly would be up for an hour of afternoon delight in a motel.

'How fast can you eat?' He pointed at her focaccia.

'We can take our meals to go.' Her tongue flicked out to moisten her bottom lip and he gritted his teeth against the urge to splay her across the table and feast on her.

'I'm not hungry any more.' He snagged her hand and brushed his thumb across her pulse point, over and over. 'At least, not for food.'

She made an odd noise, half moan, half choke. 'Let's go.'

CHAPTER THIRTEEN

POLLY HAD FELT way too comfortable opening up to Ryder while they'd waited for their lunch. He was a good listener and unburdening herself regarding her job fears had made her feel...cherished.

Which was exactly why she'd proposed they visit this motel with its rooms-by-the-hour policy.

She needed to reinforce that they were about sex, and misreading his attention for anything more was setting herself up for disaster.

She had to focus on the physical. Not such a hardship considering the dove-grey T-shirt moulding to his chest, the hip-hugging faded denim and those eyes that scorched her with a single glance.

However, wanting to show Ryder she predominantly wanted him for his body hit a snag when they entered room six at the nondescript motel wedged between a foam factory on one side and an industrial warehouse on the other.

'You sure about this?' Ryder was propped in the doorway alongside her, surveying the room, his disbelief audible.

Everything in the entire room was the colour of baby poo, an ugly mustard that hurt the eyes. The worn carpet, the faded wallpaper, a pilled bedspread— everything was awful and by the looks of the dip in the centre of the bed no way would Polly be going anywhere near it.

But the room had one thing going for it. A sturdy desk—the only clean-looking furniture in the place. It had potential.

'Come on, Pol, we can go back to my place after dinner tonight.' He placed his hand in the small of her back to guide her outside but she baulked.

She knew how tonight would play out. Dinner would be a repeat of lunch where they'd chat and laugh and grow closer, creating a false illusion of a relationship he didn't want. He'd made that abundantly clear and sex after a dinner like that would reek of intimacy.

The thought alone was enough to propel her forward into the room. She headed toward the desk and tapped it. 'Where's your sense of adventure?'

He hesitated, hovering in the doorway like he wanted to turn tail and run, so she took the decision out of his hands by sliding the top button of her black blouse through its hole, and the next, tugging the lapels open so he could catch a glimpse of burgundy lace.

His eyes widened. 'You're wearing the lingerie I chose?'

'Why don't you come over here and find out?'

In her most brazen move yet, she rested a foot on

the chair in front of the desk, making her skirt ruck up, exposing the lacy crotch.

'You're just full of surprises,' he muttered, finally stepping into the room and slamming the door.

'That's what happens when you underestimate someone,' she said, managing to sound pragmatic and breathy at the same time as she popped the press-studs on the bodysuit's crotch and peeled the lace away. 'But as an FYI, I'm not going anywhere near that bed so you can do me here on the desk or not at all.'

The corners of his mouth quirked as he advanced towards her. '*Do* you?'

'You got a problem with my quaint language?' She settled back onto the desk, splaying her thighs wide this time, giving him a view of how badly she wanted him.

His gaze zeroed in on her pussy. 'Fuck, Pol, you are something else.'

Feigning bravado, she tilted her chin up. 'Show me.'

It had only been forty-eight hours since Ryder Beale had strutted back into her life and she knew all the self-talk in the world that this thing between them would remain just sex was BS.

She wanted him for more than his body. Yet he'd made it perfectly clear that was all she could ever have.

Time to start taking advantage of it.

Her eyes never left his until he stood in front of her, between her thighs. He touched her, swiping a finger through her slick folds, sending a shock through her.

She spread her legs wider and flung her head back, giving herself over to the pleasure of having him touch her. When his tongue replaced his finger, she moaned, vibrations of lust rippling over her.

His tongue swiped her pussy over and over, slow, languorous strokes that stoked her desire quickly. He delved deeper, using his fingers and tongue in sync, consuming her until she couldn't breathe, couldn't think, a moment before her muscles tensed and her orgasm crashed over her.

He didn't give her time to recover and she didn't want it, barely aware of the tearing of foil before he was inside her, full and thick, filling her.

He claimed her mouth, nipping her bottom lip, sucking on it like he'd sucked on her clit a moment ago, and she tasted herself and the chocolate milkshake he'd had at lunch as he deepened the kiss.

Cupping her ass, he dragged her to the edge of the desk, changing the angle of his dick sliding in, setting her nerve endings alight.

She broke the kiss, wanting to watch him fuck her, a reminder of what they were about. Placing her hands on the desk behind her, she eyeballed him, daring him to drive them both towards cataclysmic oblivion.

As if sensing her need for raw sex, he gripped her thighs and drove into her, hard.

She gasped, murmured, 'More,' and he obliged, thrusting into her over and over, driving her to the edge.

When she circled her legs around his waist, his cock hit the sweet spot inside her and she gave herself over to the power of another breath-stealing orgasm that sent aftershocks through her.

He came a moment later, grunting her name, and in that moment she knew this was exactly what she'd needed: a potent reminder of what they were together. Combustible. Wanton. Hedonistic.

It would have to be enough.

CHAPTER FOURTEEN

As POLLY LEANED back on her elbows, surveying the shimmering azure of Sydney Harbour and watching mauve, sienna and pink streak the sky as the sun dipped towards the horizon, she felt like she'd entered some kind of alternate universe.

She didn't go on sunset picnics in the Royal Botanic Gardens with a gorgeous guy unpacking all her favourite foods, a guy who had a decidedly wicked glint in his eyes signalling he wanted her for dessert.

She didn't feel gorgeous and wanton in her plain denim knee-length skirt and blue singlet top.

She didn't envisage asking the guy back to her place to spend the night.

But this *was* happening to her and she resisted the urge to pinch herself.

It made her wonder: what would've happened if she'd revealed her crush to Ryder years ago.

Probably nothing, considering the minute he'd finished school he'd hit the road and hadn't looked back, while she'd been a studious sixteen-year-old wishing she were two years older and could go with him. It was wistful thinking, because she never would've done something like that. She'd had plans to go to university and she'd followed through. Chasing after Ryder on a whim would've been beyond foolish and she never did impulsive things.

After he'd left he'd popped home regularly for the first few years and she'd yearned for him even more as he acquired a worldliness she could never hope to emulate. He'd treated her the same though, teasing, taunting, driving her insane, and she'd reciprocated.

She'd never indulged in spontaneous actions back then. Now? The memory of their motel antics that afternoon made her flush from head to foot. She'd never been so bold but they were still worlds apart in savviness. He'd travelled all over the world; she'd never left Sydney. He'd conquered mountains; she was lucky if she conquered a step class once a month. He inspired people for a living; she loved juggling figures and avoiding awkward conversations.

They were true opposites in every way but one, which was why she intended to drag him back to her place later to have her wicked way with him.

Her impulsiveness this afternoon, along with the resultant sex in that motel, had empowered her like nothing else. She liked this strong, invincible version of herself, even if it was only for a short time. She intended to make every second count.

'Cider?' He held out a glass to her and she took it, smiling her thanks as she surveyed the spread he'd laid out, stunned he'd remembered all her favourites.

Camembert, rosemary crackers, dolmades, prosciutto, stuffed baby bell peppers, along with jam doughnuts, caramel swirl chocolates and Turkish delight for dessert.

'I can't believe all this,' she said, emotion unexpectedly clogging her throat. 'How did you remember? I mean, back then you and Archie would fall on any food Mum served...'

'This was the birthday feast you requested Babs serve for your fifteenth,' he said, tapping his temple. 'I guess I have a memory for trivial stuff.'

But it wasn't trivial, not to her, and the fact he'd remembered every one of the foods she loved reinforced why she had to focus on the sex. Because thoughtful stuff like this had the power to undo her.

For a fanciful moment, she wondered if this gesture meant he'd liked her as much as she'd liked him back then. Before reality intruded: more than likely his crappy home life had ensured whatever happened at their place stuck in his head.

Though she wouldn't make the mistake of asking about that again, not after the way he'd shut down last night. She had no intention of cutting this evening short. Not when she was wearing the blue satin bra and panties he'd picked out beneath her plain skirt and singlet.

'This is incredible, thank you,' she said, pushing off her elbows so she could lean up and give him a kiss.

'You deserve all the good things in life, Pol.' He captured her chin and stared into her eyes, trying to convey a message she had no hope of understanding.

The intensity of his stare, like he wanted to say more but couldn't find the words, left her reeling.

Ryder wasn't a keeper. He'd warned her off expecting anything more. He was her friend, who she was mucking around with. And while this may be the most romantic date she'd ever been on, she was under no illusions. He probably wanted to make up for last night and she was more than willing to let him. They had to keep things light and away from fraught topics like their pasts.

Starting now.

'You know what would take this evening to the next level?'

He wiggled his eyebrows suggestively. 'What?'

'You taking me up against a tree.'

'You are bad.' He brushed his lips against hers, slow and sensual, a promise of more. Her skin tingled as his fingertips skated down her arm, a feather-light touch that had her moaning a little.

But as she pressed her mouth harder against his, he eased away with a soft 'Tut-tut.'

'We're in a public place, Pol, and I'm hard for you, so please don't torture me.'

Her gaze dropped to his lap, where he'd strategically draped a napkin. 'Why not, when it's so much fun?'

He waggled a finger at her impish smile. 'You're driving me insane.'

'Good,' she murmured, with an exaggerated lick of her lips. 'I plan on torturing you plenty later.'

'Is that so?'

'Oh, yeah.' She rested her hand on his thigh and the napkin twitched.

With her free hand, she edged a singlet strap to one

side, revealing a hint of bra and his gaze was riveted to it in an instant.

'Fuck, you're wearing that sexy get-up?'

'Just for you, baby.' She readjusted the strap and patted his cheek. 'So how fast can you serve me this delicious food?'

'Eat. Now,' he growled, as he began plonking a bit of everything on a paper plate, and she laughed as half of it slid off in his haste.

'Let me.' She laid a steadying hand on his, picking up some of the morsels and popping them directly into her mouth.

His muffled groan had her eating faster.

'Watching you eat is such a fucking turn-on.'

'Maybe you should eat too?'

She picked up a stuffed bell pepper and brought it to his lips, and as he opened his mouth she popped it in, letting her fingertips linger for a moment. He licked them and it was her turn to squirm.

'As much as I enjoyed this afternoon's motel surprise, I'd intended on taking things slow tonight but this foreplay is killing me,' he said, picking up a chocolate and dragging it across her lips. 'In a good way.'

The chocolate melted on contact with her tongue and she swirled it over the tip of his thumb, sucking it deeper into her mouth.

Lust blazed in his eyes as he withdrew it and scooted back a fraction. 'I will not be arrested in my favourite park in Sydney on my first trip back in years,' he said, his voice low and gravelly.

'Though it could be kind of fun if I get to use the

handcuffs on you,' she said sweetly, snaffling a piece of Turkish Delight and lifting it to her mouth where she licked the icing sugar off it with small darts of her tongue.

He gritted his teeth so hard his jaw jutted, his gaze riveted to her mouth while he started flinging food back into the cooler.

'What are you doing? I haven't finished—'

'We're done,' he said. 'I've had enough of this harbour view. I fancy an indoor picnic instead.'

He leaned over to whisper in her ear, 'I'm going to snack on all this after I've eaten you.'

Her belly flipped and heat pooled between her legs.

With her heart thundering so loudly she could've sworn she heard the echo in her ears, she murmured, 'Hurry.'

CHAPTER FIFTEEN

RYDER HAD GRAND plans to feast off Polly's body once they got back to her place, yet once again they barely made it through the front door when they pounced on each other.

But he had to see her in that satin blue lingerie so he stilled her frantic hands as she tore his shirt out of his jeans.

'As much as I want to take you up against this wall again, I want to take things slower this time.'

She made a cute little scoff of frustration. 'Slow is overrated.'

'I'll make it worth your while,' he murmured, backing her towards the tiny lounge room. 'Promise.'

'Okay,' she said with a shrug, before pushing him down onto the sofa with surprising force. 'I'm assuming you want to see this?'

With a surprisingly deft move she peeled her singlet over her head, and gave it a swing before flinging it away. That left her sizeable C cups spilling over the top of the flimsy blue satin bra.

'Fuck,' he muttered, linking his hands behind his head, determined to enjoy the show she was putting on.

He never would've picked Polly to be an extrovert in the bedroom. Then again, he'd often wondered if she'd be a firecracker beneath her prim exterior.

They'd swapped banter for so long, had virtually grown up together, but never in his wildest dreams had he anticipated being privy to this beautiful woman's sexual revolution.

Because that was what it felt like: she was taking control and loving every minute of it. The sex on the desk in that seedy motel had blown his mind. Not that he knew much about her sexual history, but Archie had once mentioned that she rarely dated. As if a brother would know much about that kind of thing anyway. But Ryder loved taking a front seat to her sexy show, watching the girl he'd once known become the woman wielding her sexuality with power.

'You're staring at me,' she said, a coy smile playing about her mouth as she cocked her hip.

'Because I'm enjoying the strip show.' He lowered his hands from behind his head and sat forward. 'Seriously, Pol, you're sexy as fuck.'

'But it's just a bra.'

He laughed at her deadpan joke. 'It's all you.'

Colour suffused her cheeks and spread lower, down her neck and into her chest. And he instantly wondered if her being in the throes of passion would have the same effect.

'You're just sexed up from this afternoon and want more of this.' She unzipped her denim skirt, pushed it over her hips and let it fall to the floor before kicking it away. 'There. You can sit there drooling or you can do something about it.'

As expected, she rocked the blue satin combo in a big way. And her body... Curves he itched to get his hands on. Light olive skin dusted with freckles. Smooth. Tempting.

He stood so fast she gave a little squeal, and they laughed together as he snagged her hand and tugged her flush against him.

His cock throbbed with the contact but he wanted to make this first time tonight all about her, so he guided her down onto the sofa and knelt in front of her.

Her eyes widened with carnal knowledge as he nudged her knees apart and tugged on the back of them, bringing her closer to the edge.

'As much as I love those panties on you, they're coming off. Now.'

'Fine,' she said, lifting her butt so he could wriggle them down. 'I like it when you're all alpha male.'

He liked looking at her, slick with wanting him.

'You'll like this more.'

He licked her pussy with his tongue, sliding his hands under her butt to lift her closer to his mouth. She glistened, so good, so inviting... He licked her again, deeper this time, thrusting his tongue inside her. Over and over, her soft moans driving him wild.

'Ryder...yeah...so good,' she whispered, her hand resting on his head, her fingers tugging at his hair as he grazed her clit with his teeth. 'More...'

He wanted more too so he started lapping at her clit, savouring her muskiness, teasing her by alternating the pace. Slow and fast. Again and again until her hips started moving of their own volition and she thrust towards his mouth.

Her butt tensed in his hands as he sucked at her clit, hard, and she came apart on a primal yell that made him want to do it all over again right this fucking second.

She trembled as he slid his hands out from under her, already reaching for a condom in his back pocket. He'd packed several more in the cooler, hoping for a big night.

Dazed, she watched him get naked and sheathed in record time, but when he reached for her she shook her head.

'You sit. I get to be on top.'

'Fuck yeah,' he said, doing as he was told, loving the confident way she straddled him.

But she didn't lower herself. Instead, she slid her hands around the back and unhooked her bra, flinging it away to leave her breasts right in front of his face. Big nipples. Pale pink areolas. Perfect.

With a groan, he leaned forward and took a nipple into his mouth, laving it with his tongue while rolling the other between his thumb and forefinger. He loved how she tasted—sweet, somehow. As he swiped at her skin with his tongue, moving from one nipple to the other, she lowered herself onto him, one exquisite, torturous inch at a time. Encasing him in velvet heat.

She eased his head away and anchored her hands on his shoulders. 'I want to see you.'

He nodded, mute, as she started to ride him. Up and

down. With no thought for taking it slow but with sheer abandon, a woman in control, seeking her pleasure.

Biggest fucking turn-on ever.

He rested his hands on her hips but she set the pace and he revelled in seeing her get off the way she wanted to.

As she rode him faster, harder, the tension in his back intensified and his balls tightened. And as she let go, head flung back, he did the same, thrusting into her with so much force it felt like his head would explode.

When she slumped forward onto him, he took all her weight and wrapped his arms around her waist.

This felt so good...so right...

But it couldn't last. He couldn't think this way.

So he did the one thing guaranteed to get them back on track.

Releasing her, he eased away and eyed her with a cocky grin. 'Are we ever going to make it to your bedroom?'

CHAPTER SIXTEEN

IT HAD BEEN four long days since Ryder had spent the night at Polly's place, ninety-six hours since she'd come to the startling realisation this thing between them could be more than sex.

Logically, she knew it couldn't be anything more than a fling. She'd dealt with cold, hard facts for years and that meant she should be counting down the days until he left. And he would, there was no doubt. She understood why, too.

For years, she'd avoided researching Ryder online because she didn't want to see him living the high life—or who he was living it with. It was stupid enough having a crush on her brother's best friend and hearing tales via Archie, but seeing firsthand evidence would've exacerbated her feeling of inadequacy that someone like her could never be enough for a guy like him.

But with the fundraiser coming up she needed to ensure the promotion for their keynote speaker was accurate, and that meant researching Ryder.

She'd avoided it the last few days, ever since she'd

woken before him to find him sprawled in her bed and looking like he belonged there. She'd studied him, how even in sleep, with one hand under his head and the other resting on his ripped abdomen, his ridiculously handsome features slack, he looked like the hottest guy on the planet. He made sexy look effortless, while she resorted to lingerie to make her feel one tenth as wicked.

It had happened while she'd been studying him...the insidious feeling of wanting him in her bed for longer than a night. And when he'd woken and they'd had sex for the fourth time before he'd stood beside her in the kitchen helping whip up scrambled eggs, that feeling had intensified until her throat had ached with holding back the words: 'I like you beyond the sex and I want more.'

The realisation had been enough to make her bundle him out of her tiny apartment as soon as he'd finished eating and she'd cited a heavy workload to avoid seeing him since.

It wasn't a lie entirely, considering the fundraiser was taking up all her time. But now she had to proof-read the advertising for Ryder and that meant immersing herself in his world online.

The marketing junior had done a good job building him up, citing him as a world-class speaker and renowned life coach who'd faced adversity and inspired people with his tales.

The woman who had a major crush on him wanted to square her shoulders with pride at his achievements, but her logical side was curious: what had he done to deserve the accolades?

Intrigued, she typed *Ryder Beale* into a search engine and watched the hits pop up. Hundreds of thousands of them. Stunned, she scrolled through a few until one caught her eye, titled *Cheating Death*.

She clicked on the article from an extreme sports website and read. Incredulous, she read it twice to make sure she'd got the gist of it.

So that was why Ryder had changed his life after the broken leg. Nothing to do with a fractured femur and everything to do with witnessing a horrendous, fatal accident involving a car he should've been in.

Slumping in her chair, Polly blinked, surprised to find her eyes moist. Why hadn't Ryder discussed this with Archie? Or had he, and Archie had never told her? It irked that they'd reconnected this week yet Ryder hadn't mentioned this to her. Then again, scorching sex didn't encourage intimate revelations and the one time she'd dug deeper about his gran he'd clammed up.

Going through something so traumatic... He hadn't been home to Sydney since the broken leg but maybe that had more to do with the accident? Had he experienced survivor's guilt? Was the accident the catalyst behind him completing his psychology degree and turning to life coaching?

So many questions she wanted to ask him, but after the way he'd shut down on her when she'd probed into his family background, she doubted she'd get the answers she wanted.

So for the next hour she read many articles, learning

more about the man she'd fallen for. He'd been hired by people around the world, from major sporting organisations to mega corporations, to provide life coaching. He'd presented at symposiums and conferences, and had garnered quite a reputation in the field. Little wonder he'd been offered a book deal. Readers lapped up this stuff, with 'key to happiness' books hitting bestseller charts regularly at the moment.

No great surprise that in times of political and financial turmoil, people wanted to feel good about themselves. And boy, did Ryder make her feel good. But as she compared the articles with the promotion the junior office girls had done for him as the keynote speaker at the Sizzle fundraiser, she wondered what really made the enigmatic man tick.

Acting on a whim, she picked up the phone and called Archie. He answered after seven rings, which meant he was neck-deep in renovations and wouldn't welcome the interruption.

'Hey, sis. What's up?'

She heard the whir of a circular saw winding down in the background. 'Caught you at a bad time?'

'Every bloody day is a bad time,' he said. 'If I ever mention the *R* word again, hit me over the head with a mallet.'

'You love renovating.'

He snorted. 'As much as I like having you give me a pep talk. Is this urgent? Because I need to get back to butchering this wood.'

'Not urgent,' she said, wishing she'd never rung him. The moment she mentioned Ryder's name he'd know she was asking questions for more than work purposes. Archie knew her better than she knew herself. He'd picked up on her moroseness when their mum had favoured him and he'd do whatever it took to cheer her up—usually buying her a new paranormal novel but still, it was the effort that counted. 'But Ryder's doing a speech at Sizzle's fundraiser and I wanted to make sure the advertising copy is right.'

'What do you want to know?'

Here went nothing. 'Did he tell you about the car accident he nearly died in not long after he broke his leg?'

'Yeah, he mentioned something about it, but he didn't make it sound like a big deal. Why?'

Her palms grew clammy at the thought of how close Ryder had come to being in that car and she gripped the phone tighter so it wouldn't slip out of her grasp. 'I'm doing research to make sure we introduce him correctly at the fundraiser, and came across an article that said he'd cheated death because he should've been in that car.'

'Shit. Really?'

Her heart sank. If Ryder hadn't mentioned it to Archie, there was no way she could bring it up with him. 'That's what the article said, yeah.'

'Wonder why he never told me?'

'I guess guys don't talk about deep stuff,' she said, wondering if Archie picked up on how hollow her response sounded.

If Ryder wanted to offload to anyone about what he'd been through, Archie would've been his go-to person. The fact Ryder hadn't confided in Archie meant he didn't want them to know about it, but why? They could've found out about it any time by looking him up online so why hide it?

Or was she making too much of this and Ryder had omitted to tell Archie because it wasn't a big deal?

'Is that all, sis? Because I really need to get back to this so I can make it to the hardware store before closing.'

'Yeah, that's it.'

Archie paused and cleared his throat. 'Ryder's a pretty private guy when he wants to be, so my advice is to leave this alone. It could be a simple oversight on his part or we were too busy spinning shit at the time to talk about the deep stuff. But if you and Ryder are getting along, don't nose around too much. He hates it.'

She'd already found that out the hard way. 'Thanks, Arch.'

'No worries.'

He rung off, leaving her staring at the phone and contemplating exactly how far she should delve. Because despite her brother's advice she knew she couldn't let this go. She may have deluded herself into thinking Ryder was just some guy to have a fling with, a string of one-night stands that wouldn't matter once he left, but he was a friend first and foremost. She needed to know more, but she was damned if she could come up with an unobtrusive way of doing it.

CHAPTER SEVENTEEN

RYDER HAD BEEN an adrenaline junkie for most of his life and when he'd no longer been able to paraglide off a cliff or scuba dive in shark-infested waters, he'd sought his high with women. He dated, he had fun, he moved on. Women knew the score and he never deliberately misled them. And he'd certainly never do anything remotely misleading with Polly.

Which was why he currently stood outside Sizzle's offices second-guessing the wisdom in showing up here unannounced. It was a spontaneous gesture he hoped wouldn't come back to bite him on the ass.

He'd taken it at face value when she'd told him she'd been snowed under the last few days and couldn't see him. He'd seen firsthand what sort of a cow her boss was and he'd left her alone. But her short responses to his texts told a different story. She was avoiding him and he wanted to know why.

The sex had been phenomenal and usually by this stage he'd be extricating himself. A part of him had wondered if once he fucked Polly the allure would wear off, a challenge accepted and conquered. But they'd been friends for too long for him to treat her like that. Besides, he still had to do that speech for her fundraiser and it wouldn't be smart to cool things now.

With that in mind, turning up at her office on the pretext of finalising his speech for the event was a perfectly legitimate excuse. But Polly had this uncanny knack of seeing right through him and she'd know that his impromptu visit had more to do with finding out why he hadn't heard from her for days.

After their unexpected dirty afternoon at the motel, they'd spent an incredible night at her place, pleasuring each other in ways that still blew his mind. And much to his relief they hadn't been awkward with each other the next morning either. But something had changed while they'd been eating breakfast together and she'd visibly withdrawn. They hadn't been doing much—just making small talk—so it couldn't have been something he'd said, yet no matter how hard he racked his brains trying to figure out what had gone wrong he couldn't come up with a single thing.

This wasn't him, trying to figure out what made a woman tick. But this was Polly and he didn't want to hurt her. Not because of some veiled threat from Archie to dismember him if he did, but for the simple fact that she was the only woman to truly get under his skin. First as a friend, now as a lover, and he cared about her.

Inhaling deeply, he blew out a breath and strode into Sizzle. He hadn't taken much notice of the ambience the first time he'd come here, too hell-bent on saving Polly from the towering woman publicly berating her.

Now he glanced around at the sleek chrome chairs and curved front desk, the soft white backlighting on the walls and the vivid splashes of colour in the framed clothes. The place screamed hip and cosmopolitan, and far removed from any workplace in which he envisaged Polly.

Yet she desperately wanted a job here and would go to any lengths to achieve it, including put up with crap from a woman she'd usually have no compunction in dressing down—no pun intended.

Considering the way Andrina had fawned all over him the last time he'd been here, he hoped she would cut Polly some slack when he nailed the keynote speech for her precious bloody fundraiser. He intended on wowing Andrina and her crowd, who, if they were half as uppity as her, would be a tough audience.

As if thoughts of the she-devil conjured her up, Andrina stepped out from behind a plush purple curtain behind the reception desk and caught sight of him. He raised a hand in greeting and she beamed, her crimson-slicked lips ridiculously plumped by fillers.

She bore down on him, crossing the entrance foyer quickly despite her towering five-inch heels. 'Ryder Beale, what a delight.'

'Andrina.' He offered a terse nod. 'I'm here to see Polly.'

'Great, I'll take you to her office.' She touched his arm, a lingering gesture that left him wanting to take a bath. 'She's very busy with the fundraiser.'

'She's a good worker, you're lucky to have her.'

She made a face, half-grimace, half-surprise. 'Yes,

well, she's proving her worth, especially by convincing you to be our keynote speaker.'

Ryder hid his distaste for this woman with a brief smile. He knew her type. He'd met people like her all around the world, people so filled with their own self-importance they only valued others who they deemed to be on their level. Everyone else was beneath them and treated accordingly.

He hated the hypocrisy. Just because he came from a moneyed background, had built a reputation as a daredevil, then lucked into the life-coaching gig where people actually wanted to hear what he had to say, people like Andrina revered him. What would they think if they knew the truth? That he had more insecurities than most and was plagued by self-doubt on a daily basis—about his family, about the choices he'd made over the years, about everything.

'How did she convince you anyway?'

Of course she'd ask something like that. Her implication was clear. How did an unimportant subordinate warrant a visit from him, let alone secure his participation in a Sydney fundraiser when he'd commanded audiences around the world?

He decided to toy with her and hopefully teach her a lesson. 'Polly has connections everywhere and, as I'm sure you've learned, she's very hard to say no to. She's one hell of a woman.'

'Yes, well...' Andrina blustered, lost for words, and he bit back a grin.

Take that, you bossy old bat.

Thankfully, they'd arrived at Polly's office. 'I'll take

it from here,' he said, dismissing her by turning his back on her.

'Nice seeing you again, Ryder.'

He didn't respond and instead knocked on Polly's door, glad when he heard a soft 'Come in'.

Polly's startled expression had him biting back a second grin in as many seconds.

'Not pleased to see me, Pol?'

She reassembled her wits quickly, he'd give her that. While her smile appeared forced her eyes didn't lie and they glowed with warmth. 'You can't drop in like this. You'll get me fired.'

'On the contrary.' He winked and jerked a thumb over his shoulder. 'Your boss has a lady boner for me.'

She wrinkled her nose. 'Yuck. That's gross.'

'But true.' He strolled towards her desk and took a seat opposite without asking. 'Now that I'm here, aren't you going to admit you're pleased to see me?'

'But I don't lie.'

She widened her eyes in faux innocence and he laughed. Damn, he loved it when they played like this, swapping banter like the good old days.

The Scanlons had never pressured him for answers regarding his occasional foul moods, they'd never asked why he spent more time at their place than at his own, and they'd never made him feel second best, a feeling he'd grown up with every single day with his grandparents.

He couldn't pinpoint the exact moment he'd felt like a burden to his grandparents but the gnawing feeling of being unwanted and unloved had grown over the years with every harsh putdown from his grandfather until he couldn't wait to escape. While he never regretted leaving Sydney behind he did regret not spending more time with his friends once he'd escaped.

'Well, I'll say it for the both of us then,' he said. 'I missed you.'

'It's been four days.' She rolled her eyes but he saw the pleased flush in her cheeks. 'And I seriously doubt you're the pining type. You miss the sex.'

'Ouch.' He clutched at his heart in mock outrage. 'You wound me, Pol.'

'Yeah, right.' She ducked her head but he glimpsed her smile as she added, 'Hide like a freaking rhino.'

He laughed, glad that the tension of the other morning had faded away. 'How's work?'

'Good, apart from unexpected interruptions.' She sent him a pointed glare. 'Everything's ready for the fundraiser.'

She paused then glanced away, before refocussing on him with renewed purpose, like she'd come to a decision he might not like. 'I've been going over the final copy for your introduction.'

'And?'

'Why didn't you mention the accident?'

His blood chilled like it usually did when the subject of the accident was brought up, the same frostiness that enveloped him when he still woke with a start in the dead of night all these years later, hearing the screams for help of those car occupants before the ear-splitting yells faded to nothing.

'You've been doing some research.'

The statement was delivered in a monotone that earned a raised eyebrow. 'It's my job so yeah, I did. And it surprised me that you never mentioned it to Archie either.'

Fuck, he hadn't come here to be interrogated. He didn't need this shit. Rehashing the pain of the past would be nothing but detrimental.

But then he risked a glance at her face, saw the worry in her eyes, concern for him deepening the grooves bracketing her mouth, and he realised they were more alike than he'd thought.

He'd come here to find out what made her tick, to get to the bottom of her withdrawal the other morning. How was that any different?

Reaching out had nothing to do with the two of them hooking up and everything to do with friendship. If he'd come back to Sydney after the accident he would've told her about it, Archie too. But he'd distanced himself for a reason and while he wasn't quite ready to open up to her about that, he knew he had to give her something because she clearly cared.

'The accident shook me up. Badly. It took a long while to get over the guilt that I wasn't in that car when I should've been.'

He didn't need her pity but he understood her sorrowful stare.

'I read a bit about it. Will you tell me what happened?'

'A party of us had been travelling together, doing an informal extreme sports tour. When I busted my leg they stuck by me, so I decided to tag along when they headed to their next cliff. One of the girls fancied a guy in the first car, so we swapped out…' He shook his head, hating the inevitable tightening in his chest as he remembered the exact moment he had made the decision.

Jules had been her name, a boisterous South African who had never shied away from a challenge. Long blonde hair perpetually in a loose bun on top of her head, a large nose, freckles. She'd had a laugh like a braying donkey and the gang had loved it. Spontaneous, warm, adventurous, she'd be the first in line to abseil down a mountain or jump off a cliff.

She'd all but hauled him from the car that day, insisting he'd be more comfortable in the larger van and he'd laughingly agreed when she'd winked and jerked her head at the tall Swede in the front seat on whom she had a major crush.

Ten minutes later, he'd watched that car become a mangled mess, the screams of his friends obliterated in a fireball when it exploded.

'Survivor's guilt,' Polly murmured, and he nodded, the simple action making his rigid neck muscles ache.

'It messed me up, but it also changed my perspective on life.'

He hadn't stopped chasing adrenaline highs out of fear but from gratitude. Watching that fatality, seeing how close he'd come to death, had made him re-evaluate everything in his life and scaling down impossible cliffs or jumping out of planes hadn't seemed so important any more.

'So a changed perspective meant you embraced a second chance?'

'Something like that.' He shrugged, like it meant little, when his entire life had changed courtesy of a split-second decision. 'I saw a shrink for a while afterwards who helped me gain perspective, and seeing that guy work a miracle on me made me want to complete my psych degree, and with Archie's encouragement too, I did.'

She wanted to ask more. He could see it in the slightly arched brows, in the way she opened and closed her mouth. To her credit, she didn't push.

'After that, I fell into the life-coaching thing after word spread about the adrenaline-junkie-turned-nerd.'

At least, that was the version he told people. Nobody knew how hard he'd striven to get where he was today and he wanted to keep it that way.

'You've been through a lot,' she said, clasping her hands on her desk and he had the distinct impression she was interviewing him for a position he didn't want. 'I'm always here for you, if you want to talk.'

'Now who's the shrink?'

She didn't laugh at his joke. 'Seriously, Ryder. We've always been friends and when this thing between us is over I don't want you to feel like you can't talk to me any more.'

Of course their fling would end sooner rather than later. They'd both known that going in, which made it all the easier for him to assuage his guilty conscience that he was taking advantage of the situation.

But something in the way she said 'when this thing between us is over' was so matter-of-fact that it made him wish for something different for once in his life.

It was crazy, because he couldn't stay in one place for too long; it wasn't in his DNA any more. And considering the bad memories associated with his upbringing in Sydney, the harbour-side city would be the last place he'd put down roots.

But having Polly onside, having her look at him like he hung the moon and stars after opening up to her the tiniest amount, made him wonder what it would be like to come home to someone like her every day.

It was a ridiculous thought, because he knew what he was like. For him, Polly represented the ultimate challenge, a woman who'd never shown overt interest in him, who'd done her best to take him down a peg or two for most of their lives. And he knew, deep down in his gut, that now he had her he'd soon tire and move on, seeking the next challenge. It was what had driven him since the accident and he couldn't change. He didn't want to. He guessed he had his grandparents to thank for that, because not feeling worthy of a long-term relationship had stemmed from them.

No, he could never be anything more than a good fuck and a childhood friend for Polly. Imagining anything else was masochistic and he'd been through enough pain in his life already.

'Thanks for the offer, Pol, but talking is overrated,' he drawled, determined to lighten the hell up. 'Sex is better.'

He expected her to chastise him or blush or parry with one of her famous quips.

So she surprised the hell out of him when she stood and held out her hand, an eyebrow arched, her gaze brazen.

'I couldn't agree more.'

CHAPTER EIGHTEEN

RYDER WASN'T THE only one to turn escapism into a fine art.

She understood now why he hadn't come home to Sydney for the last five years. He'd been running since that heart-breaking accident and hadn't stopped.

She'd escaped feeling second best by turning to glossy magazines and had ended up bonding with her mum a little because of it.

They'd never had a close relationship but for those few hours on a Sunday afternoon when her mum would bring home the latest releases they'd sit together at the dining table or in the far corner of the backyard under a towering eucalypt and pore over the fashions and the make-up and the celebrity gossip, eagerly tearing out tiny sachets of sample perfumes or foundations.

She may not have ever dabbed those perfumes behind her ears or slathered foundation over her face, but keeping them in a small treasure box under her bed had made her feel like she had a connection with her mother, who had used both liberally.

Facts and figures grounded her but fabrics and fashion had always been her escape.

Like now.

Ryder needed a distraction, badly, and she knew just the way to provide it.

'Where are you taking me?'

'You'll see,' she said, shooting him a flirtatious glance from beneath her lashes. 'Why? Don't you trust me?'

He leaned down to murmur in her ear, 'After the filthy things you did to me at that motel and at your place later that night, I'm never trusting you again.'

She laughed and squeezed his hand. 'Lucky for you, I'm feeling particularly filthy again.'

That silenced him and as they reached a tiny storeroom at the end of a long corridor, she unlocked the door and tugged him inside.

She released his hand to lock the door and pocket the key. 'I'd planned on doing some inventory in here today so I'm the only one who has the key.'

He quickly cottoned on to the importance of her declaration, if his decidedly wicked smile was anything to go by.

'Are you saying—?'

'Yeah, I'm saying exactly that.'

She placed a hand on his chest and pushed gently, guiding him to a low-slung velvet chaise longue in the corner. It had seen better days, had probably been in the reception foyer at some stage, before being relegated to this back room. But it would be perfect for what she had in mind.

She loved this room, overcrowded to the point of stifling with random cast-offs of fabric and clothing. There was a shocking-pink taffeta ballgown that looked like something out of a Bollywood movie hanging from the ceiling, swathes of emerald-green velvet cascaded from a roll and slashes of silks in a rainbow of colours were draped over every available surface.

She hadn't lied earlier when she said she'd planned on doing inventory in here today—not because it was part of her job description but as a way to ground herself.

If Ryder hadn't shown up, she'd been in danger of going in search of him. She'd been angsty all day, wishing she hadn't been so curt in her responses to his texts, wishing she had the chutzpah to follow her heart and tell him about her burgeoning feelings.

Then, to make matters worse, he'd opened up to her, revealing more than she could've anticipated, and it had made her fall even deeper.

She needed a distraction and the one thing guaranteed to take her mind off her insane urge to spill the truth was to drag him into her favourite room and go for it.

'What is this room?'

'My go-to place.' She snatched up a daffodil-yellow satin stole, draped it across her shoulders and batted her eyelashes at him. 'You like?'

'Babe, I like you in anything, anywhere.'

'You're quite the charmer.' She flashed a coy smile. 'But two can play at that game.'

His eyebrow arched. 'What do you have in mind?'

'I'm going to charm the pants off you.' She flung the stole away and advanced on him, only to kneel at his feet. 'Literally.'

He sucked in a breath when she reached out and snagged his zipper, before tugging it down slowly.

'Babe...'

'Lift your butt and wriggle down your jeans,' she said, sounding breathy yet commanding.

She eyed the rigid outline in his jocks before raising her gaze to meet his, smug that she could turn him on this much.

'Whatever you're thinking, I like it.' His gorgeous mouth quirked in a lopsided smile. 'I like it a lot.'

'Then you'll like this even more.'

She slid her hand into his jocks and wrapped her fingers around his cock. He moaned as she eased him out and slid her hand up and down the shaft, her grip firm.

'Yeah, just like that.' He gasped as her thumb brushed the head, a second before she leaned forward and licked him.

It was a long swipe of her tongue from the base to the tip and back again. Over and over, savouring the musky taste of him.

'Pol...fuck, yeah...'

He didn't say anything else as she sucked him into her mouth, swirling her tongue round and round. Her hand clutched at the base of his cock, just above his balls, gently squeezing as her head bobbed. Sucking him in. Easing him out. Again and again and again, until his hips were thrusting upwards and his hand rested on her head.

She didn't need the guidance. She didn't need anything but him filling her mouth, making her feel powerful and in control. And when he tightened a second before coming on a guttural groan, she knew she'd never forget this moment.

Blowjobs had never been her favourite thing, but with Ryder it gave her a sense of power, like she could do anything and be anyone. With him. Only with him...

The realisation had her easing away to slide a tissue out of her pocket and dab at her mouth while he zipped himself back in.

She wasn't this woman.

She didn't have sex up against a wall or sex on a desk in a sleazy motel, or four times in a night, or give head in a storage room at work.

But with Ryder, she was. What would happen when he left?

Would she revert to being absorbed in a world of figures, relying on statistics to get her through every day?

Would she start wearing sensible cotton underwear again?

Would no guy she dated ever measure up to the one guy who'd always held a piece of her heart, even if he didn't know it?

'Hey.' He reached out, placed a finger under her chin and tipped it up. 'What's wrong?'

Everything.

So she reached for a monstrous lie and summoned her best acting skills by forcing the mother of all smiles.

'Nothing. You've just made one of my fantasies come true and I'm a little overwhelmed.'

'You and me both, babe.'

He hadn't bought her excuse; she could see it in the knowing glint in his eyes. But thankfully he let it go.

'My turn to return the favour—'

'I can't.' She made a grand show of looking at her watch. 'I have a meeting with Andrina in three minutes and she hates to be kept waiting.'

'Okay. I'll see you later tonight?'

She hesitated and saw his jaw clench.

'What happened to the uncomplicated sex, Pol? Because it feels like you're avoiding me.'

Admiring his bluntness, she nodded. 'I know. But I'm a chicken—'

'The Polly I know is the bravest, smartest woman on the planet and she doesn't shy away from the tough stuff.' He leaned down to brush a soft kiss on her lips. 'We can do this. It's not complicated.'

Polly had no idea what he was referring to and was too terrified of her out-of-control feelings to ask.

CHAPTER NINETEEN

IT DIDN'T SURPRISE Ryder when Polly had to work late that night. After blowing his mind by blowing him in that storeroom at Sizzle she'd withdrawn from him again, in the same way she had after he'd spent the night at her place.

It confused the hell out of him.

He hadn't meant to open up to her about the accident but he'd known he had to give her something otherwise she'd keep pushing. Surprisingly, she hadn't, and instead had tried to distract him in the best way possible.

She might've had a meeting with Andrina but then why start something up in that storeroom? Unless revealing hidden truths about the accident had made her feel sorry for him? He hoped not. The last thing he wanted or needed was a pity fuck.

But he knew her better than that and deep down he recognised that wasn't what that blowjob had been about. Polly wanted him as much as he wanted her and for her to do something so brazen at work, she must've got off on the illicit thrill as much as he had.

He wished he could've returned the favour. Instead,

he'd left satisfied and she'd gone off to her meeting with her cheeks flushed and a determined gleam in her eyes. He hoped she'd given Andrina hell.

He loved her contrasts: studious and fastidious at work, with a hidden impish side that came out to play in a big way when he least expected it. Every time they'd hooked up she'd been an uninhibited and generous lover, and he couldn't stop thinking about her.

He knew his shitty grandparents had driven out all hints of emotion from him, obliterating any chance for him to make a deeper connection beyond the physical with a woman because he'd never felt like he deserved happiness. And with a woman like Polly, he'd never be good enough, which meant he had no right thinking about her beyond the sex.

There was only one way to get him out of this funk: spend time with Archie. Though he knew his best mate; he'd want to go out and get drunk, and he wouldn't put it past Arch to test him by trying to pick up women. Yeah, that would be just like his mate, to see if Ryder would do the dirty on his sister.

Then again, hanging out with Archie would guarantee he could take his mind off Polly, because no way in hell would Arch want to talk about his sister.

Before he could second-guess his decision, he fired off a text. A response pinged back in under a minute and Ryder was outside Archie's door in another twenty with a sixpack of his mate's favourite boutique beer under one arm and a bag of Thai takeaway in the other.

Paint fumes seeped out from the semi-open door

so he entered, calling out, 'Hey, bozo, I brought re-freshments.'

'In the kitchen,' came the response, and he strode down the hallway, admiring the new walls and floors.

Archie had accomplished a lot since he'd first walked in here over a week ago to find Polly with her cute ass in the air as she sanded. Arch had always been a good handyman so it was no surprise he'd done a building apprenticeship when he'd finished school, and it looked like this labour of love would turn out beauti-fully. Archie had created a real home and it made him wonder if there was a woman in the picture he hadn't heard about.

The old Arch wouldn't have kept stuff like that from him, but he'd stayed away for five years and despite their regular phone calls and emails, Ryder knew things had changed between them. It was his fault, not Arch's, and it rammed home how he'd unintentionally ostra-cised the only people to ever really care about him.

Though Polly had welcomed him back with open arms and while on the surface Arch appeared the same, tonight would be a good opportunity for the two of them to reconnect.

He strode into the kitchen to find Archie descend-ing a ladder, covered in paint splatters and dust. But his wide grin said it all: he was loving every minute of the renovations.

'You look like shit,' Ryder said, dumping the Thai takeaway and beers on the table.

'We can't all be pretty boys like you.' Archie poked

at the bag and sniffed. 'But considering you brought Thai you're forgiven for being a dickhead.'

'Takes one to know one.' Ryder slipped two bottles from the cardboard holder and held one out to him. 'Beer?'

'Love one, but give me two secs to get cleaned up.'

Ryder nodded, popped the top off his beer and took a deep slug. The brew had a pungent yeasty flavour and it catapulted him straight back to the first time he'd tasted it in Archie's backyard, when the two of them had finished year eleven. Archie had been working part time at the local hardware store for a fortnight and though Ryder could've afforded to buy them alcohol any time they wanted, he knew what it meant to his friend to be able to pay for the beers with his first wage.

They'd sculled five beers each and ended up spewing into his grandmother's precious rose bushes over the back fence; no way would he desecrate Barbara Scanlon's trees. With his head spinning and his stomach rolling, he'd lain next to Archie on the grass, staring up at the cloudless sky, laughing as they'd tried to outdo each other with outlandish proclamations.

'I'm going to scale the Eiffel Tower barefoot,' had been one of his.

'I'm going to find the biggest opal in Coober Pedy and make a fortune,' had been Archie's.

'I'm going to date three Danish supermodels.' Lofty aspirations indeed; he'd been lucky enough to date one early last year.

'I'm going to construct an eco-friendly house that's

going to win architectural awards worldwide.' Archie had always had a thing for building.

And so it went on, until they'd ended up dozing beneath the trees, to be woken by a disapproving but forgiving Babs who'd instructed them to throw the beer bottles in the recycling bin and never drink again until they turned eighteen.

Interestingly, they'd both kept their promise. That was how much he'd respected Babs and cherished Archie's friendship. So why had he let the friendship lapse? He'd been too scared to make himself vulnerable to Archie by sharing what he'd been through and how screwed up he was because of it? Because articulating what had happened with that accident made him relive it all over again? Because he couldn't stand the inevitable pity?

Whatever his rationale, he intended to start making amends now. Tonight would be all about Arch and what was driving his mate to remodel this place into a home.

Archie padded into the kitchen barefoot and reached for the beer. He'd had a quick shower and changed into clean shorts and a T-shirt, but paint spatters still dotted his hair like confetti.

'Man, I needed this.' He twisted the top off, raised the beer to his lips, and drank the entire bottle in a few gulps.

'Thirsty, much?'

Archie flipped him the finger and reached for another. 'Been working like a dog all day and didn't stop for lunch.'

'You'll end up spewing, you moron.'

'Thanks for the advice, Mum.' He tipped the bottle in his direction before taking another few slugs.

'Speaking of that, how's Babs?'

A strange flicker of emotion crossed Archie's face. 'She's good. Travelling around northern Queensland at the moment.'

'Alone?'

Archie shrugged. 'Who knows? She's always been secretive about boyfriends and hasn't mentioned anyone this time around.'

Ryder sensed he'd touched a nerve but having Archie mention significant others gave him the perfect segue. 'What about you? Seeing anyone special?'

'Not really.'

Archie's response came too quickly and his gaze darted away.

'Come on, mate, I may not have been around for a while but I can still read you like a book. What's her name?'

'There's nobody,' he said, but his goofy grin gave him away. 'You'll be the second to know, after her, when there's anything to tell.'

'Is that what the renovations are about?' Ryder gestured around the kitchen. 'What you've done here looks amazing. You've created a real home.'

A tell-tale blush crept into Archie's cheeks. 'Thanks, mate. Maybe it's turning thirty soon that got me thinking, who knows? But I realised last year I've had this place for a while now and it looked like a dump, so what woman's going to take me seriously if I'm still living like I don't give a shit about anything?'

Ryder grinned and clinked his beer bottle against Archie's. 'Wow, my boy's all grown up.'

'Fuck off,' Archie said, returning his grin. 'What about you? Are you treating my sister right?'

Ryder had expected Archie to grill him at some point during the evening. Not that he'd tell him much but he owed the guy something.

'Polly's amazing.'

'Yeah, but you still haven't answered my question.'

Ryder huffed out a breath. 'Already told you, boof-head, I won't do anything to hurt her. So, yeah, I'm treating her right.'

But was he? If she kept pushing him away after they'd been intimate then her actions signalled a prob-lem, and rather than confronting it he was avoiding her by hanging out with her brother. Dumbass.

'She called me, asking if I knew about the acci-dent.' Archie pinned him with an accusatory glare. 'Gotta tell you, mate, I felt like an idiot not knowing what the hell she was talking about beyond the fact that there was one.'

Ryder grimaced and swiped a hand over his face. 'I didn't keep it from you deliberately. I just didn't want to talk about it.'

'Yet we talk about everything else?' Archie shook his head. 'It sounded pretty bad.'

'It was.'

Two short syllables that hid a world of pain and sadness and guilt. He knew Archie, knew his friend wouldn't push him to reveal anything he didn't want to. But he'd come here tonight deciding to be a better friend and that meant trusting Archie with the truth.

'I should've been in the car when three of my friends got killed. I swapped out at the last minute. So I got to witness them die...' Emotion tightened his throat and he cleared it before continuing. 'It mucked me up.' He made circles at his temples. 'Up here. Until a shrink helped me. You'd told me to finish my degree, and that guy pretty much inspired me, so that's why I finished my degree and set about helping others.'

Archie seemed to deflate before his eyes. 'That's some serious shit you dealt with on your own.' He jabbed a finger at him. 'You should've told me.'

'I should've done a lot of things, but I guess we're always wiser in hindsight.'

Archie paused. 'Does Polly know all this?'

He nodded. 'I told her.'

Archie eyed him with respect. 'Wow, so it's serious between you two.'

Ryder bit back his knee-jerk response of, *Not really.*

Because he couldn't have feelings for Polly. He'd only end up hurting her if he did and she didn't deserve that. Viewing Polly as anything more than a lover was far scarier than dealing with any residual guilt from the accident.

'She's great,' he said, desperate for a change of subject. 'But I'm not going to discuss her with you, so why don't we eat?'

Archie's gaze flicked between him and the take-away containers, and thankfully his hunger won out.

'Sure, I'll have a double helping of everything.'

However, as Archie got plates and cutlery and they started dishing out the food, Ryder's appetite vanished. He didn't like what Archie had implied, that sharing the truth about his accident with Polly meant things were serious between them. They weren't. They couldn't be. He wouldn't allow it.

Sex, he could do. Anything remotely involving feelings, not a chance in hell.

CHAPTER TWENTY

THE LAST THING Ryder had said to Polly in the storeroom at work was that they could do this, whatever that meant. He'd accused her of being a chicken, which was true, and it had sparked something within her. Not about discussing their relationship per se, but with her life in general.

What was she doing, sucking up to Andrina, taking her crap, when she could be proving her worth by doing what she'd wanted all along, wowing her with figures?

She'd depended on her brain her entire life—making smart decisions, using logic, calculating probabilities to ensure the best outcomes.

With the fundraiser prep running smoothly and little left to do, Polly had time on her hands and rather than pick up the slack from some other lazy-ass co-worker she could use it wisely and prepare to wow Andrina. She'd been up most of the night, nailing a presentation that would hopefully secure her the job she actually wanted.

It helped to stay focussed and keep her mind off Ryder and his 'it's not complicated' throwaway remark.

Maybe not for him, but she was in danger of creating a giant complication if she ever told him the truth.

He'd surprised her with his honesty in revealing more about the accident. It made her wonder if they'd moved past screwing for screwing's sake.

She had known the danger all along, the inevitability considering their longstanding friendship, but she was fast losing hope that she could walk away from this at the end and revert to just being friends.

She'd fake it, for Archie's sake, because she'd never put her brother in the position of having to choose between his sister and his best mate. But she knew that every time she saw Ryder for the rest of her life she'd remember their brief fling and wish things could've been different.

He would obviously stay for the fundraiser next Saturday night and Archie's thirtieth on the Sunday, but would he leave straight after? It made sense, considering his nomadic lifestyle of the last decade, but in revealing so much of himself to her she'd wondered if he'd changed.

Would he stop running once he'd dealt with his guilt? Would he confront his past now that he'd returned home? She figured much of his avoidance of his home city had to do with his grandmother and as far as she knew he hadn't visited her yet, which spoke volumes. And while she didn't want to interfere, maybe it wouldn't hurt to give him a gentle nudge in that direction?

Then again, who was she to talk? She hadn't spoken to her mum in weeks, not since she'd landed the job at

Sizzle. Her initial excitement at working for the premier fashion house in Sydney had given way to wariness when it came to telling her mother. Would she appreciate the importance of what this job meant to her daughter? Would she downplay it, expecting Polly not to last beyond her trial? Or would she reiterate an old insult, that a girl like Polly couldn't possibly fit into the world of high fashion?

Barbara had dropped that particular doozy on her the night of her twenty-first, when Polly had been high on champagne fizz and had articulated her dream of mixing statistics with fashion to improve companies' bottom lines. Her mum had laughed at her, sent a pointed look at her plain black dress, and said she'd never fit into that kind of world.

Polly had been gutted.

And more determined than ever to prove her mother wrong, using her mum's low opinion of her to drive her harder to achieve what she wanted.

Starting now.

She squared her shoulders, tugged down her jacket and smoothed her skirt, before striding into the conference room where Andrina waited for her. Polly had scheduled her presentation for nine sharp and she had two minutes to spare. Not that it stopped Andrina from glancing at her watch and frowning, but Polly wasn't in the mood for her games today.

Today she was going to kick ass.

'What's this about, Polly?' Andrina stared at the laptop Polly opened as she prepared the electronic version of her presentation, as if expecting it to spontaneously combust. 'I haven't got all day.'

'This won't take long.'

Andrina's eyebrows rose at Polly's commanding tone, far from her usual deference.

'I prepared this last night and once you take a look I'm sure you'll be convinced I can drive this company's financial growth even further.'

Polly resisted the urge to swipe her clammy palms down the sides of her skirt, took a deep breath and launched into the spiel she'd mentally rehearsed.

She spoke with clarity, making concise points, using her presentation to back up her proposal. If Andrina was bamboozled by the figures she didn't show it. Instead, for the first time since Polly had started working at Sizzle, Andrina looked at her with genuine interest.

Last night, Polly had timed the presentation to keep to a brief twenty minutes, but with Andrina asking countless questions, by the time she finished it was closer to forty-five.

'That's some impressive work you've done there.' Andrina pointed at her laptop. 'Did it really only take you an evening to prepare?'

Polly nodded. 'I'm good with figures. My degree's in statistics and I can see gaps in the market and ways to improve any company's bottom line.'

Andrina's brows knitted together. 'I'm guessing you're wasted as my personal assistant.'

'Yes.'

Polly's voice didn't quiver and she didn't glance

away. Instead, she eyeballed Andrina and squared her shoulders, a woman in command of her fate and going after what she wanted.

Andrina glared at her with grudging admiration. 'In that case, it's time we found you a position more suitable to your skills and talent.'

Polly wanted to leap out of her seat, punch the air and do a hip-swivelling victory dance. She settled for a sedate, 'Thanks. I know I can make a real difference to Sizzle's bottom line.'

Andrina offered a brief nod. 'Can I ask you something?'

The fact her boss was actually looking her in the eye, let alone treating her like a human being, was shock enough, but now she wanted her opinion?

'Sure.'

'Why did you apply for the job as my PA if you knew you were overqualified?'

'Because I love fashion. Sizzle is the best in Sydney, and I wanted some hands-on experience before showing you what I'm capable of.'

Andrina tapped her bottom lip, admiration in her gaze. 'For what it's worth, you're the only PA I've ever had with half a brain and I'll be sorry to lose you.'

Wow, praise too. Polly couldn't help but grin.

Andrina waggled a finger at her. 'But don't get ahead of yourself. You've still got to make sure the fundraiser runs smoothly, then we'll discuss your new role next week.'

'Sounds good to me.' She stuck out her hand. 'Thanks for the opportunity, Andrina. I won't let you down.'

Her boss grunted as she shook her hand, releasing it quickly. 'You've certainly made an impression on Ryder Beale. He speaks very highly of you.'

Polly hoped her cheeks wouldn't flush crimson. 'I'm sure he'll do a fine job as keynote speaker.'

Andrina looked like she wanted to ask more but the last thing Polly felt like doing was revealing how well she knew Ryder and for how long.

'I'd better get back to work.' She closed her laptop and gathered her things.

Thankfully, Andrina took the hint and left the room, leaving Polly wanting to jump up on the conference table and dance a jig.

She'd done it.

She'd confronted her demon boss and impressed her enough to get the job she coveted before the end of her three-month trial period. She really should be dancing a jig, a highland fling and a hustle.

But Polly knew she had a much more difficult confrontation looming and she hoped Ryder would be as receptive to what she had to say.

CHAPTER TWENTY-ONE

RYDER HAD SCALED mountainsides with just a few ropes keeping him from plunging to his death. He'd shot down rapids in tiny boats not deemed safe enough for white-water rafting. And he'd skydived more times than he could count.

But none of those daredevil activities terrified him as much as standing outside the front door of the house he'd grown up in, ready to confront his grandmother.

He'd had no intention of doing it this soon, but after hanging with Archie last night, then poring over the information for his book today, he'd known it was time.

For the simple fact he felt like a fraud.

Putting so much of his life into a book for public consumption when he had unresolved issues from the past made him feel like an imposter. Who was he to give advice to people on how best to lead their lives when he was actively avoiding the tough stuff in his own?

He had survivor's guilt, commitment issues and—the doozy of them all—a deeply strained relationship with his family.

He had to start somewhere and seeing his grandmother seemed the logical place. He'd avoided her for too long, had blamed her for too much. Hopefully, with some kind of resolution, he could start dealing with the rest.

He could've called ahead and warned her but he didn't. He hadn't wanted to give her the opportunity to come up with an excuse or not answer the door. This confrontation was long overdue and he had to do it for his own peace of mind.

Inhaling and exhaling slowly, forcing air into his lungs like the shrink had taught him, he calmed his rampant nerves and knocked on the door.

Swiping his palms down the sides of his jeans, he waited, willing his grandmother to have enough decency not to turn him away.

His heart raced and a stabbing pain jabbed at his chest, so he took slow, deep breaths, quelling a possible anxiety attack like the shrink had taught him. Back then, the chest tightness, pain and light-headedness would come on with no warning. One minute he'd be using an elastic band to rehab his weak leg, the next he'd be gripping the walking bars so he wouldn't slither to the floor in a heap.

The worst flashbacks were confined to his dreams but the panic attacks terrified him because he had no control over them even when he was awake. He had feared that made him less of a man, and he'd wanted to talk to his gran about it. When he'd reached out and called his grandmother to tell her about his broken leg and the accident, he'd expected her to welcome the contact because it had been so infrequent.

Instead, she'd dismissed him, as cool and callous as

ever, and he'd taken it as a sign to move on. But maybe he should've fought harder. He hadn't given up when physical challenges had seemed impossibly difficult in the past and he sure as hell hadn't given up after the accident, no matter how much he'd wanted to. He'd confronted those fears, had learned to live with them the hard way, even if he acknowledged he'd never fully be in control of the guilt that dogged him. He lived, others had died, and he needed to make the most of that.

The thing was, he'd let this relationship lapse as much as she had. He'd been quick to blame her when things had deteriorated between them and had severed all contact. She may not have reached out but he hadn't either, and he had to cut her some slack or tonight wouldn't go well.

He heard footsteps, surprised by a wave of nostalgia as he remembered how Gran never wore slippers even at home. She wore black patent leather court shoes with a tiny kitten heel, ensuring she made clacking sounds wherever she went.

It had been helpful in the past because it had meant he'd been able to avoid her. Strange how a sound that had once driven him to hide from her now seemed like the most welcoming sound in the world.

When the door swung open, the nostalgia grew stronger, making his lungs seize.

She looked the same.

Older, with more wrinkles around her eyes and mouth, but essentially the same: shoulders back, head straight, perfect posture, with a steely blue-eyed gaze that missed little.

For one crazy second he swore he glimpsed pure, unadulterated joy in her eyes before she blinked and peered at him.

'You've come home at last,' she said, and surprisingly her tone held no judgement.

'Hi Gran. Can I come in?'

She nodded, swinging the door open and as he crossed the threshold and the familiar smell of floor polish and her favoured gardenia-scented candles hit him, his throat tightened with emotion.

This house held nothing but bad memories. Memories of being ignored by the only family member he had left, memories of silent dinners with a woman who virtually ignored him, memories of long, sleepless nights when he wished he had the guts to run away.

But for all the bad stuff there'd been good too, namely Polly and Archie next door, and they'd saved him even if they hadn't known it.

'Would you like something to drink? Tea? Coffee? Something stronger?'

She sounded perfectly normal, like he was just another guest she had to entertain, and even though he hadn't expected a welcoming gesture he lamented the fact they'd grown so far apart that they couldn't hug after five years of absence.

'I'm fine.'

'I'm not,' she muttered, shooting him a hesitant glance. 'A brandy is definitely in order.'

'In that case, make it two.'

He followed her into the lounge room, where he spied a basket of knitting next to the chair she spent her evenings in. That was new. After Pop had died she'd spent countless hours staring into space or trying to read, looking at the print without turning a page.

He knew because he'd be lying on the couch reading and shooting the occasional glance her way, the only time they'd co-existed in the same room with some kind of peace. She'd ask him the occasional question about whatever book he'd been reading, though she'd frowned when he'd read comics. Those evenings reading together in here were the only good memory he had of this house.

'It's good to see you, Ryder.' She handed him a brandy balloon and raised hers, waiting until he'd tapped it before saying, 'Welcome home.'

Stunned by her easy acceptance of his appearance after all this time, he sipped the brandy, savouring the burn down his throat. Anything to ease the emotion threatening to well up.

Brandy made him think of Polly, and how she loved doctoring chocolate milk with it. She'd always been quirky and cute, and he hoped that once he made an effort to resolve issues with his gran he could do the same with her. He had to leave soon, and telling her would be tough.

But he needed to take one confrontation at a time and for now he had to focus on Gran and setting the past to rest once and for all.

'Let's sit.' She gestured to the sofa and he sat, expecting her to resume her usual seat, but she sat next to him instead. 'You haven't said much. Everything all right?'

'Fine,' he said, making a mockery of that when his

hand shook and he quickly tossed back the rest of the brandy before placing the balloon on a nearby coffee table.

She cocked her head to one side, the same mannerism he'd seen countless times in the past when she'd looked at him as if she couldn't quite figure out what he was doing living in her house. 'Then what brings you by?'

Typical. She thought he'd only visit if there was something wrong. Did she have no feelings? No sense of family? Nothing?

'I haven't seen you in over five years. Isn't that reason enough?' He sounded bitter but didn't care. They had to talk, and rehashing the past was bound to bring up his latent feelings of resentment.

The Edie Beale he'd known would have compressed her lips and preferred not to answer. They'd existed in silence for so long after his grandfather had died he'd given up trying to make her talk back. As for showing emotion, she'd never let him get close. He'd wanted to offer comfort, to tell her everything would be okay with just the two of them but she'd closed off and eventually he'd given up trying.

He'd expected more of the same tonight so when he glimpsed the sheen of tears in her eyes he couldn't believe it.

'We have a lot of catching up to do,' she said, placing her brandy balloon on the table before clasping her hands in her lap. 'A lot to talk about.'

'I'm surprised you want to.'

She didn't flinch at his bluntness. Instead, she nodded, but the way her knuckles stood out beneath the fragile skin indicated tension she was struggling to hide.

'You must think I'm some kind of monster,' she murmured, blinking rapidly. 'Your parents entrusted your care to Fred and me, and we let you down.'

Stunned she'd broached the subject before he did, he shook his head. 'You're not a monster. But I'd like to understand what happened to us. One minute we were okay, the next Pop died and you pretended I didn't exist.'

She stared at her clasped hands in her lap for what seemed like an eternity before raising her eyes to meet his and they held a world of pain and regret and sorrow.

'I didn't like the way Fred treated you, but losing your father, our only child, broke something in him and stupidly he blamed you.'

Great, more survivor's guilt.

Thanks for nothing, Pop.

'Nothing I could say got through to him, so I lavished the attention on you that he couldn't.'

Yet it wasn't enough. Sure, she'd paid him attention and come to a few functions at school like the art fair and athletics day, but Pop had always come first in her eyes and if it had come to a choice between the two of them she'd always chosen Pop.

Gran had loved him though. She may not have been overly demonstrative but she'd shown him affection in myriad ways that had gone some way to making up for Pop's appalling treatment. So it had been harder to fathom when Pop had died and she'd withdrawn from him totally, when they should've been there for each other.

'I appreciated the effort of you trying to make up for Pop's terrible treatment, but it didn't really change anything,' he said, remembering his grandfather's put-downs, his callous indifference, his deliberate coldness. 'I ended up hating him.'

'And that's why you acted out.'

He nodded, not proud of some of the stupid things he'd done to taunt his grandfather in the hope he'd garner attention, even negative attention. It had become a game to him after a while, a stupid, self-sabotaging game of one-upmanship. In his younger years he'd swap out the sugar for salt or bicarb soda, childish stuff that had earned scolding and criticism. Later, he'd rebel by doing the opposite of everything Pop said, from playing his music too loud to deliberately failing maths when it had been his favourite subject.

She eyeballed him and he couldn't fathom the emotion behind her stare. 'When his heart gave out too young, I blamed you.'

Shocked, Ryder ran a shaky hand through his hair. 'Why?'

'You gave him constant trouble and it was easier for me to think you drove him to an early grave than consider other possibilities...' The corners of her mouth drooped, accentuating the deep lines bracketing it. 'I could've done more to snap him out of his grief. Losing your father gutted us both but I was more resilient. Then when he turned on you, I hated him a little and I shut down too. I withdrew from him emotionally. We were virtual strangers when he died...'

She trailed off, swallowed several times and reached

for her brandy. He waited until she'd taken several sips before asking, 'It seems contradictory. You hated how he treated me yet you irrationally blamed me when he died?'

'It's not logical, I know, but I felt so guilty for treating him badly that it was easier to shift blame than assign it where it really belonged.' She pressed a hand to her chest. 'I'm ashamed for so much, but most of all for withdrawing from you when you needed me the most.'

He of all people understood the blame game; he'd been doing it himself since the accident. Acknowledging it, accepting it and trying to move on as best as he could had helped. He hoped the same would happen for his gran now she'd finally opened up.

'But what about the last decade or so? Pop's been gone a long time.'

'I thought I'd lost you.'

A lone tear trickled down her crepe-like cheek and he resisted the urge to swipe it away. 'I wanted to reach out so many times but it was easier just to provide for you financially when I had nothing to give emotionally.'

She pulled a handkerchief from her sleeve and dabbed the tear away. 'When you left Sydney, I saw it as a reprieve. I thought time apart would mellow us both. But the few times you returned you were more stilted and formal than ever, and I knew I'd pushed you away for good. So I let it be. I joined a group for grieving widows and instigated some changes in my life, hoping you would embrace your freedom and come to some realisations too.'

'Considering the lack of contact over the last five years, the only realisation I came to is that you didn't give a shit about me and probably never did.'

'That's not true…' She reached out and laid a hand over his, the briefest of touches before she withdrew. 'I'm not proud of the way I treated you, Ryder, but the fact you're here tonight means there's hope for us.'

Ryder's chest tightened with suppressed emotion as he struggled to get himself under control. He'd never been a crier but the urge to bawl now was strong.

'And thank you for the money. I don't need it, but I hoped that by withdrawing it you'd know how much it meant to me that you hadn't turned your back on me completely.' She offered a tremulous smile. 'I opened up a trust fund and deposited your money in it for the children you'll have in the future.'

He didn't have it in him to reveal his regular deposits for her had been guilt money for not having the guts to have this confrontation years earlier, so he settled for the truth.

'I came here tonight hoping for…something. Some kind of closure perhaps? I don't know.' He scrubbed a hand over his face; it did little to ease the tension making his facial muscles ache. 'I didn't expect you to open up.'

'It's long overdue, don't you think?' She sounded brusque and matter-of-fact, much like the gran he remembered from his early childhood when she'd tried to be stern before slipping him an extra choc-chip cookie.

He nodded. 'I've spent more than a decade travelling, never putting down roots, because the only time I did, with you, I didn't like it so much.'

She waited, sensing he had more to say, so he continued. 'I gave up on us the last five years. I was done.'

'So why did you really come here tonight?'

He didn't have to tell her the truth. He owed her nothing. But she'd revealed so much herself that he found the truth hovering on his lips, eager to spill out.

'Because I need to get my head on straight. I've spent a lot of my life chasing the next big thing, one high after another, but now I'm contemplating...more.'

A soft smile played about her mouth. 'This must involve a woman and she must be very special for you to go to such lengths, turning up here after five years to confront this old dragon.'

He found himself returning her smile. 'It's Polly Scanlon.'

Her eyebrows rose, the wrinkles in her forehead increasing tenfold. 'Polly from next door?'

'Yeah.'

Her eyes glinted with approval. 'I always liked how that family took you under their wing. They gave you what I couldn't.'

She blinked several times and looked away. 'I've been a useless grandmother but I hope by learning the truth tonight you can move forward with your Polly.'

Your Polly.

Ryder had no idea if he wanted her to be his, but after an evening of surprises with his gran, he knew he was closer to figuring it out.

CHAPTER TWENTY-TWO

AFTER WOWING ANDRINA and landing her dream job, Polly had tried calling Ryder. Twice. It went through to voicemail both times. So she left an upbeat message about having good news and asking him to call her.

She'd spent the next few hours scouring the research he'd sent her for his book, doing her best to collate and sort it. She approached it methodically, knowing if she got too caught up in reading the information she'd be awake all night. Besides, delving into his life would only make it harder for her to walk away at the end, something that was drawing nearer every day.

She'd known it the minute Andrina had given her a crack at her dream job. She couldn't screw it up. She'd worked too long and too hard to mess around and she knew the longer she spent with Ryder, the higher the chance she'd fall for him, thereby royally screwing up her plans. She hadn't signed up for heartbreak when they'd started their sexual liaison and she'd be damned if she allowed her growing feelings for him to muck up her dream job.

It took her seven hours to complete the compilation and after she'd saved her work into a folder and emailed it to him, she tucked herself up on the couch and ate her way through a tub of honey and macadamia ice cream, wishing he'd call.

She picked up her mobile several times, itching to send him a text, but if her voicemail hadn't been clear enough what would a text achieve?

It was interesting that he was the first person she had wanted to share the good news with. Not Archie, her go-to guy. And certainly not Barbara. Would her mum even understand what she'd achieved?

She hadn't been terribly impressed when Polly had first told her about scoring a job at Sizzle, despite gushing over their clothes in magazines for years.

Ryder had asked her why working for Sizzle had been so important and she'd given him the answer she'd mentally rehearsed for such a question.

What would he think if she revealed the whole truth?

That she still secretly craved her mother's approval after all these years? That she'd hated being second best growing up? That she hoped her mum, with her fashion obsession, would embrace her daughter's job in a way she'd never fully embraced her?

When she'd got home from work a few hours ago and Ryder hadn't returned her call, she'd rung Archie and told him the news. Her brother had been predictably supportive and said they'd share an extra drink or two at his thirtieth in a few days. But getting recognition from Archie didn't hold the same significance as getting it from Ryder—and that was the moment she'd known she was in big trouble.

She'd gone into this fling with her eyes open, but somewhere along the way the lines had shifted and blurred beyond recognition.

Their friendship was too important for her to tell him everything but she knew without a doubt that if she revealed one tenth of what she was really feeling he'd hightail it back to France or Morocco or Peru without looking back.

Her mobile rang and her heart leapt. However, when she glanced at the screen, her hope that Ryder had finally called her back evaporated.

Hesitating, she stared at the screen, wondering whether she should answer or let her mum leave a message. That way, she could call back when she felt more in control of her feelings, and not so damn down.

After the fifth ring she gave in. Sticking the spoon into the ice cream, she picked up.

'Hey, Mum.'

The faintest crackle came down the line. 'Polly, can you hear me?'

'Yeah.'

The crackle came again, louder this time. 'Damn it, I'm about fifteen minutes out of Cairns and reception here is dodgy. Anyway, just wanted to ring and say congratulations. Archie told me about your new job.'

Stunned, Polly gripped the phone so tightly she wouldn't have been surprised to hear the glass screen crack.

'Uh, thanks.'

'I'd rung your brother to wish him a happy birthday

for Sunday as I'm not sure I'll make it back by then and he told me the good news.'

Polly wasn't sure what was in that ice cream or if the combination of honey and macadamia had produced some kind of hallucinogen. 'I'm pleased.'

It was the understatement of the year, but her mum wouldn't pick up on it.

'Sounds perfect for you, combining your two great loves, numbers and fashion,' Barbara chuckled. 'Must admit, I had my doubts when you first started working there because you're too sweet to be thrust into such a cutthroat world like high fashion, but I'm thrilled you've proved to everyone, including me, that you're made of sterner stuff.' She cleared her throat. 'I never told you this, but I got a job in a fashion house once, before you were born. It was just as a general dogsbody but I was over the moon. But I couldn't hack the bitchiness so I quit after six weeks.'

Polly stared at the ice cream tub, convinced she'd entered some kind of alternate reality after eating it. Did brain freeze lead to time travel?

'Anyway, I'm proud of you and look forward to hearing all about it when I get home, whenever that is.'

The crackles grew louder and Polly didn't know if her mother heard her say, 'Thanks, Mum, that means a lot.'

But when the line went dead, she was left staring at the phone, wondering if the small, hopeful part of her that yearned for her mother's approval all these years had conjured up that phone call.

Her mother's praise didn't erase the years of feeling second best but it went some way to explaining her love of fashion and why she'd been hesitant when Polly had first landed the job at Sizzle. Her mum had been concerned, not jealous or uncaring.

It made her wonder what else she had been wrong about.

Before she could second-guess her decision, she ditched the melted ice cream, changed into jeans and a T-shirt and grabbed her keys.

She'd avoided Ryder several times now and he'd had the guts to come and see her. Time to return the favour.

CHAPTER TWENTY-THREE

RYDER HAD MISSED two calls from Polly while he'd been with his grandmother. He would've been worried if she hadn't sounded so upbeat and left a message asking him to call her. Which he would, later, because after spending an hour and a half with his gran he felt like he'd been flayed alive and he couldn't deal with anybody else.

He felt raw, exposed, like someone had used tweezers to peel his skin off one layer at a time. Polly's go-to place might be a room at work filled with plush fabrics; his was Circular Quay.

In his teens he'd often gone there to watch the buskers and the tourists, people from all over the world with nothing better to do than pose for selfies with the Harbour Bridge in the background or snap a billion shots of the Opera House. He'd liked a crowd because it had given him anonymity, a way to blend in and disappear, at complete odds with how he'd felt at home where his grandmother had had a knack for singling him out with a glare while also not really seeing him at all.

She'd explained why and, while he understood, he

couldn't forgive her. He would, in time, but too much
had happened between them for him to forget everything so quickly. She'd made him feel unlovable at a
time when he'd needed her most and that would take
a long time to get over. At least they'd parted on good
terms now and he'd vowed to visit more often and she'd
promised to call regularly. It was a start.

Tonight, striding down the boardwalk alongside a
ferry bound for Manly, he wondered if his wanderlust
was as simple as never wanting to put down roots in
a home because he'd never really had one. It seemed
too trite, too convenient an excuse, but it made sense.

So what happened now?

He had speaking gigs lined up for the next six
months in the United States. Usually he'd be looking
forward to moving on, seeking out the next challenge.
But this time it was different.

Because of Polly.

He should ring her back but with his head still aching from his grandmother's revelations he needed to
wait a little longer.

He strolled towards the Opera House where people mingled on the steps, oohing and ahhing over the
beauty of Sydney at night. The Harbour Bridge lit up
the sky like a sparkling coat hanger, with the lights of
Luna Park twinkling on the opposite shore. Mansions
worth millions dotted distant shorelines, adding to the
glitz of the panorama.

A brisk breeze blew in from the direction of The
Heads and he inhaled deeply, filling his lungs with the
familiar briny scent of home.

This city was in his blood. And maybe, just maybe, he'd made a mistake in staying away.

The high-pitched whir of a jetski snagged his attention and he glanced at the water in time to see three crazy guys zoom past. The daredevils would be arrested—if the water police could catch them. The jetskiers did a few wide loops, spraying water in their wakes, before zooming off in the direction of the Bridge.

As he watched their trails of foam, he expected to feel a pang of wistfulness, a yearning...but he felt nothing. He'd been like them once, chasing the next thrill, a guaranteed shot of adrenaline that would keep him going until the next outlandish stunt. But the accident had changed him and he'd grown up almost overnight. Though substituting chasing women as a way to achieve a thrill instead of daredevil stunts couldn't technically be classed as growing up.

Not that he didn't miss the old days. He still watched extreme sports on TV and attended the occasional event that mates were competing in. But cheating death, even if it hadn't been during one of his stunts, had given him a new perspective on life.

And he didn't want to waste a single moment.

Sliding his mobile from his pocket, he dialled Polly. He had no idea what he'd say to her or how he'd articulate half of what he was thinking but it was time to grow a pair and do what had to be done.

He had to end it between them, because the longer this dragged on and he deluded himself into believing it was all about the sex, the harder it would be. But the thought of telling Polly they were over...it gutted him.

As Polly picked up, he steeled himself.

'Hey, Ryder, everything okay?'

'Yeah, fine. Sorry for not getting back to you earlier, I was at Gran's.'

Considering how he had shut down on her when she'd initially brought up his family, he knew she'd understand the importance of his declaration. He wanted to give her some snippet, an understanding of what drove him when he told her the truth: they had never stood a chance.

After a long pause, she said, 'How did that go?'

'Better than expected, actually. Can I come over? We need to talk.'

It would take all his willpower to ensure that was all they did because every time he laid eyes on her he wanted her naked and pliant.

Another pause. 'I'd love that, but I can't. The fundraiser's tomorrow night, remember?'

'I forgot.'

He heard her sharp intake of breath. 'Tell me you're kidding. Your speech is ready, right?'

'You're still so easy to reel in, Pol.'

'Idiot,' she muttered, with a hint of amusement. 'For acting like a dickhead, I'm not going to tell you my news.'

'What news?'

'Remember I said if I lasted three months as Andrina's assistant, she'd give me a shot at pitching for a financial role?'

'Yeah?'

'Well, I didn't want to wait. I'm sick of being her lackey so I stayed up last night putting a presentation together and I kicked ass today. She offered me the job.'

Her little squeal of excitement made his chest expand with joy.

'That's great.'

He meant it, but he could hardly end things when she'd just landed her dream job. What sort of a prick would that make him? He'd have to wait until after the fundraiser and while he hated the feeling that he was stringing her along, he knew he couldn't afford to screw this up.

'How about we celebrate tomorrow night, after the fundraiser?'

'Sounds like a plan,' she said, but he couldn't miss her decided lack of enthusiasm.

Polly wasn't the type of woman to be pissed off that he hadn't returned her calls earlier, which meant there was more at play here and he hoped his plans to come clean to her wouldn't be scuttled.

'Everything okay?'

She sighed. 'Yeah, I'm stoked about the job but I just want this fundraiser over and done with.'

'You and me both.' He lowered his voice to barely above a whisper. 'Because then we get to celebrate in earnest.'

'I'm assuming you're not just talking about champagne?'

'You better believe it, babe.'

She laughed and some of the tension gripping him

eased. 'I'll see you at the hotel around seven? Your speech is at seven-thirty.'

'I'll be there.'

He'd already offered to pick her up and she'd declined, citing organisational issues but he wished he could see her before tomorrow night.

'Ryder?'

'Yeah?'

'I know I've already said this but thanks for doing this.'

'Anything for you, Pol.'

He shouldn't have said it because he heard another soft sigh before she hung up. He knew he couldn't be the guy to make Polly happy.

Polly hated lying to Ryder.

She didn't have any more work to do tonight for the fundraiser. But she did have a date with the makeover consultant he'd set her up with.

She wanted to wow him at the fundraiser in an impossibly gorgeous dress with a glamorous updo and smoking-hot make-up. However, as the twentysomething woman buzzed around her lounge room, fussing over fabrics and styles, Polly wasn't having half the fun she'd expected.

Because all she could think about was Ryder.

He'd set this up, he deserved to be here, and before she could second-guess her impulse she fired off a text asking him to come over anyway.

Her heart did a weird little jive at his response, promising he'd be around ASAP, and she refocussed her energy on the stylist, who'd changed her hair from a French roll to a chignon to a tousled updo within the space of a few minutes. When the doorbell rang she almost bolted for it in relief.

Opening it, she all but dragged Ryder inside. 'Come and save me from the fashion police,' she whispered, pulling an exaggerated terrified face. 'I had no idea what I was in for, agreeing to a makeover.'

He grinned and tapped the side of his nose. 'She's the best in Sydney, apparently, but I have some fashion expertise.'

'Oh?'

He leaned in close, his breath fanning her ear and sending a shiver of anticipation through her. 'Yeah, I'm an expert in taking off your clothes.'

She punched him lightly in the chest. 'Help me.'

He laughed and followed her into the lounge room, which looked like an entire department store had thrown up on itself. Satins, linens, silks and velvets were draped over every surface, magenta, emerald and daffodil warring with sienna, ecru and crimson. And she'd tried on almost every item over the last two hours.

'Wow,' Ryder said, glancing around the room, eyebrows raised.

The stylist offered him a terse nod in greeting, obviously not thrilled at being interrupted.

'Caitlyn, do you mind if we call it a night?'

Caitlyn frowned and folded her arms. 'But we haven't finished. You've only chosen five outfits and my contract stipulated ten.'

Ryder slid an arm around Polly's waist and tugged

her close. 'I can help you choose the other five. Putting them on, taking them off...'

Polly elbowed him away and cleared her throat. 'I'll call you to arrange another time.'

'Fine,' Caitlyn said, sounding decidedly huffy as she gathered up her paraphernalia like an expert magician stuffing tricks back into several cases.

Polly stifled a giggle as Ryder pulled ridiculous faces behind her back, knowing she'd done the right thing in inviting him over. Spending a few hours having mind-blowing sex would be better than dwelling on her burgeoning crush and what the hell she was going to do about it.

When Ryder saw Caitlyn to the door and closed it behind her, Polly breathed a sigh of relief.

'Thanks for that. I'm not cut out to be a clothes-horse.'

'My pleasure.' He gave a mock bow. 'So what's my reward?'

She crooked her finger. 'Come here and I'll show you.'

Polly hadn't had a lot of sex over the years. One semi-serious boyfriend in uni who'd never rocked her world and two other guys she'd dated sporadically since. She'd been passive in the bedroom, never particularly overwhelmed. But with Ryder, she loved taking charge because he made her feel all woman and then some.

Pushing him down onto the sofa, she straddled him. Maintaining eye contact, she undid his buttons, tearing open his shirt to mould her palms against his ripped torso.

'You feel so good,' she said, grinding her hips against him a little, savouring his sharp intake of breath.

'I love how you know what you want.' He grasped her ass, rubbing her hard against his rigid cock, rocking her back and forth until her breathing grew ragged.

'I want you. Inside me, now...' The last word came out on a croak, her pleasure building too quickly.

'Whatever you want, Pol, you're calling the shots.'

Releasing her ass, he made short work of unzipping and sliding on a condom, while she bit her lip to stop every filthy thing she wanted him to do to her spilling from her lips.

When the tip of his cock nudged her entrance, she felt a tremor run through her. Unable to wait, she lowered herself onto him, impaled and filled and beyond turned on.

As she started to slide up and down, he kissed her throat, flicking the pulse point with the tip of his tongue over and over, driving her wild.

He gripped her ass, spreading her wider, and she lost control a little. Pulling back, she rested her hands on his shoulders and rode him with abandon. He drove into her, pistoning his hips up as she came down hard. Over and over, her flesh tender yet throbbing, craving as much as he could give.

When his hands started to knead her ass, rolling her onto him in such a way her clit grazed his cock every time she engulfed him, she came so hard her head hurt like brain freeze.

'Fuck me,' he muttered, a second before coming on a long, low groan that made every hair on her body snap to attention.

They were so good together and as he wrapped his arms around her waist and drew her close, she knew he wasn't the only one who'd just been fucked.

She was too. Totally fucked.

CHAPTER TWENTY-FOUR

POLLY PRIDED HERSELF on being professional. Whatever
the job, whatever the task, she was calm and steady
and entirely too rational.

Which made the emotion clogging her throat and
the tears stinging her eyes out of character. But she
couldn't help it. Listening to Ryder's keynote speech
was like having the man she loved laid bare.

The fact she loved him wasn't so much a shock as
a realisation, and she could've done without it right
now. A small part of her had probably always loved
him, but it had been nothing like this overwhelming
drowning sensation that made her want to cling to him
and never let go.

He commanded the stage with his presence and in
all honesty she would've been captivated by his aura
even if he was reciting nursery rhymes, he had that
much of a hold over her.

He wore a navy designer suit and an ivory shirt open
at the collar. Sexy yet casual, Ryder all over. His introduction had been a brief snapshot of his life but when
he'd started talking about his broken leg and witness-

ing a terrible accident, that was when the emotion had crept up on her.

He'd already told her about what had happened, but hearing how it had pushed him into changing his life she realised how much he'd gone through. Hence the insane urge to join him on stage and wrap her arms around him.

'A coach is someone who mentors and instructs. Someone to respect and look up to. Someone who becomes your champion.' His gaze swept the captive audience of three hundred and Polly watched him, spellbound. 'As a life coach, I don't profess to have all the answers. I don't tell people how to live their lives. But I encourage them to become their own champions because in here?' He made a fist and thumped his chest. 'We've all got it within us to be the best possible version of ourselves.'

He stepped away from the microphone and lowered his head slightly, a second before thunderous applause rang out. Polly joined in, the tears she'd been battling trickling down her cheeks as she clapped so hard her palms stung.

Ryder held up a hand in gratitude and the applause intensified, a rolling sound wave that made her ears ring. She'd expected him to be good; she hadn't expected him to bring the house down.

A hand landed on her shoulder and she dabbed at her cheeks before spinning around to find Andrina grinning at her.

'Job well done, Polly. He was outstanding.'

'Thanks,' she said, knowing she didn't deserve the

credit. The only reason Ryder had initially volunteered to do this was to defend her in front of this tyrannical woman. So not only had he saved her butt, he'd wowed everyone in the process.

'I have some people I'd like you to meet,' Andrina said, eyeing her with respect. 'They'll be crucial in your new role at the company. We're all going out for drinks once this winds down and you should come.'

'Great.' She caught sight of Ryder making his way off stage towards her. 'Give me two minutes?'

Andrina nodded. 'I'll meet you in the foyer.'

Polly should be elated. Gaining Andrina's respect and finally having the career she'd coveted launched into the stratosphere should have her doing cartwheels.

Instead, the moment Ryder had wound up his speech, she'd known what had to be done.

She had to end things between them.

He had a gift for inspiring people and she now understood why he travelled the world doing exactly that. If she confessed her feelings he might be tempted to stay and she wouldn't be responsible for ruining his dream career just as hers was taking off. She wouldn't be able to live with herself.

So she fixed a bright smile on her face as he approached, hoping it didn't appear as brittle as it felt, stretching her cheeks to the point of pain.

'You were incredible,' she said, hugging him.

'Thanks, Pol.' He held her tight and her body flared to life, craving him with every cell.

It would be so easy to give in to this yearning for

him, to tell him she'd meet him after the work drinks finished, to have mind-blowing sex one last time.

But that would prolong the agony and he didn't deserve to be treated that way. She would tell him an altered version of the truth tomorrow after Archie's party, ending things between them and hopefully not shattering their friendship in the process.

'You smell so good.' He nuzzled her neck, pressing his hips against her and she bit back a moan. 'How soon can we leave and start celebrating?'

Hating that she had to do this but knowing it was the only way to start withdrawing from him, she eased out of his arms. 'Sorry, I can't. Andrina wants me to meet some important people for my new job.'

Disappointment clouded his eyes. 'How long will it take?'

'I don't know, and I can't pass up this opportunity.'

'Of course you can't.' He reached out and brushed his knuckles down her cheek, making her want to bawl again. 'If it finishes earlier than expected and you feel like catching up, drop by, okay?'

'Sure,' Polly said, hating how the little white lie slid from her lips.

Because she wouldn't be dropping by his place and she sure as hell wasn't okay.

She'd known going into this casual thing that there'd be an expiration date. They'd both known it. But knowing it logically and feeling it were worlds apart.

Ending things with Ryder had been inevitable.

But why did it have to hurt so much?

CHAPTER TWENTY-FIVE

RYDER KNEW A brush-off when he saw it—he'd delivered enough of them to women when he wanted to extricate himself—so the fact Polly had chosen work drinks over an evening with him last night spoke volumes.

He understood her keenness to advance her career but it was the way she'd delivered the news that told him something else was going on.

She wanted to end it.

He should be rapt. Having her do it saved him from being the bad guy. Yet he'd waited up for hours after he'd got home in the hope she'd drop by. By two-thirty he'd resigned himself to the truth: she wasn't coming, and he'd lain awake for the rest of the night wishing she would. One last memorable fuck before they went their separate ways.

But insomnia led to unwelcome thoughts. He'd ended things cleanly with women before, without this odd yearning for a last hurrah to say goodbye. So as much as he labelled it a farewell fuck he knew it would be more than that with Polly.

When they'd started up he'd envisaged breaking her heart. Not intentionally, of course, but because they were friends, it was inevitable feelings would develop and he'd be the one leaving. It was what he always did. He moved on before things got complicated. But breaking up with Polly felt different. She'd been a friend long before a lover and for the first time ever a small part of him would always lament walking away.

He'd make it easy for her. After Archie's party he'd take her somewhere private and start the conversation, making it easier for her to say what she wanted to say. It was the least he could do for a woman he l—liked.

That was bizarre. He'd almost thought the other *L* word. But he couldn't love any woman and especially not Polly. Not the way she deserved. She'd end up loving him back and he couldn't live with that expectation long term; he wasn't worthy of someone like her.

'So where are you taking us, putz?' Archie draped an arm around his shoulder as the boat lurched away from its mooring at Circular Quay.

Needing to focus on making this party great and stop lamenting things he couldn't change, he forced a grin. 'You'll see.'

Archie glanced around the top deck of the boat, an appreciative glint in his eyes. 'Considering half the guests you've invited are women, you'd better not be taking me to the strippers.'

Ryder elbowed him away. 'Your thirtieth will be classy all the way.'

'Pity.' Archie wiggled his eyebrows suggestively. 'I wouldn't mind a bit of debauchery.'

They laughed and took beers from the waiter wending through the crowd with drinks balanced perfectly on a tray.

'Happy birthday, Arch.' Ryder clinked his beer bottle against Archie's, glad he'd made the effort to return to Sydney for this. He owed his friend so much and while he'd never articulated it and probably never would, Archie's friendship in his teens had kept him sane.

'Thanks, mate.' Archie lifted the bottle to his mouth and took a slug. 'And if I get too drunk to thank you properly later, I'll do it now. Thanks for making an effort to come back to organise this and for being the best mate a guy could ask for.'

Shocked that Archie had virtually said out loud what Ryder had just been thinking, he swallowed to ease the sudden tightness in his throat.

'You're not going to break into a sentimental song, are you?'

'Fuck, no.' Archie drank again, his grin wide. 'But I might just smooch you.'

'Piss off.' Ryder laughed and elbowed him away harder.

'Uh-oh. Polly incoming,' Archie said. 'My cue to go chat up some of those hot models you've invited and leave you two alone.'

For a second, Ryder contemplated asking Archie to stick around. He didn't want to make small talk with Polly, not when he intended to end it later. But he didn't want Archie's party to turn into a bust, so he fixed a grin on his face and snagged a champers from the waiter as he did a second pass of the crowd at the stern of the boat.

'Great party,' she said, accepting the champagne he held out. 'Very slick.'

'Not really. We're cruising to Darling Harbour then having lunch there.'

Damn, he sounded like a party pooper when she was just making polite small talk.

'Archie's having a ball,' she said, pointing to where her brother now stood between two women, an arm draped across each of their shoulders. 'He's thirty going on thirteen.'

'Ain't that the truth?'

They smiled at each other and it struck him anew how much he'd miss this. They were in sync in so many ways, always had been, and he doubted he'd ever find the same kind of connection with any other woman.

'Sorry about bailing on you last night,' she said. 'It took a lot out of me organising that fundraiser and I was wrecked; I got home around one.'

'No worries, I understand.'

They locked gazes and he saw the exact moment she realised that he had planned on ending things too, just like she was.

They were finished.

'Can we sneak away after lunch? Find somewhere quiet to talk?'

She nodded, worrying her bottom lip with her teeth. 'Yeah, okay.'

She sounded resigned and he gritted his teeth

against the urge to say *Fuck it, let's prolong this longer until I leave Sydney.*

But he'd seen the way she'd looked at him at the fundraiser.

A clean break now would be better.

Archie waved him over and, ridiculously, he was glad of the reprieve. He hated this awkwardness between them, a hint of what was to come, and made him want to bolt.

'Archie's calling me. Catch up later?'

He touched her hand, wishing he could wrap his arms around her, wishing he could make this easy for her but knowing it would suck no matter what.

She nodded, her smile fragile, making him curse inwardly.

'Yeah, later,' she said, standing on tiptoe to kiss his cheek.

His *cheek*. Before turning her back on him and walking towards the front of the boat, leaving him with the distinct urge to jump overboard.

CHAPTER TWENTY-SIX

POLLY LIKED NOTHING better than a gourmet meal and Ryder had organised the best at the waterside restaurant overlooking Darling Harbour.

Oysters Kilpatrick for entrée, black pepper eye fillet with garlic-roasted vegetables for main and an exquisite lemon tart that melted on her tongue for dessert. She ate every morsel, making small talk with Archie's friends, faking laughter, pretending to have the time of her life.

While she slowly died inside.

So when her mum burst through the door of the restaurant in a flurry of silk and expensive perfume, Polly was already close to breaking point.

Naturally, Barbara made a beeline for the birthday boy and smothered Archie in kisses, eventually catching sight of her to Archie's right and swooping in for a surprisingly squishy hug.

'You look wonderful, Polly,' she said, beaming at her in approval. 'You're practically glowing.'

BS, considering her sleepless night spent contemplating how she'd end things with Ryder civilly, but she guessed the foundation and concealer she'd slathered on this morning were doing their job. Caitlyn the stylist really knew her stuff, her expertise with make-up and hair as good as her advice regarding clothes.

'Thanks, Mum, you're looking great too.'

And it was the truth. Barbara sported a tan that accentuated her eyes, an intense blue Polly had always coveted, while a loose coral silk kaftan draped her body and made her look like a Greek goddess. Her lipstick and nail polish matched the hue of her dress perfectly. Her mum had never looked so good.

She'd once overheard Barbara chatting to a friend on the phone, labelling her the ugly duckling. She'd been about ten at the time and had cried herself to sleep that night, wondering yet again why her mother didn't value brains as much as beauty.

'Scoot over,' Barbara said, pulling up a chair to wedge herself between her two children. 'I want to hear all your news.'

Polly saw her mother's glance zero in on Ryder at the other end of the table. 'And when I say all your news, I mean every last detail.'

Damn Archie and his big mouth. Not only had he told Barbara about her promotion, he'd blabbed about her fling with Ryder.

Glaring at her big brother, who seemed oblivious to everything but downing the boutique beers Ryder had generously paid for, she refocussed on her mother, who was staring at her with a quizzical tilt to her head.

'Something wrong, honey?'

Along with the tan, the 'honey' bit was new too. Polly didn't know whether to be flattered by her mother's attention or concerned. What had Babs been up to in Queensland that she'd decided she had a daughter worthy of acknowledging?

'I'm fine, Mum.'

To her surprise, Babs leaned in close. 'I may not have been the best mum, but I do know you and something is wrong.' She patted her thigh. 'Perhaps I can help.'

Polly gaped at her mother and couldn't help the words tumbling from her mouth. 'Maybe I should ask you the same thing, Mum. You're different.'

'When my own daughter thinks I've changed because I'm showing some motherly concern for once in my self-absorbed life, I know how shitty a parent I've been.' Barbara sighed and pinched the bridge of her nose, before dabbing at it to make sure she hadn't shifted her immaculately applied foundation. 'I met someone. He lives in Port Douglas. He's extremely close to his kids, which is why he won't move to Sydney.'

She glanced away but Polly saw the sheen of tears. 'He made me realise how I've let you and myself down by not being more attentive.'

Polly's heart twanged, spreading pain throughout her chest. 'I'm a big girl, Mum. I can take of myself, and have been for a long time.'

'That's not what I mean and you know it.' Barbara shook her head. 'For what it's worth, I'm sorry.'

Polly wanted to say *You've got nothing to apologise for.* But with her mother opening up this wasn't the time for lies.

'Did you know you fostered my love of fashion because the only time I felt close to you was when we looked at those magazines together?'

Barbara had the grace to blush. 'I treasured those times because it's the one thing we had in common.' She covered Polly's hand with hers where it lay in her lap. 'You were smarter than me from the time you started school, and I was incredibly proud of you but had no idea how to relate to you. I hate to admit it but you made me feel inadequate.'

Stunned by her mother's revelation, Polly could only shake her head. 'But why? I never said anything to make you feel that way—'

'You didn't have to.' She squeezed her hand and released it. 'You'd have your head stuck in your text books or scouring online for the answer to some difficult question, and when I offered to help you'd give me this look…like I was a dummy…'

Sadness passed over Barbara's face. 'So I gave up asking and the gap between us grew.'

'I had no idea.' On impulse, Polly leaned across and hugged her mother. 'That's why you favoured Archie, because he's a dumbass?'

They laughed in unison and Polly felt a weight that she'd been shouldering for a long time shift.

She'd always felt not good enough; it turned out her mum had felt the same. They were a crazy pair.

'How about you come by Sizzle next week and I'll give you the grand tour?'

Her mother hadn't asked for forgiveness but Barbara knew what the offer meant: a fresh start for them.

Barbara's eyes lit up. 'I'd love that.'

'Hey, what are you two gossiping about?' Archie leaned in, trying to squeeze in between them.

'None of your business,' Barbara said, playfully shoving him away. 'We're having some mother-daughter time.'

Archie glanced at Polly and winked, as if he knew exactly what she'd been going through all these years.

'Did she tell you she's shagging my best mate?'

Polly felt heat flush her cheeks as Archie stuck out his tongue at her.

'Once again, none of your business,' Barbara said, her frown lost on an oblivious Archie who'd definitely imbibed one too many beers.

'What Mum said, bozo.' Polly shoved him away, but caught her mother's knowing stare.

Yeah, he'd definitely told her about Ryder and she wanted to know more.

Which was Polly's cue to leave.

'I'm really sorry to do this, but my boss wants me to stop by the office today.'

Barbara's eyebrows rose. 'On a Sunday?'

'It won't take long. Maybe we can catch up later?'

The second the invitation popped out of her mouth she wanted to take it back. She'd be seeing Ryder later, to break up with him, and the last thing she wanted was to see her mother after that.

Sensing her recalcitrance, Barbara patted her hand. 'There's no rush, honey. You do what you have to do, I'll still be around tomorrow.'

'Thanks, Mum.' Polly stood and Archie did the same, enveloping her in a hug.

'You're the best, Pol. Thanks for coming.'

'Where else would I be with you turning into an old man?'

He gave her a noogie on the head, like he'd used to when she'd been a kid, and they grinned at each other. She knew Archie might be pissed when Ryder left and she struggled to put on a brave face, so she'd have to try extra hard not to appear too unhappy. It was a big ask but she'd known going into this that Archie would always be on her side despite his friendship with Ryder. He was the only man she could depend on and she treasured him for it, even if he drove her nuts most of the time.

'See you later,' she said, slipping out of his arms and turning to pick up her bag, only to find Ryder staring at her with an intensity that took her breath away from the other end of the table.

He quirked an eyebrow, as if asking why she was leaving, and rather than slipping out as she'd hoped, she knew she'd have to give him something. Besides, as the host of this fancy shindig it was only polite to thank him.

Giving a general wave at the table occupants—friends of Archie's with a few additional beautiful women who she assumed Ryder had invited for her brother's benefit—she made her way towards Ryder.

He met her halfway and gestured to a nook near the entry foyer. 'You're leaving early?'

'Duty calls, again,' she said, rolling her eyes. 'Not sure if this promotion is worth it considering Andrina has become more demanding than ever.'

'She's making you work on a Sunday?'

'It won't take long,' she said, mustering her meagre supply of courage to blurt, 'You still keen to catch up later?'

He nodded, glancing at Archie. 'Though knowing your dickhead of a brother he'll want to keep partying for a while yet.'

She wanted to invite him over but she knew what would happen. They'd end up devouring each other and her resolve would waver and she'd be stuck in limbo land, knowing she had to break it off but not having the guts to do it.

'Listen, why don't we catch up tomorrow? That way Archie can have you all to himself and you can keep an eye on him for me.'

A frown marred his brow. 'We need to talk, Pol, and I feel like you're avoiding me.'

'It's not that...' She faked a smile. 'Our timing sucks at the moment, but we will talk.'

'Why do I get the feeling I'm not going to like what you have to say?'

He knew, damn it, he knew.

'We'll talk tomorrow.'

She kissed him, a quick peck on the lips, before ducking past him to push through the glass door.

She shouldn't look back; it would send the wrong message.

What message is that? That you love him?

Ignoring her stupid voice of reason, she glanced over her shoulder to find Ryder staring at her with so much regret her breath caught.

Could he have feelings for her too?

If so, she had to end this sooner rather than later.

CHAPTER TWENTY-SEVEN

RYDER HAD NEVER been averse to taking chances. Big ones, too, so when he dropped a seriously drunk Archie home, making sure he made it to bed with a bucket beside it, water and paracetamol on the bedside table and the window cranked open a fraction for some fresh air, he headed for the one place he needed to be.

Polly's.

She wouldn't welcome the unexpected drop-in; he knew it, but he didn't care. He was done with her evasions.

This confrontation was long overdue and prolonging their break-up wouldn't help either of them.

Striding up the path to her front door, he remembered the first time he'd done it a few weeks ago when they'd been so hot for each other they'd barely made it inside before going at it up against the wall.

He'd been naïve to think that was all they would have—a few weeks of frantic fucking while he was in Sydney, before saying a cheery goodbye.

Yeah, only a stupid prick would think he could get intimate with one of his oldest friends and walk away at the end without hurting her.

Bracing himself for whatever was to come, he knocked at the door.

The door opened a fraction and she peered into the gap between the chain and the jamb.

'Hey Pol, can I come in?'

She glared at him, a deep groove between her brows. 'I was in bed.'

'Perfect, I'll join you.'

She didn't buy his rakish smile. If anything, her frown deepened. What more proof did he need that this would be harder than he'd anticipated?

'You can't fob me off for ever,' he said, shrugging.

With a loud sigh, she slipped the chain off and opened the door. He stepped inside and reached for her but she slipped away, leaving him seriously doubting the wisdom of turning up here tonight.

Then again, it wouldn't matter what time of day they talked; he had a feeling the result would be the same and he wouldn't like it.

She folded her arms and glared at him, the groove between her brows deepening. 'Want a coffee?'

'No, I'm good.'

But he wasn't, not by a long shot, and the sooner they had this conversation the better.

'You're avoiding me,' he said, and she turned away so she wouldn't meet his gaze.

She wore black yoga pants and a singlet top, so she'd probably lied about being in bed too.

How the hell had they come to this?

'Pol, we need to discuss what's happening with us—'

'Stop.'

She whirled back to face him, her cheeks flushed, her eyes sparking anger. 'There's nothing to say, considering we both knew this would end as soon as you left town. So please don't imply there's anything to talk about when what we had was nothing more than a fling.'

Shocked to his core at her outburst, he would've almost believed her brave little speech if not for the devastation in her eyes.

Polly had always been too easy to read. It was why he'd delighted in taunting her so much when they'd been growing up.

'You can't bullshit a bullshitter and I'm one of the best, considering I've been deluding myself for years.' He gestured at the sofa. 'Can we at least sit and discuss this like two rational human beings?'

She didn't want to. Every muscle in her body was tensed in fight or flight mode and she wanted to flee. But she eventually gave a terse nod and took a seat in a worn armchair opposite the sofa.

He sighed and sat on the sofa, hating the distance between them as much as her closed-off expression.

'Are you avoiding this discussion for a reason?'

'No.' Her mouth was downturned, sadness emanating from her. 'I know it has to happen.'

'Then what's going on?'

Her bottom lip quivered and he hated himself for doing this to her. But she straightened before his eyes, drawing her shoulders back, tilting her head up, staring him down and he almost applauded.

'The sex was great, don't get me wrong, and I don't

regret a single moment. But I've got a new job to focus on and you'll be heading off to your next gig overseas any day now, so let's not drag this out.'

Typical Polly—logical, well thought-out, factual. But she'd forgotten one thing: he'd come back to Sydney for the first time in five years because he'd sought resolutions and that meant confronting his fears. Including his fear of not being good enough for a woman like her and he wanted to know if she felt...*something* beyond the physical.

'What if I don't leave?'

She blanched and clasped her hands in her lap. 'What do you mean?'

'I mean exactly that. Sure, my job takes me overseas, but what if I returned home and set up a base here permanently? Would you want to continue our fling?'

'Why should I?'

She sounded defiant but her gaze darted away, like she didn't want him seeing the flicker of hope in her eyes.

'I'll be honest, Pol, I like chasing the next high and that means finding new challenges. This is the longest I've dated anyone and we're phenomenal together in bed, so why not prolong the fun a tad longer?'

He dragged in a breath and held it, resting his elbows on his knees, trying to appear casual when nothing could be further from the truth.

When she dragged her gaze back to his, he glimpsed a shimmer of tears. 'I'm sorry, Ryder. I'm tired of being just another conquest for you. It's definitely time you moved on to the next challenge.'

.

Reeling, he tried to assimilate her declaration. She'd implied she was merely another woman in a long list of women. It wasn't far off the truth, but why should it matter to her unless she was emotionally invested?

'Pol, I'm sorry if you've developed feelings—'

'Go,' she said, leaping to her feet. 'Please.'

She stomped towards her bedroom, pausing in the doorway. 'I can't do this, Ryder. We're over, just like we both agreed, so please leave me alone.'

He hadn't expected this to be easy but as he headed for the door he didn't know what hurt more. The fact he'd hurt someone he truly cared about or the fact he'd lost one of his oldest friends.

He'd been an idiot to imagine they could have sex and maintain a friendship afterwards. What had he been thinking?

He hadn't, that was the problem. He'd been blinded by his longstanding attraction to Polly and had let his dick override his common sense.

She wanted him to leave her alone, so he'd do it.

His trip to the United States couldn't come soon enough.

CHAPTER TWENTY-EIGHT

POLLY WAITED UNTIL she heard the front door slam before sliding down the wall and landing on her butt, hard. Only then did she allow herself the luxury of crying, great, jagged sobs that made her chest ache. Her eyes burned and her nose clogged as she mentally rehashed everything he'd said, and tried to convince herself she'd done the right thing.

He'd come here to end it, and she'd been prepared. Not tonight but for the conversation they would've had tomorrow. She'd planned it all out: wear one of her new power suits, blow-dry her hair, slather on the make-up and meet him somewhere public and impartial. Unfortunately he'd blindsided her tonight and she hadn't reacted well. She'd let some of her emotions show and that was the last thing she'd wanted.

She couldn't believe he'd actually said 'I'm sorry if you've developed feelings.' What a heartless bastard. Of course she had feelings for him, the primary one being stupid, one-sided, unrequited love.

She'd wanted to end this on her terms and he'd taken

away that option, so it had been stilted and awkward and downright awful at the end.

They'd made the final break and it was for the best, for every logical reason she'd already worked through in her head. But that didn't make it any easier on her aching, fractured heart.

She had no idea how long she sat on the floor, slumped and dejected, but when her sobs eventually petered out she pushed into standing and dragged herself to the bathroom. Glancing in the mirror was a mistake. Bloodshot eyes, red nose, puffy cheeks—a horrible testament to the lie she'd just perpetuated.

Stripping off, she flicked the shower to hot and stepped under the jets, tilting her face up to wash away the remnants of her pain. But all the showers in the world wouldn't eradicate the ache inside and she knew it would take a long time for her to recover.

The stupid thing was, five minutes later, after she'd towelled off and slipped into her oldest PJs, she wished she'd had the guts to tell him the truth.

That was the kicker in all this—being involved with Ryder meant she didn't need trendy clothes or a makeover to feel like she belonged at Sizzle. She'd achieved that on her own, with confidence and using her brain like she wanted.

He'd done that for her. Inadvertently, maybe, but seeing herself through his eyes had empowered her and she hadn't looked back.

Knowing it was dumb to second-guess her decision but unable to help herself, she reached for her mobile to scroll through photos she'd snapped at Archie's party earlier that day.

She'd known her bozo brother would want evidence of his big day but would be too busy having a good time to take any pics himself so she'd shot at random, giving him a choice of what he wanted to keep or delete.

Her finger slid across the screen, moving from one shot to the next, her heart flipping whenever she glimpsed Ryder. In all the posed photos he had a wide grin, his head close to Archie's, their arms slung across each other's shoulders. They'd been mates for a long time and it spoke volumes that even though Ryder hadn't been home in years, Archie had reached out to him to organise his thirtieth.

As tears threatened again, her finger picked up speed, swiping through the photos. Until she reached the one she'd tried to ignore earlier, the one that told her more than words ever could.

She'd caught him off guard, staring directly at her, showing more emotion than she'd ever seen.

She hadn't lingered over it earlier because she hadn't wanted to analyse it. What would be the point when she had to end it?

But now she pored over the photo, studying it, hating it when her pulse picked up tempo and her reliable logic deserted her, allowing her imagination to take over. Was that tenderness in his eyes, in the soft smile curving his lips, in the dazed expression?

Was love the emotion written all over his face?

Her finger hovered over the delete button as she willed herself to stab at the little garbage bin icon.

Her finger edged towards it…but she couldn't, and she flung her phone onto the other side of the bed and rolled away from it.

Besides, that photo might come in handy in the long, lonely months ahead when she had to remind herself she'd been right to sabotage the best thing to ever happen to her.

CHAPTER TWENTY-NINE

THE LAST THING Ryder felt like doing the next morning was giving a speech at his old high school, but he didn't shirk his responsibilities and it had gone well for the most part. Kids had heckled a tad as expected but most had been staring at him in awe, like they couldn't believe there was life beyond these hallowed stone walls.

He'd hated attending the exclusive private school growing up and had begged his gran to be allowed to go to the local high school with Archie. They would've been in the same year and it would've made his transition into the neighbourhood that much easier. But Edie wouldn't hear of it and had shipped him off to the private school five suburbs over, meaning he'd had to catch a bus.

He'd made friends easily enough but they were the type of kids impressed by money—the size of your house, your parents' portfolio and your trust fund.

Attending this exclusive school had made him aware of his social standing like nothing else, another reason why he had treasured his time spent with the down-to-earth Scanlons next door.

But as he strode through the manicured grounds, the lush green sporting ovals spread out on either side, he realised how privileged he'd been to attend a school like this. While his final grades had only been slightly above average, the fact he had fulfilled all the requirements meant he could study anywhere in the world. It had given him freedom when he'd craved it the most.

Courtesy of his grandparents' wealth and connections, he'd got an easy ride through school and he should be thanking Edie rather than eschewing everything she had stood for back then. She may not have supported him emotionally but she'd given him a good start in life.

'Excuse me, Mr Beale?'

Ryder stopped as a boy of about fourteen appeared out of nowhere. 'Yes?'

The boy, sporting trendy wire-rimmed glasses and a blazer with a plethora of badges down one side, flushed. 'I just wanted to say how much I liked your speech. You've done a lot of really cool stuff since you left here.'

'Thanks.'

The boy seemed to expect him to say more, so he continued, 'This place gives you a pretty good grounding for whatever you want to do in the future. Got any ideas what you want to be?'

'My folks want me to do engineering.' He rolled his eyes. 'I'd rather be a vet or a marine biologist.'

Ryder wanted to advise the kid to chase his dreams but it wasn't his place. Besides, what did he know about planning for the future? He'd chased adrenaline rushes and lived nomadically, running from his past.

His near-death experience had given him a wake-up call but had he really utilised his new life completely?

He'd chased one high after another, while extolling the virtues of making the right choices to thousands of people all over the world and being compensated handsomely for it.

Last night, he'd let Polly call the shots, knowing she was hurting but not wanting to make it worse. She'd made it easy for him. He should be glad. But he couldn't stop thinking about the way she'd looked at him, like he'd disappointed her... It fed into every feeling of unworthiness he'd ever had and it pissed him off.

He'd spent a lifetime running: running from difficult situations, running from his guilt, running towards the next challenge to assuage that emptiness inside. What if he stopped running?

'Good luck with whatever you choose.' Ryder stuck out his hand and waited until the kid shook it, impressed by his strong grip.

'Thanks.' The boy grinned, released his hand and strolled away, leaving Ryder to contemplate his outlandish idea.

He needed to see Polly again.

But first he had another stop to make.

'You look like someone's kicked you in the guts.' Archie opened the door and peered at him through bleary eyes. 'Which is ironic, considering my liver hates me and I feel like I've been run over by the Manly Ferry.'

'That's what happens when you consume your body weight in alcohol,' Ryder said, entering Archie's place and heading for the kitchen. 'I thought common sense might kick in when you turned thirty.'

'Screw you.' Archie clutched his head and winced. 'I said that too loudly.'

Ryder laughed. 'Had anything to eat yet?'

'Are you nuts?' He mock-barfed. 'Doubt I could keep anything down.'

'Mate, it's been sixteen hours since I put your sorry ass to bed. Exactly how much did you drink?'

'Too bloody much.' He winced again. 'Though I guess I should eat something.'

'Got any eggs and bacon?'

Archie grimaced but nodded. 'You know it's a fallacy, right, that old wives' tale about a big fry-up being a cure for a hangover?'

'Used to work in our old days.' Ryder shrugged. 'Can't hurt.'

Archie patted his stomach. 'Yeah, it can, but I've got nothing to lose at this point. Already driven the porcelain bus twice this morning.'

'Gross.' Ryder opened the fridge, which was well stocked, and grabbed the ingredients he needed.

'You didn't answer my question,' Archie said, perching on a stool at the newly renovated island bar. 'Why do you look like shit?'

'Eat first, then we'll talk about it.'

Curiosity widened his eyes but to Archie's credit he waited until Ryder had cooked and dished up a plate of buttered toast, fried eggs, bacon and mushrooms before speaking again.

'Thanks, mate, this looks good.' Archie tentatively forked a mushroom into his mouth and nibbled on a piece of toast. 'Reckon I might be getting my appetite back.'

'Eat.' Ryder pointed at the plate as he set a steaming mug of coffee in front of him. 'Then get this into you.'

Archie took a sip. 'Hmm...good.'

They ate in silence as Ryder contemplated the wisdom of involving Archie in his love life, considering the woman he wanted to win over happened to be his best friend's sister.

But if he didn't he could lose her, and he wasn't prepared to take that risk. She meant too much to him. It had taken him long enough to get to this point of actually wanting more than sex and he was damned if he'd walk away without a fight.

'This is about Polly, isn't it?' Archie forked the last bit of egg into his mouth, before picking up his coffee mug and eyeing him over the top of it. 'Everything's turned to shit as I predicted and now I'll have to kick you five ways into next week.'

'We broke up,' Ryder said, hating how his chest ached with regret rather than relief.

'Is she okay?'

'We both knew it was coming and she actually ended it before I had a chance to.'

'Good for her.' A groove furrowed Archie's brow. 'This plays right into your MO, short term, no drama, so why are you looking so bloody morose?'

Ryder didn't like involving Archie in this but he had to get some inkling as to Polly's feelings before he made a total ass of himself with her.

'It's complicated.'

'Bullshit.' Archie jabbed a finger in his direction. 'Before I drank myself into a stupor yesterday I saw the way you two looked at each other and I knew you two idiots had moved beyond a fling.'

Archie glanced at him, speculation in his eyes. 'Polly hasn't had a real relationship, ever. She's dated sporadically and has mentioned a few guys, but I've never actually met any of them.' He grimaced. 'And I've never seen her light up the way she does around you.'

He pretended to stick a finger down his throat. 'Fuck, I can't believe I'm about to say this, but if you have feelings for her and she feels the same way, you gotta go for it, man.'

Encouraged by his friend's assessment of the situation—he'd know Polly better than anyone—Ryder came to a decision. 'I need your help.'

Archie groaned and pulled a face. 'What do you want me to do?'

CHAPTER THIRTY

I T H A D B E E N a hell of a day. Mondays weren't Polly's favourite day of the week and today was no exception. Andrina may have given her a promotion but it seemed her boss wanted to drain every last bit of life out of her before she moved on from her PA position. She'd had to ring every major department store to check their stock of the latest cruise wear, personally approach fifty boutiques asking them to stock Sizzle's latest line, and sort through the CVs from applicants for her job.

It had been the pits, and all that after she'd lain awake most of the night stewing about how things had ended with Ryder.

Professionally, she may be on an upward trajectory. Personally, her life sucked, and it wouldn't improve any time soon given how long it would take to get over Ryder.

Now this.

Archie wanted her to stop by his place on the way home to check out the interior designer he was contemplating hiring. Sure, she had some expertise in the area but that was with fashion, not cushion fabrics, but she couldn't say no to her brother. Besides, she had to pull up her big-girl panties and give him the news about her and Ryder firsthand. It was the right thing to do as she didn't want to mess with their friendship and she knew once he got wind of it he'd blame Ryder for their demise.

It took her forty-five minutes in peak-hour traffic to reach Archie's place and by the time she marched up to his front door to thump on it she could've easily thumped him instead.

Her foul mood didn't improve when the door opened and Ryder stepped back to let her in.

Mustering her best acting skills, she held up her hand in a half-hearted wave. 'Hey.'

'Hey yourself. Come on in.'

He waited until she'd stepped inside and closed the door before speaking. 'Archie's not here.'

She stopped mid-stride between the sofa and the chair in the lounge room. 'But he asked me over—'

'That was me. He knows I love you and he thinks you feel the same way so he wants us to sort our shit out or he's going to clunk our heads together.'

Polly reeled from the *L* word and her hands shook as she dumped her bag on a chair and spun around. 'Since when do either of us take relationship advice from Archie? He hasn't been serious about anyone ever.'

'But he knows us well,' Ryder said, those mesmerising eyes boring into her, beseeching her to listen when she knew she should turn tail and run. 'And I happen to think he's right.' He shook his head. 'Because despite that little speech you gave me last night, Pol, and me pretending like I don't give a shit, I think we've moved beyond fucking.'

Polly darted a frantic glance at the door. She had to leave. Now. But Ryder had positioned himself in the lounge room doorway so she'd have to push to get past him and she knew if he touched her she'd be undone.

So she folded her arms and glared at him with as much animosity as she could muster.

'Please don't assume you know what I'm feeling, because you have no idea.'

'Then tell me, please.' He held out his hands to her. 'You owe me that much.'

'I owe you nothing.' She hated how her throat tightened with the lies wedged there but she had to get the words out before she crumpled completely. 'Why are you doing this? Prolonging the agony?'

'It wouldn't hurt if you didn't care.'

He advanced towards her and she scooted back in her chair. Yeah, like that would help. She craved his arms around her with every cell in her body. One hug to make it all better. But that would be her undoing too so when he got close enough she held up her hand and pointed at the chair opposite.

'I can't think when you're this close.'

To her relief he sat. 'Still got the hots for me, huh?'

'Your ego's as big as your misconceptions about my feelings for you.'

His mouth eased into the lazy grin she loved so much. 'You know you turn me on when we banter like this, right?'

She rolled her eyes but she understood, because

their sparring had the same effect on her. 'Fine. You want the truth, I'll give it to you, but it's not going to change a thing.'

His smile faded as he leaned forward, bracing his elbows on his knees, fixing her with a serious stare. 'Try me.'

Polly had made up her mind regarding them and knew nothing he said would change it, but he was right. They'd been friends for a long time and she owed him the truth.

'Everything changed for me the night of the fundraiser.'

A small frown crinkled his brow but he remained silent, waiting for her to continue.

'When I saw you up on stage, delivering your speech, I was blown away by how much you inspire people. What you've been through, how you've conquered your fears and changed your lifestyle to make a difference with others...' She pressed a hand to her heart. 'It got me right here, and made me realise I could never hold you back. You love chasing the next thrill, the next challenge, and we both know that's all I am to you. So, say we lost our minds and kept dating, what's going to happen when you get tired of me and chase the next big thing?'

His frown deepened. 'I wouldn't do that to you—'

'Yeah, you would. It's what you do.' She shook her head. 'I saved us both a lot of grief, Ryder, because I've just landed my dream job and it's all I've ever wanted. Falling for you, getting more involved, will only screw with my concentration and I won't let that happen.' She tapped her chest. 'I've worked too hard to get where I am and I'm not giving it up for some wanderer chasing highs.'

His eyes widened, a flicker of hope making her regret telling him the truth. 'And that's your reason for ending things between us?'

She nodded, gnawing on her bottom lip. 'I don't want you staying in Sydney for me, then ending up regretting it.' She shook her head. 'Tell me your career isn't everything to you.'

'It's not,' he said, quickly and decisively. 'Oddly enough, I only realised this morning after giving a speech at my old high school that I've spent my life running from my past, blaming Gran, hating the injustice of losing my folks and putting up with Pop's hatred, chasing the next adrenaline high to make me forget what I left behind.'

He stood and rounded the coffee table to kneel at her feet. 'But I don't want to keep running away any more. I've found something more important than eternally chasing something just out of reach, and that's you, Pol.'

He rested his hands on her knees, sending a sliver of heat shooting through her. 'To be honest, I didn't know I was capable of love. I've never felt worthy of it, especially from someone as amazing as you. I guess not having much of it in my life screwed me up, and while I've made peace with Gran and we're working towards re-establishing some kind of relationship, I still blame her for not showing me what love is.'

Tears welled in her eyes and she reached out to cover

his hands with hers. 'Are you sure you're not confusing our friendship for something more?'

'I'm sure, Pol, and you want to know how I know?'

She nodded, blinking rapidly so she wouldn't blubber all over him.

'Because usually I can't wait to move on to the next big thing. But this time, the thought of leaving kills me and that's all on you.'

Sliding his hands out from under hers, he stood and tugged her to her feet. Resting one hand on her waist, he placed a finger under her chin and tilted her head up.

'I love you and that means I'm willing to do whatever it takes to make this work. I'll still travel but I'll cut back a lot, focussing mostly on gigs in Australia. And once my book's finished I'll focus on promoting that here too.' He rested his hands on her waist and pulled her close. 'But none of that means anything to me unless I have you in my life. So what do you say?'

Polly could say so much but she settled for showing him what was in her heart, all the love and hope and anticipation for their future together.

Standing on tiptoe, she pressed her lips to his in a slow, sensual kiss, before murmuring, 'You have me, Ryder. You always did.'

* * * * *

COMING SOON!

We really hope you enjoyed reading this book.
If you're looking for more romance, be sure to
head to the shops when new books are
available on

Thursday 21st January

MILLS & BOON

THE HEART OF ROMANCE

A ROMANCE FOR EVERY KIND OF READER

ODERN

Prepare to be swept off your feet by sophisticated, sexy and seductive heroes, in some of the world's most glamourous and romantic locations, where power and passion collide.
8 stories per month.

STORICAL

Escape with historical heroes from time gone by. Whether your passion is for wicked Regency Rakes, muscled Vikings or rugged Highlanders, awaken the romance of the past.
6 stories per month.

EDICAL

Set your pulse racing with dedicated, delectable doctors in the high-pressure world of medicine, where emotions run high and passion, comfort and love are the best medicine.
6 stories per month.

ue Love

Celebrate true love with tender stories of heartfelt romance, from the rush of falling in love to the joy a new baby can bring, and a focus on the emotional heart of a relationship.
8 stories per month.

Desire

Indulge in secrets and scandal, intense drama and plenty of sizzling hot action with powerful and passionate heroes who have it all: wealth, status, good looks…everything but the right woman.
6 stories per month.

EROES

Experience all the excitement of a gripping thriller, with an intense romance at its heart. Resourceful, true-to-life women and strong, fearless men face danger and desire - a killer combination!
8 stories per month.

ARE

Sensual love stories featuring smart, sassy heroines you'd want as a best friend, and compelling intense heroes who are worthy of them.
4 stories per month.

To see which titles are coming soon, please visit

millsandboon.co.uk/nextmonth

MILLS & BOON

MODERN

Power and Passion

Prepare to be swept off your feet by sophisticated, sexy and seductive heroes, in some of the world's most glamourous and romantic locations, where power and passion collide.